DESPERATE DUCHESSES

 This Large Print Book carries the
Seal of Approval of N.A.V.H.

DESPERATE DUCHESSES

ELOISA JAMES

THORNDIKE PRESS

A part of Gale, Cengage Learning

GALE
CENGAGE Learning

Detroit • New York • San Francisco • New Haven, Conn • Waterville, Maine • London

GALE
CENGAGE Learning

Copyright © 2007 by Eloisa James.
Thorndike Press, a part of Gale, Cengage Learning.

Thorndike Press® Large Print Romance.
The text of this Large Print edition is unabridged.
Other aspects of the book may vary from the original edition.
Set in 16 pt. Plantin.
Printed on permanent paper.

LIBRARY OF CONGRESS CATALOGING-IN-PUBLICATION DATA

James, Eloisa.
    Desperate duchesses / by Eloisa James.
      p. cm. — (Thorndike Press large print romance)
    ISBN-13: 978-1-4104-1635-3 (hardcover : alk. paper)
    ISBN-10: 1-4104-1635-6 (hardcover : alk. paper)
      1. Aristocracy (Social class)—England—Fiction. 2. Large type books. I. Title.
PS3560.A3796D47 2009
813'.54—dc22   2009014306

Published in 2009 by arrangement with Avon Books, an imprint of HarperCollins Publishers.

Printed in the United States of America
1 2 3 4 5 6 7 13 12 11 10 09

This book is dedicated to my father, Robert Bly, winner of the American Book Award for Poetry. There were times in my adolescence when he embarrassed me by the fierceness of his love and the sheer exuberance of his joy for life. That is the extent of any resemblance between the poetic marquess of this book and my father, whose poetry — and brains — far exceeds that of the writer I depict here.

So my second dedication is to the poet Christopher Smart (1722–1771), who unknowingly offered up his poetry to be sacrificed in the name of fiction. As with any quotation pulled from its context, Mr. Smart's poetry appears here to be far more unintelligible than it truly is. In particular, "For My Cat Jeoffrey" is a cheerfully exuberant love poem to a cat; in Mr. Smart's honor I am putting the entire poem on my website. Visit *www.eloisajames.com* and enjoy Jeoffrey in his full splendor.

ACKNOWLEDGMENTS

With profound thanks to my research assistant, Franzeca Drouin, who labored far beyond the call of duty on this book. Without her perspicuity, enormous knowledge, and excellent research skills, it would be a flimsy shadow of itself. Further thanks to the large circle of researchers whom she consulted about various issues ranging from the French language to signet rings.

In addition, my assistant, Kim Castillo, made my life much easier with her organizational skills. Thank you both! Finally . . . a quick thanks to the wonderful readers who frequent my Bulletin Board. I can't wait to see what you think of my *Desperate Duchesses*!

A Prelude

November 1780
Estate of the Marquess of Wharton and Malmesbury
Knowing precisely why no one wants to marry you is slim consolation for the truth of it. In Lady Roberta St. Giles's case, the evidence was all too clear — as was her lack of suitors.

The cartoon reproduced in *Rambler's Magazine* depicted Lady Roberta with a hunched back and a single brow across her bulging forehead. Her father knelt beside her, imploring passersby to find him a respectable spouse for his daughter.

At least that part was true. Her father had fallen to his knees in the streets of Bath, precisely as depicted. To Roberta's mind, the *Rambler's* label of *Mad Marquess* had a certain accuracy about it as well.

"Inbreeding," her father had said, when she flourished the magazine at him. "They

9

assume your physique is affected by the sort of inbreeding that produces these characteristics. Interesting! After all, you could have been dangerously mad, for example, or —"

"But Papa," she wailed, "couldn't you make them print a retraction? I am not misshapen. Who would wish to marry me now?"

"Why, Sweetpea, you are entirely lovely," he said, knitting his brow. "I shall write a paean on your beauty and publish it in *Rambler's.* I will explain precisely why I was so distraught, and include a commentary about the practices of hardened rakehells!"

Rambler's Magazine printed the marquess's 818 lines of reproving verse, describing the nefarious gallant who had kissed Roberta in public without so much as a by-your-leave. They resurrected the offensive print as well. Buried somewhere in the marquess's raging stanzas describing the peril of walking Bath's streets was a description of his daughter: "Tell the blythe Graces as they bound, luxuriant in the buxom round, that they're not more elegantly free, than Roberta, only daughter of a Marquess!" In vain did Roberta point out that "elegantly free" said little of the condition of her back, and that "buxom round" made her sound rather plump.

"It implies all that needs to be said," the

marquess said serenely. "Every man of sense will immediately ascertain that you have a charmingly luxurious figure, elegant features and a good dowry, not to mention your expectations from me. I cleverly pointed to your inheritance, do you see?"

All Roberta could see was a line declaring that her dowry was a peach tree.

"That's for the rhyme," her father had said, looking a bit cross now. "Dowry doesn't rhyme with many words, so I had to rhyme dowry and peach tree. The tree is obviously a synecdoche."

When Roberta looked blank, he added impatiently, "A figure of speech in which something small stands for the whole. The whole is the estate of Wharton and Malmesbury, and you know perfectly well that we have at least eleven peach trees. My nephew will inherit the estate, but the orchards are unentailed and will go to you."

Perhaps there were clever men who deduced from the marquess's poem that his daughter had eleven peach trees and a slender figure, but not a single one of those men turned up in Wiltshire to ascertain for himself. The fact that the original cartoon remained on display in the windows of Humphrey's Print Shop for many months may also have been a consideration.

But since the marquess refused to undertake another trip to the city wherein his daughter was accosted — "You'll thank me for that later," he added, rather obscurely — Lady Roberta St. Giles found herself heading quickly toward that undesirable stage of life known as "old maid."

Two years passed. Every few months Roberta's future would pass before her eyes, a life spent copying and cataloging her father's poems, when not alphabetizing rejection letters from publishers for use by the marquess's future biographers, and she would rebel. In vain did she reason, implore or cry. Even threatening to burn every poem in the house had no effect; it wasn't until she snatched a copy of "For the Custards Mary Brought Me" and threw it in the fire that her father understood her seriousness.

And only by withholding the single remaining copy of the Custard poem did she gain permission to attend the New Year's ball being held by Lady Cholmondelay.

"We'll have to stay overnight," her father said, his lower lip jutting out with disapproval.

"We'll go by ourselves," Roberta said. "Without Mrs. Grope."

"Without Mrs. Grope!" He opened his mouth to bellow, but —

12

"Papa, you do want me to have some attention, don't you? Mrs. Grope will cast me entirely in the shade."

"Humph."

"I shall need a new dress."

"An excellent thought. I was in the village the other day and one of Mrs. Parthnell's children was running about the square looking blue with cold. I've no doubt but that she could use your custom."

She barely opened her mouth before he lifted his hand. "You wouldn't want a gown from some other mantuamaker, dearest. You're not thinking of poor Mrs. Parthnell and her eight children."

"I am thinking," Roberta said, "of Mrs. Parthnell's bungled bodices."

But her father frowned at that, since he had strong views about the shallow nature of fashion and even stronger views about supporting the villagers, no matter how inferior their products.

Unfortunately, the New Year's ball produced no suitors.

Papa could not forbear from bringing Mrs. Grope — " 'Twill hurt her feelings too much, my dear" — and consequently, Roberta spent the evening watching revelers titter at the presence of a notorious strumpet amongst them. No one appeared to be interested in whether the Mad Marquess's daughter had a humped back or not; they were too busy peering at the Mad Marquess's courtesan. Their hostess was incensed at her father's rudeness in bringing his *chère-amie* to her ball, and wasted none of her precious time introducing Roberta to young men.

Her father danced with Mrs. Grope; Roberta sat at the side of the room and watched. Mrs. Grope's hair was adorned with ribbons, feathers, flowers, jewels and a bird made from papier-mâché. This made it easy for Roberta to pretend that she didn't know her own parent; when the said plumage headed in her direction, Roberta would slip away for a brisk stroll. She visited the ladies' retiring room so many times that the company likely thought she had a female complaint to match her invisible hump.

Around eleven o'clock, a gentleman finally asked her to dance. But he turned out to be Lady Cholmondelay's curate, and he immediately launched into a confused lecture to do with notorious strumpets. He seemed to be equating Mrs. Grope to Mary Magdalene, but the dance kept separating them before Roberta could grasp the connection.

Unfortunately, they came face-to-face with the marquess and Mrs. Grope just when the curate was detailing his feelings about trollops.

"I take your meaning, sirrah, and Mrs. Grope is no trollop!" the marquess snapped. Roberta's heart sank and she tried vainly to turn her partner in the opposite direction.

But the plump little pigeon of a man dug in his heels, squared his shoulders and retorted, "Muse upon my comments at your leisure, or woe betide your eternal soul!"

Everyone in the immediate vicinity stopped dancing, grasping that a more interesting performance had begun.

The marquess did not disappoint them. "Mrs. Grope is a lovely woman, kind enough to accept my adoration," Roberta's father roared, loud enough so that no one in the room could miss a word. "She is no more a trollop than is my own daughter, the treasure of my house!"

Predictably, the crowd turned as one to examine the signs of trollopdom, the first interest shown Roberta all evening. With a gasp, she fled back to the ladies' retiring room.

Within a half hour, Roberta made several important decisions. The first was that she'd had enough humiliation. She wanted a husband who would never, under any circumstances, make a public display of himself or those around him. And he should know nothing of poetry. Second, her only chance of finding that husband was to make her way to London without her father or Mrs. Grope. She would go there, pick an appropriate gentleman and arrange to marry him. Somehow.

She returned to her seat in the corner with renewed interest and began surveying the company for the appropriate characteristics.

"Who is that gentleman?" she asked a passing footman, who had given her a few pitying glances during the evening.

He said, "Which one, Miss?" He had a nice smile and looked as if his wig itched.

"The man in the green coat." To call it green was faint praise: it was a pale, pale green, embroidered with black flowers. It was the most exquisite garment she had ever seen. The man was tall and moved with the careless grace of an athlete. He wore no wig, unlike the other perspiring gentlemen pacing through the dance. His hair was a rumpled black, shot with two or three brilliant streaks of white, and tied at his neck with a pale green ribbon. He was a dangerous mixture of carelessness and supreme elegance.

The footman handed her a glass in order to disguise the fact they were speaking.

16

"That's His Grace, the Duke of Villiers. He plays chess. Hadn't you heard of him then?"

She shook her head and took the glass.

"They do say he's the best for chess in England," the footman said. He leaned a bit closer and said, eyes dancing, "Lady Cholmondelay thinks he's the best at sport, if you'll forgive my presumption."

A snort of laughter escaped Roberta's mouth before she could stop herself.

"I've watched you this eve," he said. "Tapping your foot. We've our own ball below stairs. And it seems no one knows you here. Why don't you come back there and dance a round with me?"

"I couldn't! Someone would —" She looked around. The room was crowded with laughing, dancing peers. No one had paid any attention to her, or even spoken to her in over an hour. Her papa had wandered off again with Mrs. Grope, content to think that she was "hunting prey," as he put it in the carriage.

"Below stairs, they won't know you're a lady," the footman said, "not in that dress, miss. They'll think you're a lady's maid. At least that way you can have a dance!"

"All right," she whispered.

For the first time all evening, young men bowed before her. She invented an irascible mistress and had great fun describing her tribulations dressing her. She danced twice with "her" footman and separately with three more. Finally, she realized that there was a remote possibility that her father would miss her, and she headed back to the ball.

Then she realized there was also the possibility that he would have forgotten about her and left for the inn.

She ran down the corridor, slammed open the baize door that marked the servants' quarters — and knocked over the Duke of Villiers.

He stared at her from the ground, with eyes as cold as spring rainfall. Then he said without stirring, in a husky, drawling voice that made her shiver all over, "You must tell the butler to train you in proper behavior."

She blushed and dropped a curtsy, dazed by the pure raw masculinity of him, by his hollowed cheeks and jaded look. He was everything that her father was not. There wasn't an ounce of sentiment in him. A man like that would never embarrass himself.

Life with her father had taught her to be blunt about her own emotions, or risk having them dissected by a poet. So she knew instantly what it was she felt: *lust.* Her father's poetry on the subject filtered through her mind, confirming her sense.

He stood and then tipped up her chin. "An astonishing beauty to find in such a dim squirrel's hole as the servants' quarters."

Roberta felt a thrill of triumph. Apparently *he* didn't think that she had a beetle brow or a humped back. The lust was mutual. "Ah —" she said, trying to think what to say other than a blunt proposal.

"Red hair," he said, rather dreamily. "Extraordinary high arches of eyebrows, slightly tilted eyes. A deep ruby for a lower lip. I could paint you in water colors."

His catalog raised Roberta's hackles a little; she felt like a horse he was considering for purchase. "I should prefer not to look blurry; could you not manage oils?" she asked.

He raised an eyebrow. "No maid's apron, and the voice of a lady. I fear I misjudged your station."

"As a matter of fact, I am rejoining my family in the ballroom."

His eyes skittered over the plain laced front of her gown, with its misshapen pleats that looked as if she had fashioned them herself.

He dropped his hand. "That makes you altogether more delectable and forbidden fare, an impoverished noblewoman. I would have you without delay if you had but a few pennies to your name, my dear, but even I have a few paltry morals. Foibles, really."

"You assume a great deal," she said. She meant that he was assuming she was poor, although the supposition was fair enough, given her clothing. But he jumped to the more obvious meaning.

" 'Tis true you might not have me. Though I'll tell you the secret to my success with women, and I won't charge you ha'pence since you haven't an extra one to your purse."

She waited, cataloging the sheen of his coat and the rumpled perfection of his hair.

"I don't really give a damn whether I have you or not."

"You shan't have me," she said, stung. "Because I feel precisely the same way about you."

"In that case, I will kiss your fingertips and retire."

As he made a leg before her, she watched the skirts of his coat fall into perfect pleats. Not for nothing was she a wordsmith's daughter. Pale green wasn't descriptive enough; the silk taffeta of his coat was celadon, the green of new leaves. And its black embroidery, on close inspection, was mulberry-colored.

It was an exquisite combination. Enough to change her mind entirely. What she felt was entirely too deep for a flimsy emotion such as lust.

What she felt wasn't lust — it was love. For the first time in her life . . . she was in love.

In love!

"I'm going to London," she told her father once they were home again. "My heart is in chains and I must follow its call." Though such extravagant language was definitely not Roberta's chosen mode of expression, she felt that quoting one of her father's poems was a sound precaution.

"You most certainly are not!" he said, ignoring her literary reference. "I will —"

"Without you," she said. "And without Mrs. Grope."

"Absolutely not!"

They battled on for a month or so until the March edition of *Rambler's Magazine* arrived in the post.

These etchings were no more accurate than those of two years earlier. She was humped-backed and fiercely browed, on her knees before a man in livery, presumably praying for the footman's hand in marriage. "Like father, like daughter," the inscription read. "We always suspected that desperation was hereditary."

Roberta had no doubt that the image was selling briskly in Humphrey's Print Shop.

"My conscience is clear!" her father bellowed, once he understood the reference. "Surely you could have guessed that servants are in the pay of gossip rags? How could you not, given the fact that Mrs. Grope and myself make such frequent appearances in *Town and Country*? Someone made a pretty penny from your folly. It's no good begging me to write another poem; the powers of my literature would be of no avail."

The marquess's rage was assuaged only after writing four hundred lines of iambic pentameter rhyming "serpent's tooth" and "daughter," which is no easy feat.

His daughter's distress was diminished only by repeating to herself that she was going to marry the Duke of Villiers, order clothes of celadon silk and never listen to another poem again in her life.

She commandeered her father's second-best coach and the second housemaid to accompany her to London and left, clutching a valise filled with Mrs. Parthnell's unsightly clothing, a measured sum of money and a poem from her father, which was the only introduction he would vouchsafe her.

"Oh, brave new world!" she whispered to herself. And then wrinkled her nose. *No more poetry.* The Duke of Villiers had likely never heard of John Donne and probably couldn't tell a roundelay from a rickshaw.

He was perfect.

CHAPTER 1

April 10, 1783
Beaumont House, Kensington

"In Paris, a married lady must have a lover or she is an unknown. And she may be pardoned two." The door to the drawing room swung open, but the young woman sitting with her back to the door took no notice.

"Two?" an exquisitely dressed young man remarked. "I gather that Frenchmen are a happy race of men. They seemed so petulant to me when I was last there. It must be the embarrassment of riches, like having three custards after supper."

"Three lovers are considered rather too many," the woman replied. "Although I have known some who considered three to be a privilege rather than an abundance." Her low laugh was a type that tickled a man's breastbone and even lower. It said volumes about her personal abilities to manage one

25

— or three — Frenchmen with aplomb.

Her husband closed the door behind him and stepped into the room.

The young man glanced up and came to his feet, bowing without extraordinary haste. "Your Grace."

"Lord Corbin," the Duke of Beaumont replied, bowing. Corbin was just to Jemma's taste: elegant, assured and far more intelligent than he admitted. In fact, he would make a good man in parliament, not that Corbin would lower himself to something approaching work.

His brother-in-law, the Earl of Gryffyn, rose and made him a casual bow.

"Your servant, Gryffyn," the duke said, making a leg.

"Do join us, Beaumont," his wife said, looking up at him with an expression of the utmost friendliness. "It's a pleasure to see you. Is the House of Lords not meeting today?" That was part and parcel with the war they had waged for the last eight years: conversation embroidered with delicate barbs, rarely with coarse emotion.

"It is in session, but I thought to spend some time with you. After all, you have barely returned from Paris." The duke bared his teeth in an approximation of a smile.

"I miss it already," Jemma said, with a lavish sigh. "It's marvelous that you're here, darling," she said, leaning forward a bit and tapping him on the hand with her fan. "I'm just waiting for Harriet, the Duchess of Berrow, to arrive. And then we shall make a decision about the centerpiece for tomorrow's fête."

"Fowle tells me that we are holding a ball." The duke — who thought of himself as Elijah, though he would be very affronted were any person to address him so — kept his voice even. Those years of parliamentary debate were going to prove useful, now that Jemma had returned to London. 'Twas the reason he'd stayed home for the day, if truth be told. He had to strike a bargain with his wife that would curb her activities to an acceptable level. And he wouldn't get there by losing his temper; he remembered their newlywed battles well enough.

"Dear me, don't tell me that I forgot to inform you! I know it's a bit mad, but the plans gave me something to do on the voyage here."

She looked genuinely repentant, and indeed, for all Elijah knew, she was. The game of marriage they played required strictly friendly manners in public. Not that they were ever in private.

"He just did tell you that," her brother

put in. "You'd better watch out, Sis. You're not used to sharing a household."

"It was truly ill-mannered of me," she said, leaping to her feet, which made her silk petticoats swirl around her narrow ankles. She was dressed in a pale blue gown *à la française,* embroidered all over with forget-me-nots. Her bodice caressed every curve of her breasts and narrow waist before the skirts billowed over her panniers.

By all rights, the way her side hoops concealed the swell of her hips should be distasteful to a man, and yet Elijah had to admit that they played an irresistible part in a man's imagination, leading the eye from the curve of a breast to the narrow waist, and then driving him perforce to imagine slender limbs and — and the rest of it.

Jemma held out her hand; Elijah paused for a moment and then took it. She smiled at him, as a mother might smile at a little boy reluctant to wash his face. "I am so glad that you are able to join us this morning, Beaumont. While I trust that these gentlemen have impeccable opinions" — she cast a glimmering smile at Corbin — "one's husband's opinion must, of course, prevail. I do declare that it's been so long since I felt as if I *had* a husband that it is quite a novelty! I shall probably bore you to tears asking you to approve my ribbons."

In the old days, the first days of their marriage, Elijah would have bristled. But he was seasoned by years of dedicated jousting in Parliament where the stakes were more important than ribbons and trifles. "I am quite certain that Corbin can do my duty with your ribbons." He said it with just the right amount of disinterest and courtesy in his voice.

From the corner of his eye, Elijah noticed that Corbin didn't even blink at the idea he had just been invited by a duke to do his husbandly duty. Perhaps the man could keep Jemma occupied enough that she wouldn't cause too many scandals before parliament went into recess. He turned sharply toward the door, annoyed to discover that his wife's beauty seemed more potent in his own house than it had been in Paris during his rare visits.

Partly it was because Jemma had not powdered her hair. She knew quite well that the shimmer of weathered gold was far more enticing than powder, and contrasted better with her blue eyes. It was only — he told himself — because she was his wife that he felt this prickling irritation at her beauty. Or perhaps the irritation was caused by her self-possession. When they first married, she wasn't so flawless. Now everything about her was polished to perfection, from the color of her lip to the witty edge of her comments.

Those blue eyes of hers widened just slightly, and she cast him another of her glimmering smiles. "We really are two hearts that beat as one, Beaumont," she said.

"In that case," her brother said, "it is truly odd that you have spent so much time apart. Not to break up this touching example at marital felicity — so rare in our depraved age and, I think we'll all agree, an inspiration to us all — but can you just show us the damned centerpiece now, Jemma? I've got an appointment on Bond Street, and your friend the duchess doesn't seem to be making an appearance."

"It's in the next room, if Caro has everything prepared. She wasn't quite ready when you arrived."

Elijah caught himself before asking who Caro was.

Jemma was still speaking. "I trust her with everything. She has the most elegant eye of any female I've ever known. Except, perhaps, Her Majesty, Queen Marie Antoinette."

Elijah shot his wife a look that showed exactly what he felt about those who boasted of intimacy with French royalty. "Shall we examine this centerpiece, sirs?" he said, turning to Corbin and Gryffyn. "The duchess is considered quite a leader of fashion in Paris. I myself shall never forget her masquerade ball of '79."

"Were you there?" Jemma asked wonderingly. "I vow, I had quite forgotten." She tapped him on the arm with her fan. "Now it comes back to me. All the men were dressed as satyrs — 'twas most ravishingly amusing — but you wore black and white, for all the world like a parliamentary penguin."

He dropped her hand, so that he could bow again. "Alas, I do not show to best advantage with a satyr's tail." And neither did the asses of Frenchmen, though he didn't say it aloud.

She sighed. "Both members of my family declined to join the fun. So English — so pompous — so —"

"So clothed," Gryffyn said. "There were some knees in evidence that night that should never have seen the light of day. I still have trouble forgetting Le Comte d'Auvergne's bony knobs."

Jemma peeked through the doors to the ballroom beyond. Then she laughed and flung them open. "How wonderful it all looks, Caro! You are brilliant, absolutely brilliant, as always!"

Corbin was briskly following in Jemma's train, so Elijah grabbed his brother-in-law's elbow. "Who the hell is Caro?"

"Pestilently intelligent woman," Gryffyn said. "Jemma's secretary. She's been around for four or five years. You haven't encountered her?"

And, at Elijah's shrug, "She prepares Jemma's most extravagant escapades. Accomplices in scandal, that's the way to describe them. Prepare to be dazzled by her incomparable abilities, not that you'll appreciate them. I don't suppose that you're secretly hoping that Jemma will transform into a political wife, are you?"

"My hope is limited to a wish that she doesn't topple my career," Elijah said. "Do I understand you to say that all of Jemma's secretary's abilities are directed to the creation of scandal?"

"As I said, you won't like it," Gryffyn said. They were at the door. He pulled it farther open and moved to the side. "This is pretty standard for her."

Elijah walked through the door and stopped short.

"Bloody hell," he breathed.

"It's better than those satyrs. No tail,"

Gryffyn pointed out.

As Elijah stared into the room, he felt his hard-won calm and control slipping from his grasp. The huge mahogany table that generally stood in the dining room had been removed to the middle of the ballroom. Rather than dishes, it held an enormous pink shell, apparently made of clay. Rosebuds were strewn all about, falling in chains to the floor. Numbly he noticed that Jemma was exclaiming over how realistic the flowers appeared. "And the sea shells!" she squealed. "A beautiful touch, Caro!"

But that wasn't it, of course.

What was making his heart thud against the wall of his chest wasn't the hundreds of pounds worth of fabric flowers, nor the shell, nor even the pearls, because there were also strings and strings of pearls. God knows, he had more than enough money for whatever extravagances Jemma came up with. What Elijah treasured more than anything else in the world was his stock of carefully nourished, tenderly used, political power.

He had nurtured it day by day. Built up a solid reputation for energetic, thoughtful argument. While his wife lived in Paris for the last eight years, he built a career without the help that other men got from their wives throwing dinner parties, or hosting salons. He'd come to the top of the House of Lords, to one of the most respected positions in the kingdom, by marshalling his intellect, never taking a bribe. Separating himself from the corrupt policies and wild scandals that plagued Fox and the Prince of Wales's disgraceful cronies.

And now, when he might have only a little time left to further his work —

The centerpiece wasn't wearing a damned scrap of clothing.

And she was painted gold; never mind the pearls that were glued around her body at regular intervals.

His brother-in-law was watching her with a calculated, lustful look in his eye that Elijah despised, though he had to admit that only a dead man would ignore this centerpiece.

"At least she's not wearing a tail," Gryffyn commented.

At that very moment, the naked, gold-painted young lady bent sideways and fiddled with the little stand on which she was leaning. A huge spray of gorgeous peacock feathers burst from behind her beautifully curved rear.

"Spoke too soon," Gryffyn said happily.

"Damn it to hell," Elijah breathed.

CHAPTER 2

Roberta entered the room just as the peacock tail sprang into view. About to announce her presence, the butler froze, mouth open. She patted his arm. "I'll announce myself," she told him. "My cousin is expecting me."

He nodded and backed out of the room.

That was a stroke of luck, given that her cousin was not expecting her. In truth, the Duchess of Beaumont likely didn't even know she existed.

The duchess was much more beautiful than the sketches Roberta had seen in *Town and Country Magazine.* Her hair was tumbled into a sophisticated mass of curls, and her clothes were exquisite. In fact, she looked rather like portraits of Roberta's mother, with perfectly balanced features and deep crimson lips. But of course the duchess had a potent combination of elegance and sensual appeal that Roberta doubted her mother, buried deep in the country with a husband whom the charitable labeled eccentric, had ever possessed.

Roberta walked forward, but no one noticed her. There were two gentlemen standing by the table, gawking up at the naked woman. One had to suppose she was used to the attention, because she was smiling at them most genially. In fact, she reminded Roberta of nothing so much as a toothy crocodile, if crocodiles were endowed with large, fleshy bosoms.

The only gentleman not staring at the goddess was glowering at the duchess. He had to be the duke. Beaumont was often illustrated holding the reins of government or whipping members of the House. He looked powerful, with a sort of furious elegance.

"One of the points I should like to make," he said with icy forcefulness, "is that this preposterously tailed young woman may well destroy my career. She will undoubtedly create an interesting evening, but have you given a thought to proprieties? I count among my important acquaintances a good many people with young, unmarried daughters. After one peek at this spectacle, they will never darken the door of my house again!"

The duchess seemed unmoved. "I assure you that no one in Lords will be other than amused by my centerpiece, Beaumont. My absence has had no effect on your ability to garner support, and neither will my presence."

"Apparently your years in Paris have had no effect on your intelligence," the duke snarled. Roberta took a tentative step backward. She wanted no part in a marital quarrel.

"Apparently your manners declined in the same period; what a pity."

"He's right, Jemma. You're being naïve," another gentleman said, tearing his eyes away from the naked centerpiece. He looked so much like the duchess that he must be her brother, Lord Gryffyn, and therefore Roberta's cousin (once, or twice, or — if one is punctilious — twelve times removed). The eyebrows were darker, but his carelessly tied-back hair was the color of brandy. They had the same cherry mouth, though he had none of his sister's flawless perfection. His coat was a nice steel blue, but looked as if he pulled it on without thinking, as his waistcoat was an odd orange.

"I would guess that this particular Venus will offend the female half of the *ton*," Lord Gryffyn was saying.

"She is not Venus, but Neptune's Queen," a lady standing to the side put in. "Venus was a tired concept five years ago!" She curled her lip with such emphasis that she had to be French.

"Ah, but this isn't Paris," Lord Gryffyn said. "We're of tender stock, and we like to pretend that we don't know what various body parts look like. At this rate, Mademoiselle Caro, you will single-handedly instruct the better part of London on the composition of a beautiful pair of thighs. It's not worth it."

"Your own brother agrees with me," the duke snapped. "I will not have this sort of behavior in my house."

There was a freezing moment of silence. The cheerful smile dropped from the duchess's eyes. "Won't you?" she asked.

The duke had to be six feet tall, but to Roberta he looked at least seven. "I will not." He spaced his words in an ominous fashion.

"In that case, I suppose I shall not be the one to educate the English on the delicate matter of a woman's leg," the duchess said. "Not when you're there to do it for me, and in your own offices in Westminster."

Roberta blinked, but the duchess was turning away.

"It's damned hard to imagine Jemma as a political wife," Lord Gryffyn remarked to Beaumont. "Do naked women grace tables in Paris? I've never seen one in London." He checked himself. "Well, not in this kind of house anyway."

He looked up and met Roberta's eyes. She involuntarily fell back another step. How could she possibly —

"Looks like you have a visitor, Jemma," he said.

Jemma swung around, and so did the duke. The third gentleman was still deep in conversation with Neptune's queen and didn't hear.

Roberta dropped a curtsy. "Good afternoon," she said. "I'm afraid your butler was overcome by the event and retired to compose himself. I told him I would introduce myself."

The duchess smiled at her. Roberta was suddenly aware of her large feet. She even felt as if her overstuffed, shabby bag, dropped in the foyer by a disdainful footman, was humping along behind her.

"Please forgive us for being in such disarray," the duchess said, a wave of her hand signifying (one must assume) the naked woman and the squabble with her husband.

"Not at all," Roberta said, stammering.

"My name is Lady Roberta St. Giles." She paused.

There wasn't a spark of recognition on the duchess's face, but the duke stepped forward. "I recognize the name, madam."

Roberta breathed a sigh of relief.

"You're collecting for the Chelsea pensioners, are you not? It was most kind of you to attend me here, but I assure you, quite unnecessary." He came forward with determined kindness, clearly intending to sweep her out of the house. "I'm so sorry that you were present at a scene like this. It's enough to horrify any woman of delicate sensibility."

The duchess intervened. "If I am to be a political wife, Beaumont, I might as well begin. I gather that charity, rather than peacock feathers, should be my every thought." She tucked Roberta's arm under her own. "Chelsea pensioners are a most worthy charity, Lady Roberta," she said. "I'd be honored to hear about your work. Would you like a cup of tea?"

"You don't understand," Roberta said, holding her ground. But when she opened her mouth, she could not bring herself to tell the truth. That everything she owned was drooping in the entryway. That she had come — unannounced and undoubtedly unwelcome — to stay. To find a husband.

Without another look at her husband or her guests, the duchess began drawing her toward the door. "Please come to my sitting room," she said. "Beaumont, do you make my farewells." She didn't look at him as she said it.

The duke's voice was icy. "And your centerpiece?"

"We shall discuss it later."

"I see no reason to waste my time. A naked woman will never grace my dining table. That is all I have to say about it."

"Pish on that!" the duchess cried, stopping in her tracks and dropping Roberta's arm. "She's a work of art."

"She's a disgrace," he countered.

The duchess showed no outward signs of fear, which Roberta thought was amazing. Faced with such a large specimen of enraged manhood, she herself would have quailed.

"You're going to lose this one," Lord Gryffyn said cheerfully. "Believe it or not, Jemma, your husband is up to good works that shouldn't get mucked up by your naked ladies, no matter how luscious. What do you think?" he asked Roberta. "You're obviously a proper young lady. Would you think that a ball featuring Lady Neptune would be ill-received?"

Roberta glanced up at the centerpiece. She truly was naked: it was rather interesting how different her body was from Roberta's. For one thing, her breasts had to be three times as large. "I believe that most people will find it unhygienic," she said. "I gather that is your dining table? There's a chance that people might hesitate to dine here in the future."

Her comment was met with flat silence, and then a bellow of laughter from the duchess's brother. "She's got you there, Jemma."

The duke smiled, and Roberta suddenly felt the power of his rather icy face when it melted into a smile. "I am feeling very prone to helping pensioners," he said softly. "One good deed, etc."

The duchess gave a wry little shrug, and then turned around and called to the Frenchwoman. "Caro, darling, she needs to be clothed. Could you fashion her something appropriate?"

"Surely you jest!" she replied, throwing her hand to her brow. "Do you conceive of the diaper?"

"As long as it covers her from collarbone to ankle," the duke stated. The woman broke into remonstrations, waving her arms in the air.

"Now I really need a cup of tea," the duchess muttered, taking Roberta's elbow again. "Shall we go to my sitting room? It's cowardly of me to leave Beaumont with my secretary, but he deserves it, don't you think? I promise not to be petulant about Lady Neptune's nappy." Lord Gryffyn had turned away; the secretary's voice was escalating into a shriek.

"Perhaps Mademoiselle Caro will be able to bend her designs to the tender sensibilities of English gentlewomen," Roberta suggested, feeling quite certain that most of the Frenchwoman's designs would terrify and amaze the ladies of her acquaintance.

"And perhaps not. Then she will leave me and return to Paris, where at least three *comtesses* are slavering for her services. I've had to double her wage twice in the last few years. Which is a frightfully shallow thing to admit when you've called on such a serious business."

"Well, as to that —"

"Please, let's not talk of sad subjects until we're seated with a cup of tea. I would ring for claret; I always think that claret is a sustaining drink for unpleasant subjects, but it's too early."

They walked into a small sitting room. "I must have this redone," the duchess said, pausing a moment. "I've only come from Paris a day or so ago, or I assure you that I wouldn't bring you into such a shabby place."

The room did have a rather forbidding aspect. It was painted a drab mustard color and featured a large picture of a smiling young woman holding a severed head by its hair. "Just look at her," the duchess said. "She carries that head with all the jaunty air of a tavern maid."

"It must be Judith and Holofernes," Roberta said. "Under the circumstances, Judith looks rather cheerful, don't you think?"

The duchess strolled over to the picture. "Actually, I think she looks rather drunk. Don't you think she looks tipsy?"

"I believe that Judith first brought Holofernes some wine," Roberta said. "Before she took off his head. Though I would hate to cast disparagements on the artist's skill, her drunken aspect might have to do with the fact that her eyes do not appear to be level."

"Her face is also remarkably rosy."

"Probably the hard work," Roberta pointed out. "I would guess that it takes a strong arm to sever a man's neck."

"Good point. I can see that you are very practical. Do sit down here, Lady Roberta,

44

with your back to the severed head. I shall have it removed at my very first opportunity. I haven't lived in London for eight years, but I still wake up trembling when I think of my mother-in-law; this is her special sitting room, you understand. Thank goodness, she lives in a dower house in the country now."

Roberta seated herself. "I should explain who I am —"

"Yes," the duchess interrupted. "You are my very first encounter as the wife of a politician. So you understand that I am very anxious to get this right. How much money would you like?"

"It's not money," Roberta said. "You see, I am —"

"Not money! Oh dear, then it's that altogether more valuable commodity of time, isn't it? I'll be no use to you. Not only am I congenitally unhelpful in practical matters, but I tend to gather people around me who are as — shall we say — immoral as I?"

"Are you quite immoral?" Roberta asked, her scruples overcome by strong curiosity. The duchess didn't *look* immoral. Of course, Roberta's assessments were quite likely inaccurate, given that they were founded on years of living with her father's mistresses, women who prided themselves on a reckless disregard for conventional morality.

"Quite," the duchess said with unrelieved cheerfulness. "Absolutely. Up to my neck in it. Naked ladies on the table is only the start, I assure you. So I'm afraid that my assistance wouldn't be of the least use to you."

"In truth, I think you can be," Roberta said.

The duchess looked alarmed. "Truly, I cannot. I become irritable — fierce — when bored, and I am so quickly bored."

Roberta was thoroughly enjoying herself now. "How fierce?"

"Dastardly! Once, in the midst of a tedious dinner, I insulted the Comtesse de la Motte by being a trifle too forthright about her origins. She would have gone white in the face, but for her excessive application of rouge."

The door swung open rather violently, revealing the duchess's secretary. Her chest was heaving, her hair was disheveled, and her fists were clenched. In fact, she was the very vision of Judith, lacking only a severed body part or two. Clearly, if her wishes were respected, she would be toting the duke's head.

"Oh dear," the duchess said, under her breath.

"I return this minute — this evening —

this very minute to the shores of France, where my work is appreciated! This husband of yours is a man with no sense of the beauty in life. No sense for the aesthetic value. He has a soul of the *mud.* He bathes in the dirt, this one! I pity you!"

"Oh, Caro," the duchess said, rising from her chair. "Surely you cannot mean to say that you will leave me. *Me?* After all the glorious events we planned together? Think of the satyrs! Think of the King sending you a note after the Crystal Forest!"

"Your husband does not understand my genius," the enraged Frenchwoman hissed. "I know the type. He will be hedging me about with his concerns and his proprieties. I cannot be hedged about! I am a genius!"

"Geniuses sometimes have to work under terrible conditions," Roberta suggested, coming forward. "In fact, it is then that they produce their best, their most enviable work. Think of Michelangelo, lying on his back to paint the ceiling of the Sistine Chapel."

The maddened eye of the Frenchwoman fixed on Roberta. "Michelangelo was a foolish Italian! I am *French!* I cannot be stymied by the hidebound opinions of a petty bureaucrat!"

Behind her, Roberta heard a small snort

47

of laughter from the wife of the petty bureaucrat.

"But to turn your back on a true challenge . . ." Roberta shook her head. "It's not the action of a Frenchwoman, *mademoiselle.*" Then she decided it would be better to soothe the wild beast in her own language, and continued in the same vein in French, silently thanking her governess for her insistence on the language. *"Excusez-nous, c'est bien pour ça que Leonardo da Vinci a choisi de vivre en France. Nous étions, encore, des barbares."*

"She is right," the duchess cooed. "Your artistry has suffered naught but a small setback."

"I suggest," Roberta said, "that you think not in terms of the Queen of the Sea — so redundant, so tedious — but in terms of the great mythological figures. All of whom wore clothes. Now when I see a giant shell, do I think of Neptune? No!"

"I know," the secretary said, lip curling. "You think of Venus. I'm tired of Venus and her foolish shell."

"I think of Helen of Troy, the most beautiful woman ever to live."

"And precisely when did Helen appear in a sea shell?"

"It's not a seashell, but an *egg,*" Roberta

explained. "It can be painted white. The huge egg splits to reveal the woman who began the Trojan War. Of course, she would be wearing classic Greek garb."

"Ah," Caro said, her eyes narrowing. "Perhaps . . ."

"Brilliant!" the duchess cried. "I adore it, love it, and so will Beaumont."

"But my tail!" Caro said. "The glorious touch of the Queen of Neptune's mechanical tail, which took two days to design."

"Never fear, we can use your brilliant peacock tail for something else," the duchess promised. She ushered her out of the room and turned back with a huge smile. Roberta blinked; the pure force of the duchess's personality was unnerving. "Your pensioners, Lady Roberta, just became my special project!"

"In truth, I don't have any pensioners," Roberta said, returning to her seat. "I'm afraid that the duke mistook me for someone more charitable."

"How unusual. Beaumont actually got something wrong. I feel as if a Hallelujah Chorus ought to break out in mid-air."

"I only have myself," Roberta said. "That and my luggage."

"Your luggage?" The duchess was looking a bit bewildered now.

"I am your cousin, thrice removed. Actually more than three. At any rate, my mother looked something like you. We are remotely connected, and I was hoping that you would bring me into society." Roberta said it with a gulp. She was being remarkably bold, and as Mrs. Grope had assured her, she was likely to be thrown in the street. She clenched her hands together tightly.

"I have a letter from my father," she added. "Your father and he were very dear to each other in their youth."

The duchess didn't appear to be curling her lip in horror. "Really? I would have thought my father had no friends at all, from various pleasant little memories I have of him. It's heartening to imagine that he was once a boy," she said. "But what am I thinking; you've come to stay with me. How splendid!"

Roberta's heart thumped. "It is?"

The duchess was smiling. "Of course it is! I never had a sister, and I always wanted one. Don't worry; I shall know everyone in this benighted city within a week or two, and we'll make you a splendid marriage. If you don't mind my asking, are you connected on my mother's or my father's side?"

"On your mother's," Roberta said, feeling slightly dizzy from the relief of it. "I'm afraid

50

it's a rather faint connection. My mother was your great-aunt's second cousin's child. Her maiden name was Cressida Enright. She was rarely in London, as she married at the age of sixteen. She died when I was quite young."

"Wait a minute!"

Roberta waited, knowing exactly what was coming.

"The Mad Marquess," the duchess exclaimed. "Not — your father? The poet?"

Roberta nodded reluctantly.

"My goodness, I suppose that I knew he had a daughter. How old are you?"

"Twenty-one."

"I am twenty-eight. You're a newborn compared to me. But surely you're an heiress? Isn't the Mad Marquess —" She checked herself. "I'm so sorry, your father is Marquess of Wharton and?"

"Wharton and Malmesbury," Roberta said. "It's quite all right. No one remembers his title. At any rate, I do have a dowry, but how could I possibly marry, while immured in the country? My father refused to travel even to Bath in the last few years."

"Your neighbors are no help?"

"We don't have many. My father bought the adjoining estate to the north some years ago. And I'm afraid that he has alienated those who live nearby."

"By sending them poetry?" the duchess asked, and stopped. "You must tell me at your leisure; I shan't question you like a fishwife in your first five minutes. At any rate, you have done just the right thing. You shall be my ward. All the finest ladies in Paris had wards; they're so useful in forcing one to not malinger at home."

"I can't imagine you malingering at home," Roberta said, rather shyly.

The duchess twinkled at her. "Perhaps not *alone,* but there are certainly times when one finds oneself, shall we say, drawn to the idea of a lazy evening? And yet I consider that to be a woman's downfall. One must dress every evening, or one quickly becomes a slug."

Roberta nodded. Rarely having had an occasion to dress formally in the whole of her life, she found the prospect of a quiet night at home loathsome.

"You couldn't have come at a better time. I suppose you heard about Beaumont's collapse in Lords last fall? Naturally, I hope that it was nothing more than a case of nerves, but . . ." Her voice trailed off and Roberta thought that she actually looked rather stricken, which didn't agree with the biting dislike she'd seen between the duke

52

and duchess.

"Duty meant I must return."

Roberta nodded. Her father's response to reading of the Duke of Beaumont's collapse in the very midst of a speech in the House had been to laugh uproariously and prophesy the man was a drunk, but having met the duke, she doubted her father's diagnosis.

"I must produce an heir and all the rest of it," the duchess remarked, quite as if she were saying it might rain tomorrow. "Most unpleasant, but it needs be done, and clearly I'm the one to do it."

"Oh!" Roberta said.

"I expect you're wondering just how we shall manage the bedding part of it."

Roberta stifled a nervous giggle. Talking to the duchess was like talking to no one she had ever encountered before. "I —" she said.

"I assure you, I share your concern. The imagination quails, truly it does. Beaumont and I rarely exchange words that could be described as civil. But there, Lady Roberta, a woman's life, etc. etc. Do you play chess by any chance?"

That question caught Roberta off-balance as well. "No. I'm afraid I never learned. My father doesn't play, and my governess had strong views on appropriate activities for women."

The duchess waved her hand in the air dismissively. "Spend your time sorting embroidery yarns and generally boring yourself to tears? If you are lucky enough not to spend your days scrubbing a man's breeches."

Roberta couldn't help it; she started to smile. When Jemma laughed, one simply had to laugh with her.

"The only problem I can see with you living here," the duchess continued, "would have to do with your standards."

"My standards?" Roberta asked. The duchess was looking at her expectantly.

"Ethics . . . morality . . . that sort of thing."

"Well, I have them," Roberta said cautiously. Adding: "I suppose." In truth, she couldn't claim a great knowledge of moral strictures, given her father's propensity for lively companionship.

"Well, I have only a few." The duchess smiled at Roberta with an odd, crooked little smile. "If you are going to live with me, I simply won't be able to bear it if you are constantly peering at me in a disappointed kind of way. And if you criticize me, I'm afraid that we would quarrel directly. Among my many faults is a quite simple inability to accept that I'm wrong. Do you see how awful I am to live with?"

Roberta laughed. "I could not be disappointed, not unless you metamorphosed into Mrs. Grope, who has been my constant companion these two years. In truth, Your Grace, I can't imagine reprimanding you for anything!"

"Oh, you'll think of something. But we'd better go on intimate terms, don't you think? My name is Jemma, which is short for the worthy name of Jemima. May I address you as Roberta?"

"I'd be delighted!"

"Well, Roberta, I shall just enumerate my faults, shall I? And let me be quite clear that if you feel unable to stay with me, I have any number of relatives who will bring you out with all the appropriate rites and ceremonies. In fact, it's quite possible that you *should* do that. I'm not at all certain that young, unmarried girls are supposed to be living in houses featuring centerpieces akin to what Caro designs."

"Perhaps not the completely naked ones," Roberta admitted. "But there is a certain educational value, as your brother noted."

Jemma gave a delightful chortle of laughter. "Who knew that it would take so much gold paint to cover one chest?"

"Exactly!"

"I am just realizing that you managed Caro as beautifully as you deflected my annoyance over my husband's dictates. I suppose you are used to people of artistic temperament?"

"Life with my father was — has been —"

Very kindly Jemma cut in. "I can guess," she said. "Living in France for years, I was often behind the times with English gossip, but your father's escapades are always in circulation." Her smile was so cheerfully non-judgmental that Roberta found herself smiling back. "So, do tell me, did you feel faint when you saw my centerpiece?"

"Not in the slightest," Roberta assured her. She added, unable to resist, "But perhaps I shall once you enumerate all your faults."

"It's hard to know where to begin," Jemma said.

Roberta raised an eyebrow.

"Well, let's see. For one thing, I'm a duchess."

CHAPTER 3

"A duchess!" Whatever Roberta had been expecting in the way of Jemma's faults, this wasn't one of them. "What's wrong with that? I have always believed it is a — a *consummation devoutly to be wished.*" And given that she herself had every intention of being Duchess of Villiers, come hell or high water, she really meant it.

The door opened and the stout butler, his face returned to a normal hue, entered with a silver tea tray. "Oh thank you, Fowle," Jemma said. "That is so kind of you." After a moment of fiddling with the tray, he left. Jemma poured tea very carefully into fragile tea cups and asked, "Were you quoting poetry just now?"

"Yes, although I couldn't tell you who wrote it. My father says the phrase frequently and it stuck in my head."

"Have you had much to do with duchesses?" Jemma didn't seem to mean that question unkindly; she was fussing with the sugar bowl.

Roberta glanced down at her badly sewn skirt. "No, I have not."

"Well, I assure you that we are an abominable sort. The very title gives us license to make the worst of ourselves, and we so frequently do."

"Really?" Roberta accepted a steaming cup of hot tea.

"I have several duchesses among my acquaintances; in fact, we have formed something of a friendship based on the title itself. You see, to be a duchess means that every person you meet will fawn, if he does not positively grovel."

"Ah," Roberta said, wondering if this was a veiled way of pointing out that she had not groveled appropriately.

"It is beyond tedious. It makes one stupid."

"I believe," Roberta said, "I would hazard the loss of my intelligence. And I am fairly certain," she said, putting down her cup, "that a small amount of fawning would be a pleasant antidote to Mrs. Grope's opinions."

"Dear me, Mrs. Grope does seem to enter your conversation with some regularity," Jemma said. "Who is she?"

Roberta hesitated and then prevaricated.

"I have had a limited circle of acquaintances in the past few years, and I would love to excise her from my mind."

"And I am dithering on about duchesses. Therein another of my faults: I am incurably shallow. Truthfully, Roberta, my duchess friends are quite like myself."

"And that is so terrible?" Roberta was happily conscious that Jemma seemed almost a friend already — which surely implied that she, Roberta, was natural duchess material.

"Shallow. Fickle when it comes to men — and you should take that in the worst possible light. This is not a household in which I can imagine a gently reared vicar's daughter being comfortable. We are desperate in our affections and even more so in our general dislike for our husbands. Well, those of us who *have* husbands."

"What happened to the dukes?"

"Oh, the usual sort of things," Jemma said with a shrug. "Beaumont and I separated years ago, as you must know. My friend Harriet will pay me a visit today; her husband died two years ago, so she's a widow. I have one friend, Poppy, who is so new to the duchess-business that she is barely wet behind the ears; she's married to the Duke of Fletcher. Of all of us, I'd say Poppy is our only hope for a happy marital relationship, but she's going about that all the wrong way. And then finally there's my friend Isidore. She doesn't quite count as a duchess, since she hasn't married her duke yet. They've been engaged since birth, and she lives with his mother so if he ever returns from the Orient, or wherever he is, she'll take the title along with the man."

"Since I am not a duchess," Roberta offered, "are you quite certain that you wish my company at all? Your acquaintances sound rarefied in the extreme."

Jemma opened up her mouth to reply but the door opened and Fowle appeared. "Your Grace," he said, "His Grace begs the kindness of a moment of your —"

Belying the courtesy of the butler's request, the duke's voice rose in the near distance, his words muffled but his fury clear.

Jemma put down her teacup. "I always forget how much I loathe living with a man," she told Roberta. "Please do stay here comfortably with your cup of tea, while I reacquaint myself with the pleasures of marital strife."

"Oh dear!" Roberta exclaimed, coming to her feet.

Jemma paused for a moment, obviously

taking in the details of Roberta's costume for the first time. "Tell me that your Mrs. Grope is a seamstress and you have my everlasting sympathy."

Roberta felt herself turning pink. "No."

"We shall clothe you," Jemma said severely. "Though it pains me to say it, I would believe half the eccentricities ascribed to your father merely by examining your gown." She was at the door before Roberta could answer. But what could she say? She too thought that Mrs. Parthnell had made a mistake by pairing a bodice of melon-colored stuff with a burgundy silk skirt.

A gently bred young lady would stay in the sitting room and ignore the fracas. Roberta headed directly after the duchess.

The duke was standing in the marble entry, looking remarkably like the illustrations depicting his impassioned speeches to the House of Lords.

"He should go to the country," the duke roared. "Where he can be apprenticed to learn a decent trade."

"The child certainly will not go to the country," Jemma announced. "That is, unless Damon wishes him to do so."

Roberta blinked. Who could the child in question be? Given that Jemma explicitly announced her mandate to produce an heir, it could hardly be hers.

"Well, he isn't coming into *my* house!" the duke snapped.

"My brother is coming to stay with me for a time," Jemma retorted. "And his child, my nephew, naturally comes with him."

"For Christ's sake, send him to the care of a farmer!" Beaumont said. "You can't bring him up to your own feckless ways, Gryffyn."

Lord Gryffyn was lounging against the door to the drawing room with a muscled grace that bespoke a light-hearted demeanor rather than sober industry. "Teddy will never be a farmer," he said, apparently not turning a hair at Beaumont's fury. "You haven't yet met him, or you'd realize there's nothing of the farmer in his veins."

"What is in his veins, then?" Beaumont snapped. "Don't tell us you're finally going to reveal the name of his mother?"

"Attila the Hun," Lord Gryffyn said without blinking an eye.

"Not known for his maternal instincts," Beaumont said scathingly.

"Nevertheless, Teddy has Attila's blood in his veins," Gryffyn said. "I can't send him to the country because I have to keep him under my eye."

"May I respectfully request that you keep

him under your eye in your own house, rather than mine?"

Jemma intervened. "I asked Damon to live here, Beaumont, at least for a time, because I have missed him while I lived in Paris. And I have a nephew whom I have never met."

"Did it occur to you that the presence of an illegitimate child in my house is not precisely helpful to my career?"

Roberta could sympathize with the duke. The London papers were bound to find the presence of Lord Gryffyn's illegitimate child interesting, especially in combination with the naked centerpiece and the return of the duchess.

"Your career, Beaumont, will have to survive the presence of your family. May I remind you that we *are* that family?" Jemma said with acid indifference. "Teddy is your nephew." Her smile, a marvel of kindness, was met by Beaumont's glowering fury. She waved toward Roberta. "You mistook my relative, Lady Roberta, for a charity worker, Beaumont. I shall be bringing her into society."

Beaumont bowed frigidly in Roberta's general direction. "And precisely how will *you* do that?" he asked. "I can hardly believe that my notorious wife is going to curb her activities to suit the sensibilities of match-making mamas."

"I shall consider it if it would stop you from bleating about your career," Jemma said, turning away.

A look of such rage went across Beaumont's face that Roberta blinked. Then he bowed to his duchess's back, and once to Roberta, and was gone.

When Jemma turned around again, her cheeks had gone red and she was breathing quickly. "How shall I ever live with him?" she said, looking at her brother. "You see why I want you to move in, Damon? I can't do it, I really can't."

Her brother straightened. "I will come for a visit if you truly wish me to, Jemma, but I think it would be easier for both of you if I didn't."

"I shan't survive here otherwise, Damon. I can't live with him." Her fists were clenched. "You must stay with me so that I can have a greater acquaintance with my nephew. And — And I need you." She smiled a little tearily at Roberta. "I'm so sorry about the scenes we're played you today. We're as good as a farce. Or perhaps I should say a tragedy." Her voice wobbled a little.

Lord Gryffyn put his arm around his sister

and bent his head close to hers, murmuring something.

Roberta felt an odd twinge in her chest. She'd never had a brother or sister. Since her mother died, her closest companion had been her father, and whichever of his consorts happened to be living with them.

She backed into the sitting room and sat down. A moment later Jemma followed with Lord Gryffyn.

"You must think us hopelessly ill-mannered. I do apologize. Don't take all those cakes," she said, snatching the plate away from her brother. "My guest hasn't even had one yet. Roberta, you must have one. Beaumont has an excellent cook, and his ratafia cakes are delicious."

"I haven't even met Lady Roberta properly," Lord Gryffyn pointed out.

"This is Damon Reeve, the Earl of Gryffyn," Jemma said. "If I tell you that his best friends call him Demon, you'll know precisely how unworthy he is. Beaumont was absolutely right about his laziness: he never does a worthy action all day."

"A charming introduction," Lord Gryffyn said. "Please call me Damon. After all, we're family members, as I understand." He took another cake.

The duchess took the plate away and put

it on the floor between herself and Roberta. "Eat as many as you like," she said to Roberta. "I know him of old, and if I don't act quickly, there'll be none left for us."

Gryffyn threw her an affectionate grin. "Beaumont had a point about his career, Jemma. Both of our reputations in the same small space may well damage it, not to mention Lady Roberta's marital aspirations."

"I missed you all these years," Jemma said. "I'm not giving you up so soon, and I want to meet Teddy properly." She turned to Roberta. "Damon's son Teddy is just five years old."

"He turned six last week, you unnatural aunt," Gryffyn said. "I missed you too, Jemma. But I hardly want to cause the fraying of your marriage."

Jemma snorted inelegantly.

"Beaumont doesn't mean to be such an ass," Gryffyn added.

"He just acts that way?" his sister said. "But enough airing our linen, dirty and otherwise, in front of Roberta. You must bring Teddy and his nanny this very afternoon."

"Unfortunately, he has no nanny at the moment. Teddy has an annoying habit of escaping and the latest nanny stomped away in a temper yesterday."

"Escaping? Where does he go?"

"Anywhere but the nursery. Generally he goes to the stables during the day. And he wanders the house at night until he finds my chamber, and then he climbs in my bed. Last night he couldn't find it, so he slept in the vestibule until I came home. Marble floor. Cold, I should think."

"My father had a dog like that," Roberta said. And then clapped a hand over her mouth. "I didn't mean to compare your son to a dog, my lord!"

"Please, you really must call me Damon," he said, looking absolutely unmoved by the slur to his offspring. "Children are slightly doggish, don't you think? They need so much training, and they have a dislikable habit of urinating in public places."

"I suggest you bar the nursery door," Jemma said, "particularly now that you remind me of children's indiscriminate attitude toward hygiene."

"Can't do that," Damon said. "What if there was a fire? And Teddy, by the way, is past the age of indiscriminate peeing. He's very good at seeking out a tree, just like the well-trained puppy he is."

"Perhaps you could carpet the vestibule," Roberta suggested. "If you mean to allow him to continue in this habit."

"Remarkably uncharitable on both your parts," Damon complained. Then he looked back and forth. "How odd! I suddenly see quite a resemblance between the two of you. Don't tell me! My illegitimate child is only matched by our father's own indiscretions!"

"Actually not," Roberta said. "I'm legitimate, but from a far branch of the family tree. I only wish that I resembled Jemma."

"You have her blue eyes," he said, grinning at her.

"Roberta is going to be my project," Jemma said. "I'm going to dress her up to look absolutely gorgeous, which of course she is, and then marry her off to whomever she wishes. It'll be great fun."

Roberta felt a queer compression around her chestbone. "Are you sure?" she asked. "It will be frightfully expensive. I'm not sure how much I can persuade my father to contribute."

"Jemma's husband can manage a dozen debuts and not notice," Damon said. "I don't know why Beaumont bothers with his speechifying; he could just buy the votes he needs to get a bill passed, in the time-honored fashion. That's what father always did."

"I'm afraid that the third earl — our father — was a tad disreputable," Jemma said.

"You interrupted me, Damon. I was trying to warn Roberta that she might not want my chaperonage."

Damon looked her over so carefully that Roberta felt herself getting pink. "It's true that your reputation was marred by merely walking into this den of iniquity, or it will be once the English ladies get the measure of my sister. Jemma is unlikely to be a prudent chaperone. The Reeves have been disreputable back to the days of King Alfred, and though I regret to say it, the tendency bred true in both of us."

"Jemma has neglected to tell you that I am the only child of the Mad Marquess, to use the term the popular press prefers," Roberta said. "So the *ton* will have more hurdles than Jemma's reputation to consider when it comes to my marriage."

His eyes widened. "You grow more fascinating by the moment. Do tell me a bit of poetry."

She scowled at him, and then relented. "My father's letter to you, Jemma, takes the form of a poem in fourteen stanzas." She opened her little knotting-bag and handed over her father's letter.

"It's entitled 'Epistle to a Duchess,' " Jemma said. Roberta watched her smile fade into a look of puzzlement. "I'm not sure

I'm intelligent enough for poetry," she said, finally.

Which was a kind assessment. "It's not a question of your intelligence," Roberta said. "I'm afraid that Papa's poetry is obscure in the extreme."

Damon took the poem. "This isn't so bad. *It ever was allow'd, dear Madam, Even from the days of father Adam.* Well, I don't see much of difficulty here, Roberta. *Such stuff is naught but mere tautology,*" he continued. "What's *tautology* again? I can't remember, if I ever knew. *And so take that for my apology.* He's apologizing, Jemma."

"For what?"

"For imposing his daughter upon your presence," Roberta said firmly.

Damon was still reading ahead. "Here he's talking about the *solid meal of sense and worth, set off by the dessert of mirth.* Very nice rhyme!"

"Sometimes his poetry is quite good," Roberta said with a flash of loyalty. "He's writing an excellent poem on David and Bathsheba, for example. One can really understand what he's describing."

"Well, this poem ends with *your most obedient,*" Damon said. "I think he's asking you to bring out his daughter with all the pomp and circumstance Beaumont can afford, Roberta. My expert judgment."

Jemma took back the poem and puzzled at it for a moment. "But what's the part about a *rude ungrateful bear, enough to make a parson swear?*"

"I find with Papa's poems that it's best not to devote oneself too strictly to meaning," Roberta said.

Damon let out a bark of laughter.

"There is just one more thing that I should tell you," Roberta said.

Brother and sister turned to look at her. "Wait, don't tell us," Damon said, with his irresistible grin. "The family character bred true in you as well, remote relative though you are. Let's guess: You have a child — you, with such a young, innocent —"

"No!" Roberta said.

But before she could continue, he said, "Your turn, Jemma."

Jemma looked thoughtful. "At some time last year, you were at an inn. You gazed out of the window and were instantly struck by an ungovernable passion for my brother."

Roberta's mouth fell open but Damon didn't notice. "Very nice! Can you work Teddy into the picture?"

"More than anything, Roberta wished to be a mother, but unfortunate circumstances

71

have decreed that she will have no children of her own, therefore Teddy will become her most cherished possession."

Damon was laughing. "What about me? I want to be her most cherished possession."

Jemma turned to Roberta. "You must forgive us; it's an old game that we —" She stopped. "You did see Damon last summer! And you fell in love with him? How very peculiar. Are you sure you wish to marry my brother? I can assure you that he's terribly annoying."

Roberta started giggling. "No, I don't wish to marry your brother!"

"There's no need to be quite so emphatic," Damon observed. "I would quite like to marry you myself, although I see that I shall have to assuage my grieved heart elsewhere."

"But I saw something on your face," Jemma said. "I'm sure —"

"I went to a ball given by Lady Cholmondelay," Roberta said hurriedly, getting over the rough ground as quickly as she could. "And I did meet someone. I should like to marry him. In fact, I have made up my mind to it."

"How useful," Jemma said. "Love at first sight. I'm sure it must be most delicious. I would quite welcome it myself. I've fallen in love many times but never without thoroughly discussing the impulse with my closest friends."

Her brother snorted. "Not to mention your less-than-close friends and the other half of Paris. Although I thought it was love at first sight between Delacroix and yourself. All Paris thought it was."

Jemma looked insulted. "Absolutely not! I spoke to each of my intimate friends before I allowed myself to feel a patch of affection for the man. That is my invariable practice. A man about whom one knows nothing is invariably boring or diseased."

"There you have it, Lady Roberta. You might want to rethink your love at first sight," Damon said.

"I do know quite a lot about him," Roberta said shyly.

"If there is one thing in the world that I love it's a challenge," Jemma said. "The bigger the challenge, the better!"

Roberta took a deep breath. And told them.

She was answered by silence.

CHAPTER 4

That afternoon

Harriet, Duchess of Berrow, hadn't been in London for a year, and she hadn't been to Beaumont House in at least eight. It was just the same, of course: a huge, jumbled assortment of mullioned windows and towers that had no place in London. Terraces sprawled on two sides, in blatant defiance of the properly contained attitude of a townhouse. It looked as if it had been picked up in Northamptonshire, transported by a giant's hand to London, and plopped down on the street. The other houses around it — elegantly built in the Portland stone everyone preferred — looked positively affronted at having to reside beside such a monstrosity.

The last time she'd been here Benjamin had been alive. He'd run up the stairs, always ahead of her, and banged the knocker himself.

Then, Benjamin had leapt ahead of her in every way, and now footmen were the only men who accompanied her to parties.

The door opened and she gave herself a mental shake. The last thing she wanted to do was lower Jemma's spirits. Benjamin was gone, had been gone these many months and after she did just one thing in his memory — just the one — she would forget him. Put him away in her memories, or whatever it is you do with a dead husband.

Truly, a dead husband was an inconvenient presence, she realized, not for the first time.

The butler led her to a small dining room and then stood to the side. "The Duchess of —" he intoned. Suddenly he lunged forward, words forgotten.

Jemma was standing on a chair, with her back to them. She was in the process of unhooking a very large painting from the wall. Even as they watched she staggered back, her heel on the very edge of the seat, the huge frame waving in the air.

"Your Grace!" the butler shouted. He caught the huge gold frame just as it began toppling toward the ground.

Harriet rushed forward as well, just in time to stand directly under Jemma as she fell off the chair. They both hit the ground with a whoosh as their hoops swelled up around them. Simultaneously the butler lost his grip on the painting and it crashed into a sideboard.

"Oh no," Jemma said, laughing. "Is that Harriet?"

Harriet scrambled to her feet. Jemma's butler was shouting, presumably for a footman.

"It is indeed I," she said, smiling down at Jemma. Her friend had changed; her beauty had a modish edge that was a long way from Harriet's childhood memories. But the sleek blonde hair, the deep lip and most of all, her lit-up, intelligent eyes, those were the same.

With one practiced slap, Jemma collapsed her right pannier and then rolled to that side to get up. Harriet held out a hand. With another whoosh, Jemma's panniers exploded as she stood up and there she was: as sophisticated and elegant a French lady as Harriet could imagine.

She swallowed her up in one of the lightning quick hugs Harriet remembered so well. "You are as beautiful as ever, but so thin, Harriet. And the *black*."

"Well, you do remember . . ."

"But it's been almost two years since Benjamin died, hasn't it?" Jemma pulled back.

"Did you get my note after his funeral?"

Harriet nodded. "And I had your lovely note from Florence too, with the drawings."

"Well, it had been a year," Jemma twinkled at her. "I personally think that David has a lovely physique although perhaps slightly, shall we say, under-endowed?"

Harriet laughed a bit hollowly. "Only you would notice."

"Nonsense. It's enough to make one eye Italian males in a most suspicious manner, I assure you. After all, it might well be a national trait."

"What were you doing with that portrait?" Harriet asked.

"Ghastly thing. I stared at it all the way through luncheon and then promised myself that I would take it off the wall directly."

Harriet glanced at it, but couldn't see that it was particularly depressing; it depicted a man asleep on a bed while a woman stood next to him with a flask of wine.

"Look more closely," Jemma said. "Do you see her knife?"

Sure enough, hidden in the folds of her skirt was the wicked, curved tip of a knife. And on close observation, the woman's face was rather disturbing.

"The house is bestrewed by versions of Judith and Holofernes. I would ask Beaumont about his mother's penchant for the subject, but I'm terrified of his likely answer. In this one, she's about to saw his head off. If you'd like to see the event itself, that is hanging in the grand salon in the west wing. The aftermath — i.e., his head apart from his body — appears in various versions all over the house."

Harriet blinked. "How — how —" and closed her mouth.

"I gather you don't know the Dowager Duchess of Beaumont," Jemma continued blithely. "Let's go upstairs, shall we? We can have some tea in my rooms."

"Why, this is quite lovely," Harriet said a moment later. The walls were white with pale green trim, and painted all over with little sprays of blossoms. "Did Beaumont have the room made over for your return?"

"Of course he didn't," Jemma said. "I sent a man from Paris two months ago, as soon as I decided to return to London. My mother-in-law had this room very grand in gold-and-white. Naturally I had to have all new furnishings. I am so fond of French panniers, you know. I wouldn't have been able to fit into the chairs designed thirty years ago."

Harriet paused beside a small marble chess table. It was set out with a game in progress. "You haven't given up your chess."

"Do you remember enough of the game to see where I am? I'm playing white, and my queen is in a veritable nest of pawns. I'm almost certainly beaten." Jemma dropped into a comfortably wide chair, her panniers effortlessly compressing under her silk skirt.

Harriet sighed. It had always been so, even when they were young girls growing up on adjoining estates. She and Jemma would go for picnics, and she would come back having been bitten by stinging ants, with her hair down her back. Jemma would traipse back to the house wearing a posy of daisies and every hair in place. Sure enough, when she lowered herself cautiously into the chair opposite Jemma, her right-side hoop sprang into the air like a huge blister. She forced it into place.

"I've missed you," Jemma said, stretching out her legs. "I love Paris, as you must know. But I missed you."

Harriet smiled, a rueful smile. She'd lived a country mouse's life for the past few years. "You have been in *Paris*," she said. "You needn't tell me flummery like that. Those are the most gorgeous little slippers, by the way."

"Paris is full of Frenchwomen. They are

79

nice slippers, aren't they? I like the embroidery. I have them in three different shades."

"The fact that Paris is full of Frenchwomen surely came as no surprise?"

"That's my Harriet! I missed your peppery little comments. You always deflated my absurdities." She leaned forward. "Are you all right? You seem tired."

"I should be quite over Benjamin's death," Harriet said. "It's been twenty-two months. But somehow thinking of him makes me tired, and I can't stop thinking, no matter how I try."

"Thinking of Beaumont makes me tired, and he's not even dead. At any rate, Frenchwomen make difficult friends. They're given to thinking that Englishwomen are, by nature, inelegant and rather foolish. But even if one overcomes the prejudices of one's nationality, I have never felt as easy with a Frenchwoman as I do with you, Harriet." And as if to demonstrate her point, she stood up, reached under her skirts and untied her panniers. With a little clatter they fell to the ground and Jemma curled bonelessly back into the chair. "Go on," she said, "you do it too! You are spending the day with me, aren't you? I must introduce you to Roberta; she's a young relative come to live with me and make her debut."

80

Harriet hesitated. "You have a ball tomorrow. Surely you have —"

"Absolutely not! I have a marvelous secretary who handles all the wretched details of putting on an event. She thrives on it. My role is to stay to my rooms and keep out of the way."

Harriet got up and dumped her hoops. "How I loathe these things."

"I adore them," Jemma said. "There's nothing better than arranging huge swathes of silk just so; one always makes a grand entrance if one's hoops are large enough. This season the fashion in Paris is for smaller panniers, which in itself was a good reason to leave."

Since Harriet loathed the idea of a grand entrance under any circumstances, and particularly with huge wire baskets attached to her sides, she changed the subject. "So who is Roberta, and what is her surname?"

"Lady Roberta St. Giles. She's great fun; I am persuaded the two of you will like each other enormously. The only problem is that she's quite desperately in love and the man is rather unlikely." She reached out toward the bellcord. "I'll ask if she could join us, shall I? She's been in fittings for a ballgown but perhaps she is finished."

But Harriet quickly waved her hand. "I

want to ask you something first."

Jemma dropped the cord. "Of course."

"It's — It's about Benjamin." Whenever she brought up her dead husband, people's faces took on one of two expressions. If they knew only that she was a widow, their faces took on a practiced look of sympathy, often quite genuine. They would offer stories of aunts who were widowed and found true love a mere week afterward, as if she, Harriet, were lusting to marry over the very coffin of her husband.

But if they knew that Benjamin committed suicide, their faces had an entirely different look: more guarded, more truly sympathetic, slightly horrified, as if suicide were a contagious disease. No one offered stories of relatives who put themselves to death.

Jemma looked purely sympathetic.

"He killed himself," Harriet said bluntly. "He shot himself in the head after losing a game at which he gambled a great deal of money."

Jemma blinked at her for a moment. Then she jumped out of her chair and plumped down next to Harriet. Without panniers, the chair was more than wide enough for both of them. "That is absolutely terrible," she said, wrapping an arm around her. "I'm so sorry, Harriet. No one told me."

Tears stung her eyes. "I've gotten used to it."

"Does one? I supposed I would get over my husband doing such a thing, simply because we aren't very close to each other. But you and Benjamin — how *could* he do such a thing?"

"I don't know." Despite herself her voice cracked a bit, and Jemma's arm tightened. "He was so miserable. He was never good at being miserable."

"No, I think of him as always laughing."

"He was never very good at being formal, nor sad either. Nor ashamed of himself. He was ashamed of himself, and that's why he did it."

"Over a game of cards! And why was he playing such high stakes?"

"It wasn't cards," Harriet said. "It was chess."

"Chess!"

Despite herself, a tear rolled down her cheek. Jemma produced a handkerchief from somewhere and blotted her cheek. Harriet almost smiled. It was the softest, most elegant little scrap of cloth she'd seen in years, perhaps ever.

"It's mortifying to be crying for him," she said, sniffing a bit.

"Why? I would think you should wear your grief like a badge of honor. After all, you care enough to grieve. I can hardly imagine."

"It's mortifying because he — he was so eager to leave me that he took his own life." It came out angry.

"That's foolish, darling, and you know it. Your husband no more wished to leave you than he truly thought to give up life. I know Benjamin, remember? I was there when you fell in love."

"When *I* fell in love," Harriet said, more angry tears swelling in her eyes. "If he was in love with me, he showed an odd way of displaying his passion."

"He did fall in love with you. But Benjamin was a remarkably impetuous person. I'm sure he regretted shooting himself the moment he did it, but it was too late. He just didn't think clearly before acting."

"He should have thought about it!"

"Was the chess game public?"

"Of course. Chess is all the rage now. Everyone's playing it, in the cafés, in private houses. White's. Sometimes I think it's all anyone talks about."

"How surprising. I had no idea. I thought it was only like that in France."

"Benjamin had a tremendous passion for

chess. He couldn't just *play,* you know? He had to be among the very best."

"But he wasn't," Jemma said sadly.

"You remember that? Of course, you used to play him occasionally, didn't you? Did he ever win?"

Jemma shook her head.

"He could beat most everyone," Harriet said. "Truly. But he couldn't bear the fact that he couldn't beat the very top players. It was almost like a disease, the way he wanted to beat Villiers."

"It was *Villiers* he played at the last?" Jemma asked. "Villiers?"

Harriet dashed away more tears. "Why are you so surprised? Villiers is the best chess player in England. Or so they say."

"It's just very odd," Jemma said slowly. "I've been talking of Villiers all morning."

"Are you planning to play him in chess?" Harriet said, feeling hopefulness tighten in her chest like a vise.

"It wasn't that. It's my guest, Roberta. Lady Roberta St. Giles. She's in love with him."

"In love with Villiers?" Harriet smiled weakly. "I believe I pity her."

"Was he a friend of Benjamin's, then?"

"Villiers played Benjamin all the time, but he never allowed any stakes. Which was just a condescending way of telling Benjamin that he was unlikely to win. Then finally Benjamin challenged him and Villiers agreed to play. Benjamin played well in the beginning. But now, I think that Villiers may have been just playing along."

"I see," Jemma said, holding her hands tightly.

"And Benjamin started to raise the stakes on the game. I gather that Villiers refused and Benjamin got so angry — it was when he was winning, or he thought he was winning — that he forced Villiers to give in. That's what everyone told me afterwards."

"And then . . ."

"I don't think Benjamin realized at first. But he must have gone home and thought over the game, step by step. I was in the country, you see. I wasn't there; perhaps if I'd been in London I could have stopped him somehow. At any rate, he must have realized that Villiers had just been babying him. That he never had a chance of winning that game."

"Benjamin loved chess that much," Jemma said.

"He should have loved *me* that much!"

Jemma sighed. "Chess is a passion."

"The problem was that Benjamin was too good to play most people, and not quite good enough for the very best. He used to try to get your husband to play with him; he even said that he would trade a game for his vote in Lords."

"Ha," Jemma said. "He misstepped there. Beaumont has one god: his honor."

"Beaumont just said that he never played anymore. He doesn't, does he?"

"Not so far as I know. I only played him a few times when we were first married."

"Did you beat him? Your husband, I mean?"

"Yes. But he was awfully good."

"Is there anyone you haven't beaten, Jemma?"

"Every chess player loses occasionally. I only played one game with the French king and he won."

"King Louis? Then you allowed him to win," Harriet said with a little crooked smile.

"Prudence is part of strategy," Jemma said. "But you know I haven't played very many people, Harriet, so it hardly signifies."

"You've never played Villiers?"

"Never. I only met him once and that briefly. He was traveling on the continent during the first year of my marriage, and I've been in Paris since."

"They say he's the best player in England." She took a deep breath. "I *hate* him for what he did to Benjamin."

Jemma blinked. "What did he do?"

"He shamed him. And I think he did it deliberately. I've thought and thought about it. I think he agreed to play the game in White's, just to make Benjamin stop nagging at him. And then — and then Benjamin lost, of course, but Villiers had played it so that Benjamin thought he would win."

"But —"

Harriet wasn't finished. "He's an awful man. A positive wolf. He had *affaires* with half the *ton,* if you believe the stories, and he treats all his lovers despicably. They say he has at least four illegitimate children."

There was a noise at the door and Jemma came back with a tea tray.

Harriet drank half of her tea in one gulp. "I want you to do me a favor, Jemma."

Jemma reached to the sugar bowl. "Anything, dearest."

"I want you to shame Villiers."

She straightened. "What? Shame him — *how?*"

"I don't care!" Harriet said fiercely. "You could take him as a lover, and spurn him. Or take him as a lover and make fun of him, or something like that. I know you can do it."

Jemma was giggling. "I love your faith in my abilities," she said. "But —"

"You could play chess with him."

There was a moment's silence. "That's what this is about, isn't it? You came from the country not to see me, but to ask me to play chess with Villiers?"

Their eyes met. "I came to see you, Jemma. We're not as close as we were when we were children. You've changed; you've grown sophisticated, and even more beautiful, and I'm just a country mouse."

Jemma's eyes had assessed her brown curls and her clumsily handled panniers; she must know it was the truth.

"I didn't live in the city with Benjamin," Harriet said, though her throat was so tight she could hardly speak it. "I just couldn't make this life work, putting my hair up, and powdering it, and taking hours to get dressed. Having a maid, and a dresser, and all the rest of it *bores* me. I just couldn't stand the boredom!"

"I can understand that, of course," Jemma said. "It can be quite tedious." She smiled, but she was cooler now, more distant.

"So I left Benjamin here and I went to the country," Harriet stumbled on.

"You couldn't have stopped him from loving chess," Jemma said.

Harriet felt a wave of desperation. "You don't understand!" She almost shouted it.

"What?"

"I couldn't be around him, because — because —"

"Many couples live apart," Jemma said. "It certainly isn't your fault that Benjamin committed suicide, simply because you were living in the country. You could not have stopped him from losing a game to Villiers."

"You don't understand," Harriet said. She lifted her chin. "I had an *affaire* with Villiers."

Jemma sat bolt upright. *"You had an affaire?"*

It was such a relief to tell someone that the words tumbled out. "It was two years ago, at a ball given by the Duchess of Claverstill, about a month before Benjamin died. Benjamin was playing chess all night. Every ball has a chess room now. It's so tiresome. Some nights there aren't any partners for dancing. At any rate, Villiers came out of the chess room and, somehow, he found me."

"What is he like? I don't know much about him, other than that he was a boyhood friend of Beaumont's and they had some sort of falling out."

"I hate him," Harriet said, her voice shaking.

"Because you spent the night with him?" To Harriet's relief, Jemma had lost her air of *froideur.* She poured more tea for both of them.

"Because — he didn't really — it was just like the game with Benjamin!"

"What?"

She might as well tell the whole. "The truth of it is that we didn't really have an *affaire.* I was so cross at Benjamin that I just — well, I lost my head. Villiers was taking me home and — and — but he —"

"You're going to have to be a bit more clear," Jemma said. "Based on my rather varied experience of men, I'd say that he made an advance to you in the carriage?"

"No," Harriet said, drinking again. "I did."

"Excellent decision," Jemma said promptly. "Frenchwomen understand that a woman must pick and choose amongst her admirers rather than leaving it to the man's discretion."

"There are no men for me," Harriet said miserably. "Benjamin was the only one."

"So what happened with Villiers?"

"He kissed me for a bit, but then — well — this is so embarrassing. He did this *thing.*"

Jemma's eyes were bright with interest. "What thing?"

"With — with his hands. And that's all I'm going to say about it."

"Even if I pour you some more tea?"

"Even then. So I — I —"

"What did you do? I gather you didn't just swoon and say, *Touch me again!*" Jemma was giggling so hard that her tea was in danger of spilling.

"Well, I said, actually I shrieked, *What are you doing?* And he just did it *again!*"

"And it wasn't any better the second time?"

"What would you have done?" Harriet asked desperately.

"It would definitely depend on the thing in question. I enjoy many things that men do with their hands."

"You're so much more sophisticated than I am. I'm not like that. I slapped him. Which is just what my mother, not that my mother would *ever,* well, it's what she would have approved of, I'm sure."

"I'm sure," Jemma said, gurgling with laughter. "What did he do?"

Harriet took a deep breath. "I'm going to tell you exactly what he said."

"I'm ready."

"He said that he had always pitied Benjamin for his miserable chess-playing, but from now on he would try to be nicer to him."

"Nasty!" Jemma said looking impressed.

"And then he said that there was nothing worse than a lady whore. And that I had tried to get him to screw one of his best friends, and he must be drunk, because he'd forgotten how damn boring women like me were. And finally he said that if I told Benjamin he would kill me."

The laughter had died on Jemma's face. "That bastard!"

"And then he put me out on the street. In the middle of Whitefriars Lane and I didn't have even a ha'penny. I had to walk all the way home."

"Double bastard!"

"I never told Benjamin. I left for the country the next day because I was such a coward that I couldn't face him. I felt so guilty and so — so dirty! But then someone wrote me and said they had announced in Parsloe's —"

"What's that?"

"The London Chess Club meets at Parsloe's. They only take one hundred members, and it's frightfully exclusive. At any rate, a week or so afterwards they announced that Villiers would be playing Benjamin, in public and for stakes, at White's. So I knew why Villiers did it. Because of me."

"Perhaps . . ."

"I can't imagine why I flirted with him," Harriet said. "You'd think I would have had enough of men who prefer to caress pieces of ivory rather than me. It was so paltry of me. And how — how terribly wrong it all went."

"Life can be like that," Jemma said quietly.

"And now," Harriet said, hearing the rank desperation in her own voice, "I just want Villiers humiliated somehow. It's all I can think of. I have to make it right for Benjamin. I have to clear my slate. I *have* to, Jemma!"

Jemma reached out and took her hand. "Benjamin is gone, Harriet. There's no slate."

"Please."

Jemma sat still for a moment. Then: "I wouldn't do this because of the chess match. I can understand Benjamin's mortification at losing that match. I could never take my life, but I can understand the horror of losing. Benjamin's reaction wouldn't be Villiers's fault. Truly, Harriet. It's the chess."

"I hate chess." She said it flatly, but with utter conviction.

"I'll do it because he was an utter bastard to leave you in the road, and to say those things, Harriet. *No one* says something like that to a friend of mine and gets away with it scot-free. The only problem is that I shall have to be rather subtle."

"Why? I would prefer that he be shamed in front of all London."

"Because," Jemma said, "I told you that Roberta is desperately in love with Villiers. She's determined to marry him, and I promised I would help her."

"How on earth are you going to humiliate him at the same time as you push him into marriage?" Harriet began to wring her hands.

But Jemma was grinning again. "The two things are by no means mutually exclusive, you know. And I love a challenge. The first thing I'll do is invite him to my ball."

"He and Beaumont never speak; he won't come."

"He will," Jemma said. "Leave that to me. Now, are you coming?"

Harriet gulped. "Would you mind very much if I didn't, Jemma? I can't tell you how horrible it has been since Benjamin died. Everyone looks at me with sympathy except for people who believe I drove him to it. Lady Lacock always tells me that Benjamin was a cheerful baby, until I feel as if I could scream."

"We have to solve that too," Jemma said.

"My life? Some other night," Harriet said.

"Of course. But you must come for a council of war tomorrow morning."

"Please, Jemma . . . may I decline? I promised I would return to the country as soon as possible."

"Who did you promise? You should be here for the season, Harriet, thinking about marrying again. You can't stay a dour widow forever."

"I know," Harriet said, and then, desperate to change the subject, "I still don't think you'll be able to get Villiers to enter this house."

Jemma just smiled.

CHAPTER 5

Roberta would be the first to admit that life with her father had not been designed to turn a young lady into a leader in fashion. It wasn't that her father had no money; she rather suspected that he had quite a lot. But his priorities were directed in precisely the opposite direction than everything about which Roberta dreamed: London, balls, love, marriage . . .

"But Papa," she would argue with him at supper, "you don't wish me to live with you my whole life, do you?"

"I would love that!" he would say, beaming at her. "Who else will catalog my poetry, if not you, my dear? And your criticism, though occasionally harsh, has done much to improve my art. Much! Much! The future will preserve a warm place for you as the muse of the Marquess of Wharton and Malmesbury."

"Papa," she would say (for variations on

this theme had recurred for years), "I don't want to appear in history books as your muse, and I dislike cataloging poetry." Sometimes she would add that she didn't like critiquing poetry, either, but that depended on how recently she had torn apart one of his new poems.

At this, the marquess's face would fall into tragic lines, and he would begin to mutter about the serpent's tooth that was his only child. And if she begged a new gown, he never said no, but he would only pay for Mrs. Parthnell in the village. "If we don't employ her, child, who will?" One of Mrs. Parthnell's peculiarities was that she refused to line a sleeve in anything but white cotton duck, and due to sewing problems she routinely encountered, the white generally showed.

Even so, the faces of Jemma's French maids were almost comical in their dismay when they beheld Roberta. Her gown had once been styled *à la française,* but Mrs. Parthnell had cut out the floating back pleats and used tapes to draw up the sides around into a clumsy polonaise instead. When Roberta objected to the way the waist bunched as it encountered the new bustle, Mrs. Parthnell cut out the bodice and replaced it with one of melon-colored cotton.

Apparently, Roberta's sense that melon-colored cotton and burgundy silk were not a perfect match was correct, if the rather piercing screams of the French seamstresses could be taken as evidence.

Two seconds later she was stripped to her chemise and Mrs. Parthnell's gown was thrown in the corner. "For the beggars," Jemma's *femme de chambre,* Brigitte, had explained. "None of us could wear such a thing."

There was a cheerful little chorus of French agreements from Jemma's other two maids. Formal gown after gown was brought out, discussed at length, and ceremoniously carried back to Jemma's dressing room, which Roberta could only imagine as crammed with satins and silks.

Brigitte had explicit directions from the duchess herself. "She must look like a young lady of the utmost innocence," she dictated. After a half hour or so of gowns trundling from the dressing room to Roberta's chamber, it became clear that very few of Jemma's gowns were designed to achieve an innocent air.

The few that were tried on Roberta quickly lost their claims to innocence, though Roberta thought they were exquisite. Even catching a glimpse of herself wearing one of Jemma's dazzling French gowns made her heart sing. She didn't look like a drab country mouse anymore: she looked *beautiful.* Visions of the Duke of Villiers on his knees spun dizzyingly through her mind.

"You are too generous in the front," Brigitte stated, dispelling that dream.

Roberta peered down at her chest. She had nothing compared to the naked centerpiece, after all.

"Is excellent!" Brigitte said hurriedly. "The men, they are most fond of bosoms. Many bosoms!"

Since Brigitte likely didn't mean that men preferred women with more than two breasts, Roberta took this as a compliment. Unfortunately, her "many bosoms" made many of Jemma's gowns unacceptable. She overflowed the bodices in a fashion that Brigitte kept declaring *sensuelle,* rather than *innocente.*

Suddenly Brigitte clapped her hands. "The white silk moiré!" she announced.

There was a little flurry of conversation. One maid ventured the fact that Jemma had labeled the gown *ennuyeuse.* "Boring," Brigitte announced, "is just what is needed."

"Oh, but —" Roberta said unhappily. This was ignored, as had been every other comment she ventured to make.

It certainly was a lovely dress, embroidered with tiny sprays of flowers that looked as if they'd been scattered by the wind. It showed rather less of her breasts than the others, because the neckline was a V, and trimmed with a small ruffle of white lace. The sleeves were tight and ended in a gorgeous frill. It was exquisite, but Roberta thought that Jemma was right. It was boring.

She had no say in the matter; all the other dresses, luscious in deep crimson and striped green, were whisked away, and Brigitte got down to the serious business of altering the white gown to fit.

"You will look like a fairy princess at the ball," Brigitte said with great satisfaction. "All the princes will bow at your feet."

It seemed to Roberta that Villiers was not the sort to bow at the feet of an innocent fairy princess, but how could she complain? He wouldn't genuflect at the feet of the fleshy crocodile dressed in gold paint either; she was certain of that. She would have to study him closely in order to decide precisely how to pitch her courtship.

By the time Roberta made it out of her

bedchamber it was late in the afternoon. Her father's house was large, but Beaumont House was far larger. Within the turn of a corridor, she was lost.

Part of the problem was that she wasn't concentrating on finding her way. Perhaps Jemma was right. An innocent dress was like a suit of armor, insuring that no one would remember that the Mad Marquess lived with his courtesan, which meant that she, Roberta, had lived in close proximity with that same woman. On the whole, Roberta felt that her friendships with her father's companions had been interesting. But obviously, one might not wish to trumpet those acquaintances around a ballroom.

She had climbed another flight of stairs, and was wandering down a sun-lit corridor lined with closed doors, which she thought might be taking her back to the central part of the house, when she heard a patter of feet.

He burst around the corner going as fast as only a small boy can go.

Roberta guessed immediately that this was Damon's son, and decided there was no call to halt him. So she moved aside so that he could use the rest of the corridor as a race course, if he wished. But he skidded to a stop next to her.

Pop went his thumb into his mouth.

Roberta shuddered inwardly. She had had very little contact with children in her life, but she'd seen thumb-sucking in church. The very fact that someone would want to suck on a saliva-covered digit was disgusting.

He was staring up at her, so she smiled. He wasn't a terrible-looking child, just tousled. It seemed that no one had brushed his hair. Of course, there was no nanny.

"Feel free to continue running," she advised him.

He just stared. And sucked.

So she continued to walk. He walked right along beside her.

"What's your name?" she asked, trying to be friendly.

"Teddy," he said. In order to answer he took his thumb out with a "pop."

Roberta shuddered again. Enough polite conversation.

But a moment later he dropped the thumb of his own volition and said, "Whatcha doing?"

"Walking," she said.

"It's running, I am," he said.

"I am running," she corrected him. Perhaps that was a bit harsh, but after life with her father she had very little sympathy for inverted syntax, poetic or otherwise.

"Right," he said. At least he didn't start sucking again. But he suddenly waxed eloquent. "Don't have a nanny."

"I don't have a nanny," she repeated.

"Right. The nanny, her name was Peg —"

"The nanny's name was Peg."

"Yes, her name was Peg and her brother was sent to Bridewell Prison because he stole a sow and her piglets and then he stole a butter churn and put the piglets in it."

He paused, but Roberta had no comment about the butter churn or the piglets, and his sentence was reasonably grammatical.

So they continued like that down the hall and around the curve, with Roberta occasionally interjecting a grammatical comment, and Teddy telling her at length about various criminal deeds. Some of his stories were rather involved and, had Roberta not had a great deal of experience in decoding cryptic literature, might have been misinterpreted.

"Do I understand you to say," she said some time later, "that the housemaid with the beard, whose name is Carper, is married to a wild bog-trotting croggie, whatever that is, but she has a child by a Captain Longshanks?"

Teddy corrected her. Apparently Carper

had a mustache as well, and the signal point of his story was that she had more facial hair than the captain.

To Roberta, the more interesting point was the wild bog-trotting croggie.

Teddy admitted that he couldn't describe Carper's husband, but launched into a tale of Carper's sister, who bought an ointment entitled the Tomb of Venus, which gave her a terrible swelling.

"A dire name. She should have chosen something more propitious."

After she had explained the meaning of *dire* and *propitious,* and finally, *tomb,* Teddy said that the swelling was all in front, and Carper said that it was an ill-prepared medicine and that Dr. Jackson's worm powder would have been better.

Finally she saw the great winding stair leading down the central core of the house, so she told Teddy to run off to his nursery.

He blinked up at her and then popped his thumb back in his mouth.

"You're too old for that," she told him. "Why, you must be ten years old at the very least."

"Six," he said around his thumb.

"It's a disgusting habit," she said. "There are those who take worm powder and rub it in children's thumbs and after that they never put them in their mouths again."

He narrowed his eyes.

"Shoo," she said. "Or I'll tell your father about worm powder."

He ran.

CHAPTER 6

"An intimate family supper," Jemma said with obvious satisfaction. "How I missed this while in Paris!"

She was sitting at the head of the table, looking as enticing as a French bird of paradise and not at all like a good huswife. Damon grinned at her. "Domesticity is a new affectation for you."

She wrinkled her nose at him. "Beaumont, do you find that age is reconciling you to domesticity? You used to dine at home very rarely."

Beaumont was playing the majestic duke with particular fervor this evening; Damon couldn't blame him after the scene this afternoon.

"I shall, of course, make every effort to domesticate myself now that you have returned from Paris," the duke said. His teeth closed around a bite of partridge with an audible snap.

Damon hadn't spent much time around feuding marital couples, but he judged the best thing to do was change the subject. Jemma beat him to it.

"I suggest we exert ourselves to make a plan for Roberta's marriage," she said, throwing her new ward a smile.

Damon didn't see much need for a plan. Lady Roberta was wearing one of the most unattractive gowns Damon had ever seen, but she herself was utterly delicious. Beautiful, even given that gown. What made her devastating, though, was not her looks, but the mixture of naïveté and wit in her eyes.

"After all," Jemma said, warming up to her subject. "She has thrown me a challenge. Beaumont —"

But her voice cut off and Damon saw that Beaumont had put down his fork and had picked up a sheaf of paper handed to him by a footman.

"My deepest apologies," he said. "I must answer this dispatch immediately. If you will forgive me, Your Grace, I will read it now, since this is such an informal family meal." There was only the slightest chill of irony in his tone.

"A challenge doesn't quite cover it," Damon said, throwing himself into the silence that billowed down the table from Jemma's seat.

"Am I such an antidote?" Roberta asked.

"You'll do," he said, grinning at her. "The problem is Villiers."

"Surely the Duke of Villiers hasn't married since January?"

"Oh no," Jemma said, dropping her wifely glare, presumably because her husband wasn't paying the slightest attention. "Villiers is not married."

"Then?" Roberta asked.

"Unmarriageable," Damon said. She was a lovely little scrap, for all she'd fallen in love with the wrong man. "He's a devil with women: beds them, leaves them."

"But surely —"

"The problem is not that he's strewn a few children around the place," Jemma said. "Which he has. It's that he got at least one of those children on a gentlewoman and still didn't marry her. Do you see what I mean?"

"Not likely to be attracted to a young miss, either," Damon put in. Though he had to admit that Roberta appeared to be a long way from the milk-and-water misses he associated with the label.

"I'm not a mere miss!" Roberta said, clearly revolted.

"I think we are all happily coming to that

realization," Jemma said.

"Reeves breed true," Damon said. "Here, I've got an idea. Why don't you go to an inn and wait until a different fellow comes along to fall in love with? I could drive up with my matched grays. Any number of people have fallen in love with them."

But she shook her head. "I will never love anyone but the Duke of Villiers."

Roberta was obviously head over heels; there was a thrill in her voice at the mention of Villiers. Damon took a bite of his partridge. Of course he wasn't offended that she rejected his offer to replace Villiers out of hand. Not that he even got to make the offer.

"The only thing I can think of is the old-fashioned ploy of putting Villiers in your way as much as possible, starting with the ball," Jemma said. Her eyes were thoughtful. "In a way, this is the ultimate challenge: to marry off Villiers."

"The manly code of loyalty probably means I should warn him," Damon said. "His days of peace are numbered."

"Villiers is everything I could wish for in a husband." Roberta's hands were clasped in her lap and she had a revolting look of adoration on her face.

"You didn't set yourself an easy task, did

you?" Damon said, wanting to needle her. "Not only is he filthy rich, titled and one of the top chess players in England, if not the world —"

"The only thing worse would be if you had fallen in love with Damon," Jemma said, interrupting. "I can hardly believe it myself, but my brother is one of the most sought-after bachelors in London."

Damon didn't care for his sister's incredulous look. It was even more annoying to see an echo of it in Roberta's eyes. "I was invited to the Cholmondelay ball, and had I attended, I would have fought off my admirers to dazzle you," he told her.

"Vanity is one of the seven deadly sins," Roberta said, raising an eyebrow.

"Lust is another," he replied. "If I have one, I might as well have the other."

"From that point of view, one might think you indulge in gluttony as well." She cast a nasty calculating eye at his waist, and his sister followed suit.

"I don't have to worry about that yet," he told her. "Not like Villiers, who has to be on the far side of thirty. Likely getting a bit soft around the waist . . . just look at his hair."

"The sin of jealousy!" Jemma cried, clapping her hands.

"I pick and choose my sins like my lovers," Damon retorted. "Sloth yes, gluttony no. The more important point is that *you*," he told Roberta, "are joining a pack of young women similarly lusting after Villiers, and will have to knock them out of your way somehow."

"Stop being pessimistic," Jemma said. "I can't imagine he is so sought-after. I haven't seen Villiers for years, but there's something almost feminine about him, isn't there?"

"No, there you're wrong," Damon said, at the same time that Roberta protested, "Not at all!"

Jemma shrugged.

"You're used to obvious types," Damon said. He cast a look at Beaumont, but the duke was deaf to the world, absorbed in his dispatch. "The kind who wears black, boxes for sport, knows his way around a stable-yard and has broken a horse or two — or at least fibs about it."

"While I may not always defend my husband," Jemma said, "if Beaumont ever said that he broke a horse, it would be the truth."

"I appreciate that," Beaumont said suddenly. The gravity of his voice broke into their conversation like a bang of a judge's gavel. He turned the page without looking up. "Please disregard my presence. I merely caught those critical words: *my husband.*"

Jemma's smile hardened. She turned to Roberta. "There was a very awkward moment early in our marriage when I asked *my husband* if he loved his mistress and he told me the truth."

Damon opened his mouth but Roberta rushed to the rescue. "I have spent much of my life listening to my father's protestations of love," she said. "I am extremely tired of men in love. It turns them to fools."

"If I ever told you that I was in love with my mistress," Beaumont said, still not raising his eyes from the sheaf of papers before him, "I must have been mistaken."

Jemma ignored him. "I see just what you mean, Roberta. There is something unseemly about a man in love."

"Your father is a poet," Damon said, "and if you'll forgive me, Villiers is an altogether more complex creature. He's intrigued by clothing, and likes to wear rose colors because they look splendid with his hair, which is going white. You did notice that, didn't you?"

"Shot through with silver," Roberta said, her eyes dreamy again.

Beaumont scrawled his signature with a huge flourish and a footman whisked away his papers. "Please forgive my intolerable rudeness," he said, taking up his fork. "Do I

113

gather that in between airing the intimacies of my early marriage, we are discussing the equally delightful topic of the Duke of Villiers?"

"Precisely," Damon said. "And Jemma, you are quite incorrect. Villiers may not flaunt his sword, so to speak, but it's all the more evident for being sheathed."

"Are you saying that Villiers has fallen in love?" Beaumont asked, sounding genuinely surprised.

"Never," Damon said. "The man doesn't give a damn about women, or propriety, the niceties of life in London, or any of that claptrap. He behaves in an egregious manner and yet he is invited everywhere. It's one of the mysteries of life. Another such mystery would be how you, my dear Lady Roberta, are possibly going to get him to give a damn about you."

Jemma shot him a frown and Beaumont's eyebrow shot up.

Why the hell was he insulting Lady Roberta? Damon couldn't quite explain it, but the idea of this delicious girl chasing after Villiers made his blood curdle.

"I shall keep your good wishes in mind," Roberta said, not turning a hair. "I think that the duke and I are suited."

"Suited!" Damon said. "Not unless you

turn into a chess piece on alternate Sundays."

She didn't even pause. "I can work on that."

"It's going to be an education having you with us," Jemma said. "Creativity must run in the family. Perhaps your father can write a poem for Damon's wedding."

"What wedding?" he enquired.

"The one I'm going to arrange for you. It's past time you were married. It would have prevented the debacle of Flora's declaration."

"I haven't met a single young woman I could contemplate marrying. Most of the ones currently on the market have brains like the mills of God." He sighed, faced with two blank female faces.

"The mills of God grind exceedingly slowly," Beaumont put in. "I gather Lord Gryffyn is issuing an obscure insult to young women's intelligence."

"This is the very reason why you have reached the ripe, if not over-ripe, age of twenty-nine without marrying," Jemma told her brother. "Your jokes are obscure, and your belief in your own intelligence is far too high."

"It has nothing to do with my intelligence," he protested.

"What does it have to do with?" Roberta asked with some curiosity. "Are you holding out for a bluestocking?"

Jemma leaped to his rescue. "Damon's problem is that he's been the most eligible bachelor on the market for, oh, at least five years now."

"There was the Duke of Fletcher," Damon put in gloomily, "but he married Perdita Selby and left me to the wolves."

"The wolves being matchmaking mamas," Jemma translated.

"*And* their daughters. It wasn't Mrs. Hickman who had the idea of locking me in a privy with her daughter until we were compromised."

"It might have been Mr. Hickman," Jemma said.

He shook his head. "Elinor herself. She as good as told me so. After all, when you spend several hours in extremely intimate — and odiferous — circumstances, all sorts of revelations come to light."

"I can't tell you how many young women have marked their first year in London by falling violently in love with my brother," Jemma said.

Roberta blinked at Damon.

"I know," Jemma said, "hard to believe, isn't it?"

"Somewhat," Roberta said with a grin.

"Don't hesitate to insult me," Damon retorted.

"I certainly didn't mean to imply that you were less than handsome," Roberta said hastily.

"It's just as well that you're immune to his charms. It would be all too awkward if you joined the slavering hordes and were chasing Damon around the house with a knife in one hand and a ring in the other."

"A knife?"

"There was only one young lady with a cutting implement," Damon said, "and it was some sort of chisel for working in stone. Young Dulcit Pensington. In her first few months in London, she succumbed to a particularly virulent affection for me, and was determined to carve my head in sandstone."

"How —" Roberta caught back whatever word she meant. Probably *odd*, Damon thought. "How enterprising!" she exclaimed.

She obviously had no interest in him. Which was all to the best, just as Jemma had pointed out.

"Dulcit is a very sweet girl," Jemma said. "Not that I've seen her since she was a child, but I'm sure you have blown that chisel story out of all recognition, Damon."

"Not I," he said promptly. "For at least two weeks I couldn't leave my house without a maddened sculptress leaping from behind a bush, chisel in hand."

"Ignore him," Jemma said to Roberta. "When a man grows this convinced of his own beauty, there is no hope for him."

"I am not convinced of my beauty," Damon protested.

"What you need is a woman who doesn't even know you're alive," his sister told him. "I shall dance a hornpipe on the day you meet her."

"A fit encomium for marital bliss," Beaumont said, putting down his knife and fork. "Dancing to a tune one neither likes nor understands, with a partner who thinks you a cadaver."

As jokes go, that wasn't a bad one, though of course family loyalty meant that Damon couldn't laugh. Jemma was glaring again. Damon looked over at Roberta and saw an answering, secret smile in her eyes.

It seemed he could share a secret laugh with his new family member, which was comforting when he thought of sitting through more dinners like this one.

In fact, it was almost enticing.

CHAPTER 7

From the Duchess of Beaumont to the Duke of Villiers:
Though we haven't met in years, I should like to invite you to my ball tomorrow. My footman will await your response.

From the Duke of Villiers to the Duchess of Beaumont:
You should speak to your husband more frequently. We don't consort. No, thanks.

From the Duchess of Beaumont to the Duke of Villiers:
Would you agree that pawn-grabbing, like sin, cannot be diminished by apologies?

To the Duchess of Beaumont:
Are you offering to grab my pawn? I am charmed. No, thank you.

To the Duke of Villiers:
Perhaps I am guilty of a badly timed open-

ing? Capturing a pawn *en passant* is of course a delicious possibility, but I prefer to create a nest of mating possibilities.

To the Duchess of Beaumont:
An aggressive opening play. Does your king know of this invitation?

To the Duke of Villiers:
I was lucky enough to beat Philidor with an aggressive opening and I am fond of them for that reason. One of my weaknesses, perhaps, is that I underplay the king.

No salutation.
Are you talking about François Philidor?

No salutation.
Of course.

No salutation.
You beat François Philidor in a game of chess?

No salutation.
Many times.

No salutation.
I'll be there.

CHAPTER 8

The last person Jemma expected to welcome into her bedchamber that night was her husband. Though of course she would have to invite him in at some point if they were to embark on their heir-making activities.

"May I come in?" Beaumont said, looking furious, as always.

Jemma opened the door without saying a word. At least he didn't appear to be attired for bedroom matters. She was not prepared for that sort of intimacy with him. Not yet.

He strode over to the center of the room and stood there as if he were planning to make a speech in parliament. "Obviously, we have matters to discuss."

"I actually wanted to ask you about your health," Jemma said, rather surprised to hear herself say the words.

Beaumont shrugged. "My doctor feels that I fainted as a result of overwork and general stupidity, rather than a signal problem with my heart. But I may have less time left than I would prefer, given my father's early demise."

That casual statement gave Jemma a slightly sick feeling; for all they lived apart, they were man and wife, after all. She nodded, and made her way over to a chair by the fire.

"That is one of the reasons why I must ask you to curb any injudicious activities," he said, obviously choosing his words with care. "We are at the beginning of a revolution in the House, to be led by young Pitt, and I would not want my private life to become a distraction."

He seemed to be waiting for a response, so she said, "Experience has taught me that your idea of discussion is entirely one-sided, so you may continue as you wish, Beaumont."

He scowled but started to talk about propriety and parliament and other boring topics. Jemma began thinking about the chess game she had in progress. Her queen pawn was bottled up —

"Jemma!"

She raised her eyes. "Yes, Elijah?" It gave her an odd *frisson* to use his given name, knowing that he hated the intimacy of it. In truth, her husband was quite good-looking.

It was a shame that he was impossible to live with.

"Jemma!"

She stood up again. "Let me itemize your demands. You want me to behave with utmost propriety in every situation. You would prefer that my brother not live in the house due to the presence of his illegitimate child. In fact, you may just have ordered me to send him away although I am hoping I misunderstood you. I should also dismiss my secretary. You would prefer I entertain no lovers, take in no brothers, and chatter with no friends. Have I understood you?"

"Some version of that would be very helpful to me. Do you agree?"

"Absolutely not." She walked over to her chess table and stared down at the game as if she were contemplating a move, though to tell the truth, her heart was beating quickly with rage.

He made a sharp movement behind her but said nothing.

She turned back to him, leaning against the table. "My brother has come to pay me a visit in a house that is mine as well as yours. Obviously, you have grown mightily in your own estimation during the years I lived in Paris. You did not used to be so unilateral nor so tedious."

123

"I request" — he spat out the word — "the very minimal that any man might expect of his wife. I ask only that you not have yourself carried naked into the dining room, nor —"

She laughed. "Did that story reach London?"

"Did you think it would not?"

"I didn't do it, you know."

"Unfortunately, the truth matters little since the story arrived here with your name firmly attached to it, and all sorts of details regarding the size of the platter and the number of footmen required to hoist you into the air." His eyes raked her figure, up and down. "I would have guessed that four footmen could have managed the business, but I'm told it was eight."

She smiled at him. "My breasts and hips have grown since my salad days when you and I shared a bed. To be safe, I would have commandeered eight. But as a matter of fact, Catherine Worlée was brought in on a silver dish, and it wasn't even at a party of mine. I'm sure you would have enjoyed her company; she was something of a professional comrade to men of your ilk."

His eyes narrowed to daggers. "What a shame I never met her. Although I can imagine it would be confusing to be unable to tell my wife apart from a courtesan such as Mademoiselle Worlée."

"I doubt it would be confusing to you at all," she said. "After all, you are accustomed to paying women for the privilege of sharing their bed, are you not? Whereas I" — her heart was beating so quickly she could hardly hear — "engage in the sport for pleasure."

He turned away. "This quarrelling will get us nowhere. All I am asking, Jemma, is that you not scandalize all of London. I have work in Parliament. I know you find it uninteresting, but it is important work."

"There was a time I found it interesting. But that was before I realized that your mistress found it so fascinating that she visited you in your office to discuss it."

He raked a hand through his hair. "For God's sake, Jemma, will you forget that? I'm sorry that you opened the door. I still can't believe that the clerks let you into my office without warning."

"Never underestimate the charm of a young bride wishing to surprise her spouse."

"We have discussed this before," he said through clenched teeth. "One of the few pleasures of our marriage in the past years has been that we rarely quarreled during my visits to Paris."

"During those visits, you never questioned my decisions, nor acted ashamed of my entertainments."

"You were in Paris. Now you are here, in my house —"

"*My* house as well. I am home, and you will simply have to accustom yourself to that notion. I am home, with my disreputable friends, and my illegitimate nephew, and my entertainments. I am not a good political wife and I never will be. I will do my best, however, to tailor my flights of fancy to your hidebound notions. Luckily for you, I have no lover at the moment, nor do I intend to take one."

This would obviously be a good time to discuss the question of marital visits, but she was too angry. A mad, irresistible impulse was beating in her heart, a wish to make him sorry for describing her in such tawdry terms, for implying she was incapable of understanding politics.

There was a moment of stiff silence. Jemma sat down at her chess table, refusing to look at him again.

He walked over and looked down at the game. "You are playing, I see?"

"I have yet to find a partner in this country. Unless you would consider a return to the board?"

"My games of strategy take place on a larger stage."

She raised her head and met his eyes. They were black, marked by eyebrows that winged up at the edges. He had the straight nose and strong chin of his forefathers. "I suppose that is designed to make me feel petty. I would remind you that women are allowed no role in those larger games of strategy. Perhaps I play chess because I am not allowed to play in a larger sphere."

"How dull your life must be, to cherish one move all day," he said slowly, staring at the board. "Very pretty. A deceptively placid position. Black has some powder left, but White is nicely set up." He raised an eyebrow. "Your skill has indeed grown, Jemma. I take it your silence is an assent."

"You have never been interested in my skill," she said, without pity. "I see no reason to boast to you . . . I shall save my flights of self-congratulation."

"With whom do you play? Have you a maid who knows the game?"

"In Paris, I had partners."

"We have all heard of those partners," he said, and his voice was very even. "The practice of a gentleman and lady playing chess in the privacy of a bedchamber only reached these shores in the last year."

"How unfortunate," she said. "I was hoping to have the pleasure of setting all the dowagers' hair on end by starting the fashion myself. Since I have no partner in England, I play both sides of the game."

"So you make two moves a day?"

"When I play the other part, I am not myself."

"I would take it you are White, menacing Black's bishop."

"Unfortunately," she said, "I am Black."

He laughed.

"*You* are White."

The laughter died.

"I had no idea that I was playing," he said. "Let alone that I would win."

"Life is full of pleasurable surprises."

"Did I take my rook to Bishop Two?"

"Precisely."

"Why are you letting me win?"

"I didn't; you are winning fair and square. It was a beautiful set on your part: only five moves."

"You must be very fair to play like this."

"The hard part is not being fair, but playing as if I am you."

"Because?" He looked at her, eyebrow raised.

"You are an excellent chess player. Better

128

when *I* play you than you used to be on your own."

He gave a bark of laughter.

"Given that proviso, I rarely win against you."

"Oh, have we played often?"

She nodded. "Whenever I am without another partner, I turn to you."

He picked up the rook. "I am, then, a way station between partners?"

"You seem to be confusing bed partners with chess partners," she said. "Men who can play chess are so infrequently worth the time in bed. It takes a different kind of imagination."

"Describe my play — at chess?"

"You have foresight, detail and courage. Your fault is that you are not daring enough, but you excel in outwitting, cornering and demolishing your opponent."

He was silent a moment but she saw a smile in his eyes. "I think my opponents in Lords would agree with you. Your play?"

"I am more brilliant, and more erratic. In our last four games, played by myself, of course, you have won three. I tend to take far too much delight in risk."

"How interesting that by pretending to be me you curb your own impetuosity."

"I don't consider myself impetuous,"

Jemma said. "I assure you that when I win, my moves are beautiful. I frequently win, except when I play you. Monsieur Philidor was the only person who beat me on a regular basis, but I also beat him, many times."

She felt his eyes on her, but refused to look up again. When he spoke again, his voice was rather stifled. "I realize that you didn't have to return to London, and that you left a great deal behind you in Paris, Jemma."

"True."

"I am grateful." The words seemed reluctant.

"It is no more than my duty."

"I confess that I am reluctant to see the estate go to my nephew."

"Is he still as foolish as ever?"

"He wears a great quantity of false hair," Elijah said. "False teeth, and — so he tells me — pads his stockings to give himself a proper leg. So false legs as well."

"I am not yet ready to engage in the intimacies that will lead to an heir," Jemma said, still not looking at him. "I am accustomed to pleasure for its own sake. Nor am I happy about the inevitable unpleasantness involved in carrying a child. Perhaps after the season. We can retire to the country." And won't that be fun, she thought.

He bowed. "I am at your convenience."

CHAPTER 9

April 11
Nine o'clock
Beaumont House

There hadn't been such excitement over a ball since Princess Charlotte attended her first public fête at Windsor Castle. Though many were certain that the Duchess of Beaumont would lose her reputation within weeks of arriving in London — after all, they'd all heard stories of the many lovers she deserted in Paris — she had not yet been rejected from society, and thus everyone with an invitation was free to attend.

"We have to take advantage of it," Miss Charlotte Tatlock said to her sister May. "Lord knows, the duchess may be *persona non grata* by next week."

"I wish you wouldn't speak in riddles," May replied. She was looking out the carriage window, trying to see whose coach was following theirs.

"That's not a riddle; it's Latin."

"I see no difference. And besides, I know why you wish to attend the ball, Charlotte."

"For the pleasure of it?"

"Because you're hoping that her uncle will have come to town to see his niece. Lord Barnabe Reeve."

"I had forgotten about him," Charlotte said, less than truthfully. "Didn't he retire to the country? Of course he won't be there. You know as well as I do that he's not right in the head."

"Like all the Reeve family," May said. "Did you hear that the duchess is bringing the daughter of the Mad Marquess into society? I expect there are bets in White's about her eccentricities, to put it kindly. Naturally the Mad Marquess and the Reeves share some part of their family tree. It only makes sense."

May had the most annoying titter in the entire world. "I want to see the duchess's arrangements," Charlotte said. "I heard that she intends to serve a table of fruit embedded in Parma violets. I've seen fruit embedded in moss; haven't we all? But violets? That must cost three hundred pounds."

"I am more curious to see her clothing," May said. "That is, if she wears any. She may repeat herself and be delivered on a platter."

"I discount that tale entirely. It would be most uncomfortable, as one would be in constant danger of falling to the ground."

May looked unconvinced, but just then the carriage drew up in front of Beaumont House. "Well, you can't tell me that you have forgotten the Duchess of Claverstill's ball. Not after making an exhibit of yourself dancing all night with Barnabe Reeve."

Charlotte had a low opinion of her sister's intelligence, and this question did not improve it. How could she — Charlotte — have forgotten that ball? 'Twas the one at which she fell in love with Barnabe Reeve. Though he'd never asked for her hand, and left London shortly thereafter, she hadn't forgotten.

There was a cacophony of noise around them as carriages unloaded and footmen shouted. May was dressed most becomingly in blue, with moderate hoops. Charlotte, who prided herself on being elegant, was resplendent in sprigged silk. Unfortunately, the best they could hope for in terms of compliments were words like *becoming* and *resplendent.* It was a far cry from the ball when Charlotte danced all night with Lord Barnabe Reeve, dance after dance, certain she would be married within months.

"Let's enter, shall we?" she said, adjusting her drape of Anglican lace around her elbows. "We have a duchess to see!"

But in fact the first person they saw was not the duchess, but the duke.

"He's glowering," May whispered, as they approached the receiving line. "I cannot think why Her Grace returned from Paris. They cannot be happy together."

"Perhaps she was tired of France. I've heard that it can be miserably hot in the summer."

"There *must* be something more to it," May murmured, with the kind of intensity that suggested she would spend the entire night talking of nothing else.

"Good evening," the duke said, bowing before them.

They curtsied.

"The duchess has made her way into the ballroom," the duke said, looking glacially disapproving. "I know she will be most happy to see you, Miss Tatlock, Miss Charlotte."

"Goodness," May whispered as they hurried past him. "He couldn't be more forbidding, could he? Is that Villiers on the other side of the room? It can't be. He never speaks to Beaumont."

"He might know the duchess . . . How

135

interesting *that* would be!"

"What?"

Sometimes May was quite dense. "If Villiers made a set at Beaumont's wife," Charlotte said patiently. "Villiers hasn't a mistress at the moment, has he?"

"Who would know? The only thing that man really cares about is chess."

"I know, but he seems to cut a wide swathe through the female half of the *ton* in between matches."

"He's so rude!" May said. "I simply can't abide him." She plumped up her hair. "Perhaps I shall grant Muddle two dances tonight. Here he comes."

Charlotte groaned inwardly. Her older sister finally had a beau, Horace Muddle. I'm happy for her, she thought. I'm happy for her.

Why not be happy? They are both muddled and muddling; they will live together in happy muddlestown. And I shall live —

She turned away. One of her friends was hailing her from the side of the room, so she smilingly made her way over to sit among the young matrons, all of whom were her age and spent an inordinately large amount of time discussing their offspring. At least to Charlotte's mind.

But not tonight.

"Did you see what she's wearing?" Lady Hester Vesey asked immediately.

"I haven't seen her at all. She had left the receiving line and Beaumont was irritably doing the honors on his own."

"There she is," Hester breathed. "Over to the right."

Charlotte took care not to appear to be staring. She straightened her wrap, and smiled at an acquaintance to the left, and then let her eyes drift in the other direction.

The Duchess of Beaumont had dressed her hair very high in a mass of curls, marked by jeweled flowers. She was exquisitely gowned, so much so that Charlotte felt slightly faint with envy. Her gown was lemon-colored Italian silk, the petticoat puckered all over and sewn with roses.

"Do you see who she's talking to?" Hester whispered.

"Ah," Charlotte said, her eyes narrowing as the duchess laughed. "It's Delacroix. I thought she had left him in Paris."

"He followed her."

"Did you hear that her brother has moved into Beaumont House with his child?"

Charlotte's eyes opened at that. "I'm amazed the duke would allow such an irregularity."

"It's got everyone talking again about who the mother could be. Lady Piddleton claimed yesterday that she knew for a fact it was Mary Strachey's child. But then there's others who say his mistress took off for America and left him with the babe."

"America? That seems unlikely."

"Well, that's what everyone says. I can't imagine why he didn't simply stow it in the country like any decent man would do."

"I've never seen him with Mary Strachey."

"*That* means nothing," Hester said, with irrefutable logic. "Her acquaintances are legion, as it says in the Bible, or at least it says something like that. Your sister is looking very intimate with Muddle."

"Yes," Charlotte said. "I'm hoping for a wedding in the family."

"Next we must turn to you," Hester said comfortably. "It's never too late!"

Charlotte silently ground her teeth. "I live in hope."

"Well, that might be —"

But whatever bit of wisdom Hester was going to offer was swept away as her husband bowed before her and bore her off onto the dance floor, ignoring her protests. "There's a chess game brewing between Corbin and Villiers," he told her. "I'm not missing that, so we're having our dance now."

Charlotte sighed. There was nothing very appealing about the marriages she saw around her, but it was hard not to long for a spouse anyway. She sat still and tried to look as if she wasn't alone. You'd think she'd be used to it. A few chords sounded . . . a polonaise was beginning.

Suddenly a pair of polished shoes stopped before her. "If you please?" A gloved hand paused before her face . . . she looked up. It was the Duke of Beaumont.

"Your Grace," she said, rising and curtsying deeply.

"Miss Charlotte. May I have the pleasure of this dance?"

Her heart skipped a beat. Of course, he was a married man, but he was so dreadfully handsome. She rose and placed her hand in his. A moment later they were gravely pacing down the dance floor. Charlotte resisted looking about to see whether anyone had noticed she was dancing with the host.

Instead she looked up at him. Of course, he was famously short-tempered, and it would be foolish of her to provoke him. But then he achieved such remarkable things in the House of Lords.

She had two choices: they could engage in twenty minutes worth of silent dancing, or she could speak. He clearly considered his duty to end with the dance itself. "I read the description of your recent speech in the House of Lords, Your Grace."

He looked marginally more awake. "In the *London Gazette*? I'm afraid that the majority agreed with the opposition, more's the pity."

"Are you quite certain that you are right about Mr. Fox's intent to make the East India Company accountable to commissioners?"

"Am I certain that it's a blatant attempt to seize the Company's wealth for themselves? In a word: Yes." He didn't look very pleased by her question anymore.

"I mention it because I was greatly struck by the wording of the actual bill. I am in sympathy with your wish to force an election, but should not companies be accountable? Someone must look over their shoulders, Your Grace."

"The Whigs look over the Company's shoulders only to seize its wealth."

"How hard it is to tell the difference between an anti-corruption measure and greed," Charlotte said. "It did occur to me —" She stopped.

"What occurred to you?" He looked interested, bending down slightly, and Charlotte's heart thumped again. "Curses, we're going to the end of the measure," he said. "Don't forget your thought."

A moment later they were reunited. Charlotte looked at him over their raised hands. "You understand that I have only read the accounts in the *Gazette.*"

"They have been fairly accurate, which is unusual."

"I thought that perhaps you might emphasize the question of treason in your next speech," she said. "As I understand it, you are trying to drum up support against Fox. But if I were you, I would swing this particular discussion to support *for* the King, rather than antagonism *against* the Secretary of State. Fox is so very popular."

His eyes narrowed. "I suppose I could. But Fox is the problem and he absolutely must be removed."

"Tell the House of Lords that anyone who votes for the bill would be regarded as the King's enemy. Don't even mention Fox."

For a moment he lost his step in the measure and then recovered. "Miss Charlotte, I'm grateful indeed that I asked for this dance."

Charlotte's heart sped up again. He drew

her to the side of the room. "Did you have a chance to read the debate published in the *Gazette* between Lord Temple and Fox?"

Roberta knew that she should be in the ballroom. She knew that all she had to do was walk down that last flight of stairs and she would enter the buzz and hum that was drifting through the house. She had been dressed for at least forty minutes.

The problem was that her dress was all wrong. She stared at herself in the mirror again. "You will be a perfect *jeune fille,*" Jemma had told her that morning. "We'll dress you very simply, some rosebuds here and there, a strand of pearls."

"I don't want to be a *jeune fille,*" Roberta had protested.

But Jemma had been firm. "I realize that you are a Reeve at heart. But your first appearance in the *ton* must be as an exquisite bud of young innocence. Later you can show your true colors. After you're married."

Roberta sighed. She had dreamed of going to a ball. But it was difficult to pretend to be docile and modest. She tried casting down her eyes again. No one could be innocent who had lived with her father for long. She felt like a fool. A wolf in lamb's clothing.

Just then the door burst open. "There you are," Jemma cried. "You look adorable!"

Roberta looked back in the mirror. Her hair had been carefully curled and powdered by the lady's maid assigned to her. She was wearing pearls, and there were sprigs of apple blossom in her hair. Her panniers were large enough to be elegant, but not large enough that she would have trouble dancing in them. And she had just a faint shading of pink to her lips and her cheeks. She simpered at herself.

The only thing she really liked were her slippers: they were exquisite, and pink.

That and the little patch high on her cheekbone.

"You don't like the way you're dressed, do you?" Jemma asked, appearing at her shoulder.

"Oh I do!" Roberta said hastily. "It would be most ungracious of me to dislike it, and I promise that I love it. I've never looked so wonderful in my life! In fact," she said in a burst of honesty, "this is the first time I've ever worn powder."

"Itchy, isn't it? I avoid it whenever I can," Jemma said sympathetically, "but one's hair simply must be powdered on occasion."

"Truly, I am so grateful, Jemma."

Jemma narrowed her eyes as she stared at the mirror. "What do you wish you were wearing?"

Roberta knew the proper answer to that. "Exactly what I am wearing! Shall we go downstairs now?"

But Jemma was smiling. "Fancy yourself a *séductrice,* do you?"

Roberta caught another glimpse of the pretty shepherdess in the mirror. "I'm not sure," she said.

"But you'd like to find out?"

"I don't think that Villiers will be interested by maidenly docility," Roberta confessed. "He's not the type to court young girls, is he?"

Jemma laughed. "Absolutely not."

"So what good is it to wear this clothing? It's not going to work with him," she said desperately. "And I don't care about the rest!"

"You need to fool the *ton* before you take on Villiers," Jemma said. "They are invariably sheep-like and once they get a fixed idea in their head, it's hard to move it. If you act in an innocent and demure manner tonight, that is how they will see you. All talk of your father's companions will die quickly. Then — and only then — will you receive invitations to the parties where you will find Villiers. He's downstairs, you know."

"He is?" Roberta felt a wave of dizziness that spread from her toes to her hair line.

"Succeed tonight and tomorrow morning invitations will shower on your head. Villiers will be at most of them."

Roberta snatched her gloves. "I am ready."

Jemma smiled. "Be docile."

Roberta simpered at her.

"Very good," Jemma said. "Innocent?"

Roberta cocked her head to one side and gave her a brainless smile.

"Not quite *that* innocent," Jemma said. "You are obviously quite accomplished at prevarication, though how you learned it while penned up in a house with a poet, I don't know."

"There are many opportunities to prevaricate when one lives with a poet," Roberta said. She walked down the stairs by herself, as the width of Jemma's skirts did not allow her to walk beside anyone. "It would not always have been advisable to inform my father of my true opinion of a given poem, for example."

"Fibbing is an extremely useful sport," Jemma said. And as if to prove it, she paused just inside the ballroom door and introduced Roberta to a group of matrons

145

as a close relative, whom she'd known for years. Then she leaned closer and Roberta caught the word "heiress."

One of the mothers produced her son, a lanky boy, out of thin air and introduced the two of them. Roberta obediently simpered at Lord Rollins and set off into the dance.

By an hour later, she felt fairly confident that all of London thought she was an innocent, albeit rich, maiden from the country.

"Which you *are*," Jemma said in passing. "Remember the eleven peach trees."

"I don't need peach trees," Roberta said. "I'm sure that Villiers has his own orchard."

"A woman should always have an auxiliary target, a man in the wings, as it were."

But Roberta had no man in the wings. Villiers was everything she wanted in a husband. She glimpsed him briefly, across the room, and her feeling of rightness was almost overwhelming. He was resplendent in a coat extravagantly embroidered with poppies, a cloth that might seem feminine on another man. But his dark, coiled features turned the delicacy to a jest.

She was no fool. Villiers wasn't going to be attracted by simpering innocence and powdered curls. If she meant to marry him, she would have to play a very tricky game indeed.

CHAPTER 10

Jemma had to acknowledge that if her husband was beautiful, the Duke of Villiers wasn't. His face was long, with narrow cheeks and black eyebrows. He had a rakish look, like a buccaneer of Queen Elizabeth's time. He wore a patch high on his cheek, and his lips were the same deep red as the poppies on his coat. It made her consider lip color — was that possible? Yet his hair was just pulled back carelessly from his forehead, unpowdered, no wig.

Beaumont and Villiers were as dissimilar as night and day. Jemma surveyed Villiers from across the ballroom floor for an hour or so without approaching him. He didn't dance; he prowled. Elijah danced. She saw him doing his duty with every unattached woman in the room. The only woman in whom Villiers showed interest was Lady Nevill. Jemma didn't know her, other than by reputation, but she had to admit she was delicious, with her satiny smile and sleepy eyes.

Jemma bided her time. The whole business of avenging Benjamin's suicide had taken on its own pleasurable edge, giving her a flare of excitement. Would she seduce? Or would she merely beat him at chess? Or both? She danced near Villiers, and he didn't look at her.

Then, quite suddenly, those heavy-lidded eyes lifted and the shock of it went down her spine. The glitter in his eyes was that of a chess player, the same light she'd seen in Philidor's eyes, but only when he watched her queen take his pawns.

She whirled away into the steps of the dance, and found her corset felt unexpectedly tight around her ribs. She looked one more time, and he was murmuring in the ear of Lady Nevill. He wasn't nearly as handsome as Beaumont, but he had an irresistibly wicked look that her strait-laced husband could never achieve.

Roberta danced by, smiling beatifically at a young squire. He looked besotted, as well he might. Roberta raised a cynical eyebrow over his shoulder.

At that same moment, Jemma realized something. Her revenge wouldn't run parallel to Roberta's pursuit of Villiers. It would be an integral part of it. She, Jemma, would wrap up the man whom all London had tried to tame — and deliver him to Roberta as part of Harriet's revenge.

Marriage laid the ground for a hundred — nay, a thousand — petty humiliations of the type that Harriet longed to visit on Villiers.

It was the ultimate revenge.

Suddenly Villiers was in front of her, eyebrow raised. "A black bandit knight at your service."

"Not a king?"

He took out a cheroot. "Let's go outside, shall we?" And without waiting for her response, he walked straight outside onto the balcony. He shook back his deep lace cuffs and lit the cheroot from a torch on the balcony. The light flickered against his face. His skin was startling clear and white against the black hair, sleekly pulled back from his face. No, he wasn't handsome.

And yet he wasn't the sort of man who would find himself in a friendly cuffing match with the lads down at the pub either. He was altogether more refined and intelligent. No wonder he was the best player in England.

Every instinct told her that he would be a powerful partner. For a moment she couldn't distinguish between the wish to play him and to have him. A challenge — and what a challenge! Villiers was famous for drifting from woman to woman with limpid disinterest. If Roberta was to marry him, she would have to take the law into her own hands, or rather use the law on her side, because he would never propose due to love.

The truth was that he *was* in love . . . with chess. A man bound to the chessboard has little left over, as poor Harriet had found to her distress.

Villiers stood silently, drawing on his cheroot and watching her. Jemma said nothing. She disliked opening conversations. It was such an immediate way to give away one's strategy. Women, she found, were generally too eager to rush into flirtation.

Instead, she turned and looked over the gardens. The great elms were putting out new leaves that looked almost blue because of swathes of bluebells planted beneath them.

"Black King by a smothered mate," came a drawling voice behind her.

"An old but pretty trick," she said, turning around. She was conscious of a slight feeling of disappointment. Did he really need to test her knowledge?

"Do you know," he said softly, watching her unblinkingly over the glowing end of his cheroot, "that I often walk into Parsloe's and find there is no one worth playing?"

She shrugged. What was his point? She rarely had a partner at her own level other than Philidor.

"You'll forgive me, then, for seeming brash in my enthusiasm."

"Benjamin, the Duke of Berrow, used to play a fine game," she said, testing him.

His whole face changed. His cheekbones hollowed and his eyes looked haunted. "He was a good match. Better five years ago . . ."

"Has your skill fallen, as did his?"

"I was best when I was twenty," he said, taking a long draw on his cheroot. "And you?"

"I am best now," she said. It was the truth; she met his eyes and knew that he understood it.

"What did Philidor make of you? I heard little of a female chess player in France though" — he paused — "I heard much of *you.*"

"You'll find, if you travel to Paris to play him — and you should — that he is ranked among my lovers. We played almost every day, in my bedchamber, at a table beside my bed."

"I take it he had no interest in that bed," Villiers said. His eyes were dark, too dark to read.

"Of course not," she said tranquilly. "We would play a game, or sometimes make a match last by playing only one move a day."

"That must have been a remarkable pleasure."

"Indeed."

"Who do you play otherwise?"

"Generally, I play myself."

"All by yourself?" he asked, and suddenly she was unsure whether he was talking of chess or bedroom matters.

"Life is so much less complicated by oneself," she said, sighing.

"I wouldn't know," he said. The smoke drifted past his eyes. "I find partners at Parsloe's or White's. I would prefer to play with strangers — or those with less skill — than find myself holding my own pawn in the safety of my bedchamber."

"The difference between a man and a woman perhaps," she said. "For myself, I find that my knowledge of chess comes from long moments of self-study."

He grinned at that, the flash of a tiger's white teeth when it spots its prey.

"I think this game will be very interesting," he said. "Because there is to be a game

153

between us, is there not?"

She held his eyes. "Let's make it a match. Two out of three games."

"You are a formidable opponent," he said.

There was a rustle of the silk hangings and Elijah came onto the balcony, accompanying a young girl who was feeling faint, apparently. Her mother rushed after them.

Elijah glanced in Jemma's direction and froze. A second later, the girl was wilting in her mother's arms, and Elijah was standing beside them. "What an inestimable pleasure," he said. "My boyhood friend enters my house."

"That would be I," Villiers said indifferently. "The one you don't speak to. Your wife — who invited me to your ball — and I were just extolling the benefits of the solitary life."

"Really?"

They were like night and day. Beaumont burned with the raw intensity that fueled his political ambitions, that had propelled him to the most important cabinet place under the Prime Minister, that had given him the ear of the King. Villiers drooped against the balcony, his cheroot held in long, lean fingers, his eyelids half open. He had a frown line between his brows and wrinkles by his eyes. Yet Beaumont still looked as he had in his early twenties, though he surely had as many late nights in politics as Villiers did in gaming.

"She tells me," Villiers said, "that she beat Philidor many times."

"To be fair, Philidor beat me as many times," Jemma remarked.

Elijah lifted an eyebrow. "You must have improved."

A slow burn went through Jemma's chest. Since her husband had played her only a few times, in the earliest days of their marriage, how could he know whether she had improved? She said nothing.

Villiers's eyes slid back to her like sweet honey. "Our match is on, then?" he said, flicking his cheroot into the air. It flew through the evening sky like a glowing spark, landing on the gravel path below. Of course Elijah's eyes followed it. He would never do such a thing. Why make work for a servant or possibly cause a fire?

"Of course," she said. "Shall we play one move a day? The match will be slower, but all the more satisfying."

"If there's a tie with the first two, the last game blindfolded."

She couldn't help a little smile at that. She had played herself blindfolded, but it

155

would be much better to have an opponent.

Villiers bowed with careless ease. His coat was as beautiful as one worn by the finest dandy in Paris.

Elijah was in unrelieved black.

When Villiers walked away, Jemma saw that his hair was tied back with a poppy-red ribbon. It looked shocking against the dark silk of his hair. He must be setting his own fashion; in Paris men used only black ribbons.

"Where will you play chess with him?" Elijah asked. His voice was even, but his eyes were burning with rage.

Jemma mentally shrugged. Elijah was a creature of anger. "I suspect I shall play him precisely where I played Philidor."

"And where was that?"

"In my bedchamber."

With some pleasure she watched his eyes smolder. "And the prize?"

She shrugged again, one languid movement that showed her shoulder to creamy advantage. Though why she should bother with such a thing around her husband, she didn't know. "Need there be a prize?" she asked, and made to leave.

But he was blocking her way. He'd grown bigger in the past eight years. When she had left England, he had lean legs and large shoulders. But now he had turned into a proper man. Jemma pushed away that thought with irritation.

"I gather that you are the prize?" To do him credit, his voice was silky.

"I am no prize of any man's," she said, meeting his eyes to make sure that he understood. "I'm a free gift . . . to those upon whom I choose to bestow myself."

"A gift many times given is cheapened by its traffic."

"Dear me," Jemma said. "It seems to me I've heard that before. Yes! It must have been in church. How unusual to find a politician quoting the catechism. Perhaps you missed your calling."

"If you are playing chess with him —" Beaumont said, and paused.

Jemma was already past him, but she stopped. And then turned, slowly. "You would play chess with me simply because I have scheduled a match with Villiers? Surely you jest."

"Cannot a man play a game with his wife?" His mouth was set in a firm line. "I see nothing particularly interesting about the fact."

She laughed. "And will it be on the same terms? One move a day for each of us; best of three games; final game is blindfolded, if played at all?"

He shrugged.

"But Beaumont, you have not played chess, to the best of my knowledge, in years. Is it not ill-advised to wager so much on a rusty skill?"

"What do I wager? As you say, there is no prize."

She closed her lips. Far be it from her to point out that he played from the dislike he felt for Villiers. "You'd have to speak to me civilly," she pointed out, "and come home every day to play. As I understand it, there are many nights when you sleep in your chambers."

They both knew that he did not sleep alone when he stayed in his apartments in Westminster.

But he shrugged. Of course, a man in his thirties was presumably not quite as active as a man in his twenties. The day she discovered him on the desk with his mistress, he had risen from her bed but a few hours earlier. It was rather dismaying to realize that the memory still gave her a moment's heartache, even so many years later.

"I'll play you," she said over her shoulder. "But I shall allow you a handicap."

"I need no handicap." He said it evenly.

The memory of that day was still like a coal under her breastbone, so she smiled at him. "To make our match a challenge."

There was a faint color, high in his cheek, that betold rage. But Elijah was much better at containing himself than he had been when they were young.

"No," he said steadily. "Remember: when you play *as me,* I frequently win. I would venture to say that I can equal that performance."

Either he thought to humiliate her, or he completely underestimated her current skill. The latter made much more sense.

She curtsied. "By all means, Your Grace. Shall we begin the game tomorrow?"

"There is an important vote in Lords. But I suppose Villiers will lose no time attending you."

"Gentlemen rarely do, once I admit them into my presence."

He bowed. "Tomorrow."

CHAPTER 11

The news spread throughout the ballroom within a few minutes. The Duchess of Beaumont was engaged in *two* chess matches: one with her husband's enemy, the Duke of Villiers, and the second with her husband himself.

"They say," May said at one in the morning, "that she's a remarkably fine chess player."

"Perhaps that's the case," Charlotte said, thinking of the intense eyes of the duke. "But she's making a fool of herself to play with Villiers."

May laughed. "Then you must be settling into old age indeed, sister. Even I can see that Villiers is a man to savor." She looked slightly startled, as if such a word could not have come from her lips.

"The duchess's young ward, Lady Roberta, seems entirely acceptable," Charlotte said, changing the subject.

"Yes, a naïve little slip of a girl, isn't she?"

Suddenly Charlotte realized that May was gazing at her hand. And there, crammed over her glove, was a signet ring.

A ring.

It seemed that she would now be the only old maid in the Tatlock family. She snapped out of her momentary bleakness, embraced her sister and said all the proper things. In the flurry of congratulations, the docile young ward of the Duchess of Beaumont was quite forgotten.

In truth, Roberta had been forgotten by most of the players of this comedy. She obediently circled the ballroom throughout the night, moving from one gentleman's arms to another. At first she danced like a feather, and later she began weaving a bit because her toes hurt.

She retreated to the ladies' retiring room because Jemma's exquisite French slippers caused blisters, not because she had no one to dance with.

A whole flock of girls were there, chattering like magpies. Their voices died when she walked in.

But then a girl with a sweet, plump face stood up and smiled. "I'm Margery Rowlandson; we met earlier this evening."

"Good evening," Roberta said, and curtsied.

Margery introduced her to everyone, and soon she was a part of the giggling group. One girl who couldn't be more than sixteen was expecting an offer on the morrow; another had danced twice with a young courtier.

"But you're so lucky!" Margery exclaimed, turning back to Roberta. "I just realized that you are staying in Beaumont House, aren't you? That means you are *living* in the same house with Lord Gryffyn."

"Yes, he is here," Roberta said.

"Along with his — his — his —" Roberta thought her name was Hannah. She was giggling so hard that she couldn't voice it. Among the foolish, she would take a crown, to Roberta's mind.

"His son is in the house as well," she said evenly.

"I don't know how you can!" a shrill voice said. "Why, my mother said that if she'd known of his presence, she might not have let me come to this ball at all!"

"He's only a child of six years old."

"You haven't met him!" That was Margery, her eyes round with horror.

"I met him briefly and there was no sight of devil's horns anywhere," Roberta said gravely. "But then, I do not care for children."

"Neither do I," the shrill-voiced girl said. "Especially ones of this nature, who should be kept out of sight."

"I don't care if Lord Gryffyn does have an illegitimate son," Margery sighed. "He's so adorable."

"I suppose one could think that," Roberta said. "I believe I prefer someone older . . . say the Duke of Villiers?"

There was a moment of horrified silence.

"Hasn't anyone told you of his reputation?" Hannah gasped. "Stay away from him!" She punctuated each word with a stabbing motion of his finger. "Stay away! You haven't a mama who can tell you these things. Stay away from him!"

Roberta almost fell back a step. "I will. I promise."

Never had she felt more lonely.

The girls all took her for precisely what she appeared to be: a docile young heiress, brought from the country to be launched onto the marriage market under the aegis of her cousin the Duchess of Beaumont.

Their mothers seemed equally accepting. The dreadful illustrated pictures of her and her father in *Rambler's Magazine* were brought up several times, but only by kind matrons intent on reassuring her that no one knew of their existence.

All night Roberta danced and looked for the Duke of Villiers. Then, finally, she curtsied to a partner who had trodden all over her wounded toes, turned away and there he was.

"You must forgive me," he said. His deep, purring voice went through her like a bolt of lightning. "I might almost have knocked you down."

She curtsied. "Your Grace."

"I gather you are a new lamb brought to languish in the London season. Or to triumph over it, as the case may be. Do tell me your name, now we meet again?"

"Lady Roberta St. Giles."

"My father died some years ago," he said, in a striking non sequitur. "I can only suppose that yours has come to some unfortunate end since you are consigned to the duchess's tender care."

She raised her chin. "My father is enraptured by the duchess's kindness toward me."

"Shall we dance? It will come near to ruining your reputation, I should warn you. But I believe I already gave you a warning, did I not?"

She raised an eyebrow. "Indeed? I must have forgotten."

He knew she was lying, but she thought he liked it. "I never seduce impoverished young ladies," he said, his voice silky and sweet, "but I am more than available for young ladies of ample means."

"I believe," she said, allowing just the right amount of time to pass, "that my virtue can withstand the assault of partnering you in one dance. But it is *so* reassuring to know that if I am overcome by a desire for ruination, you are willing to accommodate. It warms the heart."

He threw back his head at that and let out a peal of laughter. "Hoist with my own petard! I deserved that. Come on, then. You're not as wholesome as you look."

"Since I gather that chastity would set no edge on your appetite, I shall not pretend to horror and dismay."

"*The Rape of Lucrece,*" he observed. "Do you play Lucrece then, with beauty and virtue striving in your face?"

"That sounds like an armada in full battle. Absolutely not. Had I been Lucrece, that dagger would have made its home in Tarquin's heart."

"Bravo! But have no fear, Lady Roberta, I have never yet had to lower myself to Tarquin's violent tactics."

"Ah," Roberta said. "It's useful to know

that ruination does not always result in feeling like a *polluted prison.*"

"A terrible use of alliteration on Shakespeare's part," he said, frowning. "I assure you, Lady Roberta, that ladies leave my care as assured of their own divinity as they were the day before. If perhaps slightly more so. I find — don't you? — that pleasure is a divine gift."

They walked into the ballroom. The main pleasure on Roberta's mind was the slightly hungry way in which other women looked at Villiers.

"I don't suppose you play chess, do you?" he asked suddenly. "I am finding myself rather surprised in that respect this evening."

"I have never played the game," she said. The chess board had languished in her father's drawing room forever; it had never occurred to her to study it. If only she had known it was so crucial to London entertainments.

He seemed to guess at her thoughts. "Almost no one in this house" — he nodded at the brilliant silks crowding the dance floor — "can play the game worth a damn, if at all. It is only I, and perhaps your hostess, who seem to have a curious affinity for it."

166

They paused just inside the ballroom, waiting for a new measure.

Villiers seemed to feel no need to entertain her. He dropped her arm; when she looked at him he was exchanging looks with a young matron who had an entire ship balanced on top of her hair.

"A nautical miracle," he murmured, seeing that she had followed his eyes. "And Madame Moore is so very light herself that it's a miracle she doesn't capsize more often."

He was bored by her, and why shouldn't he be? "As I understand it, light frigates are very easy to board," Roberta said, unrolling her fan and fluttering it before her face. "I assume that is an attraction for those too clumsy to attract a less sluggish vessel."

"Definitely unexpected depths," he said, and there was a strain of amusement in his deep voice that made her lightheaded. A strain of trumpets signaled the beginning of a minuet. He bowed before her; she snapped shut her fan, and curtsied. The steps of the dance kept them apart, turning toward him and his heavy lidded eyes, turning away. Her breath was coming quickly.

At the end of the dance he gathered her hands, kissed both of them, and made a magnificent leg. "My title, Lady Roberta, is the Duke of Villiers. I fancy I may see you one of these days, as I have undertaken to play a prolonged chess match with your hostess."

Of course she knew he was the top chess player in London; but now it occurred to her that he was deeply competitive in all things. And that such competitiveness was a weakness.

She smiled. "I wish you luck."

"In seeing you, or in playing chess?"

She let her eyes slide away from him. She was playing the game of her life, and it would never do to appear eager. "In chess, of course, my lord. I am frequently absent from the house, and would not wish to raise your hopes that I shall choose to be ruined, as you so charmingly offer."

She turned and then glanced over her shoulder, caught sight of his white teeth — he was laughing — and slid into the crowd. So far she had been dancing rather indolently with whomever presented himself. But now she realized that in order to catch Villiers she must be the very top of the *ton*. The catch of the season. The most desired of all marriageable women.

He would have to win her over the hands of many men — or he would show no interest whatsoever.

Jemma's brother appeared before her around an hour later. She had three young lords vying to offer her gingerbread wafers and champagne. In comparison to Villiers, they were easy to enchant. All three of them were giving her swooning looks, and judging from the sullen glances she'd had from young ladies, she was plucking chickens meant for someone else's supper.

Damon cut her from the crowd adroitly, which she rather appreciated because it was good for her swains to see that she wasn't theirs for the asking.

"Where are we going?" she asked. He nipped out of the ballroom and down a corridor that she hadn't even known existed.

"To my sister's sitting room," he said, grinning down at her. "Back way."

He pushed open a door and sure enough, there were the mustard yellow walls (minus Judith and her platter). But just as Roberta entered, she realized that the room was not unoccupied.

Directly before her, leaning over the arm of a chair, was a woman. All she could see was a creamy, rounded bottom because the lady's violet skirts had been tossed over her head, undoubtedly so they wouldn't be crushed. There was a gentleman there, of course, and he was —

He was doing her a service.

Roberta clapped a hand over her mouth and froze. Behind her, she heard Damon's low chuckle.

Roberta just stared. It was almost violent and yet strangely intoxicating. The man was caressing his partner at the same time that he . . . well, he . . . The woman, whoever she was, was clearly enjoying herself, given the noise she was making. Roberta didn't recognize the gentleman; he was rather tubby. But she couldn't help noting that his thighs were strong, and he too was obviously most happy, and as she watched he shaped his partner's bottom in his hands and pulled her higher and —

Damon's arm came around her waist and pulled her silently backwards into the corridor. He was still laughing as he closed the door. Roberta didn't feel in the least like laughing. She felt odd, as if all the air had been crushed out of her lungs.

Damon peered at her in the dim light of the corridor. "Shocked you to the bottom of your boots, I see. Come along then. We'll go to the library; there'll be no one there because it's so damned hard to find." He took her hand and pulled her along through a corridor and a turn, and finally through a door.

It was a monstrously big library, all lined with books and hung in somber crimson velvet.

Roberta walked forward feeling slightly unsteady on her legs. There was a sofa before the fire, and Damon pushed her into it. "A brandy, that's what you need," he said, going over to the sideboard.

He tumbled a few glasses about and said, over his shoulder, "I take it that was the first tupping you were ever witness to?"

Roberta opened her mouth but no sound came out.

"Poleaxed," he said cheerfully, coming back and handing her a glass. "Drink that."

Roberta took a fiery swallow and coughed. "What is it?"

Damon was laughing again. "First brandy, first tupping."

"*I* didn't tup anyone," Roberta said, taking another sip. She quite liked brandy. Although it made her realize that her stomach was disconcertingly hot, and the drink only made it more so.

"True," Damon said, throwing himself down next to her. "So, are you shocked, horrified, stricken to the bone?"

Roberta turned and looked at him. He was remarkably like his sister, though his hair was burnished a darker brown, whereas his sister's was golden. Not that she could see his hair under his wig. He had Jemma's eyes and her deep lower lip. "It's rather unkind of you to make jest of me."

He grinned unrepentantly. "I don't see why you should be so horrified. It's entirely natural, after all."

But was it? Previous to this, Roberta thought she had the facts of procreation and marital intimacy firmly in mind. One of her father's courtesans had informed her that the man climbs on top of his partner, inserts his private part into the appropriate area, and continues. What exactly *continuing* meant was rather fuzzy to Roberta, but she certainly understood the mechanics.

Until this.

Because the mechanics might have been — she had to suppose they *were* — reproduced in a different position . . .

Under Damon's interested eyes she felt herself going pink in the cheeks. "It works in many different positions," he said helpfully.

At this evidence that he knew precisely what she was thinking about, she turned pinker still.

"Any other questions? I am your cousin, after all."

"Five times removed," Roberta said rather crossly.

"Actually, it's more like seven," Damon said. "As I work it out in my head, you're about as much related to me as most of the people in the ballroom."

"Are you implying that I am taking advantage of your sister?"

"If Jemma didn't want to bring you out, she wouldn't. Believe me, no one talks Jemma into doing a single thing that she doesn't care to. Thus, her eight years in Paris."

"Do you understand why she came back to London?" Roberta asked, desperate to change the topic to something other than tupping peers.

Damon stretched out his long legs. The current fashion for tight knee breeches suited him. His breeches were of a dark crimson and they made his legs, in cream stockings, look remarkably virile.

Roberta caught herself. What was she thinking? It was all the effect of seeing that performance in the sitting room. It made her feel peculiar. *Most* peculiar, she thought, realizing just what kind of messages her body seemed to be sending her.

"She has to make an heir," Damon said, "because Beaumont might drop dead at any moment. He collapsed in the House last fall, didn't you hear? Fell to the ground and everyone thought he was dead. But he wasn't. Still, the prospect is not too pretty. Fainting is not a healthy man's activity. His father stuck his spoon in the wall at thirty-four due to something wrong with his heart. Beaumont is living on borrowed time."

"He looks healthy enough," Roberta said.

"Doesn't he? I'm hoping it was an aberration. I like the man, and I think that it's better for Jemma to have him here to fight with, rather than buried, if you see what I mean. Did you meet the Duchess of Berrow, Jemma's friend? She was here yesterday afternoon."

Roberta shook her head.

"She used to be a smiling little thing, and then her husband died — killed himself in truth — and she's like a little bird with a broken wing now. You can't coax a smile for love or money."

"How sad," Roberta said softly.

"Jemma had to return from Paris and do her wifely duty."

The words wouldn't have meant much to Roberta before this, but now she could feel herself getting pink again.

Damon's mouth curled into a wicked smile. "I don't imagine Beaumont doing the business in the sitting room with his breeches at his ankles, do you? He's far too proper."

A mad choke of laughter came from Roberta's chest. "No!" Now Villiers . . . She felt almost feverish at the thought. Villiers she could easily see dragging down his breeches and turning someone over the arm of a chair.

There was a touch on her cheek and she turned, to find Damon looking at her. "You're not thinking about my brother-in-law," he said, his eyes slightly narrowed. "So who, my dear Roberta, cousin and relative, are you thinking of?"

She gasped but said nothing.

"It's Villiers, isn't it? I forgot that you'd already found the love of your life."

He still held her chin and it seemed to Roberta as if the world stopped spinning and froze, with the two of them but a hair's breadth from each other.

"Of course I was thinking of Villiers," she said, pulling backward. Pulling herself together.

He raised his glass to hers. "To many lazy afternoons spent in the drawing room with your husband."

"You shouldn't say such things," she scolded, taking another delicious sip from her glass.

"Why not?"

He had green eyes. She'd never realized that before; she thought they were blue, like those of his sister. But no, they were green, and beautifully shaped, with a little turn upward at the corners. "Because I am a young lady," she said, looking at the fire again.

"I suppose that young ladies don't think about disreputable people tupping in drawing rooms?"

"Never."

"But you, Roberta, aren't you rather extraordinary among young women?" There was a thread of laughter in his voice.

She shook her head. "Not at all." She almost choked when a large sip of fiery liquor went down the wrong way.

"I thought you were . . . For one thing, I thought you told the truth."

"Well, of course I tell the truth," she said. She dared to look at him again. There was something different in his eyes, something daring and delicious and altogether not like the Damon of yesterday. She was shivering with excitement, and yet she hadn't the faintest impulse to leave the room. Which she ought to.

"As to the truth," he said, stretching out

his legs again, "I found the whole scene rather arousing. Didn't you?"

She couldn't think what to say. One had to suppose that *arousing* covered feelings like the queer warmth in her legs.

"Look at that," he said, obviously thinking the conversation was no more important than an exchange over muffins. "Lady Piddleton ran my stockings."

There was a large snag running through the clocks splashed on the outside of his stocking. And then she noticed that higher up, where his tight breeches turned into a waistband, there was —

One had to pretend to be a virtuous young lady and not have even seen that.

"What was she doing in such a position as to scratch them?" Roberta asked, and then felt herself going purple as all sorts of thoughts as she'd never had before came to mind. She stared at the mantelpiece so that she wouldn't accidentally gaze at his breeches again.

He let out a peal of laughter. "Lady Piddleton, Roberta! Coming into fifty years old, with a face like the back of a rusty saucepan?"

"I merely wondered how it came to pass," she said with dignity.

"Jeweled heels," he said. "Belying her age,

she rubbed her shoe against my leg under the table at supper."

Roberta blinked at him. "In an invitation?"

"Are you so surprised? That's a notable insult!" He made a mock scowl.

For a second, she saw him as Lady Piddleton undoubtedly did, a big muscled man who moved lazily but in perfect control, whose eyes had a wicked, laughing tilt to them.

"No," she said. "I suppose not."

"These are things you will have to learn quickly if you wish to marry Villiers — you do wish for marriage, don't you? Because —"

She was quite sure that Villiers would do her quick honors in the sitting room as well. "Marriage," she said firmly.

"You'll have to trick him into it," Damon said.

"I will?" She had been thinking the same thing.

"You're beautiful, and you're in a fair way to being the most delectable young lady on the market this year. But Villiers isn't *on* the market. He shows no sign of wanting a bride, not at all. And there's all those children of his to take into account."

Roberta nodded. "Four?"

"I think it's only two," Damon said. "But one of them was fathered on an unmarried girl, daughter of Lord Killigrew. So it's not as if you could just let him spring you a babe, and hope that would get him to the altar."

She nodded.

"Seduction is out of the question, then," Damon said, and she felt him turn toward her. "But you don't know a thing about that business, do you? Have you ever kissed anyone?"

"Actually, yes," she said, enjoying the tiny shadow of surprise in his eyes. "I may not have seen anyone tupping before, but I have certainly been kissed."

"And have you kissed, as well?"

"Of course," she said, though frankly she wasn't sure what the difference was.

He put down his glass of brandy on the floor next to the couch. "Being kissed is like this," he said. His mouth came down on hers gently, persuasively.

"You shouldn't be kissing me," Roberta said a second later. Her heart was thudding in her chest over the impropriety of it all. "You're my cousin —"

"Not really," he interjected.

"Well, you know what I mean," she said. "I'm in *love!* I'm really in love, Damon. You have to understand that. Ladies don't sit around and kiss other people when they're in love!"

"Ah," he said thoughtfully, "I've met so few people in love that I likely haven't learned that particular lesson yet."

"Well, it's true," Roberta said, feeling rather regretful because he looked disconsolate. "I can't kiss you. I'm supposed to be kissing Villiers."

"Did he offer?"

Roberta blinked at the intense green of his eyes. "Not yet. We just met and danced but one time." She couldn't help smiling. "He's coming to the house to play a chess match with Jemma and he said he would see me as well."

"Ha," Damon said. "I suppose you've heard about the dual chess matches?"

Roberta nodded.

"Trust my sister to add yet another utterly disreputable story to a long and checkered career in my family."

Roberta thought it was very nice of Jemma to lure Villiers to the house, but she kept her mouth shut.

"Now I kissed you," Damon said, "so why don't you kiss me? Because you're going to have to understand kissing in order to catch Villiers. The man has slept with most of the

180

women in London."

"Are you saying I need to practice?" she asked suspiciously.

"Something along those lines. And who better than with a family member?"

The glint in his eyes told her that his flimsy justification was nothing more than that. But there was nothing unpleasant about Damon, after all, and practice might be a good idea. So she leaned over to him and placed her lips on his, just as he had with her. And as Angus Pilfer had done, last year in the cow lane, and as the squire's son had done at the village dance the year before that.

"Is that your best try?" he asked, pulling back.

She looked at him. There was something dangerous about this, but it was fun, not nearly as unnerving as talking to Villiers. "I gather you think my performance was inadequate?" she asked. "Then, sir, I defer to your teaching abilities."

His eyes glinted at her. "Kisses are preludes. That couple we saw in the sitting room started with just a kiss, I've no doubt."

The image flashed back into Roberta's mind and she shivered.

"They both enjoyed the kiss," he went on, "and so things progressed."

"Well," Roberta said, not wanting to sit there silently like a little girl, "I could certainly see they were enjoying the progression!"

He laughed. "Who would have thought Lord Gordon had it in him?"

"Who is he?"

"A horse-loving, stout Englishman. Did you see how his wig was askew?"

She nodded.

"An intelligent gentleman always removes his wig for a true kiss."

She knew she was out of her depth; she knew it. He tossed his wig on a chair, and suddenly his hair swung forward, all bronzed brown and shining.

"So, kiss me," he commanded.

She leaned toward him again. He smelled clean and fresh, not like some men she'd danced with this evening who smelled like lilac hair powder or, worse, sweaty locks. She put her lips onto his and kept them there for a moment. Was she supposed to do any different?

But then somehow his mouth yielded to hers, though she had not asked such a thing, had not understood such a thing. The sweetness of it clanged through her body and she pulled back. "What do you think?"

he asked, as if they hadn't — as if she
hadn't —

But Roberta's mind was clashing with im-
ages. "*That's* what you meant by a prelude,"
she said, surprised to hear how very collected her own voice sounded.

"Precisely," he said, sounding pleased, as
if she were a good student who had solved a
difficult mathematics problem.

He curled a large hand around the back
of her neck. "Let's do that again, shall we?"
he said. His head came toward hers. She
closed her eyes this time, smelling the male-
ness of him and tasting him at the same
time. He was holding her still, and suddenly
he was doing the kissing, rather than she,
and this was different.

No prelude, this, she thought dimly,
because he was part of her, he was inside
her, he was tasting her — and how different
it was. She had to stop kissing him. She was
in love with someone else.

But somehow she leaned back against the
sofa and he leaned toward her, and still he
kissed her. His mouth was madness, like
cherry wine in midsummer: sweet, intoxicating, drugging.

He kept kissing her.

It made her feel restless, as if small sparks
danced between her legs, as if the pooling

warmth she felt in her stomach after leaving the sitting room were turning into something altogether more embarrassing and more — more dangerous.

There was a dim question in her mind about the nature of kisses. And then, as if a curtain lifted, she realized that she was *being* kissed, and she rather thought she would like to *kiss*. So she curled her hands into the silky locks of his hair and pulled him a bit closer and kissed him.

It all changed again.

His body felt heavier against hers, hotter, charged with a weight that made her feel achy where she had felt warm.

As if he could hear that drugged thought whisper through her mind, he pulled back.

Roberta didn't open her eyes immediately.

"Have I shocked you?" He didn't sound in the least sorry, just curious.

She opened her eyes. "No," she said, meaning to shock *him* for once. "I am interested in how kissing feels."

His eyebrow flew up. "Feels?"

She smiled, and knew it was a siren's smile, a gamester's smile.

"You would appear to have learned something."

"If not from you, from the sitting room," she said. She stretched, knowing that the plumpness of her breasts above the stiff fabric of her bodice was tantalizingly close to his finger.

Being Damon, he did the unthinkable. He ran a long finger over the curve of her breast. "Very nice," he said, and she heard the hitch in his voice with approval.

His finger burned a sweet trail. But she batted him away. "A salutary lesson, and I thank you for it," she said, rising.

He rose too and she couldn't help checking his breeches. But alas, the heavy line of his coat swung into place.

He caught her looking and laughed. "Well-designed coats, aren't they? Any number of women can caress my legs under the table and no one will know if I respond. I hardly need say that I did not respond for Lady Piddleton, but if you stroke me under the table, it would be another story."

Roberta walked over to a mirror on the wall rather than answer this nonsense. The glass was long enough to give her an excellent view of the way her silk gown had been crushed when he leaned against her. There was nothing to be done about that, but she tucked an errant curl back into place.

Damon appeared in the mirror behind her, bewigged once more. He was so warm that she could feel his body just behind her.

" 'Twas a dangerous game we played to-night," he said to her reflection. "I am no Villiers, Roberta. If we ended up with a child, you'd have to marry me."

"We were a long way from that!" she said.

"Not so very far. Trust me."

She concentrated on repositioning a spray of apple blossoms that was hanging drunkenly over her ear. That ache low in her belly told her that he was right. He leaned close to her ear.

"You know how we watched that couple?" he said to her.

She nodded and repressed a shiver.

"It's possible to watch oneself make love in a glass," he said.

Rosy color flooded her cheeks. "I declare that you have made it your pleasure to shock me this evening!" she said, taking as sophisticated a tone as she could muster.

He met her eyes and her next sentence died on her lips. Still watching her, he bent his head and kissed her neck.

She shivered in his hands, as if she were a newborn bird fallen from its nest.

Then he held out his arm, and they left the room.

CHAPTER 12

It wasn't until nearly morning that Roberta was able to pull Jemma into the ladies' retiring room. "Playing a simpering fool definitely won't win Villiers," she told her.

"We know that. But you did a magnificent job of it tonight," Jemma said. "Everyone has told me how sweet you are. And most of them added the pious wish that I not corrupt you."

Roberta smiled at that. "Since seduction will be ineffective, I'm going to have to trick him into marriage."

Jemma looked thoughtful. "You think so?"

"Absolutely. He's all of what — how old is he?"

"Not so very old," Jemma said. "He and Beaumont were boyhood friends, as I understand."

"And now they don't speak?"

"Rarely. They did exchange a few words tonight. I suspect they have little in common by now."

"Well, how old is your husband?"

Jemma looked blank. "Thirty-three," she finally decided. "It must be in our marriage lines, I suppose. We were engaged when I was the tender age of two, and I think he was seven."

"So Villiers is likely thirty-three as well." A very nicely preserved thirty-three, Roberta thought to herself. She felt a pulse of longing. "I'll have to attend any ball where he might be."

"We can always bribe one of his footmen, you know."

"A pleasant thought, but I might end up with a child and no marriage," she said dubiously.

"Did you think I was suggesting we bribe the footman to give you entry to his chamber?"

And at Roberta's nod, "You're more likely to corrupt me," Jemma said, laughing. "You aren't much of an innocent, are you?"

"Not particularly," Roberta said, with a helpless shrug.

"We'll bribe a footman to let us know which invitations he accepts," Jemma explained. "The more important question is how to trick him. You can't simply —"

"I know," Roberta interrupted. "He

spurned a lady carrying his child so that would be ineffective."

"Though Damon would likely challenge him for you," Jemma said. "I probably do not need to mention this to you, Roberta, but you have noticed how my brother is looking at you, haven't you?"

"He has been all that's kind."

"I'm sure," his sister said. "But . . ." Her voice trailed off.

"In fact, we had a discussion about Villiers," Roberta said. "He fully shares my opinion that Villiers must be tricked. And it was he who warned me about Villiers's refusal to marry the lady carrying his baby."

"Oh, in that case . . . I must be mistaken," Jemma said. "I don't know Damon as well as I used to. He visited me often in Paris, far more than my husband, but still, one's siblings grow up and change, don't you think?"

Having never had a sibling, Roberta didn't venture to comment.

"As I said, the important question is how to trick Villiers in such a way that he cannot back out. He cares nothing for scandal. In truth, I think the only way for him to marry would be if you simply married him, if that makes sense."

"How so?" Roberta asked.

"Well, we know he's not going to marry under his own aegis. And yet he's famous for breaking every sort of law of decency and morality in order to get his own way with a woman. Did Damon tell you what Lady Caroline said after it all came out about the child?"

Roberta shook her head.

"She maintained that Villiers had married her in secret, a sort of Fleet Street marriage. But it seems that the marriage certificate was false, because her father would have forced him to acknowledge the marriage if it were all true."

It was rather depressing to think of her future husband's unethical behavior. "If the wedding certificate were false, wouldn't her father have done something about that?"

"What could he do, other than challenge Villiers to a duel?"

"He could have done that! My father would have —" The mind boggled thinking what Roberta's father would have done. It would have been violent and noisy.

"Women are invariably more decisive than are men," Jemma said, yawning. "I think we should sleep on the possibilities."

"I don't understand how he got away with it," Roberta said.

"He doesn't give a damn."

"What?"

"I expect he got away with it because he really doesn't give a damn what society thinks. The only thing he cares about is chess, and Roberta, you really ought to think about that. I'm not as obsessed as Villiers, and yet when we first married Beaumont loathed the fact that I thought about chess far more than I thought about him. Or listened to him. Villiers will be just the same."

"If I were Lady Caroline's father . . ."

"What could he do? Villiers is an excellent swordsman. Almost all chess players are. If there's one thing a chess player can do, it's master a game of strategy."

"Then *you* are my secret weapon," Roberta said.

Jemma blinked.

"I suspect that you are a better chess player than Villiers."

"Haven't you heard that women can't play chess?" Jemma opened her eyes very wide.

"Your brother told me you are a master. With a strategist pitted against him, Villiers cannot win."

Jemma looked marginally more awake. "There's a play we call the poisoned pawn. We could allow Villiers to lure you into a false wedding, during which you would produce a real certificate, and then he'd be caught."

"But how could we ensure that he would offer to marry me with a false certificate?"

"Of course we can't . . . but men are invariably repetitive. If he offers a secret marriage, we'll know what he's planning. It worked with one young lady, so why not with another? I don't mean to be pessimistic, Roberta, but are you sure you wish to marry such a man? I find my husband tedious, but not dishonorable."

Roberta nodded. "It's my heart's desire."

"In that case, let's plan on a wedding certificate exchange. We'll have to wait for his move. In a game of strategy, it's best to allow the early game to develop on its own rather than taking an opening gambit."

CHAPTER 13

Finally the ball had dwindled to the point at which Jemma decided that they could go to bed and leave the few remaining revelers to greet the dawn alone.

Roberta started off for her chambers dreaming of being a duchess. Villiers's duchess. His behavior didn't bother her much. How could it, since she'd grown up in a household dominated by her father, whose madness, as she knew well, was not exaggerated by report? Chicanery of Villiers's type seemed positively wholesome by contrast.

It took a while to get ready for bed, as her maid didn't immediately understand that she couldn't go to sleep with powder in her hair. Perhaps she should just wear a wig the way Damon did.

So it wasn't until she'd had a bath, said goodnight to her maid and drew back the heavy rose curtains around her bed that she had a shock.

She wasn't alone.

There was a male body in her bed.

He was very small and sweaty. He was curled like a little wood-louse, the kind you find when you turn over earth in the springtime. His hair was the exact color of his father's, a kind of brandy-brown, but all in ringlets. And he was snoring.

Roberta sat on the edge of the bed and stared at Teddy for a moment. She didn't have much of a propensity for children; indeed, she had several times thought that her instinct toward maternal love seemed strangely muted. She never felt like doing more than coo over the estate children when they were presented for kisses.

She didn't even feel like cooing over this one.

She was bitterly tired, and there was a sweaty, snoring man, albeit a small one, in her bed.

With a sigh she reached out and pulled the cord by the bed. A housemaid appeared and clucked. "They've been looking for that child all over the house," she said. "His lordship is that worried!"

"Well, tell him to come fetch it," Roberta said, unable to make her tone more enthusiastic.

A minute later Damon himself appeared. His face had lost all its easy charm of earlier; he barely looked at her, Roberta noted with a pulse of irritation. Instead, he half-lunged at the bed and then stared down at his son.

"Christ," he said. It sounded half a curse, half a prayer.

"Well, you can't have thought he'd left the house," she said, letting irritation drip into her tone.

"I didn't know where he was. I couldn't find him," Damon said, not turning to look at her. "Christ, what a couple of hours it's been."

"Could you possibly take him with you now?" She was feeling more and more irritable. Damon had kissed her earlier, and now he acted with as much interest as if she were a housemaid he had bussed in a side corridor.

He was already folding back the covers, but he stopped, and looked at her for the first time. "I'm sorry, Roberta."

"What?"

He scooped up the sleeping child and she saw exactly what he meant. Where the boy had nestled — in her bed — there was a dank looking spot. A very large, wet spot. And the smell that arose from it was everything one might expect.

Her maid let out a little shriek.

Damon smiled at her ruefully and Roberta registered exactly how adorable he was, at the same time she felt a swell of irritation that almost had her screaming along with the maid.

"I do apologize. It only happens when he's in a very deep sleep."

"Is that a compliment to my bedding?"

He nodded. "You are right to be annoyed. I'll return immediately." And he made a leg while holding the sleeping child, which Roberta had to admit was quite a trick. Particularly since the rose-colored sleeve of his brocade coat was, quite likely, getting ruined.

The only good thing about it, Roberta thought as the housekeeper and a flock of maids burst into the room, was that it confirmed that vague sense she had that children were undesirable.

The headache pounding behind her right ear said the same.

Two minutes later, Damon reentered the room and pulled her unceremoniously to her feet. "Come on," he said.

"I gather you didn't hear that it will take some time to air and make up another room," Roberta said.

"So Mrs. Friss, the housekeeper, told me. We came up with a solution."

Down the hall they went, until they turned into a room. It was beautifully made up, linen sheets turned back and looking so inviting that Roberta almost fell into them directly.

"Thank you!" she said, and only then did she realize that a rather rotund individual was hastily sweeping away an assortment of masculine looking accoutrements. "Oh, no!"

"Oh, yes," Damon said. "That will be all, Martins. Thank you."

Martins took himself and a collection of neck clothes out of the room.

"I couldn't take your room," Roberta said. But she felt as if she were swaying in place.

"Of course you could. These mattresses are all old, you know. Wool, most likely. Yours is going to soak up Teddy's urine like a flower in the sun. You don't want to sleep in that bed until the mattress is replaced."

Roberta shuddered.

"You look like a ghost but more sickly looking." Then, before she quite knew what was happening, he undid the knot at her waist, pulled off her dressing gown, ignoring her protests, and bundled her under the covers.

"I feel like a larger version of your son,"

she said, peeping at him from under the covers.

He sat down on the bed — which was vastly improper — and said, "You don't resemble Teddy in the slightest."

"I suppose that is something to be grateful for. Why was he in my chambers?"

"I imagine he was on his usual search for my room and thought he'd found it. Jemma's mother-in-law didn't waste any inspiration decorating the bedrooms; they're all precisely the same."

Roberta cast a bleary look at the walls, and sure enough the crest of the Beaumonts marched around the top of the walls, and a painting that looked remarkably like Judith holding a platter was directly opposite the bed. She shut her eyes.

He kissed her so swiftly that it might have been a dream.

Perhaps it was.

CHAPTER 14

April 12
Day one of the Villiers/Beaumont chess
matches
Beaumont House

Early the next afternoon, Beaumont House was brimming like a stagnant pool full of brine shrimp wearing heels and velvet jackets. The only problem was that the residents weren't in a position to receive them.

The duke had left the house early in the morning, bound for a meeting with Pitt and then the House of Lords. Teddy woke up at seven in the morning. Damon rose just long enough to push his son in the direction of a maid, and then collapsed back into bed. Teddy migrated to the kitchens, and from thence to the little shed where the gardener kept his spades and the cat kept her kittens. Roberta woke briefly at nine, groaned, and went back to sleep. Jemma was one of those people who only needed five hours of sleep, but never left her room before three in the afternoon on principal. Philidor had given her a book by an Italian chess player named Greco as a goodbye. She was working through the combinations and finding them surprisingly unambitious.

In consequence, flowers were dropped in the duchess's sitting room until it resembled nothing so much as a royal funeral. Carriages drew up and left with the regularity of traffic to a new apothecary promising miraculous increases to one's bosom.

Finally, the duchess decided that she would receive. "Two of them may come up," Jemma said to Brigitte.

"The Duke of Villiers didn't wait but left a card," Brigitte said.

Jemma picked up the beautifully embossed card, as elegant as the man who owned it. His hand was nothing like Elijah's impossible scrawl. *At the time you choose,* it said.

Very nice. There was a certain lack of eagerness there that was entirely appealing in a gentleman with whom one might be embarking on an *affaire* — she caught herself hastily. Of course, she was merely dallying with the idea. Had she not promised her husband that her salad days were behind her? More to the point — since

Elijah had made no promises about his mistress — she had decided to deliver Villiers into the virtuous, if thorny, bonds of matrimony. She sighed and handed the card back to Brigitte. "Six of the clock. Inform him that he may stay to sup afterward. And do send a note to Lady Roberta informing her the same."

Of course, the servants would gossip, but servants always knew everything so Jemma saw no reason to prevaricate.

"Oh, and Brigitte," she said.

Brigitte turned as she was about to leave the room. She was as exquisite a little Frenchwoman as existed on British shores and sometimes, Jemma thought, dressed with more *éclat* than did her mistress. "You know the *écharpe* cloak that you so admire?"

Brigitte clasped her hands together. "The blue one, Your Grace, with the black lace?"

Jemma smiled at her. "It is yours in return for a small act of espionage, which I am convinced you will enjoy."

She trembled with excitement. *"Enchantée!"* Brigitte said, eyes aglow.

"Villiers comes to play a game of chess with me. He will be accompanied by footmen, naturally."

Brigitte nodded.

"I should dearly love to know every detail

201

of *une petite affaire* he had with a certain Lady Caroline Killigrew, who found herself with child."

"Quelle folie," Brigitte said, indicating with a Frenchwoman's briskness just what she thought of Lady Caroline's foolishness in not controlling her reproductive options.

"There has been a certain amount of gossip suggesting that Villiers went through a false wedding ceremony with the young lady."

Brigitte's loyalty switched sides instantly. *"Chien!"* she spat.

"Perhaps . . . perhaps not. There are so many sides to a tale, are there not? We need to know everything of Lady Caroline."

Brigitte dimpled. "I will do my best."

Before a Frenchwoman's best, an English footman is but a house of straw. "I shall accept two gentlemen to help me dress, Brigitte. Corbin, of course, and perhaps . . . oh, Viscount St. Albans. He was wearing a truly magnificent costume last night and ought to be rewarded."

Brigitte curtsied and flew down the stairs to find St. Albans and Lord Corbin, who were ushered up the stairs and into the duchess's bedchamber, where they found Jemma attired in a chemise and corset, ready for the gentlemen's skill in helping her answer delicate points to do with patches, powder, ribbons and finally her gown.

Roberta awoke to find herself in a room that looked like a copy of her original, except for the faint imprint of Damon's personality. There was a cravat flung over a chair. A book sat on the dressing table; Roberta wandered over, saw the name John Donne and dropped the poems with a thud. His clothes were in the wardrobe, of course.

He had a magnificent costume of cherry velvet lined in cream sarsenet. Taking the coat to the window, she could see metal sequins, sewn into elaborate patterns with silver embroidery. Even looking at it made her heart twist with longing. And desire. She had to marry Villiers soon, so that she could buy a gown in precisely this cherry color with sequins.

There was a scratch at the door and Roberta hastily dropped the coat onto the bed. But as the door opened, she didn't see her maid. In fact, she didn't see anyone until the door closed again and Teddy appeared around the end of her bed.

"You shouldn't be here," she said by way of greeting.

"Gotta apologize, my papa says."

"My papa says — appropriately — that I

should apologize," Roberta corrected him.

He grinned at her. "Brought you — *I* brought you a present."

Roberta summoned up a smile. Of course she ought to be touched by whatever grubby, bent flower he was about to produce from under his coat.

It wasn't a flower, but a struggling, spitting kitten. She felt no inclination to take it from him.

"Perhaps you'd better put it down," she said after the charming feline gave Teddy another red welt across his hand.

He dropped it and the kitten landed on its splayed-out feet with a rather pitiful mew of protest and then streaked under the bed.

"It was much nicer when it was in the shed," Teddy said, with an edge of apology in his voice. "I thought you might like it. Since you have to sleep alone. Cats are good company."

"I like sleeping alone," Roberta informed him.

He wandered over. "That's Papa's French coat," he said. "France is in Paris."

"Paris is in France," she said. "You need to retrieve that kitten and take it back to its mother."

"It's *yours* now. Besides, I wanted to tell you about the gardener, he works in the gardens and —"

"The gardener works in the gardens," Roberta said automatically, moving over to pull the cord.

"His name is Rummer and he used to be a prize-fighter. Rummer used to stroddle his opponents and once he almost spent five guineas for a wife —"

"For a wife?" Roberta said, rather startled by that. She had seated herself before the dressing table and began brushing out her hair.

"Yes, indeed. Rummer was at a fair in Smithfield and a man was auctioning his wife, and he wanted five guineas to start, and Rummer thought about it hard, but then he decided that the life of a prize-fighter was no place for a wife because" — Teddy finished triumphantly — "lady's gowns are pinned so high these days that you can't see their heads for their tails." And he broke into a mad fit of giggling, and repeated the head and tail part two or three times for the pure naughty value of it.

Roberta just kept brushing. It was rather sad to think about the wife auctioned off for five guineas, but when questioned, Teddy didn't know her fate, only that Rummer hadn't bought her.

"That's two things you need to discover,"

Roberta told him. "What happened to the wife, and what a bog-trotting croggie is."

"I likes you!" he said, beaming up at her. "I likes you —"

"*Like* you," Roberta said.

"I like you because you listen to me. Papa says that I'm a gossip who could out-rattle fifty porters."

"I agree with him." Finally there was a knock at the door and she called, "Enter. I didn't know it was *you*," she said rather crossly.

"Papa, look at this," Teddy said. "The lady's new kitten likes your red coat."

Sure enough, the kitten had clawed its way up on the bed and was nestled in velvet with silver embroidery.

"I'm not dressed," Roberta said with dignity. "I'll thank you to take your son out of this room — once again — and allow me to continue dressing."

He raised an eyebrow. "At this very moment my sister is undoubtedly entertaining at least two gentlemen in her chambers as they aid her in choosing the day's costume. Why don't Teddy and I do the honors?"

Roberta realized she still had her brush in the air and put it down in exasperation. Teddy had picked up the kitten, who actually seemed to be purring.

"I very much doubt that your sister is allowing gentlemen into her bedchamber while she's" — Roberta glanced down to make sure that her dressing gown was still tied tightly — *"en déshabillé."*

"But that's precisely the fashion these days," he said, taking a chair and swinging it about so that he could sit on it facing her. "It would be a dismal thing indeed for a lady to dress herself. Generally one has a maid or two in the room as well. They throw the clothes on you, while Teddy and I advise you where to place a patch, if you wish one, and face color, and ribbons — that sort of thing."

"I do not believe that unmarried ladies invite gentlemen into their rooms while they dress. And I don't wish to wear a patch!" Roberta said, feeling rather discomposed. She prided herself on her lack of naïveté, but she was beginning to realize that being sophisticated in comparison to Mrs. Grope was nothing in relation to the Reeve family.

Damon's eyes were even greener in the sunlight.

"I think we should go onto the river," Teddy said. "This kitten would like that."

"I doubt it," his father said. "Roberta likely has important things to do."

The river? In truth, Roberta had a singular

longing to see more of London. "I have to return to the house by early evening," she said cautiously.

"Ah, the great Villiers chess match," Damon said, rising. "Come on, scrap. Let's give Roberta some time to put on a gown without our help, and then we can all go on the river. Haven't you ever been out on a river?"

Roberta shook her head.

"On a picnic?"

Roberta did not feel like explaining her disinclination to picnic with Mrs. Grope, so she just shook her head again.

"A woman with much to learn," Damon said, with a wicked smile that spoke of kisses, not picnics. Then he was gone, leaving behind a red velvet coat with small white hairs sprinkled across the front.

Roberta untied her dressing gown. Perhaps she shouldn't be going on the river, whatever that signified. Perhaps she should stay at home so that she was definitely here when Villiers arrived.

But she wasn't quite certain what she meant to do *to* or *with* Villiers in order to make him marry her, although the very thought of him made her heart speed up again. Her maid burst into the room, carrying another of Jemma's gowns. It was a pale blossom pink, and Roberta forgot all about Villiers as she learned the intricacies of a skirt draped *à la polonaise.*

Some two hours later, Viscount St. Albans bowed his way out of Jemma's room and minced his way down the stairs. He was a slender man who made the very best of himself. This afternoon he was wearing a magnificent suit of lemon-colored iridescent silk, set with enameled buttons. His coat curved away from his waist; he left it entirely open, displaying all twenty buttons on his waistcoat (matching enamel, naturally). The waistcoat was judiciously padded over the chest, which repaired the one small fault he found with his own physique. Well, that and perhaps the fact that his eyes were just a trifle too close together.

He picked his way down the stairs carefully because there is nothing worse than polished marble when one was wearing high heels, and he judged that height was always desirable. But his mind was racing far ahead of him, already at the coffee house reporting the pleasurable fact that when he announced a previous engagement that meant he *must* take himself off, though naturally he perfumed the fact with many compliments, Corbin had made no move to leave the duchess's bedchamber.

In fact, he had left the two of them in a cozy discussion of some chess player from Poland, a god-forsaken country that did not interest the viscount in the least. He wrinkled his nose at the thought of how they tried to fool him into thinking they were actually talking of chess. Clearly, Corbin and the duchess had bored him to tears in an effort to make him leave, which, frankly, he was more than happy to do.

Far be it from him to separate two love birds. Although he would do his best to ascertain just how long Corbin and the duchess would stay in unchaperoned harmony.

He reached the entryway and demanded a mirror. As a footman held the glass for him, he carefully placed his Macaroni hat on top of his curls at a jaunty angle. Then he noticed that a rosette was falling from his shoe; ten minutes later he was seated in an elegant little chair while the duke's own valet sewed the rosette into a better position. After that, of course, he must needs readjust his stockings in private, and finally, he ended up in front of the glass again, rearranging his hat.

Just when he was about to give up altogether, he heard a brisk clicking of heels and down came Corbin. *

"Still here?" Corbin said, with a cheerful grin that — to the viscount's mind — signaled far too much cheer for a mere discussion of chess.

"I suffered the greatest imposition to my shoe," the viscount said, taking care to lisp slightly in the new fashion. "It is of all things annoying; these rosettes are prone to falling on the wayside, do you not think?"

"I never wear such things," Corbin remarked.

"I see that," the viscount said, larding his voice with disapproval. "Your waistcoat would look so much better with a small fringe."

"Yours would be greatly improved without it," Corbin said, with such a gentle smile that at first the viscount didn't take his meaning, and by the time he did — and would have rejoined sharply with a sharp comment about those buttons! — Corbin had slapped on a round hat and taken himself out of the house.

The viscount huffed and minced his way down the stairs to his waiting carriage. In his mind, there was no question. While the duchess did not seem to be carrying a child, she was clearly carrying a lover. He tittered to himself at his own jest.

In their wake, a perfumed, powdered and altogether delectable duchess wandered downstairs, leaving her bedchamber, strewn with silks and ribbands, flowers and shoes, to be made presentable for her upcoming chess match with Villiers.

To her surprise, her husband was just coming in the front door.

She halted halfway down the stairs, hand on her heart. "Good lord, Beaumont," she said. "What an odd start to see you here."

"I finished the day's business," he said, looking up at her.

Jemma tripped down the last few steps, conscious of being glad that she looked her very best. Which was a sad reflection on the tedium of her life, if she considered such a thing in connection to her husband.

"Would you like to begin our game?" he said.

"Of course!"

"You play Villiers in your chambers," he said. "I would suppose that mine must do the honors for our game. If you'll give me a moment, I'll remove my wig." And then, when she didn't move, "You do know the location of my chambers, don't you?"

Jemma didn't glance at the footmen who lined the wall, their faces blank and their ears straining for every word. "I shall

212

endeavor to find my way there."

Elijah watched her go back up the stairs. She was wearing a gown light enough to flutter in the breeze. It was indisputably French, designed to make a man break into an instant sweat.

He couldn't think of Jemma's sensual appeal if he meant to win this game. The one thing about his wife that he had never underestimated was her intelligence. In truth, his memories of their early beddings were not that interesting. It was so long ago that he could hardly remember, and everything took place under the covers, and that rarely.

It wasn't her fault, exactly, that she was a tedious bed-partner. Obviously, he'd been a poor teacher. But it had meant that his mistress Sarah's bouncing, erotic pleasure in his company provided a sharp contrast to the wife his father picked out for him when he was a lad of seven.

He started up the stairs. Would it have turned out differently had Jemma not found him in his chambers in Westminster with Sarah?

Perhaps.

And perhaps not.

Neither of them appeared designed for the narrow straits of matrimony.

213

She entered his room a few minutes later, as he was setting out the pieces. "Ah, your grandfather's chessboard," she said. "I hadn't remembered it until now, but of course I played many a game on it during our first year of marriage."

"Who did you play with back then?" he asked. He had been so feverishly excited by his burgeoning role in the House that he barely remembered being at home. Not that things were much better now. All day long people had elbowed him, and smirked at him, and asked him what he was still doing in Westminster. Until finally they drove him to come home some four hours earlier than was his usual practice.

"The second footman was a fairly good partner: remember Jacobs? He had a long face, like a bulldog. I was saddened to hear that he had died."

"He died?"

Jemma nodded. "How gorgeous this chess set is." Each piece was a delicate marble fantasy of medieval warfare. The paint had long ago worn off, except for faint touches of red, in the fury of the king's eyes, on the queen's lower lip, in the bishop's robe.

"You think I don't remember your game," Elijah said. "I do. I am ready for attack, if you please." He moved a pawn to King's Four.

Jemma smiled and moved her pawn to King's Three.

"The pawn is my favorite piece," Elijah remarked.

Jemma sat back, their moves ended for the day. "I could have guessed that. So lowly and humble as you are."

"A pawn is crafty, versatile, and in pairs, they sometimes prove irresistible."

"There's little flair in a pawn," Jemma said, picking up her queen to examine her faded robes.

"Your game is all about flair, as I recall."

"That sounds remarkably dismissive."

"I didn't mean it so."

"I prefer to think of my strength as being in the area of assault."

Elijah watched his wife's delicate fingers. "What I remember of your game," he said slowly, "was that you would attack, but in the event of opposition, you would sacrifice. Run. You sometimes lost on that account."

Jemma replaced her queen with a little click. "How gratifying to know that you remember the intricacies of my failures."

CHAPTER 15

Around three in the afternoon
The Fleet River

"I told you that the kitten wanted to come," Teddy said.

"But I disagreed," his father said. "And I thought my sentiments constituted a mandate."

Roberta watched footmen pack a sturdy basket into a flat-bottomed boat. It was a very pretty boat, with a roof of flowered muslin that rippled in the breeze, little benches for seats and rolled canvas walls that could be lowered from the roof in case of a sudden shower.

"This is Mr. Cunningham," Damon said, introducing a serious looking young man who apparently arranged for the boat. "Ransom, this is Lady Roberta St. Giles. Ransom is my brother-in-law's secretary. We know each other from years of debauchery at Cambridge."

"Hardly debauchery," Mr. Cunningham protested.

Damon ignored that. "More to the point, Ransom knows every bend of the river, and he has been kind enough to eschew the duke's company for ours today."

Roberta smiled at Mr. Cunningham, and thought that he had lovely dark eyes, and that it was a nice thing to go onto the river with two handsome young men.

Well, one could say three. Or two and a half.

The kitten was the only interloper.

Roberta could see precisely why Teddy was sleeping hither and yon, in beds where he had no call to be. Damon was attempting to be charming to his son, which, while a nice impulse, was the wrong tactic. Of course Teddy ignored talk of sentiments and mandates.

The fact that Teddy was reasonably entertaining company did not excuse the fact that he was a child, therefore, by definition, a lower species.

She cut directly into Damon's courteous discussion of the kitten's likely distaste for boating. "Perhaps we should see if he likes to swim."

Teddy clutched the animal to his breast, his eyes rounding as he reassessed her as a homicidal cat hater.

"Just to see if he likes it. Your father can fish him out if he doesn't."

Teddy shook his head.

"If he's not a swimming cat," Roberta said, pausing a little to make clear her opinion of small kittens who professed no skills at swimming, "then he'll stay in the carriage until he learns to know better." And without further ado, she plucked the cat from Teddy's arms and handed it to a footman.

"Are *we* going swimming?" Teddy asked, trotting along next to her as she walked down the stone steps to the waiting boat.

"I certainly hope not," Damon said, handing her into the boat.

Roberta settled herself under the awning and they set out. The Fleet River was much smaller than the Thames, no more than a sleek and sinuous little stream, gleaming and sparkling in the sunlight. Mr. Cunningham moved them along by stabbing a large pole in the water and drawing it back out. Every movement caused the water to chatter and boil around the pole, which enchanted Teddy.

Damon kept himself occupied by ineffectively remonstrating his son for crimes such as getting wet, and Roberta trailed a hand in the water and watched the ripple of the water. Presently a family of ducks joined them.

"If only we had your kitten now," Roberta said to Teddy, "we could throw him in and he could catch us a nice fat duck for supper."

He shook his head at her. "My kitten, he's too small."

Roberta corrected his grammar, and Teddy allowed as how the kitten would have liked a ride on a duck's back. "I'm going to catch a fish for his supper!"

Damon grabbed him back into the boat just in time.

The backs of large pleasure gardens stretched to the river; it was as if they were in Bath, or another more slumberous place than the great city of London. Just where green turf came to the water's edge, one could see brown tree roots jumbled at the surface of the water. There was a squeal when Teddy discovered that sleek silver bodies flashed among the roots.

"You'll have to catch a minnow out here if you want one," Damon said.

"Mr. Cunningham," Roberta said, "do people boat on the Thames as well?"

"There's too much river traffic," Mr. Cunningham explained. "The Thames is no place for anything other than a large pleasure craft. Unfortunately, they're talking of covering over the Fleet, which would be a great shame."

They drifted past a field all glossy and yellow with buttercups just as Teddy managed to catch a large amount of dripping weed. "Look!" he said, "I'll give this to my kitten because Rummer says that cats eat grass sometimes, did you know that?"

Damon said fiercely, "Drop it, Teddy."

Mr. Cunningham was laughing. "You need to teach your son how to swim, Damon. He'll swim like a minnow on the first try."

"I'm sure that I would," Teddy put in.

"The water's quite shallow around the curve over there," Mr. Cunningham suggested. "Mud flats. We could simply drop him off the boat, just as Lady Roberta suggested for the kitten."

"That would be good," Teddy said, nodding so vigorously that he didn't notice his father pulling the seaweed away, although he promptly plunged his hand back in the water to try to rescue it.

"Teddy, I told you not to get wet," his father said. "And Ransom, do I understand you to be volunteering for the pleasure of such instruction?"

Rather to Roberta's surprise, Mr. Cunningham didn't say no outright. "Swimming involves disrobing, which wouldn't be appropriate for ladies," he noted.

"A boy never shows a girl his pizzle," Teddy informed Roberta.

"I'll keep that in mind," she said.

"But once you're married, you can look at all of 'em that you wish."

"I assume that is a philosophy learned at Papa's knee?" Roberta enquired.

Damon stopped laughing to say that perhaps the field would be a good place for their picnic.

Mr. Cunningham agreeably began steering the boat in that direction and a moment later they were on the bank. Teddy let it be known that he would like a private visit to the trees, and he and Damon set off in that direction. Roberta busied herself with setting out the picnic basket under a tree while Mr. Cunningham fashioned a landing post out of a sapling.

By the time they came back, Roberta had discovered that a rug on top of bumpy ground is not a comfortable seat. They all seated themselves except Teddy, who danced around them like an impatient dragonfly.

Damon drained his glass of wine with a slightly desperate air. "Parenting is exhausting," he said.

"That is because you have insufficient help. Weren't you going to find a nurse-maid?"

"The Registry Office is sending a new one tomorrow," he said. "I only have to survive today."

Roberta looked at him and couldn't help a tiny smile. His hair was standing on end, and his arm was wet to the elbow from pulling Teddy's hand out of the river. He was pouring himself another glass of wine as if it were the elixir of life. Mr. Cunningham had deserted his uncomfortable seat and was swinging Teddy in a circle until he shrieked.

"Perhaps Mr. Cunningham would be kind enough to go through the grove to the mud flat?" Roberta asked. "He can teach Teddy how to swim and we'll sit in this vastly uncomfortable spot and wait for them to come back, sparing me the sight of a minia-ture pizzle."

Damon blinked at her for a moment and then leapt to his feet. "Ransom!" he called.

Roberta finished her glass just as Mr. Cunningham and Teddy set off through the grove.

"He won't drown, will he?" Damon said, sounding not terribly concerned.

"I think it's unlikely. Where did Mr. Cunningham learn about children?"

"Likely he has siblings," Damon said. He lay backwards and then sat up with a curse. "Damn it, where have you placed us, Roberta?"

"In a field of buttercups. Tables and chairs are unaccountably missing."

"I've been in many a field," Damon said, "and this is the most uncomfortable of my experience." He brought Roberta to her feet. Then he picked up the rug and kicked at something underneath.

"What is it?" she asked.

"Cowpats," he said. "You put the rug down on a lovely collection of them. In fact," Damon said looking about, "this entire field is dotted with cowpats."

"Do you suppose a bull will be coming along?"

"In a month or so when the grass is high enough. I'm going to have to sacrifice my gloves, which will give Martins palpitations, but what can I do? Back up, Roberta."

Two minutes later, cowpats started sailing across the field.

"See if you can get one in the river," Roberta suggested.

The river lay gurgling in the sunshine, about ten yards away. Damon pulled back his arm and then let the cowpat fly.

It struck the bank just before the river. Roberta very loudly said nothing.

"I can do better than that," Damon muttered. "Here, help me take my coat off. I don't want to soil it with my gloves."

She helped him pull off his beautiful coat. It was a misty grey, lined with scarlet silk that trimmed the sleeves with a huge open cuff. His breeches were the same scarlet, very tight. His waistcoat followed until he was wearing nothing but the breeches and a linen shirt, so fine that she could see the swell of his muscles as he threw another cowpat. But it landed a good foot before the edge.

"Do gentlemen invite women into their chambers to help them dress, the way ladies do?" she asked with some curiosity.

He shook his head. "I'm aiming at that duck, Roberta —" And he gave a little whoop. "Hit it!"

"Perhaps, if it hadn't dived first." And then, answering his gesture, "No, I am certainly *not* going to hand you a cowpat."

"I'd never ask such a thing of a proper lady, but that's the great thing about you, Roberta. You're not so ladylike."

"I don't think that's a compliment."

"Only because you have no idea how

tedious ladies can be. For one thing, they have no sense of competitiveness. And having grown up as Jemma's brother, you can imagine how boring I find that."

"Is Jemma competitive?"

He laughed. "Jemma is the best female chess player in England and France, and quite likely better than all the men as well. She kept beating Philidor, and he is the best in France."

"Who's the best in England?"

He blinked at her. "You don't know?"

She shook her head.

"Your lover," he said with relish. "Villiers. Though I suppose I shouldn't yet call him that. Now, do you suppose I could hit the sapling we tied the boat to?"

"No."

"You're not very encouraging," he complained and then leaned back as far as he could and let go with a mighty fling. The pat fell far short.

"I'll try," she said.

It was very gratifying; his mouth actually fell open.

Clearly, the right shape of cowpat was essential. It had to be disc shaped, as opposed to some of the balls Damon was hurdling around; they lost their shape in midair and fell to a pile of dust.

Finally she found just the right one and, saying a silent apology to Jemma's beautiful lilac gloves, crossed her hand over her chest and spun the disc as hard as she could.

It didn't quite hit the sapling, but it went further than any of Damon's.

"How in the hell did you know how to do that?" he said, a gratifying shock in his voice.

"Your sister may be the best chess player in two countries," she said, pulling off her soiled gloves, "but I shall claim the title of best cowpat thrower."

"It's yours. So where did you do your training, Lady Roberta?"

"No training," she said, grinning at him. "Just the ability to assess the mistakes of those who went before me."

"Piss on that," Damon said, finding a disc-shaped cowpat for himself. Of course, when he tried the spinning method it went past the buoy. "Still, you were there first," he said, very fairly. "I think that's cleared a spot for a rug; what you do think?"

"I think we should walk through the woods and see how Teddy is swimming."

"You don't want to lounge in the dappled shade with me and practice your kisses? I could quote some poetry and ply you with wine."

"I've heard enough poetry in my life," she

said wryly.

"Ah, but this is — with excuses to your father — a different brand of poetry. *Come live with me, and be my love,*" he said, with exaggerated emphasis. *"You will be my buttercup and I will be your — your — parsnip."*

"I don't want to be your love," Roberta said, giggling.

"You could give it a try." He put an arm around her waist and before she knew it she had her back against an old apple tree. His mouth looked very delectable, but —

"Are you really trying to seduce me?"

"Of course," he said, leaning over to brush his mouth against hers.

"You smell a little bit like a cowpat," she said.

"I could say the same to you."

"Don't. I prefer to think of myself as perfumed."

"I prefer to think of you as naked," he said, his voice a husky murmur against the sound of birds singing.

She let him kiss her. Why not? He was a rogue, but such an enjoyable one. She relaxed against him, letting him slip into her mouth, start a game that made her heart pound. He had his hair tied back, so she pulled on the ribbon until all that loose silk fell into her hands, the way it had the previous night.

He was kissing her with a breathless intensity now, his mouth slanting over hers, invading her, retreating. His lips were hot and beautifully full. She licked his lower lip and he let out a little noise, like a muffled groan.

It was so odd that she pulled back to stare at him.

That was a bad idea because Damon seemed to have shed his friendly exterior. He snatched her back so quickly she lost her breath, and kissed her hard, so her knees buckled. He had her against the tree trunk, and she could feel every hard curve of his body.

"Don't push at me," she gasped. "This tree has bumps on it."

"We can lie down."

"No."

"Then I'll have to protect you from those evil bumps," he said, sliding his hand over the curve of her bottom and pulling her against his body. He had bumps of his own, and her body welcomed each of them with feverish delight.

It made her feel weak and silly, capable of collapsing against him and squealing, *take me,* or something foolish of that nature. That dim suggestion was just enough to bring her thoughts together.

She pulled back and this time he let her go, bracing his arms on the tree on either side of her. Kissing made her feel delicate and fragile, all those things she wasn't and never could be.

"Are you trying to seduce me?" he demanded. "Because, damn it, Roberta, you're about as close to success as I've ever come with a marriageable young woman."

"No, I'm not," she said, pushing his arms away. He had no reason to look quite so shocked at the idea that she might be seductive. "You know I'm not."

He straightened. "Because you're in love with Villiers, right?"

"Among other reasons," she said, straightening her skirts.

He still sounded a little stunned. "If you weren't in love, you still wouldn't want to seduce me?"

Roberta looked up at him. He had a look of utter disbelief on his face. He stood there, muscled and lean in his white shirt, his hair tousled by her hands, and his eyes narrowed. She started laughing.

"I'll kiss you silent," he threatened.

So she sobered. "It's just that — well, you *will* fall in love someday, Damon, and then you'll see what I mean. You're awfully handsome and very sweet, funny and all the rest of it. Just not for me."

"Sweet and funny?" He ran a hand through his hair and it looked even wilder. "Damn it, what happened to my ribbon?"

She picked it up and watched as he pulled his hair back and tied it off his face. The style suited him; it made his cheekbones even more prominent.

"Haven't you ever been in love?" she asked.

"Of course I have," he said, smirking at her. "Many a time."

"No, really in love."

He pulled on his waistcoat. "Of course I have been, you wench. The first time was a lass named Susan, and I'll have you know she was lovely."

"Someone from the village?" she guessed, thinking of him as a young lad with a buxom barmaid.

"Lord Kendrick's daughter," he said, pulling on his coat. "Married a squire and lives in the country."

"Really? And did she love you back?"

"Oh, she did."

"Well, then —"

"For at least a week. She sent me a letter drenched in scent. Which brought us to a tragic close, because our butler informed my father that I was receiving mail from a lady, and he cut off our friendship."

"Goodness. He didn't want you to marry your Susan?"

He grinned at her. "I was fourteen. And he'd arranged my marriage already, though the poor lass died before we got to the point."

"How old was Susan?"

"An ancient woman of seventeen."

"Quite precocious on your part."

"I shall watch Teddy like a hawk. Speaking of which . . ."

They walked across the buttercups to a small grove of spindly trees. They were about half way through when Damon said suddenly, "You never told me why you wouldn't wish to seduce me if Villiers wasn't in the picture."

"Because I intend to marry. And unlike Susan I have enough sense to see that you are not the husband for me."

"I'm not fourteen any longer. I have a title. Why would I be ineligible?"

For some reason she felt like reassuring him, even though it was obviously all a jest. "You're very good looking. And very skilled at kissing."

He grinned down at her. "Thanks for those words of praise. But?"

She shrugged. "You don't want to marry me; you explain it."

"I'm a man. No good at explaining things."

"The moment I saw Villiers, I *knew* he was perfect for me."

"Because he's an old stick who will never embarrass you?"

"I like you hugely, Damon. You can tell that I do. But I feel as if you are a family member, a cousin."

"If you were really my cousin I wouldn't be kissing you under an apple tree."

"It's just that it's all easy with you. And funny." She stopped, hands on her hips. "Do you really think that you'll find yourself having a cowpat throwing contest with your bride?"

He raised an eyebrow. "No?"

"Absolutely not. When you fall in love, your heart will pound so much that you won't be able to throw a mouse, let alone a cowpat."

"I don't think I could throw a mouse now. I dislike the idea of scrabbling little feet in my palm. Unless they were yours, of course."

"That's just what I mean. You wouldn't be so silly if I were the right person for you.

You'd be too afraid to do or say the wrong thing."

"Whereas with you I don't give a damn?"

"That is my distinct impression," she said, walking a little faster because there was sunlight just a few trees away.

"Well, in that case," he said, and a moment later she was spun around against a tree again and he was kissing her. Hard. When Damon kissed, there was nothing cousinly or funny or sweet about him.

At first she struggled a bit; had he no concern for the fact that she was marrying another?

But Damon was the sort of kisser who claimed mastery. Lord of his realm, etc. There was no fighting him when he —

She lost the thought. His fingers were warm on her back and his touch was singing through her dress.

Plus he was pushing against her again. Dimly, she realized that pushing was definitely part of male strategy. Mating strategy, one had to assume.

Fine.

She liked it.

She wiggled a bit in response, and then noticed that his breathing got a little ragged, and she thought, *aha,* and did it again.

The trouble with Jemma's too-tight gowns

was immediately clear when Damon wrapped his hand around the part of her breasts that plumped above her bodice. The bodice promptly lost its moorings and took her corset with it, leaving her whole breast open to his caress.

Dimly, Roberta knew that this had to stop.

For some reason Damon was taken with the idea of kissing her, and acting as if he wanted to seduce her — all right, she was willing to admit that he *did* want to seduce her. But he wasn't the man she was in love with.

She jerked away from him.

He made an odd little groaning sound, and then: "I was enjoying that."

"Do you really want to kiss a woman who's thinking of another man?" she asked him, angry for some reason.

He froze for a second. "I suppose not. Particularly, I must admit, if you were thinking of Villiers. All that passion for chess. All that white hair. No, thank you. I like my hair as it is, and I find chess deadly boring. Don't you?"

"I've never played."

He shuddered. "My father made Jemma and myself play for hours and hours when we were children. Some pieces go one way and others go the other way. It's all about the queen, which" — he grinned at her — "I found tedious and Jemma did not."

"I shall learn to play."

"No point. Villiers will find it monotonous to play you, since you're a beginner. And he's not the type to suffer fools gladly."

"I shall think of ways to make it interesting for him," she said obstinately.

He looked amused but said nothing. A tale one of her father's courtesans had told her came to mind. "We'll play naked," she said.

He stopped short. "Roberta St. Giles!"

She dimpled at him. "Reeves breed true," she said, and took off with a toss of her head. They walked through the spinney to discover that Teddy was swimming like the proverbial fish, and Mr. Cunningham had taken an unlucky spill into the water.

"Do you know what I found?" Teddy shouted. And he pranced out of the water, his little pizzle waving for all the world to see, uncurled his fingers and showed her his discovery.

"A treasure?" she asked. For a little boy, he was really quite beautiful. He had his father's tawny hair but his eyes were darker, and shot with amber specks.

His treasure was a piece of bottle glass, worn smooth.

"Hmmm," she said.

"Do you think it's beautiful?" he asked.

"Not particularly. Do you?"

"Yes, because" — he stuck a plump finger at the middle of it — "a star is there, just there. Do you see?"

Roberta leaned over and sure enough, in the very middle was a tiny, lopsided etching of a star. She thought about correcting his sentence structure and dismissed it. "That *is* beautiful," she said.

When he smiled, one noticed that he was missing several teeth, which was a surprisingly attractive look. "I expect this piece of glass was owned by a smuggler," he said. "That's what I expect."

"Where did the star come from?"

"That's a mystery," he said. And ran away.

CHAPTER 16

When Jemma took a bath, she invariably thought about chess. Once, six years ago, a Frenchman joined her in the bath and diverted her attention, but generally speaking, chess and the pleasures of warm water were intimately connected.

But this evening she couldn't seem to focus. Of course, both games had just begun, and there was much to think about. She had no idea what Villiers would play next, since they both made conventional pawn openings. Nor could she say what Elijah would do, though she could presumably hypothesize based on the games they played in the past. Jemma remembered every game she had played, and if she paid some attention, she could visualize the chess pieces moving, as if the years hadn't passed. Yet she and Elijah had played only three games, all in the first month of their marriage, before she discovered him tumbling his mistress.

She had won all three, but not easily. He played with a brilliant sense of forward strategy, but he was far more protective of his pieces than she was.

She played through one of their early games in her head and then leaned back with a sigh and wiggled her toes. She would beat him again. In all likelihood, he hadn't picked up a piece for years. Unless his mistress played.

One had to wonder whether his mistress was still *au courant,* as it were. Was her husband a man of loyalty? Did he have the pleasant, if foolish, habit of keeping to one mistress these many years, or had he moved on to a younger, fresher version of the same?

The thought made her feel sad — stupid emotion! — so she shook her head. "Brigitte, did you get a chance to speak to any of Villiers's footmen?"

Brigitte smiled the dimpled, triumphant smile of a Frenchwoman who eats English footmen for *son petit déjeuner.* "I have met a certain Joseph," she said. "He is not terrible. Red-haired, which my *maman* always called the mark of Cain. But not terrible. He is taking me to a certain gardens next week, where I will ask him the correct questions."

"You are brilliant," Jemma said. "I do hope you enjoy your evening."

"He has nice shoulders," Brigitte said. "But here is a question. The butler, that ungraceful one by the name of Fowle — an abhorrent name — asked me to inform you that he has received several solicitations to disclose the state of your various chess games."

"The games with Villiers and my husband?"

"*Oui,* those. The requests come from various newspapers, and also from a club called White's. They propose to pay Fowle a sum of the money if he will inform them every day of the position of the games with His Grace and the Duke of Villiers."

Jemma slid down in the water. "I see."

"Of course, Fowle cannot do so without my assistance," Brigitte said. "And frankly, I told him that the thing cannot be done without your permission. The duchess plays many games of chess at the same time, all in the head, I told him. Bah! He does not understand chess, that one."

Jemma thought about it. There was only one reason to keep the information to herself that she could think of: the scandal of it. Elijah would loathe having the matches tracked in the press, or bets placed on his victory at White's.

"I'm afraid the answer is no," Jemma said. "I'm sorry, Brigitte. I know that the newspapers would have paid well for the information."

Brigitte shrugged philosophically. "Fowle would likely have feathered his nest with most of it. Besides, I have Joseph to keep my feathers warm." And she laughed as only a Frenchwoman can.

CHAPTER 17

Day two of the Villiers/Beaumont chess matches
Beaumont House

Elijah woke the next morning as the very first light came through his windows and almost groaned aloud as the details of the day before him burst into his head. Actually, they had been in his head all night long, because now he realized that he had been in the middle of a terrible dream in which the inner circle of Pitt's advisors had been invited to breakfast. He had found the room, but left to use the privy. And then wandered for hours through labyrinthine passageways under Lords trying to find his way back to breakfast. At one point he was in a room lined entirely with costumes, and a smirking Lord Corbin told him that a man of wit would always triumph over a laborer. Which, Elijah realized belatedly, referred to himself.

The day was when he would bound out of bed, eager to get to the House of Lords and tackle the enormous complexities of moving large groups of men to do exactly what he wished them to. These days he felt as if he staggered to the carriage.

His fainting episode last autumn didn't help.

He tried not to think about it too much; what man wants to contemplate his own mortality? But imperceptibly it crept into his thoughts and dreams so that it poisoned his every moment. The morning it happened he hadn't slept more than a few hours for two days. He was running on energy and will power, laying the groundwork for Pitt's takeover of Parliament.

And now Pitt was almost there. He was a good, solid man. Fox would have to retreat to his country house, St. Anne's Hill, and live with that courtesan he took with him everywhere. Pitt would usher in a new era without corruption, without scandal . . .

Except for the scandals attached to Jemma, of course.

He ended up sitting on the edge of his bed, head in his hands. The truth of it was that he wasn't the Prime Minister and never would be. He was an attendant lord. A necessary one. An impassioned man at his best — except he hadn't been at his best since last October.

The House of Lords had been in session. He was standing, talking of the madness of acceding to Fox's demands. Before him rose serried ranks of white wigs, beneath them the little faces with their mouths moving as they chattered to their neighbors, listening to him, listening to them . . . as was the custom. And yet he soldiered on, making his points for the fourth or the fifth time, because he'd discovered that no one seemed to hear him the first, and sometimes even the fifth time.

And then it felt as if those little moving faces under the white wigs were disappearing, leaving rows and rows of wigs. He blinked and kept going, but the wigs were getting bigger and then there were no faces at all. And then, thankfully, it all went away.

He was grateful. He didn't care to be lecturing to nothing more than empty rows of wigs.

Some six months had passed since that morning. The House went into recess and came out again. He showed no further signs of keeling over, though Pitt viewed him, he thought, with a certain veiled anxiety.

But he couldn't stop thinking about all

the empty wigs, and the tiny chattering mouths under them. The fact that his father died at thirty-four didn't help. That gave him only one year, measured against his father's life.

His valet bustled into the room. "There's quite a commotion below, Your Grace," he said. Elijah was quite aware that without Vickery's reports he wouldn't have the faintest idea what went in his own household, although before his wife returned from Paris, these reports were brief descriptions of Cook's lumbago, or the second footman's propensity for pocketing silver.

"Teddy?"

Vickery laughed. "No, the devil himself is already out of the house. His lordship hired the nursemaid sent by the Registry Office this morning, and she's taken him to the park. I've my doubts of her tenure, as do we all. She's a prim one. And Master Teddy is fairly focused on" — he lowered his voice — "bodily processes, if you don't mind the comment, Your Grace."

Elijah snorted. "So what's the fuss about, if not Teddy? Are we having another ball?"

"Lady Roberta's father sent a message saying he'll arrive this afternoon. Him as they call the Mad Marquess. It's luncheon with Mr. Pitt and the King today, isn't it,

Your Grace? And a meeting before that. And then in the afternoon . . ."

"Committee for abolishment of the liberties. Then the Serene Company of Cloth Workers at their hall in Mincing Lane."

Vickery was a snob. "Why must you meet them?" he demanded. "Waste of your time, and they ought to make do with someone lower."

"They are frightened that their workers will be committed to the poor house," Elijah said wearily. "They are afraid that the cheese makers are weaving their own muslin and so will make inroads into their business. In short, they are afraid."

"They should be afraid in private," Vickery said with withering emphasis. He had the bath all ready. "If you please, Your Grace."

"Why is Lady Roberta's father coming?" Elijah asked, settling down as Vickery poured warm water over his head.

"I couldn't say," Vickery said, although this was nothing more than a diversion, since he always gave his opinion. "I do believe he's thinking of staying for a time, Your Grace."

Elijah closed his eyes as Vickery massaged his head with a liquid soap that smelled of orange flowers. It was his one indulgence: a woman's soap, and a woman's practice of bathing every day. There were times when he didn't think he could go on, morning till night, without these two minutes of watery peace.

"Will you be home after the cloth makers?" Vickery enquired, once he began rinsing away the soap.

Elijah sat there, eyes closed, in the peculiarly vulnerable position of one who is being washed rather than washing. "No," he said. "After the cloth makers there's a group of diplomats from America regarding the peace treaty. I can't miss that."

Vickery muttered something acid about jumped-up colonials that Elijah didn't quite catch, but he knew what the gist of it was — that he was working himself to death.

It was an odd thought.

Death.

Or working and death in the same moment.

By all accounts, his father's heart stopped in mid-sentence. At least, Elijah thought, it must have been painless. His faint had been painless. One minute he was standing before a row of empty wigs; the next he woke up covered with cold water flung by a hysterical clerk. It would be so, presumably: in mid-sentence, without time for regrets or second thoughts . . . from light to darkness.

There was a small rebellious voice in his head that sounded louder these days. Elijah was very afraid that the voice was saying something about his father enjoying himself before he died.

"Has there been much conversation about the duchess's propensity for chess?" Elijah asked, feeling unutterably weary.

Vickery launched into a discussion of scandal that bounced from the duchess's various matches — "There's been quite a lot of interest about that, Your Grace" — to the presence of Lord Gryffyn's illegitimate child, to the disputed centerpiece.

"But she was respectably clothed and depicting Helen of Troy," Elijah protested. "What could possibly have upset anyone about her, unless they found her songs disreputable?"

Unfortunately, Vickery disclosed, Helen of Troy had voluntarily disrobed in the latter part of the evening. "It was almost dawn and there weren't many people left in the ballroom," Vickery said. "By all accounts, she was most remarkably painted. With pearls glued to her bosoms, as I heard it. Fowle said it gave him palpitations, but the footmen were more celebratory, if you conceive my meaning."

Elijah slumped back in his bath. "Is the duchess aware this happened? Was she there?"

"Oh no, Your Grace," Vickery said. "She had already retired to her chambers. As I said, it was very late."

There were so many scandals brewing, Elijah thought. What was the addition of a mad marquess? With a sigh, he stood up and reached for a towel.

"No one can blame you for the situation," Vickery said, clearly meaning to be comforting. "Fox treats his Mrs. Armistead as if she were his very wife, and the world knows she is not."

Yet Fox's indiscretions had worked in Elijah's favor. He had convinced certain straitlaced gentlemen to question Fox's judgment, based on his inordinate love for a courtesan. Lord Holland once promised him his support purely on the basis of Fox's indiscreet relation with Mrs. Armistead. "Will Fox never learn the importance of character?" Holland had demanded, looking like a plump pigeon who had eaten a worm not to his liking. Elijah could just imagine what Holland thought of Jemma. Not to mention the naked centerpiece, if news of her pearls and paint was abroad.

Clearly he should no longer count on

votes from those scandalized by impropriety. "If you have the Americans after the cloth makers," Vickery said, "when will you be playing your chess move, Your Grace?"

Elijah tossed him the towel and ran his fingers through his hair. He kept it short as possible to make his wig more comfortable.

He felt slightly better, though it was truly disturbing to realize how much he would have liked to retreat to bed or perhaps wander downstairs for a chat with the marquess. He liked poetry as much as the next person, though come to think of it he hadn't opened a book of poetry for years. "I don't know when I'll fit it in," he said vaguely.

After a man and master have been together for years, they grow attuned to each other's moods. It was clear to Elijah by the time he had his stockings on that Vickery was not happy.

Vickery chose the moment when Elijah was positioning his wig to burst into a flurry of exclamations, all of which led to a few key conclusions:

The Duke of Villiers would play his second piece without fail.

The majority of the household had bet in favor of their master winning, Vickery included, and said master needed to play in order to win.

And, finally, missing a day's play would be taken by all of London as a sign of weakness.

When Elijah thought about it in the carriage, he realized that missing a day would presumably be akin to an admission of impotence. He leaned toward his private secretary, Ransom Cunningham.

"I must return home before the cloth makers," he said.

Cunningham opened his mouth to protest.

Elijah raised his hand. "The chess game," he said.

His secretary's mouth snapped shut. Elijah almost asked him if he had bet on Villiers or himself, but decided it was better not to know. "Do you have any idea how the betting is going in White's?" he asked casually.

There was a moment's hesitation. Then: "Well, Villiers is ranked first in England, Your Grace," Cunningham said with a look of pained apology.

"Humph." Elijah settled back in his seat.

It had been years since he played a game of chess. But he knew its lineaments and its bones. There had been a day when he had been Villiers's only serious opponent. Of course, they had last played when they were seventeen, but still, he fancied he had an advantage.

Not because he had once played Villiers.

But because he was Jemma's husband. To know an opponent was to be able to defeat him. Or her. It was exactly like politics, though he could never seem to make that clear to some idiots in government. He would meet the American diplomats and the cloth makers because, once he knew them, he could move them like little pawns around a chessboard of his own making.

The idea was rather soothing. In fact, one could say that he was better practiced for a game of chess than he had ever been in his life.

The only point that gave him the slightest hesitation was the tingling sense that it could be that he understood Americans and cloth makers better than his wife.

But that was a problem that could certainly be overcome. He added it to the great list of tasks that lived in a corner of his brain, and was consulted every hour or so. The list ranged from the small to the very large, from check the cellars of the house in Portman Square (for he had holdings all over the city) to strengthen connections with France, and Pitt be damned. Somewhere in the middle of the list he added:

Get to understand Jemma.

He thought about it and then annotated the entry.

Get to understand Jemma quickly before she wallops me and costs the loyal parts of my household their annual salaries.

Chapter 18

The Duke of Villiers spent the morning at Parsloe's. He played a mediocre game of chess with a Russian who happened by, and then spent a solid three hours discussing queen sacrifices with Lord Corbin. It could be that Corbin might become a regular partner, which Villiers hadn't had since Berrow shot himself.

Damn it.

Regret always struck Villiers as a foolish emotion, suited to poets and those who had nothing better to do with their time than weep over missteps. As in chess, as in life: it was all a vast game of attack, and one should waste no time regretting mistakes. He found it preferable to excise them from his memory.

But that game, that final game with Berrow . . . His memory stubbornly refused to forget it.

It had started simply enough. He was

focused on pawns that year, and soon had his black pawns swirling around Berrow's white queen like a swarm of hostile ants. It was a brilliant tactical game, played against a weaker opponent, but not the less enjoyable for that.

Except . . . could he have done it differently?

Could he have headed off the moment when Berrow took himself home and put a gun to his head?

The question nagged and nagged. It visited him in his sleep sometimes, leading to dreams full of black pawns. If Berrow had taken his rook in the fourth move, his pawn attack would have collapsed.

But perhaps he shouldn't have pointed that out to Berrow after the game was over. Villiers hunched his shoulders, striding down the block toward Elijah's house. Odd that he still thought of the house as Elijah's, though the two of them had barely exchanged a word in years, and weren't on speaking terms, let alone the intimacy of first names.

Yet to all appearances, they were now playing for Elijah's queen. Whom Villiers didn't really want. All he wanted was someone to play with.

Or perhaps: all he wanted was Berrow to

play with.

It was a maudlin thought and had Villiers banging the knocker with such a fierce scowl on his face that the butler fell back a pace. "Her Grace awaits you," he said.

But Villiers was already on his way up the stairs. He shook off paltry regrets. Yesterday Jemma had played a pawn to King's Four, as had he. Likely she would move a knight.

She moved a pawn to Queen's Four; he promptly took her pawn with his from the day before.

He sat back. "May I see your husband's board?"

The duchess shook back her delicate ruffles. She really was a remarkably beautiful woman, he noted with a certain detachment.

"No."

"Tell me about Philidor's mode of play?"

"He's a round little man with pince-nez. He is quite bald and —" Her eyes laughed at him.

"He looks like a pawn," Villiers guessed.

"Slightly. One of the most interesting games I ever saw him play was one in which he was challenged beforehand to checkmate using his queen's bishop."

"A contract game . . . and such a difficult one. Fascinating!"

"He sacrificed his queen, two rooks, a knight and a bishop, but he did it."

Villiers sat for a moment, imagining the chess pieces flashing from place to place. He couldn't be certain how that game had gone, naturally, but he could see the beauty and complexity of it.

"He taught me a great deal about sacrifice," she continued. "In one game he took from me, he sacrificed his queen, promoted a pawn to a new queen, and won my queen rook."

"Did you sleep with him to celebrate his victory?" he enquired.

She seemed unoffended. "No."

"I think if I met someone who could play like that I would do everything in the world to bed her," he said, watching her.

"Would you?"

She looked like a classic Greek statue, every feature in perfect symmetry. "Playing chess is like music and passion. It gives one a reason for living. Surely to combine two of them would be heaven."

"I have made love while a violin played," she said. The secret smile playing at the corner of her mouth turned his blood hot.

"But have you made love to a master chess player?"

"It depends on one's definition."

"I fit the definition. Philidor as well."

"A chess master with a resemblance to a pawn is not in my purview. And I feel I should add that Philidor is happily married and Madame Philidor would likely resent any encroachment upon her king."

"Unfortunate," he said. "Though I should warn you that I myself have never viewed queens as being possessed by a king. Queens have so much more flare and daring: they move in every direction; they attack and counterattack."

"They can certainly operate independently," she agreed and rose.

Villiers rose as well, conscious of a feeling of disappointment. He didn't want to leave. He wanted to stay in Jemma's bower, talking in double talk about chess and desire. "Why don't we play a game on the side?" he said impulsively. "A private game . . . one that is not being played out by days? Or do you only play games involving a daily move?"

"If you mean by that do I need an entire sunset in order to think out my next move, the answer is no."

"Then play with me," he appealed. "I'm tired of playing idiots. I have nothing particular to do. Let's play together."

"I should have to offer my husband the

same courtesy."

He shrugged. "Do so. My impression is that Beaumont has no time for the games of mere mortals."

Jemma sat down again before the board. "He did once say something of the sort to me."

"He told *Gentleman's Magazine* that his chessboard was England." He started putting the pieces in place before she changed her mind.

Jemma turned back the ruffles that fell over her fingers, leaving her slender fingers and wrists free.

"So intriguing," he commented, watching her closely.

"Why do you say so?"

"It makes me think of undressing you. Women wear so much clothing . . . one lusts for the small amounts of flesh that make themselves visible."

"I am beginning to think that you find everything sensual."

"To my mind, there are two things worth doing, one out of bed and one in. Perhaps we should change the rules of the final game?"

She turned the board around. "Your advantage this time."

"The final game blindfolded," he said,

"and in bed."

"And how precisely would that work?" she said, her mouth curving in a delicious lopsided way. "Would my maid stand beside us, moving the pieces? You did say blind-folded, did you not?"

"I never pay the slightest attention to servants. But if you would feel discomposed by her presence, we'll set up the chess board in the corridor and I shall call out our moves." Villiers caught himself before he started begging like a bishop blocked by a pawn. What was that about? He never begged. He took.

He scowled at the board and leaped his knight over the row of pawns. He didn't believe for a moment that she was as good as she claimed.

It incensed him that something in her eyes suggested she knew precisely what he was thinking.

"Do you ever resist the feeling?" she asked some time later, as he was frowning down at the board. Her queen had just taken one of his knights. There was no good move that he could see.

"Resist what?" he asked absentmindedly. Perhaps if he moved his queen to Bishop's Two . . .

"Resist women. Or a woman. Resist a

259

woman whom you desire."

He looked up at her. She had to know that her intelligence made her more luscious. She made no effort to hide it, never simpering or giggling, as far as he could see. Yet there was something odd about their match prickling the back of his mind. Why had she summoned him to her ball? Why was she challenging him?

It might have been simply for the pleasure of a match, of course. He looked back at the board.

She leaned toward him, and the curve of her breast was enticingly plump above her stiff bodice. "Do you ever resist desire, Villiers?"

"Very occasionally. I have felt impulses that I have not pursued; I feel that impoverished women would come to my bed with desperation, and the emotion is enough to dampen my appetite."

He bent forward and moved his pawn to take one of hers.

"Women resist desire as a matter of course," she said almost dreamily, taking a pawn of his in return.

"There are so many more consequences for the female sex." Suddenly he was scowling down at a game that had flipped from comfortable to . . . otherwise.

"Damn it," he said. It was the first comment either of them made for a few minutes.

Until: "Checkmate," Jemma said.

She leaned back in her chair and smiled at him. "To answer your earlier question . . . there won't be a third game unless we each win one."

Villiers nearly growled. Did she really think he would go down in both games? This was nothing but a side game, and he hadn't properly concentrated.

"It would have been amusing," she said, "if you had moved that pawn to King's Bishop Three."

"I would have won," he agreed. He was already playing through all the moves in his head. "I would have won, except that was the moment when you raised the question of desire."

Her mouth had a mocking curve to it that burned him to the bone. "*If* you survive to a third game," she said, rising again, "your proposition might be a very interesting one."

"What proposition?" he asked, rising automatically, but still thinking through the game.

"To play our third game blindfolded, and in bed? It certainly would amuse the staff banished to the corridor. I shall consider it."

Villiers had never come quite so close to hating someone after whom he lusted. It was true that he hated — if momentarily — every person who beat him at a game of chess, but to have that person be a woman who seemed supremely insouciant about his offer to take her to bed was infuriating.

He walked behind her down the stairs, moodily assessing her narrow frame, the elegance of her shoulders, the beauty of the dull gleam of her hair . . .

Christ.

He'd met a woman whom he really wanted — and she was the first female to beat him at chess.

Quite possibly the two facts were not unrelated.

There was still something prickling the edge of his mind about these matches. Wasn't it odd that she summoned him to play the very moment she reached England?

It couldn't be that Beaumont was behind it. He thought of his old friend's furious, cold eyes and knew that Elijah had no knowledge of his presence at the ball, nor any idea of the proposed chess game.

So it had to be for the chess.

Or did she want a whipping boy? She thought she could simply trounce him, the best player in England, by asking provocative questions at the right moment?

A flash of pure rage went through his spine. The hell with her provocative games. Had he ever resisted lust? Indeed he had. And from now on, he was going to resist her.

No woman was going to trap him, with her beauty or her chess skill.

In fact . . .

A smile grew on his face.

It was time he married. The ultimate lust killer, in his opinion. It pleased him to think that Jemma would find him planning a marriage at the same time he offered to bed her. It would keep her from refining too much on her little success.

Yes, that was the solution.

Marriage.

CHAPTER 19

Roberta greeted the news that her father had just arrived and was waiting for her in the drawing room with a feeling that could only be described as near hysteria. Surely not. He couldn't do this to her!

"Is he alone?" she asked, trying in vain to school her features into calm.

"I believe the marquess has a companion," the footman replied, his face not yielding even a flicker about that companion.

Of course he wasn't alone, she thought, despairing. Of course Mrs. Grope was with him.

"Is the duchess in her chambers?" she asked.

"I wouldn't know, your ladyship. Would you like me to enquire of Her Grace's maid?"

"Yes, please."

Unfortunately, he reported a few minutes later that the duchess was playing chess with the Duke of Villiers, although she promised to join Lady Roberta at her first opportunity.

She had to decide what to do. Figure out how to make her father leave. It was like a musical beat in her head. He had to leave, leave, leave.

"Please send Lord Gryffyn my compliments and ask him if he would meet me in the library," she said to the footman.

He hesitated. "What shall I tell the marquess, your ladyship?"

"Please convey my apologies. Tell him I am not ready to receive visitors. I shall attend him at the earliest possible moment."

It didn't help when Damon burst into laughter on hearing her request.

"Help you get rid of your father? An uncharitable act, and not worthy of a member of the family of Reeve." He gave her a lofty look.

"Please," she said. "Please! You have no idea what he's like. He's going to ruin everything." Tears were threatening.

"What can I possibly do?" He frowned at her. "No crying. Thoughtless rakes like myself can't bear to see a woman cry; it reminds us of all those we left weeping on the roadside."

She couldn't even manage a smile at his

foolery. "It's not that I don't love him," she said, gripping her hands together. "It's just that he's eccentric. He doesn't care what people think."

"Not at all?"

"Never! He never has. You'll see what I mean when you meet him. Mrs. Grope is only the latest of the courtesans with whom he has been passionately in love. She has lived with us for the past two years."

"Mrs. Grope?" Damon asked with some interest. "Is there a Mr. Grope still?"

"I have no particular belief in the existence of Mr. Grope. Except . . ."

"Who would choose that name on its own? I agree entirely."

"Please take me seriously," Roberta said, dropping into the couch. "I simply cannot stay in London if my father is here. *Please!*"

Damon sat down beside her. "Am I allowed to call you Roberta yet?"

She sniffed. "We shouldn't."

"Kissing cousins," he said, dropping a kiss on her eyebrow.

"You really shouldn't do that."

He ignored her. "What's so terrible about your father, then?"

"Mrs. Grope," Roberta said, "is something of a liability in terms of my reputation."

"There are liabilities and liabilities. One

would think that Teddy would be a liability, for example, but his presence in my home doesn't seem to have put off the matchmaking mamas a bit."

"If you don't mind deserting the fascinating topic of your popularity for one moment," Roberta said, "no matchmaking mamas are going to enter this house while Mrs. Grope is here."

"I knew you would prove useful," he said, grinning at her. "Mrs. Grope won't stop your old roué from entering the house, if that's what you're worried about."

"Villiers is not a roué!" she scolded.

"Close enough. But the point is that you can seduce him here or —"

"That is not the point. You have no idea how humiliating it is being around my father."

Damon wrapped an arm around her shoulder and pulled her a little closer. "Tell me your tales of horror and I'll do my best to comfort you."

"No!" Roberta said, but as usual he paid no attention to her. He bent his head and kissed her cheek, which wasn't very intrusive, so she ignored him. "My father is prone to falling on his knees and bursting into tears."

"Interesting," Damon murmured, kissing her ear.

"It is not interesting," Roberta said fiercely.

"I know he fell to his knees and implored the heavens for a husband who would never kiss you in public. Obviously, I would not qualify." His lips had drifted down and he was kissing her neck now.

"No," Roberta agreed. There was something oddly distracting about those feathery touches of his lips.

"That was bad enough," she said, struggling to get her mind back to her story, "but then *Rambler's Magazine* —"

At the end of that story, he stopped kissing her and actually looked at her with something approaching sympathy. For a moment she felt a thrill that he finally understood how dreadful her situation was, but: "You are nothing more than an example of incestuous inbreeding and I never noticed!" he cried. "I've sinned by having anything to do with you. Give me my sin again . . ."

He grabbed her and for a moment Roberta lost track of her complaints because he was saying things about sin in a husky voice, and his hands touched her front in an improper manner that turned her mind to smoke.

"Feeling better?" he enquired, sometime later.

Roberta blinked at him for a moment and then straightened up. "I think so," she said weakly.

Damon looked pleased with himself.

"Is this your kindly way of assuring me that you're going to convince my father to go back home so that I can marry the Duke of Villiers?"

"Will you reward me for my services?" he asked with a ridiculous leer.

"Why don't you go kiss one of those girls who want you so much?"

"Are you saying that you don't enjoy my kisses?"

Roberta burst out laughing. "Anyone would enjoy your kisses! But you know I'm in love with someone else."

His eyes had turned a dark sea green and she knew what that meant. "I think that's why you're so irresistible to me," he said, his voice deep as his eyes. "You belong to someone else."

"Oh —" she said, but he was kissing her again. And truly, she did love kissing him. In fact, she dimly thought that she could do it all day, except her father must be wondering why she was taking so long to dress.

A while later she gasped when his hand found her breast. She slapped his hand away. "I don't belong to Villiers yet, but I'm not open territory either."

"Because you don't want *me,*" he prompted, a sardonic note in his voice.

She raised an eyebrow. "Who said that?"

He burst out laughing. "Try to play a docile maiden at least until after your wedding, could you?"

"I *am* a maiden," she protested.

"So you do want me." The words hung on the air, like some sort of challenge.

Roberta wasn't going to lie. Lust, as any poet's daughter knows, is nothing beside true love. "It's not the same way that I feel about Villiers."

A moment later she felt sorry she'd clarified the point, because something flew across Damon's eyes, and she thought perhaps she'd hurt his feelings.

She tugged her bodice back into place. "Please help me send Papa back to the country."

He looked down at her and sighed. "I suppose it's no more than a cousin's duty."

They walked into the drawing room to find the marquess holding forth to a nonplussed Fowle. The butler was standing next to the door, as if he were on the point of flight. Even from the corridor Roberta could tell that her father was on one of his favorite subjects. "She was like a basilisk," he said, "her eyes killed every man at whom she has glanced." She realized with a sinking heart that her father had launched into the story of how he fell in love with Mrs. Grope.

"Mrs. Grope is a high-spirited woman," Papa was saying as they entered. With his hands clasped behind his back, the marquess looked like a rather dapper magistrate. Roberta always found it interesting how very sensible her father appeared to be, though five minutes of conversation were generally enough to convince people of his unique views.

"Papa," she said, dropping a curtsy. "What a lovely surprise this is, to be sure. Mrs. Grope." She dropped another curtsy.

Mrs. Grope had dressed her hair enormously high for the occasion. It towered in a series of curls and arabesques before being topped off by a small replica of London Bridge.

Damon came forward and swept a bow. "Papa, Mrs. Grope, this is Damon Reeve, the Earl of Gryffyn."

"My darling daughter," her father said, catching her into a hug that ignored her

271

curtsy altogether. "Lord Gryffyn, I remember seeing you in the *Tête-à-Tête* series, was it a year ago?"

"Papa," Roberta interrupted. "This is a most unexpected pleasure and yet I must ask . . . why are you paying me a visit?" That was bald, but straightforward.

"The most delightful thing, dear child!" he cried. "My book, my magnum opus!"

"A publisher?" Roberta asked, feeling truly startled.

"Not exactly — not yet — not entirely — but soon!"

"We were positively longing for some entertainment," Mrs. Grope said, putting a hand to her bosom. "Withering in the country, that's what I said to your dear father."

"But Papa, you said that London was nothing more than a nest of vipers," Roberta said, feeling as if sand was shifting under her feet.

"But then I bethought me," he said, beaming at her. "If I accompanied you to London, I could follow up on this matter of a publisher. A publisher is a *consummation devoutly to be wished.*"

"Indeed," Damon said, amusement underlying his voice. "And you, Mrs. Grope?"

"I am a creature of the theater," she said,

striking an attitude. "I live for the moment when we enter Drury Lane, scene of my triumph."

Roberta shuddered. Mrs. Grope had "trod the boards," as she had it, before meeting the marquess in Bath and returning home with them. After one quick glance at Damon, she had turned herself at a right angle to him and stood with her elegant, if rather long, nose pointed into the distance. She was wearing more rouge than usual, Roberta thought uncharitably; her flush went from her jaw to under her eyes. "Ah, the days of yore when I conquered the boards!" she cried.

"The role of Elisabetina in *The Clandestine Marriage*," Papa explained to Damon, who was doing a very credible job of keeping a sober face. " 'Tis a sad comedown for a woman of her beauty to leave the stage, especially when the Prince of Wales himself delivered his commendations in person. Yet she did me the inexpressible joy of allowing me to become her patron." He went down on one knee to kiss Mrs. Grope's hand.

"Papa," Roberta began.

"Don't worry," he beamed at her. "We won't get in your way. I'll assure the duke himself of that. And his lovely duchess. I've seen her picture many a time in the *Tête-à-*

Tête column. Many a time! I expect now we're in London, it's a matter of time before my own Mrs. Grope is appearing there, but I certainly hope my picture will be opposite hers."

"In my sister's absence, I welcome you both to Beaumont House," Damon interjected, bowing. "Fowle?"

"If your lordship would allow us a few more minutes, Mrs. Friss is readying chambers for our guests. I will ascertain her progress," he said, bowing himself from the room.

"Papa!" Roberta said pleadingly. "I really don't — I don't want you here."

His face fell, of course. That was the worst of it, and the reason why she was unmarried at one-and-twenty. His face fell, and he looked as if he were about to cry. "Don't say that, dearest. I haven't been able to sleep since you left."

"No more he has," Mrs. Grope said promptly.

Roberta threw her a beseeching look. She thought that Mrs. Grope, at the least, had understood how important it was that she find a husband. But Mrs. Grope sent her a rueful smile that admitted her total lack of influence.

"I haven't slept, and I haven't written a

274

single poem in three days," the marquess said, opening his eyes very wide. "How could I, when I had no idea with whom my child was consorting? How can I have allowed my own duckling, my little chicken, to wander the cold streets of London by herself?"

"I am hardly wandering the streets of London," Roberta said, controlling her voice to a reasonable level with difficulty.

"I woke in the middle of the night, and I knew I did wrong," her father wailed, a tear sliding down his cheek. "What would Margaret say, I asked myself?"

Damon nudged her.

"My mother," she told him.

She folded her arms and waited; from long experience she knew that her father was only now getting into his stride. "Margaret would say I was wrong — wrong — *wrong.*" More tears fell down his face. Mrs. Grope patted his face with her handkerchief.

"That is likely true," Roberta said, feeling not a whit of sympathy. "Mother would not have been pleased with my journey."

"How could I have let that happen?" the marquess said, with a sniffle. "My child . . . the dearest to my heart . . . my jasmine blossom — *in the second best coach* escorted only by servants!"

Roberta opened her mouth to say something about the poem he sent to Jemma, but Damon nudged her again. "Give over," he whispered.

Her father put a hand in his pocket and took out an enormous bundle of banknotes. "For you, dearest, for you. I know you don't like Mrs. Parthnell's sewing skills, though I cannot but ask myself who will employ her now that you are gone? But still, Mrs. Grope's patronage counts for something."

Mrs. Grope smiled grimly. Before Roberta left, she had very kindly tried to make Mrs. Parthnell's creations into something worth wearing to London. But there was the unmistakable odor of Mrs. Parthnell around Mrs. Grope's current garment. It was fashioned from lovely striped fabric, but the lines were designed to come to a V in the front of the bodice — and they didn't. It was odd, to say the least, and as Roberta watched, Mrs. Grope adjusted her arms across her chest the better to disguise the defect.

"It's for you, all for you," her father was saying, pushing the banknotes at her. "The St. Giles family has never taken charity, and there's no need to do so. After all, you are an heiress according to the mercantile standards by which people judge these things."

"Thank you, Papa," she said. The roll was far too large to fit into her pocket. Damon stuck out his hand, and she read deep enjoyment in his eyes. She handed the notes to him.

"Papa," she said, but he looked so uncertain she couldn't bring the words to her lips.

"I can't imagine why I didn't think of it before," he said quickly. "London is the path to all of our deepest hearts' desires. I expect publishers never accept a manuscript until they have made the acquaintance of its author. Why, it might be a work of the very weakest moral fiber and they wouldn't know without personal assessment. Don't you agree, my lord?" He turned to Damon.

"Absolutely," he said. "Were I a publisher, I would insist on a personal interview."

"There you are," the marquess said, as Roberta shot Damon a murderous look. "I shall be published, you shall be married, and Mrs. Grope . . . ah, Mrs. Grope."

"And what of Mrs. Grope?" Damon asked.

"She tried to persuade me against this, from the depths of her loving kindness," the marquess roared. "But I know she has ambitions. I know the truth of it. Rather than be oppressed in the country, a lady as beautiful as Mrs. Grope should be celebrated in every bookstore window, and I've no doubt but that she will be. Look at her, my dear sir, just look at her!"

Mrs. Grope was doing a very credible job of keeping her gaze on the far distance and her chin high in the air.

"I cannot fool myself that she will stay under my protection," the marquess said with a heavy sigh. "But I cannot but be oppressed by the idea that I may have caused distress to the two women I love most in the world: my daughter, and my dear Mrs. Grope, the love of my bowels."

At this propitious moment, the door opened and Fowle appeared. "Her Grace, the Duchess of Beaumont," he said. And: "His Grace, the Duke of Villiers."

Roberta would have fainted, if she'd known how.

"Please allow me to introduce my sister, Her Grace, the Duchess of Beaumont," Damon said to the marquess. "Jemma, this is Mrs. Grope, and the famed poet, the Marquess of Wharton and Malmesbury."

"How I enjoyed the poem that dear Roberta brought me," Jemma said, curtsying.

"A trifle, a mere trifle," the marquess said,

blotting a last tear. "I am not yet entirely happy with it . . . I believe I shall take out the bear and the swearing parson, when all's done. I won't publish it until it's in its finest state, when I bring out all my collected works in a folio edition. This version is for your eyes only. My gift for your kindness in sheltering the pearl of my bosom, my only daughter."

"Are your collected works forthcoming?" Jemma asked, curtsying to Mrs. Grope. "A pleasure, dear madam," she said, as Mrs. Grope's curtsy took her nearly to the floor.

"I have no doubt it will happen, in leather with pearl bindings," the marquess said. He made a leg to Villiers. "I knew your father of old," he said.

"Not always an unmixed blessing to make my father's acquaintance," Villiers allowed.

"I fear he did not understand literature. Not at all. I was in my salad days, you understand, but I already had a fine grasp of music and rhythm. Your father said something abominably rude; I shan't repeat it. But I remember every word."

"We are more and more in sympathy every moment," Villiers said. "I too have several signal lectures delivered by my father emblazoned in my memory."

"Be that as it might," the marquess said,

"it was an excellent poem. A light subject, but heartfelt in its every pentameter. I still remember it."

Roberta's heart sank. Sure enough, a moment later her father launched into fifteen verses that began, *For I will consider my Cat Jeoffry.* Even Roberta, who was well versed in literature, couldn't follow much other than the rhyming couplets that occasionally popped up like way posts in a dark night.

There was a moment of silence after he finished while (Roberta assumed) the assorted company tried to ascertain whether the poem was truly over.

"I never ask my daughter to critique my work," her father said, in a magnificent untruth, "as her literary judgment is far harsher than her pleasant exterior promises."

"Unnatural child," Damon whispered.

She shot him a squinty-eyed look and he shut up.

Just as Roberta realized with a queer little pang that her father's feelings were going to be hurt, how could they not be hurt, Damon said: "Immensely moving in every lineament and emotion, my lord. I think the line *he counteracts the powers of darkness by his electrical skin and glaring eyes,* and you must forgive me if I have that wrong, was particularly penetrating in its analysis."

Her father beamed.

"It's very sad in the end," Jemma ventured. "Did I understand that a rat bit Jeoffry's throat?"

The marquess nodded, rocking back and forth on his heels. "A sad demise for such a splendid quadruped. *There is nothing sweeter than his peace,*" he quoted, heaving an enormous sigh. "He died a few days after. Your father," he said, turning to Villiers, "was rather unkind in his assessment of that poem."

"I can see why," Villiers said, his voice as sleek as any cat's. "Father didn't like felines. If Jeoffry had been a hunting dog . . ."

"Ah now, if only he had explained that to me," the marquess said, beaming. "Some people have unusual fears of domesticated animals, as I well know. Why, Mrs. Grope is terrified, purely terrified, of camels."

They all turned like puppets to stare at Mrs. Grope. "Miggery's Traveling Circus," she said with a shudder.

Roberta felt like moaning. Thankfully, Jemma was smiling and didn't seem inclined to throw them all out.

Suddenly a large hand squeezed Roberta's. "Don't worry about it," Damon said in her ear. "This house is big enough for all of Miggery's Traveling Circus."

Even as Damon spoke, her papa was delightedly accepting the duchess's invitation to stay. "But only for a night or two," he said. "I've made up my mind to open up my house. I have one, you know, child," he said, turning to Roberta. "I expect you've forgotten that."

Forgotten? How could she possibly have known that?

"A large one it is, on St. James's Square as I recall," he said, frowning a bit. "I inherited it from someone or other. My relatives have dropped like fleas in the past few years," he told the company at large. "I'm composing a sort of universal poem of commiseration that can be applied to many occasions. It's the only prudent thing to do."

"But you will leave Roberta here with me, won't you?" Jemma asked.

The marquess frowned. "I hadn't thought —"

But Mrs. Grope proved herself a true friend. "If —" she said magnificently, viewing them all, a duke, an earl, a marquess, a duchess and Roberta — "I am to achieve the fame which I heartily deserve, I cannot be disturbed by the presence of a young lady in the house."

"But dearest —" the marquess bleated.

She raised her hand. Just so did Moses part the Red Sea. "No!"

"It *is* for the best," Jemma said.

"I agree," Villiers put in, rather unexpectedly.

"*You* think so, do you? And why is that?" the marquess asked.

"I could not pay my addresses to a young lady living in the proximity of an actress," he said, "even such an exquisite woman as Mrs. Grope."

Mrs. Grope bowed her head magnificently, as one receiving her due. Damon's hand fell from Roberta's.

"Pay your addresses, eh?" her father said, looking rather deflated. "I suppose the world is coming to a place where I might have to give my only daughter to one who doesn't understand poetry."

Villiers looked at Roberta and she felt the thrill of it to the bottom of her spine. "She has not yet accepted my hand," he said.

Roberta couldn't think what to say. Was that a proposal?

"Doubtless she will consider your merits in due time," her father said. "Roberta can look to the very highest in the land when she decides to choose a spouse."

Villiers's sardonic look indicated that he *was* the very highest in the land, but luckily,

Fowle reentered the room and announced that the chambers had been prepared if Mrs. Grope and the marquess would be so kind as to follow him.

Jemma led the way, the marquess's hand tucked in her arm, and Villiers held his arm out to Mrs. Grope. So Roberta and Damon followed. For some reason she felt rather shy about meeting his eyes.

He pulled her back as they were about to leave the room.

"Damme," he said and she could hear incredulity in his voice. "What the devil are you about, Roberta?"

"What do you mean?"

"Villiers? How did you manage that?"

She bristled. "Need there be an explanation that involves trickery?" Although to tell the truth, she couldn't quite believe what had just happened.

Neither did Damon, obviously. He raised an eyebrow at her. "What in Hades did you do to the man, to get him to the point without witchcraft?"

She turned up her nose. "Why wouldn't he wish to marry me? Don't you think I'm desirable?"

The moment she said it, she knew she had said the wrong thing.

"You're particularly desirable now that

you're almost engaged to someone else," he said, and sure enough, there she was backed up against the silk paneled wall of the drawing room as Damon pushed the door shut behind Mrs. Grope.

"There's nothing more desirable in the world than a woman planning to marry someone else," he whispered, brushing his lips against hers.

She felt as if heat struck her in the face the moment he tasted her. Or perhaps it was the moment she tasted him. There was something deliciously wicked about kissing one man when another has almost asked you to marry him.

"I shouldn't be doing this," she whispered back. He kissed her harder. She discovered she was breathing in little pants.

"I should be doing this," he said. His hands were on her breasts as if they belonged there. Her bodice skimmed below her nipples without putting up a fight. Damon was looking down at her with an odd little smile on his mouth and doing something with his hands.

"That —" she said foolishly.

"Feels good?" he asked, crooking one eyebrow.

"Interesting," she choked.

With one swift movement he pulled down

on her bodice again and it slipped below her right breast as simply as if it weren't designed to do precisely the opposite. Her breast spilled into his hand.

"Roberta," he said, and the huskiness in his voice made a strange warmth grow between her thighs. Or perhaps it was what he was doing with his thumb.

Roberta clutched his forearms. "This is scandalous," she whispered.

"You're not engaged yet," he said, sounding happy. And uncaring. "Besides, it's all the more delicious for being surreptitious."

And then, while she was still figuring out what he meant because her brain seemed to have taken a little holiday, he laughed and said, "I'm writing poetry!"

Just when she would have kicked him in the ankle, his mouth replaced his hand at her breast. Roberta was no fool. There are times in life when sagging against the wall is exactly the right thing to do, and luckily one of his arms held her up.

Arching her back toward his mouth felt like the right thing too. And whimpering when he took that delicious warm mouth away.

"Darling," he whispered

Her eyes opened lazily. "Yes?"

He pulled up her bodice and rather to

Roberta's surprise, it slid back into place as if it had always been there.

"Your father is doubtless wondering where you are. He is endearingly fond of you."

Roberta didn't feel like being a daughter. She felt like lying down, and she saw the same thought in his eyes. So she scowled at him. "You were no help to me whatsoever. I thought you were going to help me steer my father toward returning to the country."

He tucked a stray curl back into the elaborate nest of curls her maids had created that morning. "It was impossible."

"Why impossible?" she asked, feeling churlish.

"He loves you too much. Jemma and I never saw much of our parents except when my father lectured us about chess, but I can recognize parental love when I see it."

"Because of Teddy," she said as he opened the door.

"I should warn Teddy now," Damon said, looking faintly horrified. "I'll embarrass him in public, falling on my knees and imploring docile young ladies to marry him."

Roberta sighed. "If only papa wasn't so demonstrative. If only he didn't *cry* so frequently."

"The worst is over. Your beloved Villiers met him and he didn't flee from the room shrieking, so what do you care about the rest of the *ton?*"

"I would like to go to parties," Roberta said wistfully. "Our neighbors stopped sending us invitation years ago."

"Oh, you will be. Your papa will take the estimable Mrs. Grope to his house and have a lovely time guarding her against the entreaties of all those gentlemen who will want to take her away from him —"

"Don't be cruel."

"I think what would be truly cruel is if Mrs. Grope doesn't get at least one lure thrown out to her. He's so hoping for rivalry."

"He doesn't truly want rivals."

"A rival or two would make for some excellent poetry. At any rate, my point is that your papa and Mrs. Grope will take themselves off, and you will be chaperoned by Jemma. No one will close their doors on Jemma, for all she's flaunted her indiscretions for years."

"Has she indeed?"

"The fault of her foolish husband and his mistress," Damon said. "Of course, she is a Reeve. Will the strain breed true in you, do you think?"

"Why I —" She stopped. Would she have *affaires?*

"Of course you will," Damon answered her unspoken question. "Villiers is not the sort of man to demand or even desire your entire attention. You see how lucky you are that I did not appear at your New Year's ball?"

"Why?" she asked, startled.

"Jemma can tell you that I was a most annoying brother," he said. "I never share. And — I would never share you."

Roberta opened her mouth to reply but there was nothing to be said.

CHAPTER 20

Elijah came home after the cloth makers and before the Americans, instructing his coachman to dash across London as if the hounds of hell were after him, while inside the coach he bent his head over pieces of foolscap covered with Pitt's small, crabbed writing. They danced before his eyes: notes about French connections, about the mood in the House of Commons, about the recent election.

He strode into the house with a headache, to find his butler, Fowle, dancing before him in an ecstasy of impatience. "If you'll please, Your Grace."

"I have no time," he said automatically, allowing a footman to take his cloak from his shoulders and tossing his hat on the chair. He didn't take off his wig. It was beastly hot, but what was the point? Play the chess piece and leave the house within ten minutes and he had a chance of getting to the Americans at the appointed time.

"Your Grace," Fowle said, "I must speak to you!"

His tone was so desperate that Elijah paused with one foot on the bottom stair.

Two moments later he pounded up those same stairs and threw open the door leading to his chambers. She was seated before the chess table, of course.

He sat down, calming himself with a fierce interior command. Jemma looked up with a smile, but her greeting died — at the look on his face, presumably.

"Am I to understand that you have moved a woman of ill repute into the house?" he said, sitting down and moving a pawn to Queen Four. He had thought out that move in five minutes between one meeting and another, and he certainly didn't have time to reconsider it now.

She echoed his move just as quickly. Then she sat back, hands folded. "The Marquess of Wharton and Malmesbury arrived this afternoon. Surely, you were informed of his imminent visit this morning, as was I?"

"I was not informed that he arrived with a doxy in tow."

"An unfortunate omission," she said. "A Mrs. Grope does indeed accompany him."

The immense injustice of it blocked his

throat for a moment. "Do you have any idea," he finally said, hearing the harsh sound of his voice behind his teeth, "what this will do to my career?"

"I don't know. Will it cause injury?"

Her look of enquiry fueled his rage. "Don't play the fool with me, Jemma," he hissed at her. "You and I have been married far too long for that. I know that you are intelligent; I know that you can easily conceive why it would be a bad idea for a member of the House of Lords to invite a woman of ill repute to live in his house!"

She looked genuinely sorry. "There was nothing I could do about it, Beaumont."

"Send them to Nerot's Hotel!"

"I could not be so rude. There may possibly be a few straitlaced matrons who will not visit the house during her stay with us, but I am perfectly happy to hold no entertainments. That way no such matrons can have an opportunity to announce their qualms."

"How long does she stay?"

"A few days only. The marquess talks of opening his house here in London."

"I have a dislike of opening myself to entirely valid criticism of my household arrangements," Elijah said. His throat closed before he could say anything further.

"I could not turn her out. But I assure you that I hadn't the faintest idea that the marquess might pay a visit to his daughter, nor that such a person as Mrs. Grope existed."

"How could you, indeed?" he said it woodenly. His wig felt as if it weighed a good stone.

With one swift look at him, Jemma rose and walked behind him. Automatically he began to rise, but she pushed his shoulders down and pulled off his wig. It came away with a little cloud of powder. She fluttered her hands to make it go away.

"Must you?" she asked. "Villiers never wears one."

"He is hardly decent; he doesn't even powder his hair. Villiers is no one." He said it wearily, but truly. Villiers didn't have the ear of the King, nor even the ear of Fox, Pitt's great rival. He was no one.

"And you?" his wife said. Her fingers began to gently knead his scalp, touching him here and there. Her touch had the cool blessedness of water.

He leaned his head into her hands, a gesture of weakness and yet . . . She was his wife. What mattered weakness before her? She didn't love him, nor he her, but there was a bond there, between husband and wife, that was different from any other bond.

"Perhaps," she said, sounding uncharac-teristically uncertain, "you ought to reduce your appointments, Beaumont. You don't appear well."

For a moment he just enjoyed the feeling of her slender fingers working through his hair, taking away the tightness of his scalp. And then her words filtered through to his brain.

"Appointments!" He swore and leapt from the chair. A moment later he snatched his wig and threw it on his head, helter-skelter. Made a leg to his lady, filing away a thought about how very beautiful she was for some other moment, and rushed from the room.

Jemma was left, staring down at the chess table.

CHAPTER 21

April 14

Day three of the Villiers/Beaumont chess matches

Roberta felt as if she'd fallen through a hole in the wall and ended up in Miggery's Traveling Circus. Events swirled around her in which she played no part. She had envisioned a grand seduction campaign. She had planned to bribe Villiers's footmen and to trap him into marriage. She had schemed to use a substitute wedding certificate. But, in the end, what was necessary? Quote a bit from *The Rape of Lucrece,* wear a gown that was a trifle too small and suddenly . . .

Suddenly what? The Duke of Villiers had declared his intention to court her, in front of her papa, but what did that mean?

The question had kept her awake. Could it have just been an unscrupulous jest on his part? But a package was delivered the next morning. It was a soft bundle of pale blue velvet tied in ribbon, about the size of an expensive bible. When she untied it, a card fell to the floor. She snatched it up and found spiky black letters that were indubitably no one's but Villiers's.

I have no Familiarity with Courtship. Pray do not abuse your Power, Fair One. I find this trifle Reminds me of you.

A special volume of Shakespeare's poetry, she thought. There was more blue velvet. And when that fell open . . . Not Shakespeare. It was a portrait. It showed a young country girl wearing a simple dress and holding a small cage.

"Oh, how lovely!" Jemma cried, when Roberta showed it to her a few minutes later. "It's painted by Sir Joshua Reynolds, of course. How exquisite."

"Why do you suppose she is holding a mouse trap?" Roberta asked.

"Is that what it is?" Jemma peered closer and something indefinable crossed her face. Could it be longing — or — or jealousy? Roberta's heart thumped. She wanted Villiers; she wanted her friendship with Jemma almost as much.

But Jemma was gay in her answer. "Darling, it's a mousetrap because — well — you do know the old adage about marriage, don't you?"

Roberta frowned. "A trap?"

"The parson's mousetrap." Jemma's laughter sounded clear and true, and not at all tainted by jealousy.

Roberta didn't like the portrait quite as much as she had a moment before.

"Pure Villiers," Jemma was saying. "An exquisite, hideously expensive gift . . . any other man would have sent you a ruby. His present has a hidden jest."

"It's not as if he's thumbing his nose at me?" Roberta asked.

"Oh no. He's sharing the joke, don't you see? Marriage is madness, you know. He's making a joke of it, because one can hardly do otherwise."

One couldn't? Somehow . . . Roberta could see it otherwise. Though that was foolish beyond all measure, given that she was the same woman who planned to cold-bloodedly trick Villiers into marriage. And now that he was walking into the trap, and laughing at its boundaries, she felt uncomfortable?

"We'll have a dinner party," Jemma was saying. "He'll spring the question, of course, and it will be most amusing."

"Will he?"

"Of course he will." Jemma peered at her. "You do realize how much a painting by Reynolds costs, don't you?"

Roberta looked again at the odd, cunning expression in the girl's eyes, the shadow cast by the mousetrap onto the soft muslin of the girl's dress and the cat's bright eyes. "You don't think he guessed that I planned to set a trap for him?"

Jemma shrugged. "Who cares? Would you credit his earnestness if he had sent you a necklace of rubies?"

Roberta nodded.

"This is better than a necklace. Even the frame is superb. Now who shall I invite to the dinner party? It has to be just the right mix to present the proper frame for Villiers's demise."

"Demise?"

"It will seem so to the *ton,*" Jemma said. "Believe me. Ladies have set their caps at him for the past ten years, and you merely smiled at him and he surrendered. You, my dear, are about to become the toast of London."

"Even given my father's presence?" Roberta said faintly.

"Of course," Jemma said. "And Mrs. Grope. Do you know, Roberta, I'm not sure that Mrs. Grope entirely shares your papa's enthusiasm for her future career as a notorious courtesan?"

"It is my belief that she would like to marry him," Roberta said. "I don't think he understands that, though."

"Men never see things," Jemma said with a sigh. "Their marriage would cause a terrible scandal."

"Because of her loss of character?"

"Well, yes," Jemma said. "Look at Elizabeth Armistead, Fox's mistress. He openly professes his affection, and I'm quite certain that he'll marry her at some point. The bets in White's have been running in her favor these four years. Even so, she is not received at or invited to most events."

"Ah."

"The *ton* is a brutal barometer of acceptability, I assure you. I shall have to invite some respectable women to dinner, but I must speak to Beaumont first."

"About the dinner?"

Jemma seemed to have rethought whatever it was she was about to say, because she changed the subject entirely. "A far more crucial problem," she said, "is which mantuamaker should receive your patronage."

Roberta thought gratefully of the roll of banknotes her papa had given her. It made everything so much easier; she didn't feel like a horrid pauper, dressing in Jemma's clothing.

"I would suggest that we use a French-woman," Jemma said. "It's not that I am inherently prejudiced against my country-women. Well . . . perhaps I am."

Roberta burst out laughing, and in the ensuing delightful conversation, she quite forgot about the question of who was to be invited to the dinner party. "I should like a balloon hat. Do you know them, Jemma?"

Jemma nodded. "In Paris they are called *lunardi.* I'm not sure whether it will suit you, dearest. All those feathers . . . so much trimming!"

"I saw one in the park yesterday made of rose-colored French gauze with a wide brim," Roberta said. "A young lady was wearing it quite low on one side, and high on the other."

"Ah," Jemma said. "That does sound interesting. The one I have is all Italian tiffany pinned in loose puckers around the brim. I liked it very much, but then the wire poked out of the brim and stuck me in the ear one day and I never wore it again."

"Of course, the brim is wired," Roberta said. "How clever!"

"We'll address the dinner party later," Jemma said. "I think we should go to Bond

Street this very moment."

Jemma didn't think about the dinner party again until her husband appeared to play his part of the game with her. He moved as quickly as ever, knight to Queen's Bishop Three, but Jemma was aware of a slight feeling of unease. She took her time. Finally she moved a knight to King's Bishop Three.

"Interesting," Elijah said, giving her move a lightning quick glance. She was learning a great deal about her husband from their game. He seemed to grasp the connotations of her moves in two seconds. In truth, the power of his mind was astonishing.

"I thought to give a dinner party this week," she said, sitting back. He looked less tired today, although there was a deep-down exhaustion in his eyes that she found rather worrying.

"We haven't had people to sup here since you left for Paris," he said. He appeared to have forgotten about the offensive presence of Mrs. Grope. "Fowle will be ecstatic."

"I thought we could come up with a guest list between the two of us," Jemma said, "excluding anyone who would make an issue of not attending due to the marquess's companion. Harriet will lend us consequence and she won't make a fuss. Who would you like to invite?"

"From the House?"

"No! That is, not unless the person was a particular friend of yours."

"A friend," Beaumont said, almost as if he were testing the word on his tongue.

"Speaking of friends, or rather former friends," Jemma said, watching him, "I shall invite Villiers, as he is courting Lady Roberta."

Beaumont shrugged. His smile had a touch of wryness. "A prevarication? My distinct impression is that he is courting my wife, if the word can be used so."

"Most gentlemen are courting three or four people at the same time. Courting is merely an activity, like eating."

"Except that the dish in question is you," he said. But he sounded weary, not really interested, and certainly not jealous.

"So we have the marquess and Mrs. Grope —"

"Mrs. Grope?"

Jemma smiled at his bark of laughter. "Didn't Fowle mention her name? Roberta is not entirely certain that Mr. Grope ever existed. At any rate, we have eight of us, including Roberta, Damon and Villiers. It would be best if we added two."

"I met someone interesting at your ball,"

Beaumont said. "Miss Charlotte Tatlock."

Jemma frowned. "One of the daughters of Sir Patrick Tatlock? I have only the slimmest acquaintance with them."

"She seemed remarkably intelligent," he said, pushing himself up from the table.

"Are there other persons whom you would like to see at the table? Caro shall make arrangements for me, Beaumont, but I assure you that I shall curb her imagination. She can play the pianoforte for us afterwards."

He shook his head. "The devil with my reputation. If Pitt can't see that I'm hardly in the debauched company of the Prince of Wales and his friends, then he can bar me his company."

"He's no fool."

"I go to meet him now," he said with a rueful smile, made his leg and departed.

Jemma went to her little writing desk. It was frustrating to realize that she was so far out of the current of English society that she didn't know instantly who would be so overcome by curiosity as to be unable to resist the idea of dining in company with Mrs. Grope. In the end, she invited Corbin. He would never chatter about the event, even if she placed him next to Mrs. Grope.

Her husband moved his chess pieces as if there were no other move than the one he had just thought of; Villiers was far more deliberative. Beaumont calculated in a heartbeat; Villiers brooded. As a player, he was very similar to her. He clearly spent a good deal of the day thinking of dazzling possibilities. He was a swashbuckling player, and she was something of the same. Elijah was some other kind of player: taut, deliberate, incredibly fast.

Brigitte brought in the Duke of Villiers's card. "But I must tell you, my lady, that Joseph accompanies his master. He just told me that he asked, but he thinks no one in the household knows of the affair with Lady Caroline, even the duke's valet. His Grace, the Duke of Villiers, plays it very quiet to the chest, he says."

"Close to the chest," Jemma said absentmindedly. It made sense from what she knew of Villiers. He would never amiably discuss his *affaires* with a valet. "The *écharpe* cloak is yours, Brigitte. I do hope that your acquaintance with Joseph has not been too tedious."

Brigitte dimpled. "He has still to take me to these gardens. I am finding that red hair is perhaps not such a grave defect."

Villiers appeared wearing an extraordinary cloak embroidered in peacock feathers. Jemma eyed it and said nothing. He was flaunting something . . . what? His costume seemed almost a slap in the face to those who felt men should dress more soberly than did women.

She took a pawn with her queen; he moved a knight to Queen's Bishop Three; they both settled back in their chairs.

"How was your morning?" she asked.

"Terrifyingly out of the mundane."

She looked up. "Oh?"

"I pensioned my mistress."

Jemma thought about that for a moment and decided that he wouldn't mind a frank question. "How much does it cost to do such a thing?"

"It's a matter of balancing economics and affection," he said. "I am fond of her, and more to the point, she lived in a house of mine for three years."

"Was she distraught?"

"Not at all. It was all amicable, which told me that I should have done it a year ago."

"I think it must be tiresome to be a man, when it comes to these matters," Jemma said. "After all, in the last three years you have had, one must presume, some little interludes with gentlewomen of the *ton*, and at the same time, your mistress was waiting for you."

"I'm not so old yet that you need question my prowess."

She smiled faintly at that. " 'Tis the emotions that would tire me."

"Sometimes it does feel a bit complicated. Sophia is a courtesan to be reckoned with, you see. She games, she kisses, she has many demands."

Jemma toyed with a chess piece. "And thus you gave her up?"

"Oh no, I gave her up because I plan to marry." Villiers watched her closely to see whether she would show signs of jealousy.

She surprised him again, smiling at him with true appreciation in her eyes. "Then you did just the right thing."

He gaped at her. "Yes?"

"I feel that a gentleman should no longer pay for women's company once he takes a wife," she said. "I find the practice distasteful at the best of times, but dishonorable once vows are said."

He swallowed his astonishment. "Rather old-fashioned of you, isn't it?" he asked.

"Actually, I think it is the future," she said. "The Hellfire Club, with all their *fêtes* and nymphs . . . they're dying, though they don't see it yet. France was the same. The Queen herself, Marie Antoinette, is turning to settled domesticity, I promise you."

"So your husband's party will bring with

them sober behavior and settled mores? Wives who play at dairy maids rather than flamboyant courtesans?"

She laughed. "My husband and his set are as likely to have mistresses as men of other parties. They simply do not flaunt their affections, at least not as much as does Fox."

"Fox's Elizabeth is a remarkable creature."

"I met her in Paris and was most impressed."

"So I thought I would join the settled ones by marrying your ward," he said, watching her through his eyelashes.

Her smile was disappointingly genuine. In fact, Villiers was aware of an interior whisper suggesting that his revenge didn't appear particularly effective. Jemma didn't seem to give a damn whether he married or no.

"You could not make a better choice. Roberta is remarkably beautiful, as you know, but she is also intelligent and witty. The only possible defect is that she doesn't play chess." Jemma made a funny face.

"Ah, but I have *you* for that," he said, touching one of her delicate fingers. It had come to him in the middle of the night that what he really wanted from this was not, in truth, the match itself. It was she. He wanted her, that deep intelligence, and the way she sparked into sudden laughter, the

307

pure elegance of the way she moved and spoke.

Not to mention the fact that she was a brilliant chess player, a fact that fired him with a roaring lust, deep in his loins. In fact, the emotion was so ferocious that he didn't dare look at it too closely.

"I'm enjoying this," he remarked, watching as she shook down her ruffs. "Which is a terrifying thought."

"Why? I always enjoy well-played chess, even when I'm losing."

"The chess, certainly. But also" — he leaned forward — "talking to you."

Jemma hid a smile. Villiers was most seductive when he was the most straightforward, if only he knew it. She felt unshaken by his practiced raillery about her ruffs and her beauty: but when he grinned at her, and told her frankly about pensioning his mistress — then, she was in danger.

Yet she had no intention of succumbing to Villiers's wiles. All the more so now that he was almost affianced to Roberta.

She met his eyes and saw disappointment flash.

"You unman me," he said gravely. "You think me capable of such disloyalty to a friend?"

"And you think me foolish if you wish me

to believe that you have no interest in me due to my possible marriage to your ward."

She didn't answer that, and he felt a flash of anger at his own stupidity in declaring himself. Did he really want to marry? Of course, he would have no hesitation dropping the country miss as quickly as he picked her up.

Yet Roberta was exquisite. And capable of a witty rejoinder, which was rare. She was young, likely fertile, and all the rest of it. He needed an heir, for God's sake. Plus, his mistress was gone now. He needed a bed-partner.

"So you won't have me?"

Jemma smiled at him, and her beauty was almost like a blow in the face. "You're getting married."

"Perhaps," he said. "The lady may not have me." He knew that was a falsehood as well as Jemma did.

It was damnably true that it is hard to desire a person who wants you. Roberta made no secret of her desire for him. Her eyes grew slightly dreamy at the very sight of him.

He preferred Jemma's clear-eyed look.

It was also bitterly true that a person who doesn't want you is twice as desirable.

CHAPTER 22

The invitations were delivered by footmen.

"I simply can't believe you've been invited!" May said with a little gasp, looking at the card her sister held. "Do you have some acquaintance with the duchess of which I knew nothing?"

Charlotte shook her head. "The duke asked me to dance at the ball, but I never spoke to Her Grace."

"The duke?" May's round face look scandalized. "Why on earth would he invite you?" She peered at the card. "It all looks most respectable, doesn't it? I would have expected her to announce a Feast of Venus, or some such thing."

"I doubt they would invite me if they wished for nymphs," Charlotte said dryly.

"True. But how queer it is to invite you and not me. Don't you think that's queer? You don't think that he's thinking of setting you up as — as an *intimate!*" Her voice was horrified.

Charlotte allowed herself just one longing thought about the duke's lovely, tired eyes before she said, "Don't be a goose, May. Do I look like the sort of woman whom the duke would set up as his courtesan?"

"I should hope not."

"At least my life would be more interesting than it is now," Charlotte said, just to provoke her.

But May was not a bad sort, and having got over her first surprise at the invitation, was beginning to count its blessings. "You must have a new gown," she said firmly. "We'll send a message to Madame Hayes and tell her that we need that gown you ordered last month by Thursday."

"She won't do it."

"Yes, she will. She will once she hears that you are invited to this particular party," May cried. She was getting giddy with it now and waved the invitation over her head like a flag. "Perhaps *Town and Country* will produce sketches of every person invited; they might well. How exciting it all is!"

And Charlotte had to admit that it was exciting.

She kept her own preparations for the event secret from her sister; she sent a footman out to buy every political newspaper and commentary he could find.

The Duchess of Berrow's response to the invitation was rather less celebratory. With a sigh she changed her gown, had horses put to the carriage and set out for town. A mere hour or two later the butler ushered Jemma into the drawing room where Harriet waited for her.

"Darling," Jemma said, "you're just in time. I've decided to catalog all the paintings of Judith and Holofernes in the house and I would adore some help."

Harriet rose to her feet. As always, the force of Jemma's personality made her feel like a faded cutout, a cartoon from the illustrated papers. "I came to ask about this," she said, taking out her invitation.

Jemma grinned at her, leaned closer and said in a conspiratorial whisper, "Our plans are in full force!"

"The chess game? Are you winning?" Harriet asked hopefully.

"I have every expectation," Jemma said. "In fact, though it's vain of me to say so, I would bet on myself. Despair is circling Villiers on all sides. He's going to ask for Lady Roberta's hand in marriage at this very dinner party."

Harriet's mouth fell open. "Villiers? Getting *married?*"

"I can't think of a better revenge, can you?"

"But — But — are you saying that you don't like your ward?" Harriet asked, bewildered. "I thought she was a lovely person, whom —"

"Oh, she is," Jemma interrupted. "In fact, Villiers is extremely lucky to have her. No, it's marriage itself that is a punishment. He has no understanding of the state, you know. He thinks his life will hardly change: I can see that in his eyes. He's a babe in the woods."

"Not everyone's marriage is unpleasant," Harriet ventured.

"You think that I should not extend the example of my marriage to all such unions?"

"Precisely."

"Well, look at your marriage," Jemma suggested. "It was the best of matches; you both had great love for each other." She stopped.

"And?" Harriet asked dangerously. It was one thing if she bemoaned the rift between herself and Benjamin, but —

"Were there not great moments of humiliation?" Jemma asked.

Humiliating moments raced through Harriet's mind in an exhausting stream. "Yes," she said faintly.

"It's part of marriage. Inherent to the state of matrimony."

"So Villiers will be at this dinner party," Harriet said. "And I — I am to be there too? I can't."

"You must," Jemma said, taking her arm and walking into the entryway. "Now we are going to walk through this entire house and spy out all the paintings of Judith. Fowle, will you follow us and note down the pieces?"

Harriet tried to swallow her frustration. "Jemma," she hissed, "must your butler follow us? I just told you that I am not going to attend your dinner party."

"Yes, you are," Jemma said, smiling down at her. "I need you. And I need Fowle to make an inventory of these paintings."

"Why must I attend the dinner?"

"Because my brother is near to making a fool of himself. Oh look, there's a painting of Judith in the corridor. I hadn't even seen it before. Fowle, did you mark this one down?"

Harriet glanced back and saw the butler making a notation on a piece of foolscap.

"What is your brother doing?" she whispered.

"Making an ass of himself, as I said,"

314

Jemma replied, in a perfectly normal tone of voice. "Mooning over Roberta, if the truth be known. In fact, from the look in his eyes, he's halfway to thinking he's passionately in love. And I can't have that."

"Because Roberta must marry Villiers."

"Precisely."

"Well, if she's marrying Villiers —"

"No one in their right mind would marry Villiers if Damon entered the lists," Jemma said impatiently.

"You *are* his sister," Harriet pointed out, feeling a bit like laughing for the first time all day. "Don't you think you might overestimate Damon's good parts just slightly?"

"Not at all. It's an impartial judgment. Roberta doesn't play chess, so Villiers's talent is of no attraction. In fact, I'm not quite sure what she does find so attractive in him. But I also know that Damon is kissing her in the odd moment here or there, and I certainly don't want him to muddle Villiers's proposal, or Roberta's thinking about it. So you must dance attendance on him, Harriet. I am counting on you."

"I don't wish to be in the same room with Villiers."

"I'll put you at opposite ends of the table," Jemma said. "Ah, here's another. Particularly bloodthirsty, isn't it? And she put it in the morning room, in the place of honor."

They both gazed for a moment at the triumphant Judith, holding up a head. The artist appeared to have given special attention to the neck of poor Holofernes. Jemma shuddered a little. "I shall never understand the dowager duchess: never."

"When did Beaumont's father die?" Harriet asked.

"I believe he was ten years old. Perhaps nine."

"So he essentially grew up with his mother."

"That fact would go far to making me feel sorry for him," Jemma said. "But of course there's no such emotion between man and wife."

She turned away. "There's another one in the ladies' retiring room. It gave poor Lady Fibble quite a shock during our ball, or so she told me. Apparently she thought that it resembled Beaumont. I devoutly hope that is not the case. Or if it is, I assume that the portrait is of the late duke."

It was Harriet's turn to shudder.

CHAPTER 23

April 17

Day six of the Villiers/Beaumont chess matches

Charlotte could tell before she put her slipper from the carriage that Beaumont House was surrounded by throngs of people waiting to see who would enter. She took a deep breath. She was not used to traveling among the very highest circles of the *ton.* She and May were girls grown long in the tooth, hanging on the fringes with their inadequate dowries and lack of powerful friends. They were well bred, so were invited everywhere. But they didn't stand out. They never *took.*

Except, Charlotte reminded herself again, that May had now been taken by Mr. Muddle, and next year Charlotte would be doing the season on her own. It was all so dismaying that one couldn't think about it too clearly. It was like thinking about turned seams and orphaned children.

She gave herself a little shake. She looked her very best. Charlotte knew exactly what that meant: not like a ravishing goddess, but like the profile on a Roman coin. May always said her nose was refined. It was a nice shape, but far too long. "It makes you look intelligent," Mama had said. "No man wants an insipid miss for a wife."

It seemed they didn't want a Roman coin either.

The crowd around the carriage pushed and juggled as she stepped from the carriage. Most of them were trying to figure out who she was.

"That ain't Lady Sarah," she heard someone say. "Lady Sarah doesn't have —"

Charlotte was sure that Lady Sarah didn't have a Roman nose. She pulled herself taller. Her gown was of pale pink crêpe and showed off her skin and her dark blue eyes. Her hair was perfectly groomed, and as high as fashion demanded. She was the very best she could be, and that had to be enough.

"I got it — Tatlock," she heard someone say loudly, just as she began to climb the stairs to the front door. The butler bowed so low that she almost expected him to topple over.

"Miss Charlotte Tatlock," he said, backing away. The house was surprisingly quiet. "If you please," the butler said, after her wrap had been removed, "would you prefer to visit a retiring room, or would you like to join the other guests in the drawing room?"

Charlotte was, frankly, too frightened to gaze at herself again. It was best to get it over with. Surely the dinner would be large, and there would be people she knew. She could find a comforting matron and stay in her shadow.

But it was not a large party, and there was no comforting matron to be seen. Instead there was just a small cluster of people standing about holding glasses.

Charlotte almost ran, but the Duke of Beaumont turned, and smiled.

She walked forward.

One moment Roberta was chatting with Mrs. Grope about the feathers she had bought at the bazaar, and the next Villiers had swept her away to the far side of the room.

"Surely one might keep a polite distance from women of her caliber?" he said.

She looked at him.

"I realize it is difficult under the circumstances." And then, without pause: "I've never asked anyone to marry me."

Unless Roberta was mistaken, the Duke

of Villiers was about to ask her to marry him. Was doing it at this very moment, as a matter of fact. She had an unnerving sense of watching a play rather than performing in it. "I trust that new experiences are not always unpleasant ones," she said.

"I am surprised by my own pleasure in it."

It flashed into her mind that he seemed remarkably unconcerned by the question of *her* pleasure, but it was a disloyal thought, so she put an expression of pleased acceptance on her face.

Somewhat to her surprise, he did it properly. In one smooth movement, Villiers dropped to his right knee, took her hand and said, "Will you do me the great honor of becoming my duchess, Lady Roberta?"

She swallowed nervously and said, "Yes," and that was that.

He kissed her hand afterwards.

Of course it wasn't a kiss like one of Damon's wicked kisses. It was a perfectly respectable brush of his lips.

She shivered, and there was a ghost of a smile on his lips that made her feel a little vexed. The smile seemed to imply that young women always shivered when he kissed them.

"I asked your father for his permission this

afternoon," he said, rising to his feet with the lithe beauty of a large cat, like a tiger.

"Oh," Roberta said, wondering how her father had managed to keep that a secret from her.

"I requested that he not inform you," Villiers said. "Although you can hardly have had doubts about my intentions."

"Thank you for the painting of the mousetrap," she said. And then added hastily: "That is, the picture of the mouse — the picture of the *girl,* holding the mousetrap!"

He laughed. "Wasn't it a marvelous vignette, then?"

"Yes, indeed."

"Oh, come now. I know you already to be a creature of wit to match your beauty. Surely you have more to say than 'Yes, indeed'?"

Roberta swallowed a flash of annoyance. "I gather you would like me to comment on your metaphor? I found it interesting that the mousetrap contained a mouse. In fact, given the presence of a very interested looking cat in the corner of the painting, one could say that she was saving the poor wee mouse from being eaten."

He grinned at her and that smile fired desire in her heart again, for the man she'd glimpsed in the inn, for the deep weight of his silver coat, the reserve in his eyes, the sense —

She realized suddenly that she had never imagined him as domesticated. As truly married to her. She thought of him as a wild animal whom she planned to trap. And by walking straight to her hand, he seemed more docile and less — less wild somehow.

Perhaps she wanted the feral cat, and not the neat little mouse, sitting in a cage.

"So you are rescuing me, are you?" he said with a chuckle. "And what would the cat represent, do you think?"

"Age, perhaps," she said, giving in to a wish to make him sorry for making her feel young and stupid.

"Alas, age is a predator from which none of us escape."

But she knew herself to be young and he at least ten years older, and so she merely turned her head, as if it would be petty to respond. 'Twas impolite, but he made no comment.

It was better, she told herself, that he learn not to condescend to her. She was aware of a shocking urge to be rude to him, which was not proper behavior for a woman who has just accepted a gentleman's hand in marriage.

On that thought she smiled up at him, as

322

if he were a knight come to rescue her from a dour dragon. There was an answering spark in his eyes. As if he realized that she held the trap in her hand, and only she could operate the latch.

She gave him another melting smile. There was more than one way to bait a trap, after all.

CHAPTER 24

Damon was well aware that he was consumed by lust. It was a dangerous state. He'd never before experienced it as a sort of waking fever dream, as the past few days when he walked the halls of Beaumont House merely so that he could catch a whiff of Roberta's perfume, or see the flutter of her dress retreat around a corner.

Of course she was a devil of a woman, and had gotten herself engaged to Villiers, for God's sake. He'd been talking to the Duchess of Berrow when Villiers pulled Roberta to the side of the room and dropped on one knee. There, in front of all of them, although no one seemed to notice except himself and Harriet, who'd fussed at him until he stopped staring and escorted her to a chair.

It was typical of Villiers. He had no need, apparently, no wish to make his marital arrangements in private.

It was the first time in Damon's life that

he had ever felt homicidal. And yet it wasn't Villiers whose life trembled in the balance. It was hers. He had to have her. And yet . . .

Her eyes glowed as she smiled up at Villiers, that roué who would doubtless give her disease, and surely despair. She had ignored his bastards, the mistress he flaunted at the opera, the meaningless liaisons in which he had so freely engaged. There was something about him that had shattered her brain.

And that — *that* — made Damon feel deranged.

He'd never felt this emotion for a woman. He wasn't that sort of man. He had a clear sense of himself. He loved Teddy more than was seemly; he knew that. He should leave Teddy to the care of servants, and he couldn't seem to do so, and yet he was probably ruining his son in the process.

A child is like a good horse, he told himself. You should always leave a horse to be broken by a stable master. And yet somehow that was just what he was afraid of — that a nursemaid would break Teddy's spirit behind his back, when he wasn't looking.

But to return to the subject: he was a decent enough fellow. He'd never killed anyone in a duel, though he'd had reason and opportunity. He had far more money than people thought, given that Jemma played games of strategy on a board and he preferred to move his Bills of Exchange and Bills of Goods through the markets, as adroitly as any rook.

So why was he maddened — absolutely maddened — by the fact that a young woman had fallen in love and promised to marry another? Roberta thought he was all light and laughter, with no dark streak. She had no idea how furious she made him.

She wasn't his. She belonged to Villiers, and that was all there was to it. The fact that the very sound of Villiers's name made his stomach roil, made him think of the exquisite weight of a fencing steel . . . that was beside the point. If Roberta wanted Villiers, and not him, there was nothing he could do about it.

He had lost.

Unfortunately, he had suddenly realized that Roberta was the first thing in his life that he had ever truly wanted.

He would simply have to get used to it. Likely he only wanted her because she didn't want him.

Like a magnet to the true north, he strolled toward her and Villiers. "I believe congratulations are in order," he said, making a leg to the duke.

"The honor is all mine," Villiers responded, languid as always.

The butler announced the arrival of a young lady, Miss Charlotte Tatlock. Villiers glanced over his shoulder. "One must suppose Her Grace has marked this young lady for your companionship, Gryffyn." He said it politely enough, but Damon could see the No Poaching signs going up. Roberta belonged to Villiers now.

Damon walked off with a bright smile and a discovery.

The moment he knew of Teddy's existence, he understood that his life was about to change. The fact that Teddy's mother wanted nothing to do with her child did not particularly influence his decision. Teddy was his.

He just discovered a great, second truth.

Villiers could post all the signs he wished, but Damon was going to take exactly what he wanted.

Roberta.

He didn't give a damn what she thought about it, or what Villiers thought about it. She was wrong.

She was his.

CHAPTER 25

Charlotte found herself seated at the right hand of her host, which was a signal honor. The duchess had placed Lady Roberta at the other end of the table in celebration of her engagement to the Duke of Villiers, between her future husband and her father, the Marquess of Wharton and Malmesbury. On Charlotte's right was a gentleman named Lord Corbin. Across from her was another duchess, whose name Charlotte didn't quite catch. Berrow, perhaps? But she wasn't at all terrifying for someone so noble. In fact, she reminded Charlotte of a nice moorhen, although perhaps she was more of a mourning dove, dressed in soft gray. She smiled at Charlotte very kindly, though she said nothing to her directly.

In truth, the group was so small that conversations flared everywhere, in disregard of all the rules she had learned regarding proper etiquette at the dining table.

Her end of the table was quickly embroiled in a political battle. May had begged her to stay away from politics, but it wasn't her fault. No sooner had she sat down than the duke informed the Earl of Gryffyn, the duchess's brother, that she was one of his staunchest opponents.

And then, when she turned red with embarrassment and started to explain herself, the earl just laughed and started to egg her on. "I'm a great supporter of Fox," he said. "And I like the Prince of Wales. What's not to like in a man who boasts of eating twenty-four hens' eggs at one sitting? If I haven't taken my seat in the House, it's only because I'd hate to rub my brother-in-law's nose in his own foolishness."

She couldn't go along with that, so she switched sides and defended the duke's recent speech to the House about the lunacy of providing the Prince with an allowance of 100,000 pounds per year. But when the duke's eyes lit up, she felt it only fair to point out the reverse as well, that as the Duke of Cornwall, the Prince was entitled to duchy revenues as well as money from the Civil List.

The duke groaned. The Duchess of Berrow changed the subject with a comment about the need for parliamentary reforms in

Ireland, and before she knew it, the meal flew by.

The other end of the table was having a far more sedate conversation. Most of the time the marquess seemed to be reciting poetry. The verses sounded rather awful, but then they all started quoting snippets of verse at each other. She happened to meet the duke's eyes during a pause in their conversation and saw perfect comprehension there.

"I haven't read a book of poetry in years," he said, leaning over to her.

"We ought to have," she said, feeling laughter bubbling up at the pure pleasure of it. "We are very ill-prepared for a cultural conversation. Not even Thomas Gray, Your Grace?"

"Not even!" he said cheerfully.

"O ye pens and O ye pencils," declaimed the marquess from the other end of the table, *"And all ye scribbling utensils, say in what words and in what meter, shall unfeigned admiration greet her!"*

"I can deduce that was a couplet," the duke said, his eyes dancing. He was so beautiful, Charlotte thought dimly. And so brilliant.

His duchess was apparently enjoying this poetry; she was clapping her hands.

"I just figured out that it rhymes," the duke said to her. "*In what meter and greet her.*" His raised eyebrow was enough to send her into a storm of giggles. Luckily, Lord Corbin intervened to ask about William Whitehead, who was the current Poet Laureate but had refused to write poetry that conformed to government policy.

She turned away from the duke with a palpable pang. This will never do, she told herself. He's married and he's a duke. You're nothing more than an old maid, for all you somehow found yourself at this party. But she knew . . .

She knew how she found herself at the party.

Beaumont had asked to have her. The fact was like a warm blanket on a chilly night. For the first time in her life, a man was claiming her presence.

He was married, that was true.

His wife was one of the most beautiful women in Europe — and yet he had asked her to supper.

The duchess doesn't understand the political life, Charlotte told herself.

She liked paltry poetry, with terrible rhymes.

She doesn't understand him.

■ ■ ■ ■

On the other end of the table, the Marquess of Wharton and Malmesbury was enjoying himself just as much as was Charlotte, though for rather different reasons. For one thing, he had his beloved daughter to his right, and his beloved Mrs. Grope to his left. He knew himself to be a rather simple man, at heart. He expressed himself in dense rhyme and eloquent meter . . . but inside he knew that the subjects of his poetry sprang from his heart. His daughter, his beloved, his cat, cream pastries now and then.

It wasn't in his nature to keep emotions to himself. "I am not sure that I am ready to give you up," he told Roberta. She was so terrifyingly beautiful, this daughter of his: far more Margaret's than his, and yet poor Margaret had not lived to see her grow to the blossom of her womanhood. "When you were a baby, I wrote an ode to the fold of your eyelid. What will I do without your eyelids to look at every day?"

"Oh, Papa," she said, looking fussed, as she always did when he praised her.

"You'll see what I mean when you have a child of your own," he told her. Now he saw, of course, that he couldn't have kept her in the country forever. How could he think to deny his darling girl the pleasure of having her own children? Still . . . he looked across the table at her chosen husband. A duke. One could hardly complain about that. And yet there was something old and degenerate about Villiers, something of a tired soul, that the marquess did not like. He couldn't imagine how to say it to Roberta.

If only Margaret had lived. Mrs. Grope, much though he loved her flamboyant ways, had none of Margaret's subtlety. And she wasn't Roberta's mother either. In fact . . .

"Should I have raised you in a different way?" he asked, struck to the heart by sudden anguish. Mrs. Grope looked rather garish beside the ladies at the table. Lord Corbin was kindly speaking to her about the stage, and she looked like a bedazzling peacock in comparison to his sober attire.

"What do you mean, Papa?" Roberta asked.

"Should I have spared you the company of Mrs. Grope?" he whispered hoarsely. "Or Selina, darling Selina?"

She blinked at him over a forkful of green beans. "Papa, do you mean to say that you are having a change of heart about your household arrangements, *now?*"

"Why not now?" he enquired.

"Because I am twenty-one! Perhaps you should have had these qualms when I was fourteen and Selina waved goodbye to her traveling group."

"I was in love," he said, shamefaced. "Your mother had been gone for two years, and I fell in love."

She smiled a little at that, and his heart lightened. "I know you did, Papa. I know you were in love."

"But," he continued in a low voice, "it isn't because of that, because of my lack of convention that you've chosen Villiers, is it?"

"Of course not, Papa," she said. But she didn't meet his eyes.

Villiers might be a perfectly acceptable man in his own way. But he wasn't the one for Roberta. He was a cold blooded man.

"If you change your mind about this marriage," he said, "there will be many other men eager to marry you, Roberta. You've barely been in London a week. Just think who you might meet."

"Papa!" she squealed, with a glance to her right. "Don't say such things. I shan't change my mind."

"Are you quite certain of that?"

"Of course."

The marquess tried to imagine himself stopping by for a friendly supper with his daughter once she was the Duchess of Villiers and he knew without a second thought that it would never happen. Villiers was a man of rigid propriety. He would never invite an aging and foolish marquess to his house, except for those occasions on which relatives could not be excluded. Christmas, perhaps.

He felt a tear roll down his cheek. It was bad enough when he lost Margaret, but he had had his delightful scrap of a daughter to tell him that his poetry was terrible, just as her mother used to do. Without Roberta . . .

Another tear followed the first. Roberta's hand crept into his. "Papa, I promise to visit you," she said, so sweetly that he could hardly bear it. "I can't stay at home forever."

"I didn't mean you to do that," he said. "And yet I have made so many mistakes! So many mistakes!"

Suddenly he realized that all conversation around them had ceased. There was a look in the Duke of Villiers's eyes that suggested he wouldn't even be invited for Christmas dinner. Mrs. Grope, bless her heart, was eating her peas with her knife. Perhaps he should have . . .

"It must be so hard to say goodbye to a child," the Duchess of Beaumont said kindly. "I can imagine how painful it must be."

The marquess cast a guilty look at Roberta. She hated it when he made a scene, and sure enough, she was staring down at her lap. Hastily, he dashed away his tears. "When I think of all the unfeeling things Roberta has said about my poetry, my heart lightens," he said. "Do you remember, child, when I read you my masterpiece, virtually my only published masterpiece, and you said it was twaddle?"

To his sorrow, Roberta looked even more downcast. "I'm sorry, Papa," she said.

"It *was* twaddle!" he said gaily. "Utter twaddle! I read it over the other day and realized what a mistake it had been. I tried an experiment," he told the unexpressive, uninterested face of Villiers. "To write an entire sonnet, fourteen lines, with one rhyme only. Of course, Shakespeare had a scheme worked out that allowed him seven rhymes. The great Petrarchan sonneteers sometimes made do with fewer. But I think I am the only English poet to write a sonnet with one rhyme!"

"What was your rhyme?" the Duchess of Beaumont asked.

"I had to choose a rhyme with many variants," he said, "so I settled on bear."

"Ah, a nature poem," Villiers said, boredom dripping from his voice. "I would guess that the *bear* went to its *lair.*"

The marquess reminded himself that he was a grown man, and fools have always made fun of literature. "You're absolutely right," he said with dignity. "There are many useful rhymes, such as *fair, mare,* and *pear.*"

Villiers looked to his left, at Roberta. "But your daughter thought the poem was rubbish, did she? How extremely unkind of her."

His comment spoke volumes, to the marquess's mind. This man would never be able to understand a line of poetry. It wasn't that he wanted a poet for a son-in-law, but: "A man who doesn't understand poetry, cannot live poetry," he stated, hoping Roberta would understand him.

"Living poetry has never been an active pursuit of mine," Villiers responded promptly.

Roberta cleared her throat. The marquess remembered how much she hated philosophical statements. The last thing he wanted to do was embarrass her on such a special evening. His heart dropped again.

"My father was speaking metaphorically,"

she said to Villiers.

"I know of metaphors," Villiers said, glancing at Roberta with an indifference that shocked her father to the bone. "But I fail to understand the concept."

"Try to think of it as a person who lives in contact with great minds," she said to him and, gentle though her voice was, there was a sting in it. "Perhaps there were great chess players of the past, but they have left no record. There have been great poets, and we are able to enjoy their thoughts still."

The marquess sat, frozen. Roberta had defended him! Her father's chest hurt from the joy of it.

Villiers took a bite of chicken, presumably because he was so floored by his fiancée's brilliant riposte that he could think of nothing to say.

The duchess said in a very soothing way, "Who is your favorite poet, Lord Wharton?"

"Shakespeare," he said. "I am pedestrian in my admiration for the man, but to live in Shakespeare's words, to walk in his steps, gives me reason to continue." He caught sight of Mrs. Grope's plumage wagging at his shoulder and added hastily, "Along with my deep devotion to Mrs. Grope, of course."

"Of course," Villiers agreed. There was

something very unpleasant about his tone. The marquess didn't dare look at his poor daughter. Though he had been a terrible papa, and embarrassed her time and again, she still loathed it when people made fun of him.

So this time he took her hand. Because though he'd told her many a time that laughter didn't hurt him, he knew she didn't really believe him.

The sad thing was that she had never grasped the truly important thing: laughter can't hurt someone, but cold indifference can.

CHAPTER 26

The Duke of Villiers had made up his mind. While it would be acceptable to marry Roberta, he may have made a wee error. In truth, he'd be just as happy *not* to marry the lady. He certainly would rather not have her father as an intimate. His engagement didn't seem to have made a damn bit of difference to Jemma. In short, he may have made a mistake.

It was unfortunate that he came to his conclusion approximately two hours after issuing a formal proposal. But it was the work of a moment to launch a stratagem that would change the complexion of the board as it was laid out before him.

Unless he missed his bet, his old friend Elijah was flirting with a new piece, a pawn, a pawn, a veritable pawn and yet . . . who was he not to admit that pawns could be deliciously useful in their own way?

He would send Elijah's queen careening

toward the opposite side of the board. He would then sacrifice his own queen . . . it was all in the nature of the game.

"Would you care to accompany me to the library?" he asked his fiancée.

Roberta came to her feet with a pretty show of grace. She was an elegant young woman, he had to admit. They walked to the library.

"I merely wanted to make certain that we were in agreement about certain aspects of our marriage," he said, helping her to a brocaded couch.

"I am all attention," she said.

He blinked. In another woman, the comment might have an unpleasantly satirical edge, but she was smiling at him.

"It's a simple thing," he said. "Having to do with those unpleasant bits of law called torts."

"Torts?"

"Breach of contract."

"I trust you are not planning to break our engagement?" She asked it with perfect courtesy, but her eyes narrowed. Perhaps this marriage would have been the making of him. Yet it would be better to let it go.

"I would never break our engagement," he said. Such an action would be rash and clumsy, opening him up to attack by pieces not yet in play, such as solicitors. Yet it should be a matter of no particular difficulty to cause the lady to withdraw from it herself. That was the nature of a brilliant game . . . to put forward one's pieces and see what came of them.

"The particular breach I was thinking of comes after marriage," he said, "and has to do with *spurious issue* versus *lawful issue.*"

"Bastard children," she stated.

"I would prefer — nay, I must insist — that you have none."

"I had no plans to do so." She was silent for a moment.

"I trust this was not too unromantic?" Villiers enquired.

"Indeed, Your Grace, it shows a decidedly unromantic lack of faith in my character."

"I meant no imputation about your character. Did you think that we would have some sort of conventional union, like a pair of bakers who fall in love over a floury board and swear never to part?"

She shook her head. "Not exactly."

Roberta forced herself to sit for a second and collect her thoughts. Her future husband clearly loved the subtleties of rhetoric and law. "Will you do me the same honor?" She raised her head and looked straight into his eyes. "My understanding is that you have *spurious issue* with several women. Are you intending to create more of these children after our marriage is celebrated?"

"If you're asking me to start giving a damn what the world thinks, I won't and I can't. I never have."

Roberta took a deep breath. "I am asking you to be faithful to me," she said clearly.

Villiers was silent. She watched the dark shadow of his eyelashes, his swarthy, almost harsh features. "Faithfulness has always struck me as an unreasonable concept," he said, finally. "I would greatly prefer if you were faithful until we raised a brat or two for the estate. It seems unreasonable to give another man's son my grandfather's land. But a clever woman can always prevent conception."

"And after that?"

"I would give you precisely the same freedom I would take for myself. I would do you the great honor of swearing — on my honor — that I will never fall in love with a woman. That any attachments would be a matter of impulse and pleasure, never of true intimacy."

She could hardly understand what he was saying.

"You, of course, would need no excuse other than *les caprices de jolie femme,* a beautiful woman's right to commit a folly," he continued.

She looked directly at him. "Won't you be enough to captivate my follies?"

"I much doubt it."

This was a level of emotionless control that was indeed the opposite of her father's blatant adorations. She drank in the devil's slant of his eyes, the weary wrinkles at the edge of them, his palpable lack of interest. Her heart beat quickly. "All right," she whispered.

His voice lashed her. "I've seen you look at the Earl of Gryffyn with a giddy sort of pleasure that belies your words."

"That's —" she caught herself. "That's nothing. Child's play."

"No doubt," he said, sounding bored. "I would certainly have to reach some sort of second infancy to contemplate a *liaison* with Gryffyn myself."

"I do not contemplate a liaison! I would never —"

He raised a beringed hand, and the words died in her throat. "For God's sake, play me no scenes. I don't give a damn about the purity of your body or your soul. I would advise you, though, to act with a queen's munificence toward those for whom you feel desire. Any other circumstance is

344

likely to breed resentment. And resentful wives are so very tiresome, to themselves and others."

She barely suppressed her shock.

His eyes laughed at her. "Shaken, country mouse? It must be the poet's soul you inherited from your father."

That stung her. "My father does not belong in this conversation." It made her feel almost queer, to realize how much her father would dislike the whole topic. How much he would loathe Villiers, if he heard his concept of marriage.

"And yet your father has such a fascinating liberal attitude toward pleasure, given his attachment to the estimable Mrs. Grope."

It gave him obvious pleasure to utter Mrs. Grope's name; Roberta felt a flash of bitter resentment. It was so easy to make mockery of Mrs. Grope, so difficult to see what a true and loving relationship her papa and his courtesan shared.

"I would that Papa would marry Mrs. Grope," she said, keeping her voice steady with an effort.

"He won't." He wasn't looking at her anymore. In one clean movement, he pulled a long shining rapier from the interior of his polished cane.

"Oh!" she cried.

"Sword stick. Beautiful, isn't it? I had it made for me by Parisians; they understand duels in a way that no Englishman can hope to do. You see how I favor you as my future wife. You are the only person in England who knows the secret of this cane."

"You will forgive me," Roberta said, "if I reveal that knowing the secret of your cane is hardly an intimacy to which I aspire."

"I do like you," he said, grinning at her. "I never expected that in a wife."

"Why do you think that Papa won't marry Mrs. Grope?" Roberta said, ignoring what felt like a very thin compliment.

"We don't marry the women we screw," he said, running his sword across the red velvet of the sofa cushion, to polish it, she had to suppose. "You surely have noticed that I have not made any movements toward your bed, haven't you?"

She felt giddy. Was she supposed to be honored? "Because . . . Because I am not a woman to screw?"

"Not by your husband. And please do not think you must share with me the history of pleasure harvested by others." He flipped the sword and ran it swiftly against the cushion again.

He must have tilted the edge a trifle too

much because a gash followed the cut of his blade, widened, gave birth in an instant to a cloud of floating feathers. He swore.

"I wish to understand precisely what you are saying," Roberta said in a small, wooden voice. "Do I understand you to mean that my chastity — or lack thereof — is of no interest to you?"

He tossed the gaping pillow to the side. A bridge of feathers briefly shaped themselves in the air before falling to the floor, to the couch, and a single feather, to his hair. "You seem to think that chastity adds to your attractions. I assure you that your beauty needs no such ornament. Of course, until we decide to create an heir, I shall expect you to behave in an entirely circumspect manner, using precautions, as I noted before. But I would never have offered for you, Roberta, were I not well aware that you are a woman of honor. Women of honor do not offer their husbands a cuckoo."

It seemed that honor — to Villiers — had everything to do with children, and nothing to do with virtue.

"You must be sensible, of course," he continued. "Cuckold is such an ugly word, even in this easy day and age."

"Yet you are telling me to cuckold you," she said flatly.

"Cuckolds are men who are too stupid to realize that their wives will stray," he said. "I am not so foolish. Cuckolds are men whose wives make a jest of them by displaying their affections around the town. If I understand your character correctly, Roberta, you will never flaunt your affections."

She sat silent, knowing he was absolutely right, knowing that he had picked her as nimbly as she had picked him — and, it seemed, for some of the same reasons.

"I have fought several duels, though never over a woman's honor. It would be a grave disappointment to both of us if I had to defend your honor, Roberta, since I am generous enough to put it into your own keeping. I trust that you are no sprig from your father's tree. Do not cuckold me, and I will not confine you."

"I should dislike confinement," she said. Suddenly she couldn't bear another minute of his emotionless drawl. She rose, as did he. He towered above her, exquisite and controlled as the day she met him, but in truth so much more complex, scornful and erotic than she had understood. She felt young and inestimably stupid. She, who thought that life with Papa and Mrs. Grope had taught her everything there was to know about men and women. She knew nothing.

Her father bellowed and shouted and uttered his ridiculous poetry. He didn't have it in him to speak with such silken mockery. To discuss unfaithfulness as if it were no more than a moment's impulse.

Her Papa, her foolish, foolish, Papa, loved Mrs. Grope, with all her terrible head-dresses, and her grandiose ambitions to go back on the stage. Papa was the opposite of her husband-to-be. Which was just what she wanted, of course.

"Your Grace," she said, sweeping her future husband a deep curtsy.

He was so beautiful, complex and devilish, that her heart reeled slightly watching him bow. And yet . . .

And yet.

CHAPTER 27

The windows in the small back ballroom were open to the night air. Lilacs were flowering in the gardens, somewhere in the dark, and their perfume was intoxicatingly sweet.

Caro had decorated the room with lemon trees incongruously hung with crystal pendants. Now she sat at the pianoforte. Damon hoped he was the only one who realized that the dangerous sparkle in the secretary's eye had resulted in bawdy French tavern songs, translated into great sweeping dance measures. Damon danced with Miss Tatlock, and then with Harriet. He danced again with Harriet, because she was at his elbow and he couldn't say no. He talked to his sister. He talked to his brother-in-law.

Meanwhile he watched for Roberta. Where the devil had Villiers taken her? If he touched her . . .

She walked back into the room with a little wicked smile on her lips and his heart sank to his toes. He felt like vomiting.

He decided to leave, and then realized that his shoes were nailed to the floor. Villiers followed Roberta, but veered away to talk to Jemma.

"Not even one dance?" he heard Jemma say. "Oh, come, Villiers —"

And then Villiers drew Jemma's hands, both of them, up to his mouth and said something. About chess, no doubt, because a moment later they were tucked in front of a little table in the corner.

So much for dancing.

Roberta's eyes were glittering a bit too fiercely.

"Cuz!" he said to her. "I gather dancing has gone by the wayside, since Jemma is involved in a game of chess."

Roberta didn't even glance in her fiancé's direction. Instead she smiled at him. "Would you like to stroll with me?"

Damon tucked her hand into his and turned toward the door. "Always," he said. And then: "Jealousy is a dish best served cold."

She tossed her head. "I have no reason for revenge." She stopped suddenly and looked up at him. "Were you implying something about Jemma and Villiers?"

"No!" he said, hoping it was true. "Jemma would never take your fiancé. Have more faith than that."

"I'm sorry; that was horrid of me," Roberta said. "I should never have thought such an ugly thing."

Something that might have been honesty compelled him to add, "Though if Villiers wins the chess match, of course, all bets are off."

They walked for a moment and then Roberta turned a stricken face up to his. "I'm a fool. I didn't realize the implications of their chess game. I am not sophisticated enough for the life of the *ton*."

"We Reeves are particularly degenerate. But truthfully, I do not believe that Jemma intends to dally with Villiers beyond a flirtation. For one thing, they are both far too obsessed by chess to take a true interest in each other."

"You said something like that before."

"Chess is a mania," Damon said. "There are those who play with such enthusiasm that they think about it all the time, day and night. My father was one of those. He was brilliant at the game, and he devoted himself to teaching his children everything he knew. Jemma turned out to be the only one of us who found any enjoyment in the game, however."

"I can't even play whist very well," Roberta said morosely.

"Don't challenge your future husband to a game of dollymop dominoes. I have a feeling that Villiers wins every game of skill he attempts. Would you mind if we went upstairs to say goodnight to Teddy?"

"Of course . . . what's a dollymop?"

"Mrs. Grope is a refined example of a dollymop," Damon said.

"And then what are dollymop dominoes?"

He glanced sideways at her. "Dominoes with a special twist. Do you know how to play?"

"I suppose so. I played with my governess as a child."

"Not exactly the same game," he said, grinning at her. "Every time you draw a double bone, you have to take a drink."

"Bone?"

"A domino piece; a double bone has a double number. And every time you lay down a spinner, a crosswise double, your opponent has to remove a piece of his clothing."

"Oh!"

They were on the third floor and Damon pushed open the door to the nursery. "Ransom!" he said. "What on earth are you doing here? Where's the nanny?" He looked around the room rather wildly. "She hasn't quit already, has she?"

"Not to the best of my knowledge," Mr. Cunningham said, looking up from a book he was reading by the fire. "She is eating. Last night while she was at supper, Teddy evaded capture by a maid and ran from the room. So tonight she enquired whether I would watch him. He is asleep."

"I am not!" said a voice, and a tousled head popped up from the bed.

"Hello, Pumpkin," Damon said, crossing the room and plucking his son from his bed.

"Good evening, Lady Roberta," Teddy said. "Another tooth, I lost it, do you want to see?" And before she could say yea or nea, he pulled down his lip and showed her a red, gaping hole in his gum.

"That is truly disgusting, Teddy."

He grinned as if he had achieved something of notable importance. "I can stick my tongue through the space," he told her, and did so.

Since he seemed to love to see her shudder, she obliged him a few times, and then she and Damon left the room again.

The last thing she heard before she left was Mr. Cunningham's quiet voice saying,

"You're asleep now, Teddy."

"Interestingly enough, I didn't hear Teddy disagreeing with Mr. Cunningham's statement," Roberta commented once they were in the corridor.

"Ransom has a way of telling Teddy what to do that I find very instructive," Damon said. "I played spindlesticks with my son this afternoon and I'm afraid he showed rather less than gentlemanly manners when he lost the game. So I told him that he was ashamed of himself, in a very Ransom-esque manner, and Teddy burst into tears and agreed with me. It was all very satisfactory. Of course, it didn't stop him throwing the spindles across the room the very next game."

"Mr. Cunningham must have had a great many siblings," Roberta said, not without a twinge of jealousy.

"Would you like to have many children?"

"I've never thought about it. I don't know very much about children. I have to confess that I found Teddy's gum truly stomach-turning."

"Children are often stomach-turning," Damon said gloomily.

"You are a very good father." She hesitated. "How did you come to bring Teddy into your household?"

He looked down at her, his eyes dark green in the dim light. "His grandmother brought him to me. I took one look at him and, as they say, that was that."

Roberta was longing to ask about Teddy's mother, but didn't quite dare. And she felt dimly ashamed of herself as well. Would she have done the same for Teddy? The thought made her feel shallow and —

Damon took her hand. "There's no explaining it until you have one of your own," he said. "It was a moment of madness. If I tell you that his grandmother handed over an infant with a soggy nappy . . . does that demonstrate just how remarkably deranged I became?"

"Yes," she said. But she didn't think he sounded deranged.

"What would you like to do now?" Damon asked. "Shall we rejoin the party or shall we do something utterly scandalous like walking in the garden?"

"No one will even notice that we are absent," she said rather sourly.

"I must admit that the young lady whom Jemma presumably invited to be my escort shows little interest in my company." His tone was so funny that Roberta started laughing. "She is spending the evening hanging on every word that has dropped from Beaumont's lips, though it doesn't seem to bother my sister."

"No," Roberta said. "I'm afraid it doesn't. How the mighty are fallen. I'm sure you were introduced to me as the gentleman whom *all* marriageable maidens desired . . . except, it seems, Miss Tatlock."

"And you."

"I'm not marriageable anymore," Roberta pointed out. "I'm engaged to the man currently playing a game of chess for the right to your sister's bed." She clapped a hand over her mouth. "I shouldn't have said that!"

But Damon was laughing. "That's calling a spade a spade." He seemed to be steering her outside, but the last thing Roberta wanted was to walk about under the smudgy London sky smelling of coal smoke. Besides, what Damon likely wanted was to push her against a tree and kiss her senseless, and she saw no reason why that couldn't happen in more pleasant surroundings. In fact . . .

"Wait here a moment!" she said, and flew back up the stairs.

Two seconds later she was back, a box tucked under her arm.

Damon looked at it, and then his eyes widened.

"I believe," Roberta said, "there is a chess

game going on in the ballroom. Shall we take the library, or perhaps my chamber?" She knew full well that the diabolical smile in his eyes was echoed on the edges of her mouth.

"A friendly game of dominoes between cousins?" he enquired.

"Dollymop dominoes," she said firmly. "I've heard it's played in all the best households."

"I" — he said, leaning over and taking the box from her — "have made it one of my lifetime missions never to disappoint a family member."

"Then you'll need to show me a game that's truly superior," she said, making her voice into a purr and feeling a thrill at her own sophistication. "And not just your skills at the game either."

"I live to please," he said.

And since his voice brought back to mind an image of a beautifully defined chest, muscles rippling as he threw a cowpat, Roberta had no doubt but that his reputation would be unflawed by a vigorous game of dominoes.

CHAPTER 28

Jemma was a trifle irritated. She and Villiers played a side game of chess, but it was over almost before it began. Villiers set two traps for her simultaneously. She saw the chance to capture his bishop, but missed the chance to capture his knight. Either way, she lost her queen.

The moment she rose from the table, Harriet pulled her over to a small sofa. "Things are going so well," she said happily.

"They could be better," Jemma replied. If she had moved her knight to Queen's Bishop Three in the fourth round . . .

"I don't mean the particular game," Harriet said. "I mean your strategy. Villiers is set to be married. It was such a brilliant twist to invite your husband to play a game at the same time."

"I didn't invite him; Beaumont challenged me."

"Challenged you! Perhaps he is hoping

that your marriage will improve."

Jemma shrugged. "I take one look at his John the Baptist face and I feel the weight of every one of my sins. There's no possibility of that."

Harriet hesitated. "You wouldn't fall in love with Villiers, would you? I should feel terrible if I led you into something that might hurt you."

Jemma laughed. "You think that Villiers will cause some overset of my reason?"

"I don't know. I still feel such shame about the night that I — that I gave in to him," Harriet whispered. "It's almost as if Benjamin died that night."

"Listen to me," Jemma said, leaning forward. "You did not betray Benjamin. You were close to it, but that is not the same. I know. I've betrayed Beaumont several times, though never before he did so to me. And the first time was shocking."

"Do you know what grips me to the heart?" Harriet said. "What if Villiers told Benjamin? What if —"

"Benjamin did not end his life because of a stolen kiss in a carriage," Jemma snapped, truly alarmed at the strained look in Harriet's eyes.

"But what if he did? What if Villiers did not tell the truth of that evening?"

"Do you accuse Villiers of embellishing his account?"

Harriet's eyes were agonized. *"What if he did?"*

"I don't think it of him. He is not an unscrupulous player, nor is he a canny one. His play is actually similar to mine, which is why I will win the match."

"I know it's petty, but would you dedicate the match to Benjamin? No one talked of the fact that Villiers drove Benjamin to it. No one."

"I will do my best," Jemma said. "Please don't worry, Harriet. Would you like me to ask Villiers if he spoke to Benjamin about you?"

"Of course not!"

"Chess is the most intimate game in the world. It's like making love. By the time we finish our first slow game, I will know all his thoughts."

"What's different about a slow game from a quick one?"

"I think about his move, and my move, all day long," Jemma said. "It lurks in the back of my mind, a hundred intriguing possibilities. I shall know him to the core when this game is finished, let alone when we have played out a match."

"Good," Harriet said. "Stab him in the back!"

"Bloodthirsty wench."

"The engagement went off just as you planned," Harriet said, changing the subject. "But you're right about Damon. I had a hard time getting him to stop looking at Roberta for all of five minutes."

Jemma frowned. "My brother is so used to being chased by marriageable maidens that I'm afraid he can't quite accept the fact that Roberta thinks herself in love with Villiers."

"Does she?" Harriet was silent for a moment. "I'm sorry for her."

"I'm not. Being in love is great fun, don't you think? It may not last forever, but she's enjoying herself."

"I don't know," Harriet said sadly. "I have only been in love with Benjamin, and now I'm so angry at him that it poisons all my memories. Isn't that awful, Jemma? To be so angry at someone who is dead?"

"I am angry at him too. He should never have treated you so lightly. Nor life either. But that doesn't mean you didn't love him, Harriet."

Harriet's eyes were all shiny with tears, but she gave Jemma a kiss and made her way out into the darkness. The door of the carriage slammed shut and it moved off through the fog, the sound of horses' hooves growing indistinct immediately.

Of course she would win. True, Villiers had beaten her today, in a very pretty stratagem. But she would win the match.

Jemma went inside, but when Fowle stepped back, thinking she would rejoin her guests in the ballroom, she shook her head and asked Fowle to give her excuses. She had seen enough of Miss Tatlock giggling at her husband's every word. Roberta and Damon had disappeared at some point, possibly together, which was a complication she didn't want to consider. And frankly, a little of Mrs. Grope's company was more than enough, although her tip about using ceruse to prevent wrinkles was interesting.

What she would prefer would be to work through a few of Francesch Vicent's *100 Chess Problems.* She headed up the stairs.

Forty minutes later she was bathed and wrapped in a comfortable dressing gown, with her hair bundled up in a towel. "You may go, Brigitte."

"Your hair, Your Grace," Brigitte said. "It will dry with curls in it."

But Jemma was seated before her chess board, with a glass of French brandy and her copy of Vicent. She smiled apologetically, and Brigitte (who had strong views about the supreme importance of appearance) banged her way out of the room.

"Come in!" Jemma called impatiently, an hour later, or it might have been two. She expected a weary maid, but instead her husband stood there, looking as perfectly groomed and attired as he had at the beginning of the evening.

"Beaumont," she said, moving her bishop. "Is there something I can do for you?"

He walked over and looked down at her book. "Vicent?" he asked. "I haven't thought about that book in years. Villiers and I worked our way straight through it at some point."

Which was all the more reason for Jemma to do just the same if she meant to beat Villiers as soundly as she wished. Not to mention Beaumont himself.

He sat down without being asked. "What about moving your rook to King's Four?"

"Two moves with his rook and I would be in check. Are you thinking of setting up that young woman as your next mistress?"

He raised his head from the board, and the look in his eyes almost made Jemma flinch.

"She's a well-bred young woman," she

said. "I thought you hoped to avoid a scandal."

"I have no need of a mistress."

Heat scorched Jemma's spine. "Of course not," she said, nodding. "I was not implying that the position was open, but I didn't expect such loyalty on your part. Your mistress is still with you, then?" She schooled her face to an expression of benign enquiry.

"She is not."

"But she's been replaced. You soothe my spirits, Beaumont. Watching you with Charlotte Tatlock I feared that you were about to flare into true scandal."

His mouth barely moved when he spoke. "I am not intending anything untoward with Miss Tatlock. I merely enjoy speaking to her about politics. She is, you see, interested in what goes on in England."

She gave him a faint smile. "Unusual in a woman."

"Quite."

Without looking at the board again, he said, "Queen to King's Three and you have him in four moves."

She frowned at the board, saw what he was talking about. "Not if black moves his rook to block me."

"It's possible, but it's the only move I see

that will open up your board."

"You like it because it counters black's attack," she said.

"I dislike finding myself under attack, it's true. At the moment, I am one move away from open warfare on a number of fronts."

"Due entirely to my return from Paris?"

"Imminent scandal," he said. "I now house a woman of ill repute and an illegitimate child, and my last ball featured a nearly naked Helen whose songs were hardly proper. My wife is widely believed to be playing a game with the Duke of Villiers, in which she herself is the prize."

She felt anger sweeping up her spine, making her head reel. "You simply wish everything to be kept silent, is that it? You have your mistress, and flirt with a young unmarried lady until she looks at you with stars in her eyes, but that's not a scandal, because to you neither woman matters. All I do, Beaumont, is live my life without hypocrisy. Perhaps that is something a politician cannot understand."

"You live your life with the easy arrogance of someone who has never cared a damn for anything or anyone except yourself." His tone was crushingly blunt. "I suppose you care for chess, Jemma, but from what I gathered, you never really gave a damn for those men you partnered in Paris."

She sprang to her feet. "How dare you suggest that I didn't care for them? You know *nothing* of my relations!"

"I know you were sleeping with Monsieur Philidor for a matter of years," he said, rising in his turn. "I could only hope there was no payment involved; his regular visits to your house suggested a relation embellished by francs."

"How dare you!" she cried. "Philidor —"

"I really don't wish to know what Philidor was to you. Let's just assume that I underestimated your ability for emotion and you care a great deal for the man. Should I, as your husband, applaud that?"

"Let me see if I can get this straight. You are suggesting that Philidor was my courtesan? Forgive me; I don't know the correct term for a male. Paramour, perhaps. Could I ask exactly how my taking a paramour would differ from your relation with Sarah Cobbett?"

And when he didn't reply, "It's only been eight years, Beaumont. Surely you remember the name of your former mistress?"

"I am merely surprised that you know it," he said.

"Believe me," she said with a shrug, "there were many people happy to tell me all her circumstances after I realized the truth of our marriage. Did you think to keep it secret?"

And when he said nothing, "I see you did. How very odd. Even had I not discovered the two of you in such an awkward way, someone would have told me in the near future. I found myself glad of it, afterwards. Do you know: I was so stupid and young, that I might not have believed it without visual proof? I don't believe I would have understood that you might bound from my bed to hers — at least figuratively, since you bedded her on a desk."

She was possessed by an icy fury that no one except her husband had ever inspired in her. "That is quite different from you, Beaumont. *You* have no difficulty whatsoever believing that Philidor was somehow in my employ, even though you never saw me lying beneath him."

"That's enough."

"Since you show so much curiosity, I will reward you with the gift of information. I have never paid a gentleman for his favors; unlike you, I seem to be lucky enough to attract lovers who need no payment. And I have never led on a man who did not understand the game at hand. Perhaps you are blind enough that you did not see the

368

way Charlotte Tatlock looked at you tonight. I don't know why I was so surprised. Surely I could simply look back at myself eight years ago and recognize her stupidity."

"Those are harsh words."

"I am sure that you will be able to dismiss my criticism of your private life. It caused you no distress in the past."

"If you will forgive me," he said, "I have many appointments tomorrow morning."

She fell into a deep curtsy. "Good night, Your Grace."

He bowed, and was gone.

Jemma stood for a moment, chest heaving with rage, and then pulled on the cord. Brigitte appeared a few minutes later, correctly interpreting that angry peal as commanding haste.

"Tell Fowle that you will deliver the chess moves to him every night," Jemma said. She scribbled on a piece of paper. "Here are the moves so far. There are perhaps four days left in each game, possibly longer in Beaumont's case. I don't suppose that Villiers is still in the house?"

Brigitte dropped a curtsy. "If you please, my lady, he has been partnering Miss Charlotte in a game of whist with the marquess and Lord Corbin, and they are just leaving now."

Charlotte Tatlock? Why not? Why shouldn't the woman play with both Beaumont and Villiers? It made sense in a queer sort of way.

"Ask him to step upstairs, if you would," she said.

Brigitte was far too wise to ask any questions. She dropped into a curtsy and left the room before Jemma could say another word.

Jemma swept the chessboard clean and sat down to wait for Villiers.

CHAPTER 29

In the end, they settled in a small sitting room, the same one to which Jemma had first brought Roberta. Damon rang the bell while Roberta wandered over to say hello to Judith's foolish, tipsy face, but she had been removed.

"If we're going to drink," Damon said, "and since it's an essential part of dollymop dominoes, we are, you should eat something. You didn't touch your food at supper."

"I'm not fond of ornate food," Roberta said. "I would grow very thin living with a French cook."

"You prefer apples and hard-boiled eggs?"

"Not that, but our cook at home is gifted at simple dishes."

"Beaumont's cook is definitely French, with the temperament of a devil, or so Ransom tells me."

"Isn't it odd that your school friend would

end up secretary to the duke?" she asked.

"Not at all. I recommended him for the post." The door opened. "Ah, Fowle," Damon said. "May we please have a small repast and a bottle or two of champagne?"

"I do not like champagne," Roberta said. "Some other drink perhaps?"

"Do you like wine?"

"If it's sweet."

Damon shuddered. "Intolerable. We have nothing of the sort in the house, and if we did, you'd have a terrible headache in a couple of hours."

"Ratafia?" Fowle suggested.

"Absolutely not. I don't want our guest casting up her accounts tomorrow morning."

"In that case, I would suggest a gentle concoction of champagne and strawberries, my lord. Strawberries just arrived from the country, and I believe it will make the champagne tolerable to Lady Roberta."

"Champagne with fruit doused in it," Damon said morosely.

But Fowle was right. It was delicious.

"I shall ring if we need anything further," Damon told Fowle and then, turning back to Roberta, "There's no better way to nurture gossip among the servants."

Roberta shrugged. "The servants in this

household have so much to occupy them; I'm sure we're at the bottom of the list."

"It is true that your engagement should keep them talking for the evening," Damon said, cautiously sipping his drink. "It's pink," he said with disgust, "and there's sugar in it."

"I like it," Roberta said. "Champagne always bites the back of my nose, but this is lovely."

Damon brought over a small table and placed it between them. "Do you know how to play dominoes?"

"You asked me that before," Roberta said, giggling. She had finished her glass and the world seemed a much more cheerful place. "In fact, I always beat my governess."

"Superior skill at matching sixes?"

"I have very good luck," she said smugly. "I often draw doubles."

"I shall prepare to disrobe," Damon said, loosening his cuffs.

Roberta froze for a moment. Then she picked up her pieces. Her mind was a little fuzzy but she was quite certain of the important things. Her fiancé had said that chastity was tiresome. That same fiancé was playing a game of chess whose outcome had everything to do with loss of clothing.

"Let's just see what happens, shall we?"

she said, smiling at Damon.

He sat opposite her, looking a little perplexed. That was because he was a man. She turned all the pieces face down and prepared to draw.

"Wait a minute!" he said, and the wicked gleam was in his eye. "I'll bet you were cheating your poor old governess by memorizing where the doubles were." He shuffled the pieces.

She managed to keep a pitying smile off her face because when a man is about to lose all his clothing, he needs his composure.

She drew the highest piece, a six, so she pulled all her bones first. She didn't draw a double in her original three, which was a wee bit disappointing.

She played and sipped her drink.

Damon handed her a tiny square of iced cake. "You should try this, Buttercup. It's just as sugary as the champagne."

It was lovely, so she ate it while she drew her next piece, a double three. She didn't tell him, though, until two moves later when she put it down crosswise as a spinner.

"Wait a second," he said startled. "You're supposed to tell me when you draw a double. You have to drink."

"I have been drinking," she pointed out.

His glass was still full, but she threw back the last drops of her second glass and fished out the slice of strawberry with her tongue. He seemed to enjoy watching her do that, so she licked the edge of the glass.

He wrenched his eyes away. "Well, so you put down a spinner —"

"Which means that you have to take off a piece of your clothing."

"No need to be quite so eager. I'm wearing a great deal of clothing."

"I'm not eager," she said loftily. "Just curious."

He pulled off his jacket and threw it to the side. Underneath he wore an embroidered waistcoat and a linen shirt.

"That waistcoat doesn't quite match your jacket," she pointed out.

"My valet made the same comment, but it was too late. I already had it buttoned." He selected a new piece. "Oh, no. A double. That means I have to drink." He took a large swallow and shuddered visibly.

"How could you not like it?" Roberta said. "It's absolutely delicious. I feel quite swimmy."

Damon put down a piece but it wasn't his double. "There's no place for my spinner, but you should beware."

Meanwhile Roberta drew another double

and put it down directly as a spinner.

"I can see there are benefits to your sort of luck," he said. His waistcoat followed his jacket.

She glanced at him from under her lashes. His shirt was so fine it was almost transparent. He had beautifully cut muscles in his shoulders. As she watched he rolled up his sleeves. "Though why I bother," he muttered. "I don't suppose I'll have this shirt on my back much longer."

Roberta smiled to herself.

But to her vexation, it was she who began to lose clothing next. Damon put down the spinner he drew earlier. She was experiencing the most deliciously fuzzy feeling, so rather than lean over, she simply pointed a foot at Damon.

"Very small feet," he said, holding her ankle. "And sweetly turned ankles." He drew off her right shoe.

A moment later she lost the left one as well.

"I had better not lose any more," she said, sitting up straight.

She put down a spinner. "It seems that I'll have to take off my shirt," Damon said. His voice was as sweet as strawberry champagne and far more dangerous.

Roberta put down her drink. After all, this

was her very first male chest, and she might as well have a good view.

He played right along, smiling at her as if he exhibited himself to young ladies every day. First he took his time pulling the shirt from his breeches, and then he slowly pulled it up over his head.

Roberta's lips made a silent O. He was so beautiful. Smooth muscles rippled as the shirt flew to the ground. Her fingers twitched, wanting to touch them.

"Your move," Damon said gently.

Roberta dragged her eyes away from his body. She reached forward and picked up a domino piece, cool and long in her fingers. She knew it was a double without looking. She turned it over, thinking that he would have to take off his breeches —

It was a three.

She made a little, disappointed sound before she realized and he let fly with a bellow of laughter. "One of the things I really like about you, Buttercup, is that you're almost transparent."

"No, I'm not," she said, stung. "I can be very Machiavellian when I want to."

"Oh really?" he asked, his eyes dancing over the edge of his glass. "I bet you're no good at lying whatsoever. You look like a girl who never told a decent lie in her life."

"I certainly have," she protested. "Why, I regularly tell Mrs. Grope that her hair is remarkably elegant."

Damon visibly shuddered. "So you tell white lies. But have you ever told a lie about something you really felt deeply about?"

"Yes! I feel deeply about Mrs. Grope's hair!"

"I can understand that. Now look me in the face and tell me a lie about something you really care about, something you feel desperately about."

What did she feel desperate about anyway? The champagne had made her so cheerful that she didn't feel desperate about anything . . . except, perhaps, seeing Damon take off his breeches.

She must have looked blank, because he said, "Tell me that you're not in love with Villiers. Go on!"

"I'm not in love with Villiers," she said slowly.

"Terrible!" he said. "Your eyes went all soft and moony even mentioning his name."

In Roberta's opinion, her eyes went soft and moony because — the horror of it — for a moment she couldn't remember who Villiers was. Champagne was dangerous.

"I don't want to draw another double," she said, keeping her voice firm. "Absolutely not. I will simply *faint* if I draw another double."

Something flared in his eyes that made her belly fire in response.

"And why is that, Buttercup?" he asked. He pulled a two from the pile and played it.

She kept her voice casual. "I'm afraid that you'll take this game too seriously. That you might have misunderstood me."

"What?" Apparently this took him by surprise.

"I'm afraid that you'll think I'm like all those other young women, chasing after you in hopes of marrying you."

He gave a bark of laughter. "I can distinguish a mountain from a molehill, Roberta!"

"Just so long as we're in agreement. Now if I could just draw a two . . ." She turned over the piece.

"Double two's," she said cheerily. "And — how lucky! — I can create a spinner from the two you just played."

His eyes were unreadable. "I seem to have lost track of this conversation. Were you exhibiting an unexpected brilliance at fibbing, or are you really afraid that I'll consider you a marital prospect?"

"I'm hardly a marital prospect," Roberta said. "I'm in love with someone else, and I'm engaged to marry him."

Damon reached down and pulled off a shoe. "Then why are you here?"

"Shall we make a bet that you won't be able to tell whether I'm lying or not?"

He shook his head. "I've lost all faith in my ability to read your mind."

Roberta took another delicious swallow of champagne. "My fiancé and I are going to have a sophisticated marriage," she told him.

"Sophisticated?"

She nodded. "That means that we don't have to be prudish and chaste and tedious things of that nature. It's not as if I'm a baker, you know!" She opened her eyes very wide.

He pulled off another shoe, even though it was his turn to move, but she decided not to mention it. It was too much fun to look at his chest.

"Your muscles are quite beautiful," she said. "Do you take exercise?" He didn't seem to hear her, perhaps because he was putting his stockings to the side.

Roberta's heart was beating quickly.

"We're being absolutely straightforward here," he said with a slow smile. "I will not fear that you are hunting my considerable assets —"

She giggled.

"Instead, I take it that you are here with

the laudable desire to gain some experience before encountering Villiers in an intimate setting. After all, such an older man —"

"He's not old," she protested.

"Perhaps it's just his style. He always strikes me as bored by life. Enthusiastic only about chess. Though, of course, perhaps it will all change when he gets you alone in a bedchamber. God knows, we're not in a bedchamber and I'm finding it a challenge not to leap on you like an untamed dog."

He sat down and pulled a five from the pile.

Roberta felt a flash of chill. It went without saying that Villiers would never compare himself to an unmannered mongrel. He would never sit opposite her, wearing nothing but a pair of breeches, looking as easy as if he were born to be naked.

Damon put down his piece and then looked up at her. Her heart almost stopped at the look in his eye. "I dare you to pull a double from that pile," he said.

"Maybe I should go to my chambers," she said. "It's late."

"Bedtime?"

Roberta wasn't sure what she was doing. She was teasing him, even though she didn't mean it, or did she? Her mind seemed to be drugged by the very sight of Damon. And it wasn't as if there was anyone who thought she *shouldn't* be here. Villiers had said — had said —

"I suppose we ought to finish the game, since we started it," she said. Her heart was thudding against her ribs.

"I always finish a game once it begins."

Roberta didn't think Damon was talking about dominoes. Was she ready for this?

"The world is a different place than I believed it to be while growing up," she said, pulling a four from the pile.

One of the intoxicating things about Damon was the way he looked so interested in her opinion. "Really?" He pulled a blank. "What did you think the world would be like? It must have been rather remarkable, growing up with Mrs. Grope. I would hardly have thought you had a conventional upbringing."

"Well, it wasn't conventional," Roberta said. She couldn't fit any of her pieces onto the board. "We're getting all cramped on the right side of the table."

He ladled a bit more strawberry champagne into her glass and pointed. "One of us needs to start a spinner with that four."

Roberta was feeling suddenly shy. She drew a one. "Mrs. Grope has only been a friend of my father's for the last few years."

"Before that?"

"Well, there was Selina . . . an actress."

He looked up at her, startled. "You can't mean Selina Trimmer, currently the lead actress at Drury Lane, not to mention *inamorata* of the Prince of Wales?"

She nodded.

"I gain a whole new respect for your father," he said, snagging a three from the pile. "Selina is remarkably beautiful. Is she as temperamental in person as in reputation?"

"Oh yes," Roberta said. "She found it very hard to live in the country and I'm afraid it had a wearing effect on her composure."

"Then why on earth —" he said, and checked himself.

"She was in the grip of a passion for my father," Roberta explained, feeling a little thrill of parental pride. "She met Papa when the Drury Lane traveling company visited our estate. He persuaded her to stay for a brief visit."

"How brief?"

"Two years."

"You lived with Selina Trimmer for *two years!*"

"She wasn't a Trimmer at that point," Roberta explained. "This game is so irritat-

ing, Damon. I don't think I can move anything."

"Yes, you can. Put your one there," he
said, pointing.

"We knew her as Selina Le Faye. But
Selina felt that she would do better with a
more English-sounding name, so when she
decided to go to London, we concocted the
name Trimmer."

"You mean that it was an amicable part-
ing?"

"There was no rancor. Of course, my
father wept voluminously."

"My dear Roberta," Damon said, "why on
earth are you the least bit surprised by the
goings on in this house? To put it bluntly,
you have grown up in a household whose
attention to conventional mores seems to
have been fragile, to say the least."

Roberta had to think about that for a moment, which was just as well, because Damon had drawn a piece that he didn't seem
to know what to do with. "It's not that I'm
surprised by intimacy outside of marriage,"
she said finally. "But my father was deeply
in love with Selina, and then with Mrs.
Grope. He *loved* them, both of them. It
broke his heart when Selina decided that
she could not continue to be happy in such
a remote location as our home."

"But he didn't take her to London."

"I believe that Selina felt it was time for something new, perhaps?"

Damon grinned. "Nicely put."

"The truth is that I know something of what goes on between men and women," Roberta said. She could feel herself going a little pink. "I hadn't actually seen anything until the other night, but I have —"

She broke off, seeing the utterly fascinated look on his face.

"You have what?"

"I suppose that I am in possession of a rather unique amount of information about pleasuring men. At least for someone like me."

"A virgin, you mean."

She nodded.

He put down his piece. "It seems that I, Roberta, have drawn a double four, which I shall place as a spinner in the one available spot."

"Oh," she said, feeling her heart speed up again.

"What will you take off?" he asked. His grin was absolutely devilish.

But Roberta had already thought this through. She stood and pulled up her skirts in the back, where he couldn't see. With a sharp pull, she untied the ribbon that held her hooped petticoat in place. It fell to the floor, and Roberta stepped neatly out of the frame.

Damon's face fell. "That was sneaky," he said, getting up. Before she realized what he was doing, he picked Roberta up in his arms and sat back down on his chair.

"What?" she yelped.

"I love holding a woman who isn't wearing an iron-wrought frame around her body," he said.

"My hoops aren't made of iron," Roberta said. He smelled so good that it was hard to think. Instead she just snuggled into his chest. It was soft, like velvet but not velvety. She ran a finger over the contours of his chest.

"Buttercup," he said in a husky whisper. "It's your turn to move."

"In a moment."

He busied himself by kissing her ear, and Roberta flattened her hand against his chest. He was warm, hot, in fact. And smooth chested.

"Will you grow hair as you age?" she asked, running her hand over his chest again. It was intoxicating. He had a nipple, which she wouldn't have expected. His was flat, not like hers. She ran her fingers over it again. And again.

His voice sounded a little strained. "I don't think so. Why? Do you hanker after chest hair?"

She giggled. "No. The only male chest I've ever seen belonged to a groom, and he had white hair all over his front."

"I'm sure Villiers will have all the white hair you want," he said. And then: "I'm sorry, Roberta. That was entirely uncalled for."

She squeaked. "What are you doing?"

"Making up for my rudeness," he said, his voice entirely serious. "It's the least I can do."

Roberta thought about that, but none too steadily because his fingers were sliding up her leg, and farther. It was as if she could feel her skin as he felt it, curved, smooth, rounding under his fingers. His breath was coming faster and his fingers —

She cleared her throat.

"Yes?" His fingers slid forward again.

It felt so good — too good. She jumped to her feet. "My turn to draw a piece!" She sat down hurriedly, avoiding his eyes. He uncoiled himself, leaning forward, all taut male muscle. She snatched a piece and then stared down at it.

His hand plucked the piece from her fingers. "Another double four," he said. His eyes smiled at her, and suddenly that melting feeling Roberta felt from the touch of his fingers was there, even without being touched. She blinked at him.

"You're going to have to make a spinner," he said. Quietly. As if it were an ordinary invitation.

Roberta looked him over. In the candlelight, Damon was all golden skin and shifting muscles. Her father always said there was only one reason to act impetuously: if she really wanted something. Roberta had heaped scorn on her father's maxim, given that following his whims was so frequently antithetical to the mores of polite society.

But now she saw the wisdom of it all.

What she wanted was to lose her inconvenient virginity to Damon. Then she would marry Villiers and embark on a life of reckless sophistication. But at the moment . . .

"I can see that you are likely shy," she said.

"I am?"

"It's difficult to expose yourself for the first time."

"The first . . ."

She was standing up, and his voice trailed into silence. First she pulled off her stockings. They dropped to the ground, frail and silken, with a gleam like trapped sunshine. Damon's eyes followed them with some fascination, she thought.

She waited until he met her eye again, and then slowly, slowly, she began unlacing the front of her gown.

He didn't move. In fact, he looked as frozen as a man might be who was trying to lure a fawn into eating from his hand. But Roberta didn't feel like a fawn. She felt like a powerful woman doing exactly as she wished. Her bodice gaped open as she bent to pick up her glass.

He turned slightly red. Roberta took a drink and surreptitiously checked his breeches . . . yes. He was interested. Very, if that look in his eye were any indication. She bent to put her glass down again, thought about kissing him, and decided that she might as well get rid of her gown first. So she gave an easy roll of her shoulders.

It fell to the ground, all embroidered silk and gold lace. "It was heavy," she told him. He didn't look as if he would disagree; his eyes were eating her up.

"Those stays are heavy as well," he said.

"They lace in the back." She turned around and waited.

He must have leaped to his feet, because she heard a bang, as if he knocked against the table, and then his long, clever fingers were at her back. She held the stays against

389

her and turned around before she let them fall to the floor. The bodice of her chemise was extremely low, the better to accommodate the neckline of her gown. In fact, it barely covered her nipples at all. And it was made of fine lawn edged in lace.

"Your next move would surely be a spinner," Damon said. His voice was smoky, almost sleepy. He pulled his breeches down and put them away.

Roberta was afraid to look. Her heart was thudding against her ribs, dancing a rhythm that she hardly knew and yet recognized with an age-old wisdom. That same wisdom was in her smile as she put her arms around his neck and then, still without looking, brought her body against his.

He made a muffled sound, like a groan, and his lips were in her hair and his hands were against her back.

"Buttercup," he whispered, "there's no going back from this. You do realize that, don't you?"

"Yes," she said. She'd discovered his ear and was doing exactly what he'd done to hers earlier: kissing it and then, daringly, touching him with her tongue.

"No," he said, and put her away.

Roberta grinned at him. He was having male scruples, no doubt. She'd watched her father wrestle with those for years, and in her opinion, the wrestling always ended up in the same way: her father did exactly what he wanted to. Her job was to make sure that Damon wanted to do exactly what *she* wanted.

So she lifted her arms and started pulling pins from her hair. It had been coiled and curled and pinned all over. She pulled pin after pin, and he said nothing. Finally her hair tumbled beyond her shoulders. She bent over and gave it a good shake to get rid of the powder.

Damon stared at Roberta's sweet little bottom as she bent over and had the feeling of a man drowning — with nary a soul to throw him a life buoy. Kissing Roberta was one thing . . . but her virginity? He'd never done such a thing.

He could only do it if he were intending to marry her.

But she didn't want to hear that yet. She was giggling, and the sound went to his heart and his blood sang with joy.

She was his, whether she wished to acknowledge it or not.

Roberta straightened up and turned around. Dark red curls tumbled all over her bare arms, but it was those crazy arching eyebrows and dark plump lips that caught his heart. No one could say that she looked innocent. Hell, after growing up with Selina, she probably knew more about bedding than he did.

Except . . . he remembered the stunned look on her face when they walked in on that couple tupping in the sitting room.

She was an enchanting mixture of innocence and sophistication.

"I shouldn't do this," he said, knowing the truth of it. "It's not right, Roberta."

"What's not right?"

"Bedding you. I can't do this. I can't take your virginity when you're not married, and you're in love with someone else, even engaged to him."

Her eyes turned a shade darker blue and Damon instinctually felt that was a bad sign.

"Why?" she demanded. "Do you think that you're taking advantage of me?"

"You don't understand the ways of the *ton.* Hell, your father was crazy to let you come to Jemma's house. She's no fit person to take care of a young woman. She's *married,* Roberta. Married. And playing chess with —" Too late he remembered that Jemma was playing chess with Roberta's fiancé.

She had her hands on her hips. "Jemma, whom I adore, by the way, and am not in the *least* jealous of, is playing chess with Villiers. To whom I am engaged to marry. Villiers told me that my chastity was unattractive, and that he didn't give a damn who I had slept with, as long as I don't give him a cuckoo to raise. Damon, do you know how to prevent conception?"

"Yes," he said, "but —"

"Good. Because so do I, but my understanding is that male participation makes it much more effective."

His mouth fell open. "You know?"

"Selina lived with us from the time I was fourteen to the time I was sixteen. I loved her. She gave me a great deal of advice, sister to sister."

He snapped his mouth shut. "You had sisterly conversations with Selina Trimmer." He wrenched his mind away from the *Tête-à-Tête* report of Selina's latest party, in which it was reported that she had filled her bathtub with vintage champagne and invited several guests to watch her bathe. It was also reported that two of them joined her in the tub.

"Do you need some education?" Roberta demanded, hands on her hips.

"What did you learn?" He shook his head. "Forget I asked that. The point is, Roberta, not how much you learned from Selina, but how much I would take away from you by making love to you."

"Perhaps you're right," she said. "You're practically a family member, after all."

"Yes! Your cousin."

"I shall find someone else," she said. "In case it isn't clear to you, Damon, I shall not be carrying my inconvenient virginity to bed with Villiers. After all, I'm in love. I wouldn't bore my husband with such a task, and if you don't feel like taking it on, there's no point in crying over it. I shall simply find another man who is more eager."

Damon almost laughed at that. He'd never felt so damned eager to do anything in his life. In fact —

She was laughing at him. Still a little angry, but laughing. Christ, she was magnificent. Her chemise was of fine lawn, and it barely skimmed her leg, stopping just above her rounded kneecap.

"You go to another man only when I'm dead."

She clearly didn't realize that he'd just declared himself. "I realize that you are used to women tripping over themselves, trying to woo you into marriage," she said, eyes sparkling. "But don't you understand that I'm not like them? I don't want your ring, or your money, or your title."

"Because you have Villiers." Saying his name aloud steadied Damon.

She nodded. "You need to understand that. I'm a terribly hard-headed woman, and I always have been. You can ask my father. I knew the moment that I saw Villiers that I wanted to marry him."

"Why?" He had to ask. "And don't say because you're in love. I'm not a big believer in love at first sight, and I'm not entirely sure that you are either."

"It doesn't matter how you put it," she said. "I look at Villiers and I know exactly what sort of marriage we will have, and it's exactly the sort I want to be involved in. He is controlled."

"Controlled?" Damon was stunned. "You're marrying Villiers because he's *controlled?*"

"He will never embarrass me. He will never launch into gushing flights of emotion. He will never write a poem to my toe, or any other part of my body. He will never weep."

"Well, you're right about that," Damon said. "It could be your funeral, and Villiers would just stand there with that snarling little smile of his."

She walked over to him and put a hand on his arm. She didn't even seem to feel the slightest bit of embarrassment at being in her chemise, nor at the fact that he was next thing to naked. She truly wasn't a normal virgin. Whatever that was. "Villiers is right for me. And I am lucky that he recognized the same in me. We will be an excellent match and I think we'll live together happily for years."

Damon's teeth were so tightly clenched he thought he might break his jaw. "Fine," he managed. "Married bliss. I see it. You and Villiers will get old together except — hold on a moment! — he's already old, so I guess you'll be a happy widow."

Her eyes turned a dark navy again, and every bit of native caution he had in his body warned him that was an even worse sign.

He was right.

"You're an ass. I have no idea why you are being such an ass, but I've learned over the years that men are impossible to understand, and so I shan't try to fathom you. There's something I want from you, Damon."

His mouth went dry. "There is?" Every inch of his body knew exactly what she wanted, and those same inches were straining to satisfy her.

With one swift gesture, she pulled her

chemise right over her head and tossed it to the side. Then she looked at him, and for just one moment, there was a flash of uncertainty in those beautiful eyes of hers.

That was enough. Every ethical sense that Damon had in his entire body melted like sugar in hot water.

"You're sure, Buttercup?" He had her in his hands when he said it, his palms sliding over her round derrière.

"I choose you for my first experience with men," Roberta said, sounding far too logical for the moment.

He almost said something about her first man being her last, but he caught it back. She didn't want to hear it yet. She was hanging onto the dream of a controlled marriage.

Obviously, it was up to him to teach her the bliss of losing control.

He shut the thought off and dragged her against his chest. Little Miss Inexperienced Know-It-All was about to find out what it was like to actually sleep with a man, as opposed to talk about it.

Chapter 30

He had spread out the huge silk skirts of her gown and put her on it, but she wouldn't stay there. She was supposed to lie back and let him gently introduce her to the fruits of pleasure while she trembled and shrieked, *"No, no!"* In fact, experienced matrons had done that on occasion, because he was the kind of man who thought that every inch of a woman tasted good.

But Roberta?

She did squeal, and even squeak, but he hadn't heard a single "No, no." Sometimes he couldn't understand exactly what she was saying, but it sounded an awful lot like "Yes!"

So he let a bit more guilt slip away from him, and turned back to nuzzling her breast. What she liked best was when he sucked her nipples into his mouth. He kept doing that, and then pulling back and shaping her breasts in his hands, and even giving her little bites, and nibbles, until she was all calmed down — of course, he wasn't; he'd never been harder in his life — and then he would suckle her again and her back would rise just like that, and she would start gasping and crying. He didn't even want to think about what would happen when he made his way down her body.

He was sliding his fingers there now, slowly because so often ladies didn't want to be touched, or rather, they had no idea what they wanted.

But he wasn't getting much resistance from Roberta. He slid his fingers a bit lower, flicking her nipple with his tongue so that she didn't notice what he was doing. But then she shocked him because one of her beautiful slim legs slid up and she sobbed, "Damon," and her knee fell open.

And if that wasn't an invitation?

Damon was a man who considered making love to be a work of art. You prepared the canvas (kisses) and then threw on some background (special attention to certain parts of the body) and then you painted the main event. With your brush, ha ha.

In other words, he never made love without generous attention to the woman, and in general he believed that she should come before he did.

Which must be why he found himself absolutely mad in this case, unable to stop himself. Because Roberta had the sweetest, reddest, most —

He couldn't stop himself. He couldn't. He was poised over her and she curled up against him with a little puffing wail of desire and even though he was a man who never came before the woman . . .

He did.

He thrust where no man had been. Into her plump sweetness, and the only thing he had enough self-possession to do was rub a thumb over her breasts at the same time.

Her eyes got huge, but he wasn't thinking, he couldn't think. His entire body was concentrated on the most glorious sensation of his life, on the sleekest, wettest, tightest experience of his life —

She wasn't saying "yes," anymore, but Damon didn't know it. He threw his head back and plunged forward a few times, almost sobbing at the exquisiteness of it. It was all too much, though, and he came with a muffled groan wrenched from his chest.

He collapsed on top of her but managed to catch most of his weight on his elbows. "Oh God" — he was babbling — "you were — that was — Roberta, are you all right? I'm sorry." She didn't look angry, just kind of perplexed. "You don't know what I'm talking about, do you?" he said, feeling a rush of protectiveness and affection such as he'd never experienced before. "You'll see, Roberta. Just let me have a moment to gather my strength and next time you'll . . . see . . ."

He closed his eyes to recover his strength.

Roberta St. Giles found herself lying next to a sleeping man.

She looked down at herself. There was no sign of blood, which was reassuring. She'd heard various stories about gushing blood and then the opposite, from Selina, who told her that women over the age of twelve never felt a thing.

"Surely not — under twelve?" she had asked. There was something closed about Selina's face that didn't allow her to finish that question.

Roberta sat up. Her body had a faint tingling sensation about it still. The whole experience was quite interesting, really. She looked down at Damon. He was peacefully sleeping.

She was no longer a virgin. That statement meant about as much to her as she had thought it would. Virginity, like many things connected to men, was obviously vastly overrated. And frankly, so was sexual intimacy.

No wonder Villiers didn't care if she'd had previous experiences. It was all a matter of a minute at most. Yet there was something alarmingly intimate about it, for all its speed.

Damon's shoulder, for example. He was lying on his side, and his shoulder had a beautiful curve. She ran a finger along it. What she wanted now was a bath. There was a sticky feeling between her legs that she disliked. And, in truth, the experience wasn't entirely comfortable. In fact, she likely wouldn't do it again until marriage.

"Thank you," she whispered, touching his face. The angle of his cheek was beautiful. For a moment she thought about kissing him again; somehow, he'd started touching her breasts, and they'd never really kissed, and that was her favorite part of it all.

But if she kissed him, he might wake up. And though it was kind of him to offer, she didn't feel like doing that again.

So instead she teased her gown out from under his body, holding her breath when he seemed as if he might wake up. When she got it free, she stood up and wrapped the gown around her like an enormous towel.

The servants in her father's house had

been used to all sorts of extraordinary behavior; she could only hope — and in truth, expect — that Jemma's servants were equally imperturbable. There was one footman standing in the hallway, so she gave him a smile and sailed up the stairs.

Once in her room she dropped her gown and rang the bell. Her maid appeared, looking rather sleepy, and quite surprised to find her mistress wearing a dressing gown. After all, she couldn't have removed her stays by herself.

"Ellen, I've left some of my clothing in the yellow sitting room," Roberta said, not wasting breath on feeble explanations. "We should probably send someone to fetch it, but not yet."

Ellen nodded, showing that she was just as well trained as Roberta would have expected. "Would you like a bath, my lady?"

"Absolutely," Roberta said. "Thank you."

A few minutes later three footmen staggered in carrying a zinc bath and buckets of water, and Roberta was able to climb into the scented water with a sigh. Ellen helped her wash her hair, and then Roberta told her she could go to bed. "You must be exhausted."

"Oh, I couldn't leave you in this state," Ellen said, looking sleepy. "How will you prepare for bed?"

"The same way I got myself into bed these last twenty years," Roberta said. "My maid at home was quite old and couldn't manage late nights, and so I always tucked myself in bed. In fact, I prefer it."

"Will you call a footman to remove the water?"

"Of course I will. You go to bed."

Ellen curtsied and left. Then she stuck her head back around the door. "I forgot to say that everyone below stairs is that pleased that you will be a duchess?"

Roberta smiled at her. "Thank you."

"And no one will think the less of you for anticipating the wedding night, my lady . . . I'll ask Martin, the second footman, to fetch your clothing in an hour or so. He can stow it where no one can see."

Roberta's smile was a little crooked this time. One had to hope that Damon would get himself out of that room without being seen by Martin or anyone else.

The moment the door closed she leaned her head back against the edge of the bath with a sigh. She was half asleep by the time she pulled on a dressing gown and called a footman to remove the bath.

The bath was gone, and she had just sat down on the bed, still in her dressing gown,

and was thinking about where her nightgown might be when the door swung open.

"Oh," she said, blinking up at him. "It's
you." And then, with a squeak as she woke
up, "What are you doing in my bedchamber?"

CHAPTER 31

Villiers stood quietly in the doorway, one eyebrow raised.

Jemma deliberately looked him over from head to toe: the sulky bottom lip, the dramatically streaked hair, the languid yet powerful stance. He was wearing a plum-colored coat embroidered with fire lilies; his hair ribbon matched. He wore one patch, high on his right cheek. He looked inexpressibly elegant even to her, who had lived for eight years in the shadow of the French court.

There was something about Villiers . . . about his penchant for clothing embroidered with peacock brightness, about his patch and his colored hair ribbon, about the deep intelligence in his gamester's eye, and the coiled power of his body.

"Do come in," she said, indicating the chess board. "A game, another side game, if you are not too tired?"

His heavy silk coat sounded like a distant seashore as he walked. He closed the door behind him and then swept into a magnificent bow, as low as that one might give to a queen. "You do me too much honor, Your Grace."

"Jemma," she said.

His heavy-lidded eyes paused on her face for a moment. "Jemma." Her name sounded odd on his lips, and Jemma suddenly remembered the first time she was unfaithful to Beaumont. It had been in Paris, of course, after she fled England in rage and tears. Two years after she moved to Paris, it finally became clear to her that Beaumont was not coming after her to beg her to come home — fool that she was, she had thought he would. In fact, he didn't even pay her a visit for three years, and by then it was too late.

She had fallen into bed with a merry French gentleman who taught her the pleasures of her own body and his. And yet that first night, her heart had been as heavy as it was now.

Why should it be heavy? She had the right to do precisely as she wished. She watched him sit opposite her, tossing his coat-skirts behind him so they wouldn't crease. "You may perhaps think that I do you more honor than I intend," she said.

"Dear lady," Villiers said, "I will take whatever scraps you throw from your table."

More of his curfluffle. Perhaps she should just tell him that she disliked his practiced gallantry.

"A game?" she asked. "I have given you the advantage, as you see."

He played a piece and so did she. Again, and again. The rhythm of the game soothed her, wrapped her in the sweet complexities of knights and rooks and the powerful queen. Slowly her rage and mortification ebbed as her focus on the game sharpened. Her bishop was menaced. She rushed to save him, only to find that her queen's pawn was threatened. A troublesome move . . . she slowed to think. Paused, her fingers still on her rook, until she suddenly saw a path, took his rook.

He fought back, but her bishop took his queen . . . four moves later it was over. She won.

Then they parsed the game, playing it backwards.

"When your rook took my pawn . . . that was a beautiful play," Villiers muttered.

"What if you had threatened my queen, so?"

"No, because knight takes bishop . . ."

It was almost more fun dissecting the game than playing it. Almost, but not quite. At the end, he leaned back and smiled at her. "Sometimes I think that chess is better than sex."

"I think so always," she said, startling herself.

"Someone should change your mind on that subject."

She reached out and turned his hand over. "Perhaps you could be the one to change my mind," she said, tracing a path on his palm with her finger. "That is, I would be pleased, but you are Roberta's fiancé, and the bonds between friends are stronger than those between lovers, in my opinion."

"I have few friends. The closest friend of my life was your husband, and that many years ago."

She glanced at him, but he was staring at her fingers on his hand. "I know that you were close once . . ."

"In the way of boys and small animals. Without thought for the future nor our differing personalities. But still, I find I have a fragment of honor left in me. I am not the person to show Beaumont's wife that the body is greater than the mind, and games of chess pale next to games in bed." He took her hand and kissed it, and there was something so sad in his eyes that she didn't even mind the fact she had been turned down.

Though that had never happened before.

"Why don't you speak to him?" she asked impulsively. "Elijah needs friends. He needs someone to tell him to slow down, to drag him away from his work."

His smile was rueful. "He and I are centuries apart, in personality and taste. In all honesty, and without offense, I wouldn't wish to be particular friends with the Duke of Beaumont now. If it were a matter of being fourteen again, and playing a game of chess by the river . . . that I do miss. But those days are gone."

"I have no wish to be fourteen again."

"Life was simpler. I do not let myself entertain regrets nor think about mistakes. My father always said, and he was right, that regret is a useless practice. But I find that in my thirties, regrets chase me down the street sometimes. It's not so easy to shrug them away."

He was talking about Benjamin, perhaps. She thought about whether to mention his suicide too long, because Villiers asked her, "What do you regret, Oh Duchess?"

That made her grin. "So many things!"

"Such as?"

"The absurd Italian hat I bought yesterday in Bond Street with Roberta."

"Ah, Roberta."

His eyelids dropped and she couldn't see his expression. "Your fiancée," she prompted.

"A charming young lady."

"I gather," she said wryly, "that the dew is off the rose, for you."

"Yet another regret." He sighed. "They are like bad dreams; once you allow one, they come as thick and fast as leaves in autumn."

"She will make you an excellent wife."

"I did it to make you angry." He raised her hand and put one kiss in her palm, and then replaced it on the table, all without looking at her. "I admit with some shame: You won our first game of chess."

She shook her head at him. "You asked someone to marry you out of pique?"

"Are you suggesting that I take this game too seriously?"

She found herself laughing, and then he joined in.

"One never knows," he said a moment later. "There's many a slip between an engagement and the church."

"She loves you, you know."

"Or something of that nature," he agreed.

"It would take an act of God," Jemma said. "But I think she will be the making of you, Villiers. Perhaps you will have the real marriage that I can only imagine."

"Unfortunately, I cannot imagine such a thing," he said with some disdain. "I shall pray for an act of God." He was at the door when he turned and said, "I have had many lovers, Jemma."

She raised an eyebrow. "I am the more disconcerted to be left out of the legion, then."

"That's not what I meant. I've had many lovers . . . but few friends."

And he was gone, before she thought how to reply.

Chapter 32

"What happened to you? Where did you go?" Damon demanded.

Roberta blinked. "What are you talking about?"

"Why did you sneak off like a housemaid in the night and leave me in the sitting room?"

She couldn't help laughing a little. "Are you telling me that you wanted me to stay around and watch you snore? Perhaps until the footman came in to bank the fire? I took a bath, just as you apparently did," she said, looking at his wet hair.

"I didn't get a chance to show you what making love can be like."

"Oh, yes you did," she said hastily. "I thoroughly enjoyed it. Truly. I was simply —"

He swallowed all her words, and her protests, and her sensible points, just by pulling off his shirt, and then his breeches.

A protest died in her throat. Without a word he lowered his hard masculine length on top of her. It was unsettling. A sort of hunger settled deep in her stomach that made her feel uneasy.

Then Damon started kissing her, and with a little moan, she opened her lips to him. She could taste his hunger, as if they passed it back and forth to each other. The uneasiness in her stomach was turning into something else, some sort of restlessness that brought her hands up to his powerful forearms. Her fingers trembled as she traced his muscles.

The feeling alarmed her, and with a sudden twist she rolled out from under him and sprang away from the bed. "I'd prefer not to be intimate again," she said, dismayed to realize that her breath was coming fast.

Damon didn't even seem to hear her. He started padding toward her, without a word, like a predator.

Roberta backed up as far as she could go, against her little armchair. "Damon!" she cried, trying to make her voice sound commanding. "I prefer not —"

But he was kissing her again, fierce in his possession, and all her flimsy words blew away because the mere touch of his hands had her shivering.

"No," she gasped, but it was like throwing kindling on a fire; he laughed, deep in his throat and kissed her again, kissed her until she was trembling, her mind swirling, her body rocking against his, her voice strangled with the need to beg him —

She never begged.

Never.

But then he stopped touching her and suddenly her body raged with the memory of his large hands shaping her breasts, rubbing her. He was just kissing her. That's all. As if —

Of course, she wasn't touching him either. They were standing together, and the only thing touching was their mouths and it wasn't enough.

"Damon," she said, her voice husky.

"I've never lost control like that."

"It had nothing to do with your control. I think I just didn't enjoy that part of it very much. It's — It's so fast, isn't it? And not —"

He groaned. "Can we talk about aberrations?"

"What?" she said, confused.

But he was there, scooping her up. "This one's for you, Buttercup," he said, putting her back on the bed and sitting down next to her.

Roberta was still trying to think what to say when he pulled open her dressing gown. Instinctively, she grabbed it back. "No!"

"Yes." His eyes were full of slumberous intent, but she hung on. "Roberta," he said slowly, "if you don't let go, I'm going to bite you."

"What!"

He put a finger on her breast and it sizzled, straight through the silk of her dressing gown. "Here," he said, his voice husky. "And perhaps" — his finger wandered down, leaving a trail of fire in its wake — "here."

"You'd bite my stomach?" Her voice squeaked, so she sounded as foolish as she felt.

He laughed at her. "I thought you learned so much from your informative discussions with Selina?"

"She never talked about *biting*. And I'd really rather not do that again," she confessed, though her cheeks turned pink.

He looked down at her, eyebrow raised, and there was such a flare of desire in his eyes that she instinctively moved her hips. But they encountered something hard and hot, and she shrank back. "I bathed," she said. "Please, could we just *not?*"

He groaned and his eyes shut. "I'm such

an idiot."

"No, you're not," she said reassuringly. Her fingers trembled as they slipped down his arms onto his broad back. "I thought it was very interesting. Not at all as Selina described it, but —"

"How did Selina describe it?"

"Well," she foundered, "I thought it — it —"

"It would take longer," he said grimly, his mouth a straight line.

"No," she said, frowning at the look on his face. "No, not at all. It was just as she described it, that way."

He groaned. "Wonderful. What else did Selina say?"

"She said that a woman has to take her own pleasure," Roberta said, "but I don't think there was any pleasure for me to take that you didn't give me, Damon." She didn't like that look on his face at all, so she arched up against his body to kiss him, her lips sliding over his lips to his cheek. "Truly," she said anxiously.

"You," he said, "are an innocent."

"No, I'm not!" she said, flopping back down on the bed. "No one raised in my father's household could call herself an innocent!"

He suddenly grinned. "All right." He

417

pushed back on his forearms and rolled away to lie next to her on the bed.

"What?" she asked, confused.

"Take your pleasure."

"What?"

"That's what you learned from Selina. And believe me, Roberta, you didn't get a chance to do it downstairs. I took all the pleasure there was to be had." His eyes had a shade of self-condemnation that she hated.

"I don't know what you're talking about," she told him, "but it was enormously pleasurable. Truly."

In response he just flung his arms above his head. "Go on," he said. "Take your pleasure."

Roberta was confused. Selina had never been entirely clear about what she meant, but Roberta had (obviously mistakenly) formed the conclusion that a woman should demand that her partner kiss her . . . in an intimate spot. But that didn't seem to be what Damon had in mind at all, as he had made no move to kiss her anywhere other than her breast and her lips, and now that she thought about it, that kind of kiss would be so tremendously embarrassing that she had to be wrong.

She could feel the color creeping into her cheeks at the very thought. What if she had asked Damon to do such a thing? Not that she would have, but —

"Roberta," he said patiently, and her eyes flew open. "I'm waiting."

Roberta looked down at his hardened length. Just what was she supposed to do?

As if he could hear her thought, he said, "Your pleasure, not mine."

Roberta was starting to feel a bit like a failure. How was she supposed to know what to do? "And we won't do the rest of it again?" She really didn't want to take another bath. It was too awful even to think of summoning her maid again.

"We won't do anything you don't ask me to do."

Satisfied, she moved a fraction of an inch closer to him. "But what do you expect me to *do?*" she said, a second later, unable to think of anything.

"Think about pleasure," he said to her, his eyes slumberous and dark. "What gives you, Roberta, pleasure about me? About my body? Is there anything? Because it's yours. You can touch me however you wish. If you tell me to do something, I will. If you don't tell me, I won't raise a finger."

A shiver went through her. "Go on," he said. "You're not showing Selina's tutelage to the best advantage."

Roberta bit her lip and put his teasing out of her mind. Her pleasure? And what did she particularly — well, like? She had been absolutely wrong about Selina's advice, obviously, so what was Selina actually saying?

She didn't meet his eyes because she didn't want to discover he was laughing at her naïveté, after she boasted of learning so much from Selina. So she looked at his arms instead. They were broad and muscled, as unlike her slender ones as possible. She reached out a hand and placed it on his arm, slid over the bunched muscle there to the strength of his shoulder, to the breadth of his chest.

Suddenly she noticed something. He quivered under her hand. Perhaps . . .

She tried it again, running her hand over his muscles. Her fingers brushed his armpit and touched his nipple. He did it again. He shook, just slightly, from her touch. She scooted over on her knees so that she was just beside him and could use both her hands to touch him.

She flattened both hands on his chest, and then drew her fingers down his chest to his taut stomach. That was . . . pleasurable. The feeling of powerful muscle under her fingers, rippling slightly under her touch was pleasurable. The low sound that came from Damon's chest was definitely pleasurable, though she didn't look at his face. She was too busy swirling a finger around his nipple, and listening to his breathing grow short and hoarse. She was smiling now. *This* was what Selina meant! Selina meant that she should learn to take pleasure from her lover's body, from making him react to her touch.

His stomach was rock hard, not flat, because it was covered with organized bumps of muscle. She'd never seen anything like that. Her father, as far as she could tell, had a nice flat stomach for a man coming perilously close to the age of fifty. But she'd never dreamed that men had such very different stomachs from her own.

She actually glanced down at her own stomach, but her dressing gown was still firmly tied. In the sitting room, he had kissed her breast. Could Selina have meant her to do the same to him?

Finally she looked up at his face, her fingers still caressing his abdomen. Damon's face was dark and taut. There was a fierce hunger in his eyes that made her blood sing. Yes, *this* was pleasurable! Suddenly she knew exactly what she wanted to do: she wanted to drive him mad with desire.

She didn't know it, but the smile that touched her lips made another groan slip from Damon's lips . . . her smile had the slumberous joy of a woman who had just surrendered to her own sensual nature.

She bent her head and her glossy hair fell over her shoulder and brushed against his nipples. Damon's hands stayed at his sides, but he bucked his hips into the air. Roberta was so startled that she froze. Then slowly, her smile growing, she picked up a lock of hair and rubbed it over one of his nipples. "Roberta!" he said, and his hips arched again.

"Yes?" she asked sweetly.

"If you sat on top of me . . ." but she was experimenting with rubbing a little harder, and the words died in his throat.

Still, she heard what he said. "Would you like that?" she whispered.

"Aye."

"But you won't leap on me, or something of that nature? Because," she felt silly telling him again, but it had to be said, "I really don't wish to become messy again. I'm sorry."

He shook his head. "I will not do anything you don't ask me to do."

Satisfied, she pulled up the silk of her dressing gown and straddled him. He groaned out loud this time, and Roberta froze. Suddenly, she was feeling his muscles with a whole other part of her body. It made her feel feverish, hot, as if she were melting.

When he had kissed her breasts earlier in the evening — it was shocking to remember it, and yet the memory sent a twist of liquid heat down to her thighs — he didn't just touch her with his tongue. He suckled her, as a babe might its mother, at least so she thought. It was a strange idea and yet . . . She lowered her head to his chest.

It wasn't at all like being a baby. He twisted under her mouth, and made a hoarse groan, and the sound sent another wave of liquid heat down her body. So she suckled harder, and he writhed under her.

Which had the most peculiar effect on the place between her legs.

"Roberta," he gasped, "would you please ask me to touch you?"

"No," she said immediately, straightening up.

His eyes were fevered with desire, but there was a lurking smile too. "I can't stop moving if you do that," he said, his voice rasping.

"All right," she said, her fingers brushing over his nipples again, just to see what he would do.

What he did was arch up, which made him rub against . . .

She gasped and clutched his shoulders.

"Not that!" she cried.

"No?" his eyes were so disappointed.

"No."

"Sometimes I can't stop it," he whispered achingly. "When you touch me, Roberta, I feel mad, out of control."

That was a very pleasurable thing to hear. So Roberta kissed him again, and a groan tore from his throat and he was moving under her. *That* was rather pleasurable as well though not, of course, in the way that Selina was talking about.

"May I touch you?" he gasped.

"No!" But she wanted to touch more of him, even . . . even that part of him. So she moved backward, careful not to touch him, and sat on his legs instead.

Damon instantly propped himself upon his elbows, watching her. That part of him was like smooth velvet, hot to the touch, jerking against her hand.

"Don't you have control over it?" she asked curiously.

He groaned. "Normally I do. That was an aberration."

"What aberration? Look, every time I touch it, it moves." She cupped her hand around him, and he fell flat back and that hoarse sound came from his throat again.

One had to wonder, Roberta thought, what he would do if she — of course, she couldn't do that. It wasn't done, she was sure. Except that she had a fragile memory of something Selina said . . . something about just this subject.

She'd thought it was disgusting at the time, but now, looking at Damon's rigid face and the way he was breathing quickly and harshly, she rather thought that it would give her a great deal of pleasure to make him mad, as it were. Perhaps even lose control.

She tried touching her tongue to it first. It was smooth and hot on the top. Just like the rest of Damon . . . sleek and muscled. She actually licked it. The sound he made sounded almost like pain. She jerked up her head.

"Is this wrong? Should I not —"

"Oh God, please don't stop."

He tasted clean and slightly sweet.

"I think you are designing this whole night to make me understand my limits," he gasped.

She smiled and tasted him again.

"Roberta." Damon's voice was strangled, dark, coming from some deep place in his chest. "Don't you want me to touch you at all?"

Confused, she sat back up. "What?"

"This is about your pleasure," he said, up on his elbows again. "Yours. If you'd let me touch you, the way you've touched me . . ."

Roberta thought about that. Her body didn't have to think about it. She shivered all over instantly.

"Please? Please, Roberta, may I touch you?" The aching sound in his voice made her shake even more.

"All right," she whispered. "All right."

In one smooth movement, he sat up and lifted her off his legs. "You tell me."

"Tell you what?"

He gently pushed her backwards. "Tell me what would give you pleasure."

"Oh!"

"Shall I kiss you here?" He put a finger on her wrist.

That seemed acceptable. Roberta nodded. He didn't just kiss, though, he nuzzled her wrist, and licked it.

"Your hand?"

Something like an assent came from her throat and he was kissing each of her fingers, and then swirling his tongue around the tips of them, and even suckling them, which against all commonsense made her shiver. He pressed a kiss into her palm.

"Where next?"

She blinked at him.

"If you don't tell me, I suppose I could just make a choice for you?"

There was something violent and tender in his voice that made her lose her head. "Here," she gasped.

"Where?"

Her hand touched her breast. "Here."

"I'll have to untie your dressing gown. May I?"

"Yes," she whispered.

"Because I could kiss you straight through the silk." His large hand pulled the frail silk taut against her breast, and there was her nipple, puckered, straining against the fabric. Roberta could feel herself turning crimson, but she was so hot it hardly mattered.

She tremblingly untied her dressing gown.

"I'll take that as an assent," he said, a tone of deep satisfaction in his voice.

She didn't tremble or gasp when his mouth came to her breast. She shrieked. It was a small shriek, but still —

Roberta clapped a hand over her mouth.

He was laughing, of course. And then kissing her again, sweet and rough, and her body arched toward him precisely as his had toward her.

"Oh," she said, helpless in the face of delight. "I . . ." but the words slipped away from her. He was moving from one breast to the other, expert and slow. Just when she thought she couldn't bear it another moment, he would move back to the other breast, and his rough fingers would replace his lips.

"I can't — I can't —" Roberta said, those little screams building up in her throat until she couldn't keep silent. She couldn't —

"Roberta, may I kiss you in other places?"

"Wha—"

His fingers trailed down her body. "Just to demonstrate," he told her, his fingers leaving a fiery trail. "I'd like to kiss you here." The sweet mound of her stomach, so different from his.

"Here." Her hip.

"Here." The inside, secret curve of her upper thigh.

And finally, "Here." He put a finger on her curly patch of hair and slowly, deliberately, drew it downwards.

Roberta shook like a sapling in a storm. His finger lingered, slipping deep, tutoring her body to a kind of pleasure she hadn't imagined.

"Roberta?"

She sobbed in response, and he must have taken it as a yes, because a moment later he started following the path he had laid out. Roberta's mind sank into a haze of desire. His lips brushed the skin of her stomach, and she squeaked. He migrated to the curve of her hip, and his hands slipped underneath her and shaped her bottom.

"How does that feel?" he asked.

She could hear the control in his voice now, the way he'd taken charge. All she could do was moan. He kept his hands there but his lips went lower and now he was skating across her thigh, nipping her a little, and she was breathing in little pants . . . which would have been embarrassing but there wasn't a place for that emotion, not even when he pulled her legs apart and settled between them like a man dedicated to one cause.

Her pleasure.

From the moment his tongue touched her, she surrendered. He may not have known it, but Roberta was lost in a fever dream that had tongues of fire licking in her body. Her hands clenched in the sheets, she was sobbing rather than breathing, when he stopped.

Stopped!

"I forgot to ask permission to kiss you

here," he said, his fingers tracing a particular sensitive spot.

"Yes," she sobbed. And oh, it was coming again, she was climbing some mountain toward —

He stopped.

"I apologize, Roberta. I forgot to mention *this* place." His thumb brushed another sweet fold.

"Oh — *yes!*" she cried.

The feeling grew in her like a gathering calm before a storm. She was twisting against his hand now and gasping for air. He put a hand on her breast, and the fury broke in her blood, rolled like thunder through her legs. He didn't stop — he didn't stop — she arched her back and cried out, let the sweet storm roll over her again and again and again.

Slowly she opened her eyes, and Damon was above her, on his knees.

"You," she said foolishly.

"Did you like that?" His eyes were dancing and she felt a wave of some emotion she didn't want to catalog, some emotion that made her wind her arms around his neck and pull him down into a kiss.

His hard body came against hers, and for the first time she realized that a woman's body is a perfect cradle for a man's, and that the whole silky soft warmth of her was shaped perfectly for the hardness of his.

He was there . . . there . . . "Roberta," he said, his voice hoarse. "May I?"

There was no thought of baths in her mind. "Yes," she whispered, her fingers cupping his face. "Yes."

His eyes darkened, and he kissed her as he thrust into her . . . which meant that he caught her scream on his lips.

Damon had never felt anything like this. In a life not starved for sensual encounters, he had never experienced anything like making love to Roberta. She was gripping his arms as if he were her savior in a strange land. Perhaps it felt that way to her.

He knew only that she was breathing in deep breathy sobs that brought him to the edge of control. Even without the silky clasp of her body. But if there was one thing he was going to do, it was stay in control.

And he did.

He thrust into her again, and again, and again — fiercely, softly, trying this, adjusting that, listening to her squeaks, and then her cries, and finally, her pleas. When she started pleading, his proud, lovely Roberta, pleading, he put his hands on her sweet bottom and pulled her up, bringing their hips together in a volley of passion. His chest

431

burned, and his whole body was fighting for release but he held back, guided her over the brink, watched as her eyes flew open and she clenched her hands in his hair. Watched her luscious breasts arch toward him as she rode him up, up . . . up.

And still he didn't lose control, though his teeth were clenched and he was panting like a stallion after a long ride.

He settled, though, let her body rest for a moment . . . till her eyes opened again and she smiled at him, all wonder and the shadow of joy there.

"I forgot," he said.

"Forgot what?" Her voice was husky; it made him pulse inside her, and he had to wage another silent battle with himself.

"I forgot to show you something," he said. He slipped out of her, not without an internal groan, picked up her boneless body, flipped her over and slid her off the bed so her toes touched the ground. And came around behind her.

"Oh," she said, startled.

And then, when he rubbed against her, slipped into her impossibly silky depths, *"Oh!"*

Damon didn't say anything. He couldn't. It was taking every ounce of control he had to keep plunging into her while he shaped her breasts in his hands, feasted his eyes on her heart-shaped rear, counted to forty, counted to forty again, and then finally, slowly, she started moving back toward him a little bit, arching and then — finally — she began breathing in that little sob that he knew he would listen for his entire life.

She understood now and was pushing back at him with the same strength with which he thrust into her, giving her everything he had, until she convulsed with a little shriek.

And yet he still didn't lose control because he wanted to see her, this first time, this first real time.

So he turned her over and slid back into the place where he belonged most in the world, and simply let go. Took her mouth in a kiss that was as savage and possessive as his thrusts. Her hands twined in his hair, and he couldn't hear for the thundering sound of his own blood in his ears, so he gasped her name, thrusting again and again. Filling her; filling him, if only he'd had the words for the emotion that flooded him.

The room was silent for a long time.

"You're marrying me." His voice was deep and certain.

Roberta didn't answer. She nuzzled into the strength of his arm around her and sighed blissfully.

"Just so you know," he said.

But she was asleep.

CHAPTER 33

April 18
Day seven of the Villiers/Beaumont chess matches

Roberta woke up alone.

She stared at the bed curtains, realizing that she ought to think about serious subjects, like her marriage to the Duke of Villiers. But she didn't want to think: she wanted to dream about Damon . . . about the way his large hands spanned her breasts, and then slid between her legs, and . . . everything else.

Until she suddenly woke up again and realized that her heart was beating fast, her breasts were tingling, and her maid would be there any moment to draw back the curtains.

She felt rather foolishly blissful. Almost poetic, in fact. Which was surprising enough to make her rethink the whole idea of poetry.

She wandered down to breakfast to find her father there, sitting beside Teddy. He looked up as she entered. "Mrs. Grope has gone to visit her friends at the theater," he told her. "Master Teddy is showing me his collection of rocks."

Roberta sat down beside Teddy. He had a number of small brown rocks in front of him. The dirty kind that one finds anywhere.

"Very interesting," she told Teddy.

He threw her an exasperated look that was just like his father's. "The rocks aren't interesting," he told her, "it's where they're *from*."

She peered over again and then hazarded a guess. "Persia?"

"West Smithfield!" he said triumphantly.

"Yes, I will have some eggs, thank you," Roberta told the footman. "And what's interesting about West Smithfield?"

"That's where the mermaid landed. And these rocks come from there, too."

"Thank you," Roberta said, accepting some toast as well. She felt unusually hungry.

"Master Teddy and I are thinking of going to see this mermaid," her father said. "Would you like to come, dear? She's at the Smithfield Market, as Teddy says. I've never seen a mermaid, though I've read Homer's warning about their dangerous propensities, of course."

"She speaks in verse, Rummer says," Teddy contributed.

"Rummer says she speaks in verse," Roberta corrected him.

"A real mermaid!" Teddy's eyes were huge. "I hope Papa wakes up soon. I know that he will be so excited."

Just then Damon walked in the room. Roberta's heart sped up and she felt herself going pink. He bent to drop a kiss on Teddy's head. "Why aren't you in the nursery?"

"Nanny's sick as a fish," Teddy reported. "She says her stomach is turning itself inside out and" — he looked enraged — "she says it's my fault!"

"Why?" his father said, looking unsurprised as he sat down just to the left of Roberta.

The moment he sat down, even though he hardly looked at her, Damon's muscular thigh pressed against hers. Roberta took another bite of eggs. This would never do. She couldn't survive with her heart beating so quickly; she felt as hot as a housewife boiling rags.

But that's what the day was like. They set off to see the versifying mermaid, and though Damon paid her little outward attention, certainly nothing to attract her father's notice, he kept touching her. She climbed into the carriage after Teddy, and a warm hand cupped her bottom. She sat next to Damon in the carriage, and somehow his hand got trapped behind her and started to caress her back.

Smithfield Market was crowded. "Mostly horses here," Damon said cheerfully.

"Really?" her father said. "Is this a good place for horse flesh, then? I always thought that Tattersall's was the best venue."

"You were right. Smithfield is not a good place. You'll find many an old horse with dyed hair, with an owner promising he's a yearling."

"Humph," her father said, stumping ahead of them.

Roberta adjusted her parasol to keep off the sun.

"Can you see the mermaid yet?" Teddy asked.

"The marquess will see her first," his father said. "Why don't you walk with him?"

Teddy darted ahead and that very second Damon spun Roberta about and pulled her into a kiss. She gasped in surprise, his tongue slipped between her lips, and the kiss hardened. He kissed her lingeringly, possessively, as if they weren't surrounded by crowds of farmers pushing their way toward the horse auction.

"Anyone can see us!" she gasped a moment later, staring up at him.

"I'm making a spectacle of you," he said with a smile in his voice.

She blinked at him and then looked around. No one was showing the faintest interest in a pair of daft gentry kissing in the sunshine.

And even looking at his eyes made her feel hungry. Hungry . . . as if it didn't matter how people stared at her. As if —

She came up on her tiptoes and kissed him.

A man pushed by them, and shouted back over his shoulders, "Get yerself a bed, then!"

Damon laughed, of course, but Roberta didn't even flinch. "I feel like kissing you," she whispered.

His eyes flared, but he shook his head. "No more kisses. There are spectacles and then there are spectacles. And I'm wearing a French cut-away."

She frowned at him, and then followed his eyes . . . down the front of his body. Sure enough, his coat was cut back in a beautiful arch, the better to show off the twelve pearl buttons on his waistcoat, his breeches . . . and something else.

Roberta opened her mouth — but Teddy was on them like a tiny whirlwind. "Come on," he cried. "What are you doing? The mermaid is in a boat!"

"A boat?" Roberta said, allowing him to pull her away. "But this is land."

"I know, but she has her own boat anyway."

She did, indeed, have a boat. It was a round little vessel, a boat-shaped cottage. It was painted a faded blue, with curly letters on the side that read *Versifying Mermaid.* A small line of people waited restlessly outside. A burly fellow was timing the line, and let another person in every few minutes.

"Where do they go?" Teddy asked.

"Out the back door," his father said.

Roberta was looking at the line, which consisted solely of men. "Damon, go and ask that person in front if the mermaid is appropriately dressed for a young boy," she said.

Damon looked down at Teddy, dancing on one leg. "You must be joking. We couldn't leave, even if she is wearing nothing more than a fish scale on one toe."

"Yes, we can," she said firmly. So Damon made his way over to the guard in front.

"Where's Papa going?" Teddy said. "And where's *your* papa going?"

Her father was standing before a tent marked *Harry Hunks, Performing Bear.* He turned around and beckoned. "This bear can blow a whistle and dance a jig," he shouted.

Teddy was there in a second, so Roberta followed them into the cool interior of the tent. The smell of bear was overpowering, however, and she backed out directly, straight into Damon.

His arms came around her from behind. "I like that," he said. He pulled her more firmly against him.

"Your cut-away coat?" she asked, pulling away.

"There are some things a gentleman can't control," he said. "You should have seen me when I was younger."

"Really? How so?"

"Fourteen was an interesting year."

"Wasn't that when Miss Kendrick began sending you perfumed letters?"

He nodded, a lock of hair brushing his eyes. "I had absolutely no control of my body."

"You mean . . ." Her eyes slid down his front.

He nodded. "If someone had even mentioned a versifying mermaid, I would have thought about mermaid breasts and been

441

rigid for the next hour. Maybe you and I can play mermaids later?" He grinned wolfishly at her.

She smiled, but said, "What of this particular mermaid? Is she adequately clothed?"

"Oh yes," Damon said. "The man there indicated that this mermaid was pulled from the water twenty-two years ago and has been versifying ever since. He got a bit offended at the idea that she might not be proper fare for children and said that she was a vicar's daughter. Now that I doubt, but if I were a thirty-year-old mermaid, I'd avail myself of some friendly seaweed. Is Teddy in there with the bear, by the way?"

"And the smell," Roberta said.

Suddenly they heard her father's voice, loud and clear through the tent flap. "Do you mean to tell me, Mr. Clay, that you starve the bear if he doesn't behave?"

"He only misses his supper," a voice protested in reply. "And he knows, right enough, that's he's done wrong, sir. That he does. Just like any dog. Why, I hardly ever have to take a whip —"

"You whip this bear?" the marquess said, his voice rising to a roar.

People in line at the mermaid's tent turned their heads, and a few others drifted closer. Roberta's hand crept into Damon's, but somehow her usual feelings of mortification and shame at the fact her father was about to make a spectacle weren't creeping over her.

A second later, her father spilled out of the tent, followed by a lean, hungry-looking fellow, presumably Mr. Clay.

"I can't bear the stench another moment," her father said. "Not another moment. And just think what that poor bear makes of it, sir, since in the normal way of things he'd be living at the top of a tall tree, smelling nothing but the blue sky!"

They all reflexively looked up. "I does my best," Mr. Clay bleated.

"Your best isn't good enough!" the marquess said. "I'll have that bear, or I'll know the reason why."

Cutting off Mr. Clay's ineffectual bluster, the marquess produced a handful of guineas, and ownership of Harry Hunks passed hands.

"I'll fetch him tomorrow," the marquess said. "And you'd better be at your residence with the bear, Mr. Clay, or I shall have the High Constable on you!"

Mr. Clay was looking blissfully at the guineas in his hand. "I can go back home with these," he said. "I'll be there, your lordship, and so will Harry."

"I'll have more of those for you if you can find a cart to take Harry to my country house."

Damon leaned over and said in Roberta's ear, "How many bears do you have at home?"

"None," she said.

"Oh."

"But we do have a couple of deer that were supposed to be elk, but turned out to have horns glued on, a terrible weight for their poor heads, I assure you. And we have some Greenland ducks —"

"*Greenland* ducks?" Damon said with a crack of laughter.

"Hush! Papa will hear you. They are rather peculiar, and we think they're a strain of exotic chicken because they can't swim. At first papa dropped them into the lake and it was only very quick work on the part of a groom that saved their life."

Meanwhile, they had made their way back to the mermaid's boat. The marquess dropped a few coins into the guard's hands.

"He's a *pirate!*" Teddy said, awed.

Damon ducked his head as they went through the low door of the boat. Seated in the corner was a mermaid.

She was quite pretty, with long golden hair

and a sweet face. She had a glossy green tail wrapped with a net and a few artistically placed shells. Unlike any picture he'd ever seen of a siren of the deep, she wore a starched white bodice that overlapped the beginning of her tail. In fact, she looked a bit like a vicar's daughter. Except for the satin tail, of course.

Teddy marched up before her, and said, "May I ask you questions?"

The mermaid nodded at Teddy and smiled.

"I will answer whatever I can,
As a daughter of the sea to a child of man."

The marquess started rocking back and forth on his heels, a sure sign of enjoyment.

"Are you friends with fish?" Teddy asked.

"Fish were my favorite boon companions,
My very best friend was a shark,
We would whip about and have great fun,
Until I was caught by His Majesty's barque."

"Sharks!" Teddy said, eyes round. "I thought they were the monsters of the deep, and ate everything in their path."

"Have you met a shark, Oh child of the sands?

For ignorance is no excuse for those with hands."

Teddy shook his head. "I'd love to meet a shark," he said, coming closer.

"How long have you lived in this boat, oh daughter of the sea?" the marquess asked. He had his hands clasped behind his back and he was grinning like a fool.

"Your father seems to be taken by the mermaid's versifying abilities," Damon murmured to Roberta.

"Or something," she said.

She'd seen that ecstatic look on his face before. Specifically, when Selina pranced out on the stage of her traveling troupe, and when they first saw Mrs. Grope stride onto the stage in Bath.

The memory of my watery cave grows dim," the mermaid was saying, *" 'Tis been twenty years ere I swam in the deep, Now I almost think I am growing a limb."*

"Nicely put," Damon said.

The guard popped his head in and growled, "Time's up. The mermaid has others waiting for her."

The marquess turned to the mermaid.

"Could a gentleman's family lure a mer-
    maid to swim,
If we arranged it so she needn't stir a fin,
Into the shallows of a tea garden for tea,
Upon the earnest request of — of me?"

"Tsk, Tsk," Damon said. "That final
rhyme left something to be desired, my
lord."

But the mermaid dimpled and looked as
if she were blushing a little. But instead of
answering, interestingly enough, she looked
at Roberta. She nodded toward her tail, and
then toward Teddy. After a second, Roberta
realized that she was asking if Teddy would
be upset to learn that the mermaid did
indeed have limbs.

Roberta gave her a smile. "It's so hot in
here," she said, turning to Damon. "I think
I should like to go home. And Teddy, it's
time that we said goodbye to the lovely
mermaid."

Teddy bowed, very solemn. "It has been
marvelous to meet you."

*"You remind me of a shark I once knew,
called Perth,"* she said, perfectly seriously.
*"He had lovely brown eyes like yours, Oh child
of the earth."*

Teddy bowed again and took Roberta's
hand as they left through the rear. "I should

like to be a shark," he said, and he chattered so much on the way back to the carriage that he didn't even notice that the marquess wasn't with them until they got home.

Whereupon Roberta told him that her papa had gone to arrange for Harry Hunks to travel back home with him.

"I want to see Harry Hunks again," Teddy said wistfully.

"You will," Damon said, smiling at Roberta over his head. "You will."

CHAPTER 34

April 19
Day eight of the Villiers/Beaumont chess matches

Roberta stretched, feeling a pleasurable ache in all parts of her body, and then settled down to think.

Obviously, she needed to think. She plumped up the pillows to remove the unmistakable evidence that there had been two heads sleeping in her bed and thought: *the Duke of Villiers.*

My fiancé.

It was rather disconcerting to realize how fickle she was.

Ellen bustled in and began darting around the room, trailing a stream of conversation.

"A picnic?" Roberta said, belatedly catching the word. "Who?"

It seemed that everyone was going on this picnic. "Not the master, of course," Ellen said. "He's gone to his offices long ago."

Roberta thought about it. A picnic on the Fleet River sounded like a delicious way to avoid the thorny issue of her fiancé. "Marvelous," she said, swinging her legs out of bed.

"Her Grace is just playing her move with the Duke of Villiers," Ellen said.

Roberta froze. "Is the duke accompanying us?"

"Of course," Ellen said, giving her a warm smile. "I'm sure he wouldn't miss it. He enquired for you yesterday, but you were off with the mermaid. What Master Teddy hasn't told us about that mermaid!"

The picnic involved not just one flat-bottomed boat, but a whole fleet of them. Roberta climbed into a boat without any difficulty, and Teddy clambered next to her, taking it for granted that the two of them would sit together.

"I have a great deal to tell you," he said. "I talked to Rummer all morning and — this will *really* interest you, Lady Roberta — I discovered what a bog-trotting croggie is!"

Jemma almost had to have a boat to herself, given the width of her panniers, and there were a few screams when the Duke of Villiers's cane caught on the side of the boat and he fell directly into Jemma's lap.

Roberta had a difficult time keeping her

mind on the question of bogs and croggies, because it seemed to her that Villiers took a long time to disentangle himself from Jemma's lap. In fact, Roberta couldn't help wondering where her fiancé spent the night. Did his chess game shift to something more intimate?

Mrs. Grope climbed into the boat rather grimly; she was intent on telling the company at large that she was used to large pleasure boats, such as those the Prince of Wales traveled in, though Roberta doubted very much that Mrs. Grope had ever been on a boat at the same time as the prince.

"We played a lovely game of charades aboard His Majesty's yacht," she could hear her telling her father. "Why, the girls and I were talking about it last night in the green room . . ." She looked wistfully into the distance.

Damon settled himself opposite and met her eyes with a grin. "Dollymop charades," he mouthed.

Roberta couldn't help giggling. The world was a beautiful place when one was going boating with a lovely, loose-limbed man, who had done such delicious things the night before . . . She even felt a flash of approval for Villiers and his idea that chastity was an antiquated notion. He was right!

She gave Villiers a huge smile, boat to boat. He seemed rather taken aback, but nodded.

"Too demonstrative," Damon observed. "You can't go smiling at your fiancé like that. Smiles, words . . . those are for ordinary mortals. The two of you should communicate only in nods."

She turned her nose up at his silliness.

Teddy was eager to talk about a Mr. Swarthy, who often wears brown paper pinned to his white silk stockings. "Do you know why that is, Lady Roberta?"

Teddy had an endearing earnestness about him. His chin was really adorable. It was tiny with a little dimple that mimicked his father's. "I don't have any idea," Roberta said. "I wouldn't pin brown paper to my legs; would you?"

"He does it in bad weather," Teddy reported. "And he also sings 'Fair Dorinda' in the coffeehouse, and they don't like it."

They were drifting down the river. The river was more dappled and green today, sleepy in the sunshine.

"The water sounds like babies talking," Teddy said.

"I think you're going to be a novelist," Roberta told him, listening for the little sleepy murmurs of watery babies.

He beamed and slipped a damp hand into her gloved one. Roberta looked down at his plump fingers and then pulled off her gloves and picked up his hand again.

Mrs. Grope was squealing because a family of ducks was following their boat. For a moment she couldn't see what was happening, and then she realized that her father had raided the picnic hamper and was dropping cucumber sandwiches into the water.

Jemma and Villiers weren't even looking at the water; Villiers had a piece of paper and they were scribbling with a pencil and talking. As she watched, Jemma snatched the paper back and wrote something on it.

Damon followed her glance. "Working out a chess game," he said. "Jemma's chamber is always filled with pieces of paper covered with imaginary games."

"How on earth do you write out a chess game?"

"It's a series of chicken scrawls," he explained. "BK4, for example, means that someone moved his bishop to King's Four."

"Are we going to swim today?" Teddy enquired.

"*You* are going to swim," his father said. "Phillips, who is poling the boat with the marquess in it, was kind enough to offer to take you in the water. We'll drop you off at the mud flats."

Teddy whooped with joy, and in the resulting mêlée he rocked their boat so much that it would have fallen over except for its wide bottom. A few minutes later they handed him off to a cheerful-looking footman.

"Shall we follow the river all the way to the end today?" Roberta enquired, when Damon settled back into the boat. It had been easy when Teddy was with them, but now she felt prickly and strange because they were alone . . . alone except for a footman and the cheerful voice of her father in the boat just in front of them. He was reciting a poem that had to do with fish and fins.

Damon sprawled next to her, all easy grace and muscle, and didn't answer, just picked up her ungloved hand. His thumb played a tune on her wrist, and his touch, that little touch, turned her blood to liquid gold. She couldn't even look at him, so she looked straight ahead, at the way the shadows flowed over the side of the boat, reflecting off the water in pale sparks of light.

She was wearing a gown of cherry muslin, one of those sewn by Mrs. Parthnell, which meant it was of very simple construction and had no hoops. Her hair was tied up and fell in ringlets; she had blackened her eyelashes. She had never felt prettier in her life.

"What do you do all day?" she asked impulsively. She wanted to know everything about him: what he ate for breakfast, and what he named his mare, and where he met his friends.

"When I'm not making love to you?" His voice was low, so the footman couldn't hear it.

But a flush struck her face as if she had a sunburn. "Don't!"

He chuckled, and the low sound of it made her feel breathless. "I own a great deal of property."

She nodded, trying to fix her mind on property. Of course he did. It was like her father's eleven peach trees: Damon would have some peach trees of his own. After all, he was an earl. The thought slipped away from her mind and was replaced by a memory of the night before, a memory of how smooth and hot he felt in her hand.

"You see," he said, "I never could make myself care about chess pieces, but I do like to play with money."

"Hmm," she said, and peeked at him.

A slow smile curved one side of his mouth. "Why do I think that you are uninterested in my financial pastimes?"

"I am interested," she said hastily. But she could feel pink spreading down her bodice. Down to the drawstring that awkwardly separated her bodice from her skirts.

"If you look at me like that," he said, "I'll kiss you."

She couldn't not look. His green eyes fascinated her. A mere glance from him caused a tender warmth between her legs to blossom. She wanted to giggle — and gasp.

"Damn," he said, and the back of his hand touched her cheek for a moment. Then he stretched, his arms suddenly flashing up into the air. But the footman behind them was balanced on the small platform at the back of the boat, wielding the great pole.

Before Roberta could blink there was a flash of crimson livery and a splash. Cool water dashed the boat, hit the muslin roof, sprinkled her dress. She yelped, but Damon was already standing, leaning over the side.

"I can't pull you in or we'll go over," he was shouting to the footman, who was treading water and pushing sodden hair from his forehead. "Best make your way to shore and go back to the house."

The footman gurgled something that sounded like an assent, and managed to maneuver the pole into Damon's hands. He leaped onto the small platform and pushed

456

the boat forward again.

"I didn't know you knew how to do that," Roberta said, changing places so that she was facing Damon, sitting with her back to the current. He was poling the boat forward with long smooth strokes.

"Push footmen in the river, or punt?"

She was laughing so hard she couldn't breathe. The two other boats, now far ahead of them, turned around a corner of the river and vanished altogether. "Did we arrange a spot to meet them?" she enquired.

"No, we didn't."

She watched his smooth, powerful movements as he poled the boat.

"Damon, who is Teddy's mother?" she asked suddenly. "I know why you took him in . . . but who was the grandmother who brought him to you? Is he the child of your mistress?"

"I don't have a mistress," he said, shaking back a lock of hair that had fallen over his head. "I haven't had one for the past five years."

"And Teddy is just five, so —"

"No, Teddy is six. I pensioned my mistress after Teddy came to my house, and no, she wasn't his mother."

She looked at him.

"I can't tell you who his mother is," he

said finally. "I promised I wouldn't tell anyone."

"Oh," Roberta said, disappointed. "I am very good at keeping secrets."

He pulled the pole from the water and an arch of water drops flew like shining diamonds back to the water. "I'll tell my wife, of course," he said conversationally.

"Oh," Roberta said again. But the word sounded different in her mouth this time.

There was a bump and she squealed. "You've gone aground," she cried, adding hastily, "not that I mean it as a criticism." They had scooted right under the vast sheltering branches of a willow tree hanging over the edge of the bank and trailing its boughs in the water. Dappled light slid through the boughs, covering the boat with the shadows of the willow's slender spear-leaves.

Damon drove the pole deeply into the bottom of the river, and then he slung a rope over it.

Roberta didn't say a word. In fact, the whole lazy river seemed to hold its breath. She couldn't hear a sound other than the dull and smothered voice of the water, and somewhere, a lark singing.

"Our boat," Damon said, with a glance so suggestive that she felt herself grow even pinker, "has run aground."

"I see that."

"What a shame. I may have to undress in order to save us from sinking."

"Really?"

He pulled off his coat.

Roberta could feel giggles rising inside her, faster than the bubbles rising from the bottom of the river. "What do you think you're doing?" she enquired.

"Undressing."

His eyes sang to her in some language that she had just learned, but seemed to know instinctively.

"Hadn't you better follow suit?" he said, raising an eyebrow.

"I?" Roberta said. "I? Undress in a public river, in a flat-bottomed boat?"

"Be grateful it's not another kind of boat," Damon said, sitting down on the little platform and pulling off his boots.

"You can't really mean it," Roberta said, feeling very sure that he did mean it. "Anyone might happen by."

"Nonsense! Almost no one travels this river, since it goes nowhere. We're tied up to yet another cow pasture. This one has actual cows, and one must assume, fresher cowpats. It is, therefore, unlikely to host picnickers as well."

"Impeccable logic," she murmured. He pulled off his shirt. He was all sleek muscle, dappled by leaves, dusted golden by the sun, strong . . .

She reached out without even realizing and then froze again. "I can't do this," she cried. "What if someone saw us!"

"No one will," he said and his voice was as potent as brandy. He was beside her now, throwing cushions onto the floor of the boat. But he took his time unlacing her gown, and after a time she fell into the sweetness of the shaded little room they had found under the willow.

"I suppose," she whispered, "if we sit on the floor no one could see below our waists."

"If we lie down, they can't see anything at all. Don't you think it's done all the time?" He waited for her answer, eyebrow raised.

"No!" she said, with half a gasp because her dress was gone and he didn't seem to be bothering to remove her stays, his hands were running up her legs seeking that sweet spot, and she was arching toward him.

He lay down in the boat and pulled her toward him. She gave up the battle — what battle? — and fell on him with a little cry as her softness came onto his hardness, his muscles, his demands. He was unlacing her stays while he kissed her, deep and hard, and she couldn't help squirming against him, gasping against his lips.

One of his hands was between her legs, playing a rhythm that matched the sound of the water. She didn't even feel out of doors. It was as if her small cries and the deep sounds he made when she touched him were swallowed into the vast stillness of the watery afternoon, leaving their small boat as enclosed and private as a walled room. Just the lark broke its invisible walls as he kept singing, spiraling higher and higher into the sky.

"Touch me," he commanded, his mouth finding her waiting, taut nipple.

She cried out and her hands flew blindly about his body, touching him here and there, the smooth curve of a shoulder, the rippled muscles on his back. She couldn't concentrate though, not when he was doing that, so she simply let her body twist against his, begging.

"*Now* touch me," he said later, his voice thick.

He said it twice, and the meaning of it crept through her smoky brain, made her open her eyes and look down at him. "You want me to —"

"Touch me. I love it when you touch me, Roberta. No one has ever felt as you do."

461

His eyes were so dark that they weren't even green any longer; they looked black in the dappled light.

Roberta reared back, back onto her knees and looked down at him. He lay before her, like a great feast. The wood of the boat was dark brown, rubbed smooth by years. Damon lay there like a figure carved from marble, warm and golden: long powerful thighs, a flat stomach, a chest that swelled into muscles. She started there, with a fingertip, just touching.

She knelt over him, careful, her hands slipping from one set of muscles to another. He shivered when she stroked his chest, groaned aloud when she touched him with her tongue. She sat back, looking down —

"No, you don't," he said hoarsely. "I can't survive that, not in a boat."

She giggled, all the laughter inside her spilling out. She was kneeling in a boat, wearing a chemise that was made of fine lawn.

"Now touch yourself," he said, following her glance down to her chest.

She colored. "What are you talking about?"

His grin was the grin of a sweet devil. "Where you'd like me to touch you." And when she hesitated, *"Please."*

CHAPTER 35

The two boats carrying Jemma and Villiers and the marquess and Mrs. Grope poled their way along the drowsy stream. Jemma and Villiers paid no attention to the water whatsoever. Lord Wharton was composing a simple little ditty, along these lines:

All along the River Fleet,
Through the rushes green,
Swans are a-dabbling,
Up tails all!

He didn't pretend that it was a great work of literature. But it had a pretty rhythm and he knew a certain mermaid who might think it was interesting. He sang it to himself, and sang it to Mrs. Grope, and sang it again, and then set to work on another verse.

It wasn't until the poem had grown to some six stanzas, and included ducks, drakes, minnows and swifts, that he realized that his daughter was missing. Moreover . . . she was missing with that charming brother of the duchess. The earl who had quoted back a line of his poetry, and had a clear look about his eye.

That brother.

He hadn't said anything at the fair yesterday, but he wasn't blind. He saw exactly how the duchess's brother looked at his daughter.

The marquess may be mad (at least to unrefined minds) but no one could accuse him of being stupid. It was the work of a moment to stand up and roar so loudly that the boat just ahead of them, and indeed, everyone on the bank as well, paid instant attention.

"My daughter!" he roared. "She's been abducted!"

Now you may think that there was nothing but cows to hear the marquess's howl of parental distress, but in fact, he was lucky. The boats had gone so far along the river that one of those pleasure gardens stretching to the very bank belonged to a Mrs. Trimmer, sometimes known as Selina, now known as the prince's delicious tidbit (when she wasn't playing lead roles at Drury Lane).

Selina leapt to her feet the moment she

heard that familiar bellow. She and the Prince of Wales were lying on the grass, recovering after a bounteous luncheon *al fresco.* The prince had had three bottles of champagne, and Selina was considering, rather sadly, that he was probably no longer fit for an afternoon dance in the sheets, and yet she was due at the theater in less than two hours.

"Marcus!" she cried, running down to the water.

Behind her, the prince stumbled to his feet like a water buffalo emerging from a pleasant mud bath. "What! Ho!" he said, waving his arms. Three footmen chased each other down the lawn toward him and steadied him on his feet.

Meanwhile, Selina ran straight out onto the dock to which was tied her pretty little craft, the *Selina.* It had been given to her by an adoring theatergoer who hoped that a large gift would make inroads in her affection. But Selina had been loved by the best, and she no longer considered economics when choosing her bed partners. Lord Wharton had taught her that.

"Marcus!" she shrieked, dancing up and down at the end of the wharf. "It *is* you! Oh, what are you doing in London and on the water?"

"Looking for my daughter!" the marquess roared back. "Selina, my love!" He waved his arms at her.

Selina was still hopping up and down as Prince George appeared, accompanied by a whole throng of footmen. "What, ho!" he shouted.

"Your Majesty," Lord Wharton shouted back.

"In the boat!" Selina screamed. "Some villain has abducted Lord Wharton's daughter. We must go immediately."

The prince scrambled into Selina's boat followed by a flock of footmen. "Pole it lively!" he shouted at them. "Some of you swim over to those other two boats and make them move at a fine clip."

Without a second's hesitation four footmen plunged into the water and swam over to the boats. There was a bit of unruly rocking as they clambered aboard Lord Wharton's boat, especially when one of them had to swim back to Selina's boat to get some paddles, but finally all three boats were going downstream at a fine clip.

"We'll find her for you!" Selina screamed. "Little Roberta!"

"Do you know the marquess well?" the prince enquired, a note of disapproval in his voice.

466

"I was the nursemaid to his delightful child, Roberta," Selina said. "Ah, the sweet days of my innocent youth!"

"You are as youthful as a rose now," Prince George said gallantly. He was looking a wee bit green in the face from the unfortunate rocking of the boat. But he was holding up well, under the circumstances. Selina tucked herself next to his considerable bulk and smiled up at him.

"What would we do without our monarch to save us?"

"Nonsense!" he roared.

Jolted out of a lively discussion of the worst blunders they'd ever made in a game, Jemma nor Villiers said a word as their boat was efficiently turned about by dripping footmen and sent whipping down the river.

Finally Villiers said, "I believe that this is what they call an Act of God."

Jemma looked over and saw he was smiling. "You don't think that anything happened to Roberta and Damon, do you? Or to little Teddy?"

Villiers's lower lip drooped for a moment. "Forgot the child." Then he brightened. "They must have dropped him off somewhere."

"Damon did say that Teddy was learning to swim."

Villiers's smile was that of a man with a new belief in deities.

Somewhat farther down the river, and thankfully still around the curve and out of sight, Damon pulled Roberta's gown over her head and laced her up in the front. "I feel boneless," she sighed. "That was lovely." A second later, she slid her feet into her slippers, and pinned her hair back, though without the aid of a mirror, it undoubtedly looked a fright. "What shall we do now? I wonder where my father is?"

At that very moment three boats careened around the far corner, tearing toward them. But they were still far away, and the graceful branches of the willow tree blunted sound, so Damon pulled on his breeches and his boots in happy ignorance.

"What is that noise?" Roberta asked.

Damon swung around, causing the boat to rock violently. But they had both gained a certain adroitness in handling unsteady craft in the last hour, and neither fell into the water. "Bloody hell," he said, and snatched up his shirt.

But he barely had it billowing over his head before Lord Wharton's boat was upon them.

"Why are you laughing?" Roberta gasped.

"That's my father and Villiers — who's following in that boat?"

From his standing position, Damon had a better view than did Roberta. A man naturally feels cheerful when royalty and fate step in to take care of fussy little problems, such as Villiers. He pulled the pole from the mud and gave their boat a great heave.

"Oh no," Roberta moaned, as the prow swept through the long green branches and the third boat came squarely into view. "Who is —"

"The Prince of Wales," Damon said, laughing like a man possessed.

The marquess was standing in the front of his boat like a rather plump figurehead, his arms crossed and a terrible scowl on his face. "Unhand my daughter, you villain!" he shouted.

Roberta moaned again.

Damon saw immediately that his future father-in-law was enjoying himself hugely. "Displaying his considerable skills in melodrama," he muttered to Roberta, "the enraged peer advances, blood in his eye."

"Blood in his eye?" Roberta cried. And then: "Selina!"

"I wouldn't have thought it of you, Gryffyn," His Majesty said, standing up. Two footmen quickly moved into a position to

469

catch him should he topple toward the river.

"Your Majesty," Damon said, "I was overcome by her beauty."

Roberta buried her face in her hands. She was overcome by humiliation.

"You shall pay for your impetuous folly," the marquess said with magnificent emphasis. "You shall marry her!"

"I want nothing less," Damon said, looking down at Roberta.

Villiers decided that was his cue. "I relinquish my claim to Lady Roberta's hand," he announced. "She is free to wed whomever she pleases."

There was a slight diversion when Mrs. Grope realized who was in the boat next to her. She too rose to her feet, wobbling with the excitement of the moment and managed a deep curtsy, panniers and all. "Your Majesty," she cried. " 'Tis I!"

. "Bless me," Prince George said, peering at her. "Don't tell me that's pretty little Rose?"

"Indeed!"

"A more charming Desdemona you never saw," he told Selina, who appeared to have divined the reason why Mrs. Grope was in the marquess's boat, and wasn't looking too happy about it. "You must all come back to the house and celebrate the nuptial couple!"

Villiers stood up and bowed, effortlessly holding his balance in his boat. "I fear my dismay would dampen the festivities," he said. "With your permission, Your Majesty, I shall return to my house."

The prince appeared to notice he was there for the first time. "Dismay?" he said. "Dampen? What are you talking about, Villiers?"

"The duke thought to marry my daughter," Lord Wharton said, unable to stop smiling now the engagement was safely over.

"You did, eh, Villiers? I didn't think you were in the marital line," His Majesty said. "Never mind. Better to stay a bachelor. Look how much fun I'm having!" He roared with laughter, and then sobered. "I've been meaning to challenge you to a game of chess one of these days. I've got the hook of the sport now and I win almost every match. I'm ready to take you on."

Villiers bowed again. "It would be my greatest pleasure." Then, as the prince settled his bulk back into Selina's boat, he turned to Jemma. "Would you like to join the others for the celebration?"

"Indeed, I would like to congratulate my brother, so I will take up His Majesty's kind invitation." She lowered her voice. "I would feel worse for you, Villiers, if I didn't suspect that you will break out champagne when you get home."

"Only to assuage my misery," he assured her. "And perhaps to dull the thought of that chess game I just agreed to. Sometimes it's harder to fix a loss than to win."

The royal footmen nimbly maneuvered Villiers's boat next to Selina's, and with a minimum of squeaks, Jemma made her way on board and sat down next to the prince, who seemed very happy to meet the lovely Duchess of Beaumont.

"I've heard much about you," he said, "and all of it good!"

Jemma had no doubt but that her reputation was a cause for celebration to this particular future king.

Without further ado, the two boats powered by footmen started to plow through the water, back upstream, while the boat carrying the Duke of Villiers headed the other way, to the steps.

"Don't dally, Roberta!" the marquess shouted, hands cupped around his mouth, looking back at his daughter's boat.

She didn't see him. In fact, all that could be seen of her were scarlet ears, peeking out from behind her hands.

There was a moment or two of silence as the boats receded in both directions.

Damon tucked his shirt back into his breeches and pulled on his coat. Roberta still hadn't moved.

He pulled up the pole, maneuvered the boat back under the willow with one great shove, and then tethered the boat again. Finally he sat down before her.

"Roberta, you're going to have to look up at some point," he said gently.

"I don't want to." Her voice was muffled by her hands.

"I've never proposed before," he said. "I think it would be easier if I could see your face. That way if you look disgusted I can quickly throw myself off the boat and end it now."

Her hands dropped. "*Please* don't be melodramatic!" she cried. "I can't bear it at the moment." Her face was distinctly pink and her eyes were shining with unshed tears.

"I'm just fooling." He reached out and took her hands. "Are you crying because Villiers is lost to you?"

"I'm not crying," she said, all evidence to the contrary.

In one smooth gesture, he slid forward onto his knees. "Roberta, will you marry me?"

"You already told me that you *were* marrying me," she said, with a sniff.

473

He put one of her hands up to his mouth. "But this is a proper proposal. I decided to marry you about twenty minutes after we met, and I've waited a long time for this."

Her mouth dropped open.

"Of course, you were nattering on about Villiers, so I couldn't make it plain to you."

"You didn't!"

"Roberta, love, do you really think that I would take your virginity — and make love to you every chance I could get — without planning to marry you?"

"But I was engaged . . ."

"You were toying with the idea," he said. "But at the same time, you were surrendering to me."

"Surrendering?"

Her hands were at his mouth again. "Surrender," he said firmly. "You're mine, Roberta. Mine." He could see a glimmer of a smile in her eyes, so he pulled her forward into his arms. Which made the boat rock rather violently, but neither of them even flinched.

"I don't see that I surrendered," she said.

Her mouth was so pink and delectable that he forgot his point for a while, and only returned to the subject some time later. "What did you think you were doing?" he asked, his mouth sliding down her neck.

"I was — I was —"

Now that he mentioned it, Roberta couldn't remember quite what she was doing. Villiers made her angry and so she decided to lose her virginity . . . It sounded so foolish. "I was gaining experience," she said firmly.

"You were surrendering to me. You just didn't want to think of it that way," he said, even more firmly. He cupped her face in his hands. "So, will you?"

"Will I marry you?"

He shook his head. "You are marrying me. Will you surrender?"

She put her arms around his neck and those foolish tears were back in her eyes. "I think," she whispered, "that I already did."

CHAPTER 36

He was free, obviously a reason for rejoicing. The moment the boat poled back to the Fleet River steps, Villiers sprang out. His heel slipped on the slimy step; he teetered; he fell.

On his bottom.

Behind him he heard a grunt of distress from his footman, who lurched forward to rescue the poor forsaken duke who had slipped in the muck. But Villiers was already up.

The fall made the rage brewing in his stomach burst into flame. He made his way home, stripped off the coat smeared with green moss and black mud, bathed and dressed again for the evening.

It occurred to him as he pulled on tight breeches of a glorious canary that without noticing it and certainly without approving it, he had fallen into the way of thinking of himself as a man about to be married. For all of forty-eight hours, he scoffed to himself.

His valet eased a coat of saturated rose over his shoulders; he rejected it as clashing with the breeches. The man brought a waistcoat of mustard yellow, and Villiers actually swore at him. Finally he settled on a full-cut frock coat with his trademark exuberant embroidery: a tracing of leaves and yellow roses. It was, perhaps, just a trifle too exuberant, but it had an aggressiveness that pleased.

The valet cleared his throat rather nervously. "Boots, Your Grace? Or the shoes with silver buckles?"

"Red heels," Villiers snapped. "I'm to Parsloe's and then to dinner with Lord Devonshire. I can hardly tramp about in boots." Rather than his cane, he chose a proper little rapier, designed to swing at his hip. Finally he placed a patch high, just below his eye where it would emphasize his lashes.

He swept a cold look around his chamber, a muddle of rejected coats, cravats, shoes, ribbons spilling from his drawer. "Do make yourself useful and neaten this up," he said softly. "I have a mind to bring someone home later."

"A bloody animal he is tonight," his valet said later, in the kitchen with a soothing

477

cup of tea. "As if I didn't always neaten up. I'm sure I don't know what's got into him."

"The lady's rejected 'im," Cook said, wiping her hands on her apron. "I'll bet you an apple tart next Tuesday that she's turned him down flat."

"You think that because he's bringing home a dollymop?"

She had a sound of disgust. "Nothing to do with it. He's in a foul mood, he is. And he's not over at Beaumont House, is he? He's been there for three days running. Mark my words: he's back on the market again."

"I don't think he ever was on the market," the valet said dubiously.

"Could be he's not a marrying man," Cook concluded. "I'd best make up some bits and pieces for entertaining a ladyfriend tonight."

"Got rid of his mistress and all last week," the valet said mournfully. "And now the wife drops him. That's cruel, that is."

"Not his wife yet, and that's a blessing in itself," Cook said. She had firm views about matrimony, and one could not describe them as positive. "Out of the way, will you? I can't put a hand on my sugar."

Parsloe's, like any organization of its ilk, was ruled by the unspoken hierarchy structuring the members of the London Chess Club. Brilliance ruled. Chess is an odd and unlikely sport: it taxes the brains and the heart at the same time. Even a poor player might sometimes make a beautiful play, or stump a master, and thus the hierarchy is never set in stone. Only at the very top is it unassailable.

Villiers's carriage pulled up at precisely eight o'clock. It was a delicious little carriage, as sleek and beautiful as its master: painted a dark crimson, and picked out in brazen orange accents.

The door was snatched open by the duke's footman; three others joined in, standing before the door, backs straight, liveries immaculate.

One red heel emerged from the carriage, followed by a powerful, muscled thigh clad in canary colored breeches. The duke wore, as usual, not a touch of powder. He walked to the door of the large townhouse that served as the chess club's headquarters without looking to the left or the right.

As he climbed the stairs, a footman swept open the front door. Inside, he handed his hat to one, and his cape to another.

"I shall keep my sword," he said to Parsloe, who was bowing. "I am not in the mood for killing tonight."

The rules of the chess club insisted on no weapons, but what could Parsloe say? The duke ruled. And not because of his title, either.

Villiers strolled into the main room, knowing that anger was burning within him like a slow coal, and rather relishing the pure stupidity of it. He didn't want the girl, never really wanted the girl, and now he was angry because he no longer had her? Such is the foolishness of men.

Lord Woodword Jourdain looked up when he came in. "Villiers!" he cried. "You're just in time to try my new chess game."

Villiers strolled to his side and looked down at the cacophony of pieces. "How many pieces in this version, Jourdain?"

"Twenty-eight," Jourdain said eagerly. "Ten rows and fourteen columns. I had to make up a special board."

"This piece?" Villiers put a beautifully manicured forefinger on a piece.

"The concubine," Jourdain said.

"An errant piece, no doubt."

"Only held in check by two additional bishops."

"And these?"

"Crowned rooks."

"I think not," Villiers said, turning away. "I've had enough of females, concubines or otherwise . . . they are all so tiresome, are they not?"

Jourdain huffed in annoyance, but Viscount St. Albans looked up. "Do tell," he said with his usual lisp. "Has true love tarnished so quickly?"

"Ah, what is love?" Villiers said. The only person sitting before an unattended chessboard was Lord Gordon. "A game, my lord?"

"My pleasure, Your Grace."

"I'll give you a rook advantage," Villiers said gently.

Lord Gordon's face showed no response at all to this insult, merely a bovine gratitude, and Villiers felt his temper slip a notch higher.

"What is love, 'tis not hereafter," St. Albans said. "I believe that's Shakespeare, but even so, Your Grace, your experience of love must have been remarkably brief. It's been no more than a day since I heard you were engaged."

"I give you the joy, St. Albans, of being the first to know that I am no longer engaged," Villiers said.

"At least try a few of the pieces," Jourdain said, suddenly appearing at his shoulder. "You've no idea how interesting it makes the game, Villiers. Take the concubine." He plumped the piece down in the middle of the board. "Here's another for you, Gordon. She moves all directions, of course, just like the queen. Her special touch is that she can take two men in a row, but she never takes the king or the queen." He giggled madly. "She's not that sort of concubine."

"What?" Gordon's pink lips flapped like a fish on the dock, Villiers decided. "We can't play with a piece like that."

"You play with pieces like that all the time," Villiers said sweetly. "That was you I glimpsed with Mrs. Rutland the other night?"

Gordon was rearranging his pieces and didn't look up. Villiers could only hope that he remembered where they all went.

"The concubine goes in front of the king's rook," Jourdain instructed. "She's on her knees already, you understand."

It wasn't that he wished to marry. But there had been something interesting about the last few days, during which he felt part of something — of a family, one had to suppose. Yet what a family? Who would want to tie himself to that ridiculous marquess? Clearly, the man felt the same about him.

"I don't want to play with this piece," Gordon said, jutting out his lip. "I've a good shot at winning with a rook advantage. This piece will just mess it all up."

"Concubines always do," St. Albans said. He had pulled over a chair. "You should watch out for Mrs. Rutland, Gordon. Her husband was swearing to revenge his horns the other night."

"He'll have a pretty time deciding which man to challenge," Villiers said idly. He hadn't really decided whether to play with the concubine. On the one hand, it was a silly piece. On the other, it would irritate Gordon and Lord knows why he had sat down in front of the moribund fool.

"Mrs. Rutland is a praiseworthy woman," Gordon said.

"Well, you should know," Villiers said. "You may begin, Gordon." He placed his concubine in front of his king's rook. "Quite a brave little piece, isn't she?"

"She can turn the entire game," Jourdain said.

"I've no doubt. Your move, Gordon."

Gordon pushed forward a pawn and said with his customary obstinacy, "Mrs. Rutland is no concubine."

"No one said she is," Villiers said. It was his move and he decided to try out the concubine by taking one of Gordon's pawns and then his king's rook. Why not?

Gordon breathed heavily through his nose in a revolting manner. "Look here, Jourdain," he said, "how can we play a proper game with that dreadful concubine going about and sweeping up pieces right and left?"

"So true to life," Villiers said thoughtfully. "I wouldn't have thought you capable of it, Jourdain."

Jourdain turned a little pink. "Go on, Gordon," he urged. "Just think it through, man."

Gordon was incapable of thinking anything through, including his relations with Mrs. Rutland. "You might want to turn the lock next time you decide to shed your breeches in public," Villiers said, just when he considered that Gordon might be actually concentrating on a move. "Your wife would have been most distressed to walk into the sitting room and see you rutting away like that."

"Rutting Rutland," the viscount said with a simpering laugh, showing that he was ever a man who had to say the obvious.

"I don't care for your phrasing," Gordon stated, looking up at Villiers.

Villiers felt a lazy spur of interest. Finally the great walrus was listening to him. "But *rutting* is such an evocative phrase," he complained.

Gordon pushed back his chair with a scraping noise, shocking in the small room.

Parsloe rushed forward. "My lords, may I remind you of the rules of the London Chess Club? Physical interaction of any kind and the participants lose their membership."

Gordon paused. Villiers could almost see the cogs turning in his head. Finally he pulled back to the table and said, "At least I didn't almost marry her."

Villiers lifted his eyes from the chessboard very slowly. "Since I gather you are unlikely to be talking about your virtuous wife, would you like to clarify yourself?"

Gordon bent over, huffing a little, and swept his concubine forward to take a pawn, followed by one of Villiers's bishops. "After I left Mrs. Rutland at the ball, I happened into the library. My guess would be that *you,* Villiers, have lost your fiancée to the Earl of Gryffyn. Of course, I would never soil a lady's reputation by saying anything about . . . rutting."

Villiers knew quite well that the wave of rage he felt was unfair and improper. It was just that if Gordon saw Roberta in the library with Gryffyn — that would be *before* he asked her to marry him, *before* he told her to lose her chastity, *before* he decided to end their engagement. At the very moment she was doing her best to lure him to the point.

There are times when irrational feelings are insuppressible. He felt sick. That was it — sick. He looked up to find St. Albans's avid little eyes fixed on him like a pig spotting a rotten apple. Albans was watching for the slightest trace of emotion, he knew. He'd be *damned* if he allowed anyone to think that he cared.

"Queens are so unstable," he said sweetly. "They career across the board, and sometimes turn into concubines before one's very eyes."

St. Albans laughed. Gordon shook his head. "You're unnatural, Villiers. You really are. You don't give a damn, do you?"

Gordon moved forward a rook, so Villiers took it. "Check."

"Where?" Gordon bleated.

"My queen."

"I have a bishop."

"Ah, but I'm afraid the concubine will take care of the bishop, as they so often do," Villiers pointed out.

"One might say that concubines conquer all," St. Albans said, with his high cackle.

Villiers pushed back from the table. He couldn't take another moment of this god-awful idiocy. "Gentlemen, at your service," he said, bowing.

Gordon looked up from where he was glowering at the board. "I shouldn't have said that," he said, his pale blue eyes wide. "There wasn't any rutting involved. In the library, I mean."

"But there so clearly was this afternoon," Villiers said gently. "A concubine, you see, will always display her nature, and I am happy to pass my ownership to Gryffyn. Your new piece," he said, turning to Jourdain, "is dangerous."

Jourdain shook his head. "You needed the extra bishops to keep her in check."

Viscount St. Albans's laugh said it all.

No number of bishops could keep a concubine in check.

CHAPTER 37

April 20
Day nine of the Villiers/Beaumont chess matches

From Damon Reeve, Earl of Gryffyn, to the Duke of Villiers:
Your description of my future wife is all over London. Your seconds?

From the Duke of Villiers to the Earl of Gryffyn:
You're a fool. If you kill me, she will smell no less perfumed to you, and if I kill you, you will soon smell much worse.

From the Earl of Gryffyn to the Duke of Villiers:
Your choice of weapons?

From the Duke of Villiers to the Earl of Gryffyn:
Rapiers. Dawn, Wimbledon Commons, near the windmill. Tuesday. I have a chess

game planned with Lord Bonnington to-morrow and can't bother with this. You are a hot-headed Fool who clearly has no sense of the Importance of Women (none whatsoever) nor of a good Sleep (vastly to be desired). I shall, however, resign myself to killing you.

CHAPTER 38

April 21
Day ten of the Villiers/Beaumont chess matches

It was a noise beside her bed that woke her up. "Mmmm," Roberta said, reaching out — and waking up instantly. "Teddy! Are you lost again, child?"

"No," he said. He stood next to the bed like a little ghost in a white nightgown. His face, normally so cheerful, was woebegone.

"What's the matter?" she said, peering at him. "Did you have a bad dream?"

"Can we sleep with you?" he burst out.

"We?"

But it was too late. In clambered a small boy and a kitten, who promptly leaped to the bottom of the bed and curled up there, somewhat to Roberta's relief.

It took her twenty minutes to coax out of him the information that Rummer had given him. "Of course, Papa will win the

490

duel," he said, snuggling down into the covers, one hand clasping hers. "Papa always wins, that's what Rummer says."

"Rummer shouldn't have told you about the duel," she said firmly. Her mind was whirling with terror, spinning with the fact of it.

If Damon was fighting Villiers, he was fighting for her honor. And her honor, her honor wasn't worth a scrap of paper, not in comparison to the way she felt about Damon. It was as if mortal coldness gripped her heart and clenched her stomach. What could she do? *What could she do?*

She would pull Villiers aside when he came to play his game with Jemma, and she would beg him. Surely he wouldn't deny her, if only out of whatever fugitive affection that caused him to ask her to marry.

She stared into the darkness for hours, planning what to say, parsing her sentences, praying.

Mostly praying.

She fell asleep only when the light was peeking through the curtains of her bedchamber. Deep in a sleep of leaden exhaustion, she never heard Teddy scamper out of bed and return to the nursery to be roundly scolded by his nursemaid. She never heard her maid tiptoe in and then decide not to wake her, based on the white stillness of her face. She was far too fast asleep to hear the faint commotion that greeted the arrival of the Duke of Villiers, here to play his piece at chess.

She slept on.

When she finally awoke, she was aghast to see how high the sun had risen. But did it really matter? The world knew where Villiers spent his days: at Parsloe's, playing chess. He had told her so himself. She'd find him there, if she had to.

She dressed in an utterly charming affair of light silk embroidered with bluebirds. Quite in Villiers's line, now she thought of it.

She went straight to Jemma's chamber, bursting into the room, hoping that Villiers was there, only to see the blood drain from Jemma's face when she told her Teddy's news.

"Villiers said nothing to me this morning," Jemma said.

"Villiers has already been here?"

"He left an hour ago." Jemma swallowed. "Oh God Almighty, why couldn't you have kept out of Damon's bed while you were engaged to Villiers?"

Roberta sank into a chair. "I don't know, I don't know! I shall die from the guilt of it.

I love Damon so much that I lost my head. I didn't think."

Jemma's face softened. "I gather you no longer love Villiers, then?"

"I was a fool."

"It's a common condition."

"I'm going to ask Villiers to back down," Roberta said. "Do you think it might work?"

"He lost this morning," Jemma said hollowly.

"He —"

"He lost the game. All of London will know by this afternoon. He lost to a woman. To me."

There was no one in the breakfast room. Fowle informed her that Mrs. Grope had gone to the theater again, and her father had gone out. The mermaid, Roberta thought.

Damon had taken Teddy away for the day. A last day with his son, Roberta thought, and her heart flooded with such guilt that she could scarcely breathe. She would stop this duel if she had to kill Villiers herself.

Unfortunately, like chess, she had neglected to study the fine points of swordsmanship.

"I should like a carriage," she told Fowle, and a few minutes later, a smart chaise awaited her.

493

Roberta pulled on her gloves. She was icy calm now. She was going to stop this monstrous thing before it happened.

Parsloe's was a rather ordinary looking place for all the attention it got, to Roberta's mind. She was met by a butler who asked her if she was a member of the chess club.

"I am not," Roberta said, rather startled. "I didn't known there were female members."

"There are," he said with a regal bow. "May I help you, Madame?"

"I should like to see the Duke of Villiers," she said.

"I'm afraid that he is upstairs, in the Members' Rooms, and no one who is not a member is allowed therein."

"You will have to make an exception," Roberta said.

There must have been something in her eye because he stopped being a starched butler and cowered a little. "Of course, you are a lady," he said.

"I am not *any* lady," she told him. "I am engaged to the Duke of Villiers."

"In that case!" he said, gesturing to the stairs. "After you, my lady, after you."

She climbed up the stairs and a moment later found herself in a room filled with gentlemen. They were all watching Villiers, which made it easy to find him, at any rate. He was spectacularly dressed, sitting at one end of the table, his legs spread wide. He looked absorbed, elegant — and dangerous.

Roberta dizzily took in the muscled strength of his shoulders and the controlled menace in the way he put down each chess piece. He looked like a man who would slay an opponent with no more emotion than he would take a pawn.

"Your Grace," she said, coming to stand before the table. The other man looked up quickly and suddenly the whole room was on their feet, bowing and scraping. She ignored them, looking directly at Villiers. "Your Grace," she said, dropping a curtsy. "I came to beg some private conversation."

His eyes rested on her, cold, indifferent. How had she ever thought that was an attractive trait in a man? He was loathsome to her now, snakelike in his magnificence.

"I see no reason for that," he said. "I am in the middle of a match, as you see."

"Please, Your Grace," she pleaded.

But he looked at her with something akin to hatred. "If you must speak, speak here. There is nothing, it seems, in my life that is secret — is there, St. Albans?"

The slender young man standing to the side shrugged. "It is the fate of all of us to occasionally find our faces depicted in the windows of Humphrey's." His eyes lingered on Roberta, and she realized that he knew precisely who she was, and he was thinking about the cartoons in *Rambler's Magazine* that were sold in Humphrey's Print Shop. Slowly she looked about and while she didn't see hostility, she did see knowledge. They knew who she was. They knew that she had been cartooned as desperate for a husband, as begging a footman to marry her. They knew that she had spurned Villiers for the Earl of Gryffyn.

She looked back at Villiers. He stood beside his chair, his eyes impenetrable.

She walked a step forward, and then she fell to her knees.

There was a gasp in the room, and a rustle of agitation. Roberta ignored it. "Please, Your Grace. *Please* do not fight a duel with the Earl of Gryffyn. He is my future husband, and I cannot bear to see him die."

"I would not have expected this of you," he said, staring down at her and actually looking rather startled. "I thought you were of different stock than your father, Lady Roberta."

"You were in error. I find myself more like him every day. *Please.* I am begging you. I am desperate."

There was a murmur around the room, a flourishing of whispers. "Raise her up," someone said to Villiers. And: "This isn't decent."

Villiers started, and came forward. He reached out a hand but she shook her head. "Not until you promise."

"I cannot promise," he told her, and she could have sworn that she saw a flash of sympathy in those cold eyes of his. "It's no longer a matter of your honor, but that of Gryffyn's."

"My honor is worthless!" she cried.

He stooped down and brought her to her feet. "Your courage is not worthless, Lady Roberta." He kept her hands for a moment. "I will apologize," he said. "That's the best I can do, and since I've never done such a thing before in my life, you see that my apology means that I put your honor at a rather higher pitch than your own valuation."

He dropped her hands and turned away. "If you'll forgive me, milady, we have a chess match to finish."

An arm came around her shoulder, and Roberta felt herself pulled away.

"Mr. Cunningham!" she said dully. "I didn't see you."

"I often play a match during the afternoon

when His Grace is in the House of Lords."
He said nothing further, and Roberta
couldn't bring herself to say anything either.
So he accompanied her home in silence.

It had to be enough.

It simply . . . had to be enough.

CHAPTER 39

April 22

Day eleven: the Beaumont/Beaumont chess match remains in play

Dawn was curling over Wimbledon Commons, making the wheels of all the carriages disappear and look as if their fat bellies were scraping the ground.

"I shall be sick," Roberta said between clenched teeth.

"Open the carriage door," Jemma said, not helpfully. She was crying, just a little. She hadn't said anything, but Roberta saw her wipe away a tear, and then another. "Damon will be fine," she said, as if to herself.

"Does he know how to fight with a sword?" Roberta whispered.

Jemma frowned at her. "Of course he does!"

Carriages and more carriages kept pulling

up until there was a double row, and men pushed by their door as if they were going to see a cock fight.

"Villiers said he would apologize," Roberta said. "He promised." Her fists were clenched. "Should I go and remind him, Jemma?" she cried. "Should I go and see what's happening?"

But Jemma shook her head, her eyes bleak. "You've done all you can. If you shame Villiers in front of all these people, there's no saying what he might do."

"What would shame him?" Roberta asked desperately.

"To have you intervene again. And you would shame Damon."

"But he would *live!*"

"He will live," Jemma said. But her face was icy white.

"I begged him not to go," Roberta said. "He just laughed."

"That's Damon."

They waited, and still fog curled in the center of the field, and nothing happened. "What is a rapier?" Roberta said, forcing the words past stiff lips. "Do you know?"

"A thin blade," Jemma said. "It is favored by the French and considered to be agile, intelligent and supple."

"What?" Roberta said, unable to get her

mind around this cluster of adjectives. "Do you think that Damon can fight with it?"

Jemma turned her head and stared at her. "What makes you question Damon's ability so?"

Just then two men walked onto the field and Roberta gasped. They weren't Villiers and Damon, but the seconds. They seemed to be scuffing the grass, seeing if it was slippery with dew.

"Because," she said, "Villiers himself told me that chess players are the finest duelists. That makes him the finest sword fighter in the kingdom. It's not Damon's skill I'm worried about. It's Villiers's that terrifies me."

Jemma laughed, and the sound of it jarred Roberta to the bottom of her stomach. "What makes you think that Damon can't play chess?"

"He never — He —"

"He's quite likely the best chess player in England," Jemma said flatly. "My father taught us both and it was his considered opinion that Damon had an edge on me. Damon finds the game boring because it doesn't present enough of a challenge."

Roberta swallowed. "Not enough of a challenge? Then, what?"

"Have you talked of nothing, all this time

you spent in bed together?"

Roberta shook her head. "Not about the right things."

"Bills of Exchange. He plays with them, manipulates the market. He moves on a larger chess board; he's like my husband in that."

"He really can fence?"

"Of course," Jemma said irritably. "He's fought at least four duels that I know of."

"Did he win all four?"

"Of course."

"He told me last night that he had decided to strike Villiers in the right shoulder."

"There you see the thought pattern of a master player," Jemma said. "Philidor often called the piece with which he would check my king."

"But were any of Damon's previous opponents chess masters?"

There was a sigh. "No."

To the side of the field, Damon was talking to his second. "There's not so much fog that we can't see," he said impatiently. He wanted to get this over with and go back to breakfast with Roberta. He knew she was there, poor mouse, huddled in the carriage with Jemma.

The second hurried over to talk to Villiers's second, and then rushed back.

"His Grace would like to speak to you a moment," he said.

Damon dropped his coat onto the wet grass. He would fight in his old boots and a shirt, rolled up to the sleeves. He took one more look at his rapier, a beautiful length of steel from Toledo. He almost had an unfair advantage, using it. Still, he picked it up and strolled over to Villiers's gaudy carriage.

The duke was stripped to a shirt. He was bending his blade, testing its spring.

"Toledo," Damon said with pleasure. "Excellent."

Villiers lifted those heavy eyes of his and murmured, "An even match is always best."

Damon waited a moment but Villiers seemed to be having some trouble speaking. Finally, he said in an almost strangled voice, "I want to apologize."

"What?"

"Apologize. I should not have maligned Lady Roberta's honor."

Damon narrowed his eyes. "She got to you, didn't she?"

Villiers looked up again. "What do you mean?"

"Roberta. What did she do, exactly?"

"She fell on her knees in Parsloe's," Villiers said flatly. "She begged me not to fight you."

"Sounds very dramatic." Damon loved the sound of it.

"Oh, believe me," Villiers said. "It was. She enjoyed a wide audience."

"Right. Now that's out of the way, shall we start?"

Villiers glanced at him. "My apology?"

"I would have acquiesced to any demand of hers as well," Damon said. "But the fact of it is, Villiers, we're going to fight. Now."

Villiers, looking up at the earl, saw him as a man with an easy smile, a man whom he had obviously never understood. A sudden thought struck him. "Do you play chess?"

"Never," Damon said promptly. "Bores me to tears. The only partner I ever had who could give me a challenge was my sister. How's the game with her going, by the way?"

Villiers stared at him. Gryffyn was as unmoved by the prospect of a duel as he was by the prospect of death. For the first time, he felt a faint prickling. A faint warning in the back of his mind. "I lost," he said. "I lost the game yesterday."

But the earl was already striding out onto the field, hailing their seconds.

Villiers walked out more slowly, rearranging his expectations of the game. He was going to have to kill — or be killed. In the earl's eyes was the deadly cheer of a man whose future wife has been maligned and who will die to protect her honor. Except that Gryffyn clearly had no intention of dying.

Two minutes later they were circling each other, their boots leaving prints on the wet grass.

"We can wait until the sun dries the grass if you'd like," Gryffyn offered.

"No." Villiers couldn't help but remember himself, offering Gordon a rook advantage.

He started watching for an opening. The earl seemed content to circle forever. Finally Villiers swooped in with an upward-cutting *manchette* blow. Parried by Gryffyn. He tried a *pass in tierce* and a *redoublement.* Parried, and parried again. Finally Villiers fell back, deciding to let the earl make the next move.

When he did, it was supremely smooth, a twisting, swirling *demi-volte* that seemed to come out of nowhere. It was only luck that Villiers's blade caught his opponent's rapier, deflecting the blow.

Gryffyn fell back and they circled once more. But there was something different about him now; the brooding joy of a predator was in every movement of those long legs.

There was nothing so terrible about that, except that Villiers himself didn't have the energy of virtue behind him. He felt wrong.

He shouldn't have called Roberta a concubine, not after he told her to go lose her chastity. He was the one who whipped her into Gryffyn's bed, and then castigated her for it. And then too . . . there was Benjamin in the back of his mind.

Even as he parried a brilliant time-thrust from the earl, he thought about how nothing had gone right since Benjamin died. It was his infernal arrogance, that was it.

The earl tried a *prise de fer;* he knocked it to the side. Villiers felt rage rising, finally, from the bottom of his soul. What was he doing on a field in the cold dawn, fighting a duel with a man he was uninterested in killing?

"I'm not going to kill you," he said, panting, circling, watching the earl's hands.

"I'm not going to kill you, either," the earl said. He didn't appear to be even breathing quickly, which was galling. "I might have, but you apologized."

They circled again.

"I can't have Roberta think that her apology was for naught," the earl said. "The right shoulder should do it."

Villiers narrowed his eyes, but he didn't even see the *envelopment* coming. It came from above, and sang through the air with a melody like death, twisted, flicked at the last second, slid home with a terrible scrape by the bone.

Villiers's rapier dropped to the ground.

Gryffyn withdrew his blade; it was glossy with blood. Villiers bent over, breathing heavily.

Gryffyn shouted, "We could use the surgeon here!"

Villiers heard feet, and realizing for the first time how close the circle of spectators had come, straightened. Blood was running down his right arm and oddly, it felt cold rather than warm. "I regret any impunity to your lady's honor," he said, resorting to the antiquated language used by their grandparents.

"I am at your service," Gryffyn replied.

The surgeon was upon them, offering Villiers a bottle of brandy and ripping off his shirt. Gryffyn was off, running — he was actually running — toward the Duke of Beaumont's carriage.

Villiers upended the bottle for a moment with his left arm, and watched him go with disbelief. God forbid that he should ever become so tied to a woman. Or she to him. He shuddered at the thought.

The idea of a woman kneeling to ask for his life . . .

It was beyond distasteful.

Disgusting, really.

He upended the bottle again.

CHAPTER 40

They returned for breakfast to find the house full of gentlemen shouting congratulations to Damon, ladies sighing over the injury to the Duke of Villiers, servants running hither and fro with glasses and plates.

No one would know from the Duchess of Beaumont's smiling face that she had been white with terror but an hour earlier. No one would know from her husband's imperturbable calm that he too had found himself pacing the floor, unable to concentrate on the business of the realm.

She was standing with Viscount St. Albans, discussing the likelihood that Villiers would develop an infection. "A good half of the cases," St. Albans reported. "But he had the best surgeon available and the man drenched the wound in brandy. I saw to that myself. No use shirking on brandy when a man's life is at stake."

Her husband touched her on the shoulder.

"I thought we might play our piece," Beaumont said.

To Elijah's eyes his wife didn't look quite right. Her lips were rather pale. She took his arm, which she never did.

He watched her as they settled before the board. "Let's just sit for a moment," he suggested. "Does Villiers have a deep wound, then?"

She visibly shuddered. "I can't abide talk of these things. I believe not. Damon is enormously skilled and apparently he knew precisely where he wanted to place the blade. Villiers should experience no lasting effect."

Elijah watched her stare at the board and knew that for the first time he was seeing his wife when she could not concentrate on chess. He moved and said, "Check." She reached out her hand. "Wait," he said. She was going to move her king's rook, which would give him checkmate.

She looked up at him. "Let's just rest for a moment. I am frightfully tired," he said.

She frowned a little, and her hand fell back to her lap. "I do think you ought to work less, Beaumont."

"You call me Elijah sometimes," he said, hardly able to believe his own ears.

Her eyebrows shot up, so apparently she

was just as surprised. "Elijah," she said.

"How will you play your game with Villiers now?"

She swallowed. "I suppose you know that I won the first game in our match yesterday." She bit her lip. "If I know Villiers he will be chaffing horribly at confinement to the bed. St. Albans told me that the surgeon ordered him to spend a fortnight in his chambers."

Elijah's heart sank. Though why it mattered, he couldn't say.

Obviously Villiers may have lost his match but he had won something else.

"I suppose you'll have to go to him," he said, his voice as cool and controlled as ever.

She shot him a quick glance and fell to frowning over the board again. Her hand came out and she moved the rook.

"Checkmate," he said, in response.

Jemma stared at the board as if she'd never lost before.

Beaumont had the odd feeling that they were experiencing the same thing at the same time.

It was a good thing that Roberta no longer feared making a spectacle of herself, because she could not stop clinging to Damon. Her father grabbed her arm at one point. "Mrs.

Grope has decided to return to the theater!"
he said, not looking half as miserable as one
might expect.

"The theater?" Roberta said, startled into
paying attention. "As an actress? Really?"

"As a hair dresser. Apparently the manager
of Drury Lane was so impressed by her
London Bridge effect that he's invited her
to dress wigs for all the performances of the
coming season. I shall handsomely endow
her, of course. But it means, my dear, that
Mrs. Grope will no longer be part of our
lives."

Damon looked as if he might be about to
walk into another room, and Roberta didn't
want to let him out of her sight. He paused
to talk to Lord Corbin, so she turned back
to her father.

"But Papa, what of the mermaid?"

"What of her?" he said, looking a bit sly
and a bit happy.

"Will she return home with you?"

"Absolutely not!" he roared. "She's a
decent young woman, daughter of a vicar in
Somerset, not to mention a gifted poet." He
started rocking back and forth on his heels.
"Do you know, Roberta, that she began as
the versifying mermaid at only ten years of
age?"

"How old is she now?" Roberta asked, half

listening.

"I believe she is around thirty, and . . ."

She couldn't let Damon out of her sight, not when her heart was still pounding with fright. So she dropped a kiss on her papa's cheek and slipped away. Finally Damon swept her off to the yellow sitting room and offered to play her at dollymop dominoes if she would let him go to the privy.

So she did.

But by the time he came back, she was crying again, and she couldn't stop, even when he kissed away her tears, and laughed at her, and finally tickled her.

"It's just that I might have lost you," she said, hiccupping.

"Never," he said, cupping her face in his hands.

"You might have died!"

"I can't tell you *never* when it comes to death. But when I die, Roberta, I swear it to God that unless it's an accident I shall do it in my own bed, with you by my side. In other words, I wouldn't put myself in harm's way, not when I have you and Teddy and" — He smiled at her and there was something so tender in his eyes that she hiccupped again — "we might have a babe in a few months too, Roberta. Have you thought of that?"

She dismissed that thought as fit for another day. "How could you possibly know you would beat Villiers? It was all so sudden, and violent."

"Had you never seen a sword fight before?"

She shook her head. "I'm certain he almost stabbed you straight to the heart several times."

Damon actually laughed. "Sword fighting is tiresomely predictable, Roberta, and Villiers had no chance of injuring me. Truly. If he had really wished to kill me, he would have chosen pistols, because that changes the whole nature of the meeting. I knew that Villiers was an excellent swordsman. I also knew that I was better."

"How could you know that you were better?" she cried. "You haven't met him before; Jemma told me so!"

"Oh ye of little faith," he said, gathering her close. "I practice several times a week with Galliano, that's why. He's the best fencing master in London."

"It's not that I don't have faith in *you*," she said, her voice muffled against his chest. "But —"

He held her away, just enough so that she could see his eyes. "I knew I would win because I love you."

514

"What?"

"Because I love you."

"You — You wouldn't lose to Villiers because — because —"

He was grinning at her like the fool he was. "Because I love you too much to lose."

"You — You!" she cried and flew at him, but whether it was to hit him for his male foolishness or what, she never knew because he kissed her so hard that the idea flew straight out of her head.

"What about you?" he asked, sometime later, when she was clinging to his shoulders.

A crooked smile played on the corner of her mouth. "Will I win a duel fought for your honor?"

"No."

"Are you asking whether I love you?"

He didn't say anything. It was, Roberta realized, the very first time that she'd seen a shadow of anxiety in that huge, confident man, so easy with his smiles, so unassuming about his skills. So she relished it.

For a short time.

"Of course I love you," she whispered, cupping his face in her hands. "And I always will."

"Even if I take to poetry and start writing poems to your toe?"

"Yes."

"If I fall on my knees in the street and beg you to take me back to bed?"

She was starting to smile, but: "Yes."

"I *am* on my knees, Roberta. I *am* begging."

A passing footman heard laughter from the sitting room and shook his head.

Beaumont House had certainly changed since the duchess came back from Paris. Used to be the place was respectable. But now . . . wait till Fowle heard what that French piece named Mademoiselle Caro was thinking of doing for the duchess's next ball. Every one of them nekked ladies would have peacock feathers at their behinds, that's what he heard.

With a sigh he pulled the sitting room door shut so that no one would accidentally see something they shouldn't.

Epilogue

When the Villiers/Beaumont chess matches were fading in memory

"I think," Roberta said, "you might have let me win that one."

"Who do you think you are, His Majesty himself?"

"It was very nice of you to allow the prince to win last night," she conceded.

Her husband pushed away the chess set that lay between them on the bed. "You know how to play now. Perhaps we can try something else. I'm very fond of dominoes."

"You find it tedious partnering me?" She dimpled at him.

"Nothing with you is tedious, except perhaps chess." He dropped a kiss on her ear. "There are so many more interesting things to do."

"Such as?" she murmured, falling back onto the cushions.

He took her invitation in a second, rolling

on top of her and propping himself up on his elbows. "Such as kissing you," he said, suiting action to words.

"But what," she said, "if I told you a surprise? Would that interest you?"

"Can there be any surprises, after hearing that your father married a mermaid?"

"After a proper courtship," she reminded him.

"Yes, but once you've brought a fish into the family, there's no saying what will come next. Is it about Teddy? Because I think he's turning into a fish as well. His nursemaid told me that he was in the river for hours yesterday."

"What about a baby?" she whispered.

He froze for a second and then practically levitated off her body. "Did I injure you?" he gasped.

She sat up, laughing. "Damon?"

He came back to the bed and sat beside her, spreading his huge hands on her belly, his face a mixture of tenderness and love. "Are you sure?"

"Yes."

"Your belly is as flat as ever."

She started giggling. "Babies take a long time, Damon. Talk to me about flat bellies in a few months!"

He bent down and kissed her tummy

without saying a word.

"Damon?" And then, when he still didn't say anything, "Darling?"

Finally he lifted his head. His eyes were filled with tears. "But — you never cry," she said, foolishly.

"I'm happy. You make me so happy."

She wound her arms around him and pulled him back on top of her. "Happiness makes you teary?"

He smiled at that. "I've always won things fairly easy, Roberta."

She nodded. "Chess matches, fencing matches —"

"Money."

"Lucky you."

"Until you came along, and told me you were in love with Villiers, and you wanted to marry him. And that you didn't want to marry me. And then he asked you to marry him, and for the first time in my life it felt as if something important was slipping away from me and I might lose.

"Even then I didn't understand that you are the *only* important thing." The tears stood unashamedly in his eyes.

"Oh silly one," she whispered. "You *have* me, remember? I love you. I'm your wife."

"I'm not playing chess anymore because there are no games that matter next to you,

Roberta."

She kissed him into silence.

A while later the Earl and Countess of Gryffyn lay curled together like two spoons, sleeping the kind of slumber that only happens in the afternoon, after the sweetest of marital intimacies.

But in the countess's tummy a little baby was awake. She turned a few acrobatic circles and practiced swimming, an activity enjoyed by babies, mermaids and big brothers. Then she flung out her arms in a huge dramatic gesture. And finally, her tiny mouth quirked into something that would resemble a smile, except babies that small can't smile. She resembled her papa most of all . . . which meant that joy would walk beside her all the days of her life.

Especially when she fell in love.

A NOTE ABOUT CHESS, POLITICS AND DUCHESSES

One of the benefits of being a professor of Shakespeare is that one never ceases to be surprised by one's ignorance. I have forgotten the name of the graduate student who handed in a short paper on chess in *The Tempest,* but I owe him or her a great favor. When Miranda and Ferdinand are "discovered" playing chess, what was depicted was one of the few activities that a gentleman and a lady could engage in together in private. In fact, many such games took place by the sides of beds. Going back to the early Middle Ages, one can find pictures of troubadours playing games of strategy and skill with their ladies. The Georgian period was a tremendously exciting time for chess, as depicted here. New pieces were being introduced, and Philidor himself visited from Paris to play exhibition games at Parsloe's.

In the mysterious way of friendships, during some dinner party, some time, I carelessly mentioned the chess scene in *The Tempest* to my friend and fellow Fordham professor, Lenny Cassuto. It turned out that he is on the verge of being ranked a chess master. What he told me about the game of chess was so fascinating that our conversation and the many that followed led directly to this book.

For those of you who love Shakespeare references, there are bits here from *Romeo and Juliet, Twelfth Night, The Rape of Lucrece* and *Hamlet* — some marked and some unmarked. There are also traces of John Donne here and there. If you'd like to track down every reference, come onto my Bulletin Board and share your findings or ask for clues!

I am also indebted to *The Wind in the Willows*. Reading this wonderful old book aloud to my daughter inspired my descriptions of the River Fleet. Ratty wrote a version of the marquess's song, "Up tails, all!"

And finally, if you happen to be a chess aficionado, the matches played by Jemma, Elijah and Villiers are all master matches. Though I wasn't able to depict every move, if you'd like to know more about the matches themselves, please come to my website (www.eloisajames.com) and check out the Inside Take for *Desperate Duchesses.*

The employees of Thorndike Press hope you have enjoyed this Large Print book. All our Thorndike, Wheeler, and Kennebec Large Print titles are designed for easy reading, and all our books are made to last. Other Thorndike Press Large Print books are available at your library, through selected bookstores, or directly from us.

For information about titles, please call:
(800) 223-1244

or visit our Web site at:
http://gale.cengage.com/thorndike

To share your comments, please write:
Publisher
Thorndike Press
295 Kennedy Memorial Drive
Waterville, ME 04901